The Summer Guest

Emma Hannigan is the author of six bestselling novels and a bestselling memoir *Talk to the Headscarf* which charts her journey through cancer. Emma lives in Bray, County Wicklow, with her husband and two children.

www.emmahannigan.com
Follow Emma on Facebook and
on Twitter @MsEmmaHannigan

Also by Emma Hannigan
Keeping Mum
Driving Home for Christmas
Perfect Wives
The Pink Ladies Club
Miss Conceived
Designer Genes

Talk to the Headscarf

Emma Hannigan

The Summer Guest

HACHETTE
BOOKS
IRELAND

First published in Ireland in 2014 by
HACHETTE BOOKS IRELAND

Cataloguing in Publication Data is available from the British Library.

ISBN 978 1444 753 288

Typeset in Bembo by Bookends Publishing Services
Printed and bound in Great Britain by Clays Ltd, St Ives plc

Hachette Books Ireland policy is to use papers that are natural, renewable and
recyclable products and made from wood grown in sustainable forests. The
logging and manufacturing processes are expected to conform to the
environmental regulations of the country of origin.

Hachette Books Ireland
8 Castlecourt Centre
Castleknock
Dublin 15, Ireland

A division of Hachette UK Ltd
338 Euston Road, London NW1 3BH

www.hachette.ie

In loving memory of my uncle, Neil O'Callaghan.
Also for Jackie, Kate, Juliette and Rebecca.

Chapter 1

LEXIE GLANCED AT HER WATCH, MAKING SURE SHE had enough time for another cup of coffee. The remnants of breakfast festooned the table. She smiled to herself. Her husband, Sam, was such a creature of habit. As regular as clockwork, he stacked his coffee mug on top of his toast plate, with the knife neatly tucked alongside, but it never occurred to him to transport the pile across the kitchen to the dishwasher.

This was Lexie's favourite moment of the day. She flicked off the radio, posted a capsule into the Nespresso machine, placed her already used cup under the spout and pressed the brew button. She and Sam liked to hear the news headlines followed by the round-up of that day's newspapers, and after that, Lexie relished a few minutes of silence. She felt it set her up for the day ahead.

As she crossed the kitchen to the bay window seat, her leather-soled ballerina pumps made a satisfying sound as they connected with the waxed wooden floorboards. She perched on the long, spongy cushion and gazed out into the oval railed-in park opposite. The late May sunshine flooded the neatly kept communal space. Although each of the houses in Cashel Square had fine-sized gardens, the residents all made use of the wooden benches in the park. They took turns to tend the flowerbeds and keep the place clean. It was too small to appeal to gangs of youths and the absence of swings or play equipment meant it rarely attracted non-resident families.

Lexie sipped her coffee and closed her eyes to savour it. It was just the right temperature, black and strong with no sugar and a delectable covering of crema.

'I hope you don't liken your coffee to your taste in men,' Sam had joked when they first met, flexing a long arm and pulling his fingers through his auburn hair.

Luckily for both of them, Lexie's taste in men and coffee differed hugely. Soon after meeting they both realised they'd found their soulmate. They had a no-fuss registry-office wedding, with her friend Maia as chief bridesmaid, flower girl and best man all rolled into one, followed by a lunch with immediate family as the only additional guests.

Property prices were beginning to rise, so they decided to take the plunge and look for a house to buy. One Sunday afternoon, out for a walk along the promenade in the seaside Dublin suburb of Caracove, they'd happened upon Cashel Square. It comprised eight detached two-storey-over-basement dwellings set in a horseshoe, with the park in the centre, and they'd guessed it was well out of their league. The door to number three had been open and a sandwich board told them there was open viewing. They were the sole viewers and the estate agent seemed thrilled with their arrival.

'It's a wonderful property but requires a small amount of imagination,' he said.

Lexie and Sam had looked at one another and grinned. They knew that meant the place was in dire need of renovation.

'It certainly needs a lot of loving,' Lexie said, as they wandered from room to room.

'It has massive potential,' the estate agent said, injecting as much positivity into his voice as he could.

'Yes, massive potential for us to pour an endless bag of cash into it,' Sam scoffed.

'Can we have a quiet word in private?' Lexie asked, as they finished their tour.

'Be my guests,' the estate agent said, yawning.

Lexie took Sam's hand and led him back into the kitchen. 'Sam, I can see us living here,' she whispered. 'I've totally fallen in love with it.'

'It could be amazing, but it's not what we're looking for, is it?'

Sam said, as he rubbed a hand across the peeling plaster on the main wall.

'I love it,' she repeated. A giggle escaped her as she noticed the colour draining from her husband-of-three-weeks' face.

'I don't like that dancing in your eyes, Lexie,' he said, with a slow smile.

'Let's make an offer,' she begged. 'One well below the asking price and verging on insulting and see where we go.'

'We're only starting out, hon,' he reasoned. 'This is a massive undertaking. It'd be years before it's back to its former glory. And even longer before we'd manage to pay back everything it'll siphon from our bank accounts. Old places like this are bottomless pits when it comes to money.'

'Perfect!' she said. 'We have all the time in the world. We're at the beginning of our journey. Let's do it together. You, me and number three Cashel Square!'

Lexie knew Sam found it hard to say no to her. Especially when she talked incessantly about the house. Several weeks passed after the initial viewing. Instead of giving up on the idea, Lexie was verging on obsessive.

'You're annoying me and I don't even live with you,' Maia said. 'Poor Sam now knows he married a lunatic. I reckon you should rein it in a bit. He'll go running for the hills if you don't stop with the crazy house talk.' Maia was a divorce lawyer and, although she had a very happy marriage with steadfast, calm Josh, she had a habit of seeing the worst in every union.

'I've seen it a million times – couples torn apart when one or other of them becomes fanatical about something. I told you about the pair who'd been married twenty-four years when it all went belly-up,' she warned.

'You said he was a sex addict and she was a raving alco. That's hardly comparable to wanting to build a home with the man I love,' Lexie said. She had a feeling deep down that Sam was just as keen as she, but he was attempting to be the voice of reason. She chipped away for the next few days until he uttered the words she'd been dying to hear.

'All right! We'll put in a measly offer. Will that stop your nagging?' he asked good-naturedly.

To their astonishment, the offer was accepted.

'It's an executors' sale and the family have instructed us to move quickly,' the estate agent explained.

Family and friends were marvellous, donating furniture and turning up in droves to the many painting parties the couple held. 'We'll provide the materials and pay you in beer and pizza,' Lexie promised.

By the end of that first summer of 1998, Lexie and Sam had a kitchen-living room, bathroom and bedroom in liveable order. The replastering wouldn't have won any DIY awards, but it was good enough to keep the damp out and the heat in.

'It looks like an enormous monster arrived in and vomited Ready Brek all over the place,' Maia teased. 'And as for tramping about on mangy old floorboards, nah. I'm happy in my apartment.' She shuddered.

'That, my dear,' Lexie said, linking her arm, 'is where you and I differ. I would go clinically insane in that dog-box you call home. Give me vaguely lumpy plasterwork done by caring but not the most professional of friends and vast open spaces any day.'

Penelope, Lexie's mother, was probably more in Maia's camp when it came to the house. She didn't *do* mess or dust or, God forbid, mismatched furnishings. 'You can do the rest as you go along, I suppose,' she said uncertainly, as she perched on the edge of a rather saggy sofa, clutching her handbag.

'Mum, you don't have to hold your bag like a life-raft. You're not going to drown on old goose-down cushions. Sam and I are delighted to have this place and we're not in a hurry to have it looking like something from that glossy interiors magazine, *The White Book*.'

'So I've noticed,' she said. 'Still,' she brightened, 'as the children start to come along, so too will the decorating.'

'Don't hold your breath, Mum,' Lexie said. 'Children aren't even a topic for discussion between Sam and me right now.'

'Well, that's a bit of a silly thing to say, don't you think? All married couples turn their attention to having a family at some point. Anyway, we don't need to worry about it this second,' Penelope assured them. 'Needless to say your father and I are longing to be grandparents, but your brother just scratched that itch for us with the birth of gorgeous baby Amélie! I'm just *saying*, that's all.'

For the most part, Lexie and Sam kept to themselves. The neighbours in the remaining seven houses were friendly but never intrusive. They'd exchange pleasantries in passing and bid one another good day at the park. Ernie and Mary in number two fed Tiddles, the cat, if Lexie and Sam were on holiday.

Now, fifteen years later, there were still many nooks and crannies of number three Cashel Square waiting to be lovingly restored to their former glory. Lexie and Sam had made some headway, of course. They'd replaced the saggy old sofas with gorgeous cream leather ones. All the original fireplaces, ceiling cornices and floorboards had been carefully brought back to their prime. Sam had found a craftsman who'd moved into the basement for six months so he could rethread the sash windows and repair the hinges and panels of the shutters.

But the new kitchen they'd put in last year had cleared their rainy-day account. Many other rooms were still filled with junk or waiting to have the right furniture added.

Their long-term plans had changed since 1998 too. After an accident, Lexie had been forced to change tack with her career, but things were finally beginning to look up for them, despite the global recession.

Sam was now a shareholder in the computer-programming firm where he worked. But Lexie's promising job in graphic design had come tumbling down, literally. She'd been up an extendable ladder doing some careful ceiling-cornice painting when it had collapsed. She'd known by the cracking sound that her arm was broken. She'd landed on it awkwardly and it was twisted in a direction she knew wasn't natural. Crawling to the phone, she'd called Sam, then Maia.

True to form, Sam was calm and said he'd phone the ambulance. 'Stay where you are and I'll be with you in a jiffy. I love you.'

Maia was OTT as usual. 'You what? Jesus H. Christ, Lex. Is your arm hanging off or what?'

'No,' she sobbed, 'but it's really bad. Sam's on the way and so's the ambulance.'

'Well, don't go to St Mary's Hospital – they use knives and forks to sew people up. I had a client who went there to have a baby. Emergency section, baby was coming too soon, blah, blah. She had pains in her side for two months after the operation so she ended up in another hospital where they removed a fecking needle the other clowns had left there!'

'Okay.' Lexie had winced. 'I'm going now. I'm in so much pain I think I'm going to die.' She'd dropped the phone and promptly passed out. By the time she woke she was in recovery. Sam and Maia were on either side of her bed gazing anxiously at her. 'Hey,' she said weakly. 'What's happened with my arm?'

'You've had some pins put into your wrist,' Sam said gently. 'The surgical team said it was a bad break, honey.'

Maia was chewing the inside of her lip, looking agitated. Sam was smiling kindly.

'What?' she asked, turning to Maia.

'You're gonzoed,' she said. 'You're lucky they didn't saw your hand off and leave you with an unsightly stump.'

'Maia!' Sam said, growing irritated. 'Don't be so dramatic. Lexie had a horrible fall. She's going to be fine, though.'

Lexie adored Sam, but Maia was one of the only people in the world who'd tell her the truth. They'd been friends since school and, no matter what happened, they had each other's backs.

As it turned out, Lexie's injuries were closer to Maia's assumption than Sam's. 'Why did I have to break my left wrist?' Lexie wailed two days later. 'The doctors were so jubilant about the fact it wasn't the right.'

'They weren't to know you're left-handed,' Sam said, wiping away a tear. 'We'll get you the best darn physiotherapist in Dublin, and before long you'll be back in work and, most importantly, back painting your beloved portraits.'

Lexie really wanted to believe Sam. Her job was sacred to her and she was bringing so much extra business on board that her bosses had already offered her a rise. She knew it was only a matter of time before they suggested she become a partner. But all that paled into insignificance when it came to the way her painting made her feel. If a day was stressful or a week took its toll, she'd burrow away in the back room and paint.

Any time Sam suggested making the room more organised or even putting in some proper work surfaces, she balked. 'I love it this way. I know where things are and it allows me to be creative. I have to be regimented in work. This is *my* zone.'

Seven months later, despite her best efforts and many hours of painful physio, Lexie had to admit defeat.

'If things change, let us know,' Herman, her boss, said. 'The door is open whenever you get the control back in your hand.'

Lexie hugged him, accepted the farewell voucher for a massage treatment, and knew in her heart of hearts that she'd never be back at the graphic design company.

The cloud that shrouded her life could possibly have ruined everything, had Reggie, her father, not come to the rescue. She was wallowing in the house, day after day, slipping slowly into a depression when he single-handedly changed her destiny.

'I'm downsizing the company. I can't keep going with all the printing shops. Besides, lots of our customers are using cheaper on-line companies nowadays.'

'I'm sorry to hear that, Dad,' Lexie said. 'I know what it feels like when you're no longer in a position to fulfil your potential.'

Reggie patted her hand, telling her she was going to do that and more. He handed her a set of keys and told her the premises, which were strategically situated on the sea road a mere mile from Cashel Square, were hers, rent free, until she established a decent income.

'But what on earth can I do with your old printing shop?' she asked.

'How about setting up a gallery?' Reggie said.

Lexie sat back and allowed the idea wash over her. Astonishingly, she didn't feel averse to the idea. In fact, the more she thought about it, the better it sounded. 'If I'm starting my career from scratch I may as well do so within walking distance of here,' she reasoned. 'The doctors say I'll be able to drive again in a few months, but for the moment it would more than suit me to be able to walk to work.'

'Of course,' Reggie said. 'It's the perfect area for a gallery, what with the promenade, the park and the pedestrian shopping area.' He had occupied the building for more than twenty years and knew the footfall was there. 'I'll help you decorate and I'm sure your friends will too. I ran the idea past Sam and he thinks it sounds wonderful.'

'So you've pretty much set me up. All I need to do is arrive, eh?' Lexie said, grinning. Throwing her good arm around her father's neck, she let him hold her like he did when she was little. She thanked God she had such amazing men in her life.

'You're such a jammy cow,' Maia said, when they met for coffee that afternoon. 'I wish my father was like yours.' She sighed. 'But I guess I'd need to have a relationship with him and actually know him in the first place!' They giggled. Maia was blunt to a fault. Especially when it came to awkward or emotive subjects. When they'd first met, some of the girls in their class at school didn't get her sense of humour but it was the thing Lexie loved most about her. They'd been drawn to one another since the age of ten and Lexie couldn't imagine her life without Maia.

After her father had walked out on them, Maia's mother had worked a lot, leaving Maia and her brother John to their own devices. As a result, Maia had decided the only way was out. Out of the house and into a job that would pay.

'I want to earn shedloads of cash and go on foreign holidays wearing designer gear while quaffing champagne.' Nothing got in Maia's way once she set her mind to something. Although Lexie had a lump in her throat and pride in her heart the day Maia graduated from law school, she wasn't surprised. 'You did good, kiddo,' she said, hugging her.

'I'm only getting started,' Maia said, with a shrug of her shoulder and a subtle nod to the right. Lexie glanced sideways and made eye contact with a gorgeous guy.

'Let me introduce you to Josh,' Maia said. She pulled Lexie close and whispered, ever so quietly, 'Great in bed, brains to burn, and I'm going to marry him some day.'

In the early days Lexie was at the gallery morning, noon and night.

'Sometimes I wonder whether you love the art more than me,' Sam said, with an exaggerated pout. 'I know you're struggling to work with one hand a lot of the time, but I can't help feeling left out.'

'Don't be ridiculous.' She giggled. 'There are one or two pieces I like less than you.'

All jokes aside, Lexie knew she needed to push hard to make her business a success. She was determined to look after her clients and form good relationships. If the gallery were to survive and thrive, she needed to breathe life into it. She buried all her bitterness and disappointment by focusing on the job in hand. At the time she'd thought anything other than being an active artist was a come down, such was her love for painting. Owning a gallery was the next best thing and she knew it was an opportunity and the perfect way to avoid plunging into a pool of dark depression.

'The paintings and sculptures are the blood and I need to be the heartbeat,' she explained to Sam.

Luckily for both of them, Sam got it. More than that, he got Lexie. Now, nine years later, the gallery was thriving and had survived the testing recession.

Draining her coffee cup, Lexie placed it in the dishwasher with the rest of the breakfast things and turned the machine on. She adored her new kitchen and still got a kick out of closing the integrated dishwasher door. It had been a long time coming, but the gorgeous refurbishment even met with Penelope's approval. 'It's wonderful, darling,' she said. 'I'd say you're able to relax in here far more now, and it's better for poor Sam to have a proper place for his dinner.

That old falling-apart kitchen you had before must've made him feel quite depressed after a hard day at the office.'

'Sam never complained,' Lexie said, trying not to get irritated with her mother. 'In fact, I pushed for the new units more than he did.'

Taking the stairs two at a time, she grabbed a cardigan to pop in her bag in case there was a cool breeze coming in from the sea. She brushed her teeth, then checked her face in the mirror for flakes of mascara or stray spatters of eye-shadow on her cheek. Pulling her long dark hair into a clip, she decided she'd do. She hoped the short walk between the house and the gallery would kick-start her tan. She thought of poor Sam, who went the colour of a beetroot almost instantly in the sun. Even if they were sitting in the garden for a drink he had to lather himself in high-factor cream. Yesterday evening she'd brought them a glass of chilled white wine each, and tossed the tube of sun screen to him. 'From blue to burn in sixty seconds! That's my man!' she said.

They teased one another endlessly, that was their way, but underneath it, they were inseparable. The only time she knew Sam got slightly peeved was when she and Maia went too far with the sisterhood gibes. 'When God created man *she* was only joking,' Maia had slurred last Sunday, at their barbecue.

'Lex,' Sam whispered, 'don't get into the whole men-are-worms vibe. It's embarrassing for Josh and me.'

As she ran down the stairs, plucking her handbag from the hall table, the photographic portrait, taken around the time of their engagement, stared back at her. She was incredibly fortunate that their relationship had stood the test of time, she thought. So many of their friends were now either single or in second partnerships. Maia was making a very nice living on other people's failed marriages.

The second she banged the front door shut, her mobile rang. Stuffing the cardigan into her bag, she retrieved her phone just in time. 'Hi, Mum,' she said.

'Hello, love. Isn't it a lovely bright day?' Penelope said.

'Hm, gorgeous,' Lexie said, shouldering the phone to her ear as she turned the Chubb lock in the door. 'I'm just on the way to the gallery. Any news?'

'I could ask you the same,' Penelope responded.

'Not a dicky-bird,' Lexie said. 'I'll be in work until lunchtime. Kate is covering the afternoon shift and I might head out for a run on the pier later. What are you up to today?'

'I was going to see if you'd meet me for lunch,' Penelope said. 'Dad and I have been chatting. Your fortieth birthday is around the corner. Have you any plans at all?'

'It's not until September, Mum. It's May now, for crying out loud!'

'It'll be June tomorrow,' Penelope corrected. 'Poor Amélie starts her fifth-year exams in the morning. Billy and Dee are tearing their hair out with her. She hasn't opened a book, you know.'

'I'm sure she'll be fine. My niece is a clever girl. She's probably done more work than they think.'

'Well, unless they've added a study hall to the shopping centre, I sincerely doubt it. She's turned into a bit of a madam lately. Dee is at her wits' end. She'll be leaving school next year. The time to cop on is running out.'

'Lighten up, Mum, for Pete's sake! Amélie's seventeen. She's supposed to rebel against everything. I'd be more worried if she didn't,' Lexie said.

'Now, that's just ridiculous, Lexie. Amélie is in danger of becoming a problem. Billy is too soft with her and leaves all the disciplining to Dee. It's not right.'

'Mum, it's none of our business what Amélie, Dee or Billy does in the comfort of their own home. I doubt Amélie is the first teenager to find study a bore and she certainly won't be the last.'

'You treat her like one of your friends, Lexie. I'm not sure that's appropriate, considering her current behaviour. Maybe if you took a more removed approach to her it might help Dee and Billy,' Penelope suggested.

'I can't help it if Amélie thinks I'm cool,' Lexie quipped. 'Besides, she needs to feel there's at least one person batting on her team. I remember what it's like when you think the whole world is against you. I wouldn't go back to being a teenager for any money.'

'Well, that's neither here nor there,' Penelope said. 'So, can you meet me for lunch later? Why don't we go to the noodle bar on the promenade? Say, one thirty? Will that give you enough time? We can have a better chat face to face.'

Knowing her mother would probably turn up at the gallery if she didn't meet her, Lexie agreed. At least this way they'd be in a neutral venue and she could leave if necessary.

Chapter 2

AS SHE WALKED INTO THE ARRIVALS AREA OF DUBLIN airport, Kathleen felt more at ease than she had for weeks. The luggage trolley had a mind of its own and kept veering to the right. Stopping to scan the crowd, she waved tentatively at the man holding a sign with her name on.

'Kathleen Williams?' he asked.

'That's me,' she confirmed happily.

'Let me take that yoke for you,' the man said, commandeering the trolley. 'You'll do yourself an injury. It's easier to control a box of frogs than one of these things.'

Kathleen thanked him and grinned from ear to ear. It'd been such a long time since she'd heard the Irish wit first hand. Her parents had immigrated to America to find work when she was a child. Now a silvery-blonde woman of seventy-four, she'd forgotten how much she loved this type of banter.

'So let me guess,' the taxi driver said, as they sat into his car. 'You're here to find your roots?'

'Got it in one!' Kathleen said. 'I'm not totally bats, though. In my defence I was born in Dublin and lived in Caracove until I was eight. So I've got fairly fresh roots here – for an American,' she added.

'Fair enough.' He nodded. 'So what brings you home after all this time?'

'My husband, Jackson, bought me a ticket and it would've been rude not to use it,' she said.

'Didn't he want to come with you?'

'He couldn't make it this time.'

'Probably better off that way.' The man chuckled. 'Visiting old haunts with someone else is almost as bad as going shopping, if you ask me.'

Kathleen laughed.

'So where are we going?' the driver asked.

'Caracove Bay, please.'

'Ah, Caracove Bay by the sea!' he said. 'Lovely spot, isn't it? You'll see a big change, I reckon. For the better, mind you. They've done up the promenade area – paved it and built lovely glass-fronted restaurants. The big park is a hive of activity now too. The old swings were repaired and a whole host of kiddie rides and slides have been added.'

'How wonderful!' Kathleen said. 'Is the bandstand still there?'

'Indeed it is. There's music of all sorts at the weekends and during the summer.'

'That sounds gorgeous,' Kathleen said. 'What about the town? Is it still buzzy?'

'Some of the shops have closed down due to the recession, but the main street is still as alive as ever, I think you'll find. It's pedestrianised now and it works well. There was some talk of a modern shopping centre being added a couple of years back but so many of the locals objected the idea was scrapped. I think they were right, too. Caracove Bay has managed to hold on to her old-world charm without remaining in the dark ages.'

Kathleen marvelled at the changes as they made their way down the impressive motorway. 'None of this existed when I left. It's unrecognisable, actually,' she said, a little deflated.

'Ah, it's all built up along here, but once we turn off and veer towards the coast you'll see some familiar sights.'

The driver was right. Less than an hour later, as they went along the sea road, Kathleen was like a child in a sweet shop as she pinned her gaze on the sights. 'The old swimming baths! There used to be an ice-cream shop there.'

'Indeed there was,' the driver said. 'That must be gone twenty years by now. Are you staying at the Caracove Arms Hotel, love?'

'Oh,' Kathleen said, suddenly flustered. 'Would you believe I haven't made a reservation? I've had a bit of a gruelling time of it lately. I thought I was doing brilliantly just getting here. I hadn't thought ahead.'

'I'm sure they'll have plenty of room. I know a couple of the staff there. I'll see they look after you.'

'Would you mind if we pop by my old house first?' Kathleen asked. 'I've written to the owners asking if I might call some day. Do you think they'd allow me?'

'I'm sure they would. A lovely lady like yourself. Why not, eh?' he said cheerfully. 'There's no harm in asking, I'd say.'

'Yes, indeed. The address is number three Cashel Square, Caracove,' she instructed.

'No bother, love,' said the driver. 'It's literally five minutes away.'

Suddenly Kathleen was quite overcome with emotion. She wasn't sure if she wanted to laugh or cry. After all this time she was going to see her childhood home again. She wished Jackson were there to share the moment.

'Here we are, Cashel Square.'

As the driver turned the cab into the left, the park, with its white-painted iron railings, came into view. Kathleen gasped as they pulled up outside number three. 'Wow! It looks better than I remember,' she managed, her voice quite choked.

'The owners have spent a few bob on it, I'd say.'

'It certainly looks well loved,' she agreed. 'Could you give me a moment?'

'Take all the time you want, love,' the driver said, turning off the engine.

Kathleen released her seatbelt and eased herself out of the car. She was stiff from all the travelling. Inhaling deeply, she was holding back tears.

The once black door was now a cheerful shade of cornflower blue. The brass fixings were polished to a gleaming shine, and the woodwork around the window frames was flawless.

Wooden boxes were filled to spilling point with delicate blooms in varied shades of pink. The railings were expertly painted without a sign of rust. The granite steps were scrubbed, showing none of the dirt she remembered from her childhood. Memories of days at the beach, trips to the town and cold winter winds echoed through the corridors of her mind.

Afraid she'd get caught snooping and ruin her chance of being allowed inside, Kathleen pulled the letter she'd written on the plane from her handbag. Under her signature, she added the name of the hotel she was planning to stay at and popped it into the iron post-box attached to the gate. Saying a quick prayer, she hoped with all her heart that the owners would be welcoming.

'Is that it?' the driver asked, looking surprised. 'I thought I'd have time for a quick nod-off.'

'I don't want to appear too pushy,' she said. 'I'm terrified of being told to go away.'

'If they're any way decent, the owners will invite you in,' he assured her.

Kathleen stared at the square as they drove around the park and out the other side. She rattled her brain to remember the neighbours' names. 'Mrs Caddy lived in number eight,' she recalled. 'She hated children and we called her Mrs Crabby behind her back.'

'We all knew someone like that as children!' The driver laughed. 'You'd wonder why they were so cranky. I'd never bark at a small child now that I'm an adult, would you?'

'I certainly wouldn't,' she agreed. Although she was reluctant to leave Cashel Square, Kathleen was truly worn out. Jet lag and exhaustion crept over her, making her eyes burn and her limbs long to stretch out.

Mercifully the Caracove Arms had a room available. True to his word, the driver spoke to his friend and made sure she was welcomed with open arms.

'Thank you for being so lovely,' Kathleen said, handing him the fare with a generous tip.

'The pleasure is all mine. Great to meet you and I hope you have a fantastic stay.'

Not up to facing a table for one, Kathleen ordered a portion of Irish stew and a glass of cold milk to be served in her room. She managed to stay awake long enough for the meal to be delivered. The lamb was cooked to perfection. Knowing she shouldn't give in to sleep until that evening if she were to overcome the jet lag, she perched in an armchair and tried to watch the television. She toyed with the idea of turning her cell phone off and decided against it on the off-chance that her letter might prompt a response. Before long her head slumped forward as sleep enveloped her.

Dear Diary

I've been having — hash-tag — THE worst time. I know it's her job but my Mum is like so so so so *multiplied by a trillion times* ANNOYING.

All she cares about is study. She's acting as if my exams are more important than world hunger.

These exams are a total waste of space. They're not my school-leaving ones, just lame end-of-year joke stuff. The real deal is a whole year away. I keep pointing this out to my mother but she's on this mega-rant and once she gets started it's blah, blah and triple blah. They're totally meh, which roughly translates as who gives a toss?

At times like this, I wish I had a brother or sister to take the heat off. At least if there was someone else in the house I could sound off at them.

(a) That would mean I didn't have to write this diary.

(b) I could blame him/her for everything.

It's not all bad news, however. In spite of my mother I'm managing to distract myself in these times of stress. I've met this guy. He's called Elton (named after his mum's fave singer — he can totally handle it) and I can safely say he is a total mint-bomb.

When I first met him I thought he was a bit out there. You know the type, bit of a deep thinker and comes out with loads of random stuff that makes you, like, huh? But once you get to know him, he's just the bomb.

He says we connected. I totally feel it too.

There's one slight hitch in heaven. He's dating this girl Jenny.

She's in the year ahead of me in school and she's totally wrapped up in him. She's one of those foghorn types so the whole school knows she's his GF.

He says she was fun for a while but she's been buried in books for weeks and refuses to go out. He's so over her.

I feel bad that he's dumping her for me. But all's fair in love and war, right?!

I'd say she's going to be devastated. I mean, I would be if he was dumping me. But Elton says there's no time to stand and stare in this life, we've got to roll with the punches.

We kissed last night. Elton ended up with my chewing gum in his mouth. He pulled his hand through his hair, said, 'Thanks for the gum, doll,' and walked off. Slick.

He's texting me when the deed is done and we're hooking up.

I was going to wear my cropped Abercrombie trakkie bottoms with a tight vest. But I'm not sure Elton is a labels type of guy. He's not grungy but he's all about saving the whale and world peace and carbon footprints. So he may not appreciate me rocking up in gear festooned with names. He had a rant at one of the guys about his DKNY shirt. Said it's free advertising on behalf of the label. I never thought of it like that. Elton's so deep.

Other proposed outfit is yellow baby-doll dress with All Stars. Guys go for the super-cute look, don't they? Even if he's saving the planet he'd prefer to do it with a good-looking girlfriend, surely. I found a fiver in Mum's raincoat pocket yesterday. As it was left there I figured she wouldn't need it so I'm going to buy fake tan. I'll be rocking the mahogany look.

Tomorrow is going to be über-sick. #excited

Later

Amélie ♥ ✿

Chapter 3

THINGS HAD BECOME INCREASINGLY STRAINED between Lexie and her mother of late. They'd never had a huge amount in common, but Penelope seemed to have fixated on her daughter's approaching milestone birthday, a concept that was beyond Lexie. She'd always been a daddy's girl, which she knew was part of the problem. Any time Lexie thought of her father, an involuntary smile spread across her face.

Reggie was a man with old-fashioned values who treated his wife like a lady and his daughter was most certainly a princess in his eyes. He'd helped her turn her life around after the accident and she'd never forget that.

She arrived at the gallery at the same time as her first appointment.

'Lexie, great to see you,' the lady said, as they air-kissed. 'You're looking lovely as usual.'

'Thank you, Jess,' Lexie said, slipping straight into work mode. 'White linen dresses always mix beautifully with sunshine, don't they? I've always thought Ireland is the most amazing place to be when the weather is fine.'

'Too true,' Jess agreed.

'I'm dying to see your new ceramic piece. I've made a space for it over here,' Lexie said, as she unlocked the shutters and led the way. 'My clients are just loving your style. I'm so thrilled. I just knew you had an edge and your work's quality is striking.'

The rest of the morning flew, as Lexie dealt with a string of customers. Her gallery sold everything from handmade trinkets to larger, more expensive canvases and sculptures. Since the day she'd first opened the doors, her wish had been to bring art to as many people as possible. 'I don't want a stuffy place where fuddy-duddies shuffle around speaking in hushed tones, stroking their chins and pontificating in words that sound like they've just made them up,' she had said to Sam. 'I want a vibrant, bright space that's bursting with colour and loads of varied talent. I want the whole of Ireland to fall in love with art!'

By lunchtime, her tummy was grumbling and she was glad she'd arranged to meet her mother. Lexie had an awful habit of forgetting to eat and ending up with a migraine. Kate, her assistant of ten years, appeared. 'I'm delighted to say it's actually hot out there!' she said.

'Yup, real exam weather, isn't it?' said Lexie.

'For sure. Aren't you delighted you're not heading into an exam hall for the next few weeks?'

'Totally,' Lexie agreed. 'I'm going to shoot off, but if it gets too busy, just call me, okay?'

'No worries,' Kate said, and greeted a customer.

Lexie was just going out of the door when a gaggle of teenaged girls landed. Dressed identically in skimpy denim shorts, little strappy tops, zippy hoodies and stack-heeled trainers, they might have been mistaken for a girly pop group. 'Hey, girls! Hi, Amélie,' she said, kissing her niece first, then the others.

'What ya up to?' Amélie asked.

'I'm meeting Grandma for lunch. Want to come?' Lexie marvelled at the girl's long skinny legs, tiny waist and neat figure. As a tot she'd been a dead ringer for the young Shirley Temple. She still had the bouncy blonde curls, but she'd matured, seemingly overnight, into a stunningly pretty young woman.

'Oops, can't, soz,' she said, flicking her long hair over one shoulder. She held out a hand, brandishing multi-coloured nails. 'Like?' Amélie asked.

'Love,' oozed Lexie. 'How many nail polishes did you buy?'

'Uh, none!' Amélie giggled. All her friends giggled too and showed their similar nails. 'We did our usual – went into the chemist and tried all the testers!'

'God,' Lexie said. 'I'd say they love seeing you lot coming.'

'Any chance you could lend me some cash, Auntie Lex?' Amélie asked.

'Where did you get those lashes?' Lexie wondered.

'The Make Up Store. We all got them, see?' she said.

Lexie gazed from one girl to the next and tried not to wince. The lashes were long and tapered to give a cat's eye effect and Lexie knew she'd manage to wear them for about two minutes before her eyes were streaming and bloodshot. That was a sure sign she was getting old: she decided not to comment any further.

'Well, you're all divine!' she said cheerfully. 'What's the money for?'

'Ice-creams down at the prom,' Amélie said immediately. 'It's, like boiling out there.'

'Truthfully? That's what you're doing with the money?'

'Straight up!' she said, holding her hands up.

Lexie pulled ten euro from her purse.

'Thanks, Lexie. Give my love to Grandma,' Amélie said, and waved to her aunt.

Lexie waved back and walked briskly to the seafront where she'd arranged to meet her mother. She dialled her father's number. She usually rang him first thing, but her mother's call had diverted that habit for today.

It went to voicemail so she left a message saying she'd call him later.

Penelope was sitting outside one of the sea-view restaurants under a red-and-white-striped awning. 'Hello, love,' her mother said, standing to hug her. 'You look pretty. I love the lilac nail polish. It lifts all that billowing white.'

'Thanks, Mum, you look lovely as always,' she said, choosing to ignore the backhanded compliment. Her mother was immaculately dressed in classically cut clothes. She didn't do frills and never looked untidy. Today she wore cropped navy trousers with a striped polo shirt and a cashmere sweater tossed over her shoulders. Her bobbed chestnut hair shone healthily and her matching pearl stud earrings and necklace complemented her olive-toned skin. While the conservative look suited her, it wasn't Lexie's style, which had caused another bone of contention between the women.

'You're a little late, as usual, so I decided to grab a table,' Penelope said.

'Sorry. I bumped into Amélie and her friends. They're going off for ice-creams,' Lexie said.

'She should be at home with her nose stuck in a book, not gallivanting around eating rubbish.'

Lexie didn't reply. When her mother got into one of her moods she was unbearable. Lexie had learned many years ago not to fuel any arguments.

'At least she's bothered to annoy you,' Maia used to say. 'My mother treats Josh and me like an irritation she doesn't have time for.'

'You're welcome to my mother's wrath any day,' Lexie would reply.

Lexie fixed a smile on her face and decided she wasn't going to let Penelope annoy her.

'Are you okay to sit out here or would you rather go in?' Penelope asked.

'Oh, it's lovely to get some air and it would be sinful to sit indoors when the sun's shining! God only knows when it'll come out again.' Lexie reached over and poured herself a glass of water from the jug on the table. 'How's Dad?' she asked. 'I just tried his mobile but it went straight to voicemail.'

'He's golfing today but he sends his love. How's Sam? Working hard?'

'Yes, Mum. He's running like a good little hamster on his wheel, generating plenty of cash to keep his little wifey in Chanel necklaces,' she quipped.

'I can't help being slightly old-fashioned, Lexie,' Penelope said. 'I happen to think it's important that Sam looks after you. You'll always be my little girl, no matter how old you are.'

'I know, Mum,' Lexie said. She smiled because she knew she ought to, but her mother's attitude made her blood boil. Penelope didn't seem to realise she wasn't and never had been a kept woman.

'Speaking of age, Dad and I would love to host a fortieth-birthday ·

party for you at the yacht club. They seat a hundred and twenty and they'll do it beautifully, as you know from previous events we've had there. We can all invite friends. It'd be gorgeous. September is usually the warmest month in Ireland. We might even manage drinks out on the veranda. What do you say?'

'I don't think so, Mum. Thanks all the same, but I wasn't planning on doing anything flamboyant. Forty's just another number to me. I don't get the big hoo-ha with it.'

'Well, it *is* a significant age, darling, whether you choose to *get* it or not. Lord knows, I'd had you and your brother by your age. But ladies leave it longer to start families these days, don't they?'

The words hung in the air as Penelope leaned forward ever so slightly. The move was minuscule but Lexie clocked it. 'Mum, leave it, please.'

'But I must say these things. Nobody else will. Besides, look at Maia's situation. That poor little boy.'

'Mum!' Lexie said, almost shouting despite her attempt to remain calm. 'If Maia heard you referring to Calvin as "that poor little boy" she'd quite rightly have a meltdown.'

'I didn't mean to insult him and you know it.' Penelope sniffed. 'But it's not easy having a child with Down's syndrome. The risks of it happening increase with age.' She shifted in her chair. 'I'd never say anything cruel about Calvin. I'm offended you think I would.'

'Whatever,' Lexie said, gripping the side of her chair. 'Anyway, I know what you're doing. I told you the last time we saw each other that the baby issue isn't open for discussion. If and when Sam and I decide to start a family, you'll be the first to know. Please don't harp on at me every time we meet. I don't want tension between us and I don't appreciate being cross-examined. It's my life and I'm entitled to make my own decisions. Can we drop it, please? I'm starving.'

'Of course.'

Lexie's jaw flexed as she took a deep breath. Her mother was giving her that look again. Acting as if she'd been mortally wounded. Penelope was like a dog with a bone. It was as if the impending birthday had triggered a switch in her and turned her into some sort of biological-clock mistress on behalf of Mother Nature. And using sweet little Calvin as a cannon ball to fuel her debate was a low blow. Lexie knew better than anyone that there were struggles in raising a child with special needs. Maia had experienced every emotion known to woman when Calvin came along, but she and Josh were doing brilliantly now, as was Calvin. Penelope had no right to bring him into things.

Conversation during lunch was strained. Clearly her mother had come to meet her with a specific agenda in mind and Lexie's outburst had well and truly scuppered it.

'If you're in the mood for a party, why don't you and Dad have one?' Lexie suggested hopefully.

'And what would we celebrate?' Penelope asked.

'I don't know – do you need a reason? If you want a party, have one. Call it a full-moon party. They're all the rage in Asia. Renew your wedding vows – some people love that idea. Sure you and Dad are in a minority, still married after all these years. I'm sure your friends would be delighted to come and raise a glass of bubbly with you beside the boats.'

'We just thought it might be a nice offer for you. Forget I said anything.' Penelope looked down at the table.

'I'm sorry, Mum. I didn't mean to hurt your feelings. It's a kind and thoughtful offer. I appreciate it. Really I do. But I'm not a big-splash type of girl.'

'We thought you might enjoy it. Your wedding was so small. Lunch for twenty people – I'll never get over it,' she huffed. 'We thought you might have regrets and feel you missed out.'

'Mum,' Lexie took her hand from across the table, 'Sam and I had the wedding we wanted. It suited us and we enjoyed it. Sam wanted his parents and brothers home from Australia along with close friends. I agreed whole-heartedly. Once you guys and Maia were there, I was happy too. End of. I'm sorry if it's left you feeling hard done by, but I can't change who I am. Not at this stage of my life!' Lexie smiled and willed her mother to understand.

'Okay.' She sighed heavily. 'I tried.'

'And I love you for it. But it's just not me. Friends?'

'Yes, of course,' Penelope said, managing a flicker of a smile.

'Sorry, Mum,' Lexie said, glancing at her watch and pushing back her chair. 'I have to rush off. I got a call from an out-of-town artist and she wants to show me some work. I'd better go – I don't want to keep her waiting.'

'I thought you had the afternoon off. Well, your business must take precedence, I suppose,' Penelope said, standing to kiss her cheeks, while waving away the offer of money. 'Will you at least say it to Sam about the party offer this evening?'

'I will, thanks, Mum.'

Lexie was a good ten feet away when Penelope called after her: 'And don't forget your biological clock is ticking. It could be good to mention that at the same time.'

Halting momentarily and squeezing her eyes shut, Lexie bit her bottom lip. She didn't grace the comment with a response, just continued walking, trying not to mutter obscenities under her breath. As far as she was concerned, motherhood was not on the agenda. Sam had agreed from the start. It was one of the reasons she'd allowed herself to fall in love with him, hook, line and sinker. He was on the same page.

What Lexie hadn't banked on was her mother taking on the role of fertility Führer.

Chapter 4

LEXIE STOMPED HOME. SHE DIDN'T REALLY HAVE A client: she just knew she couldn't spend another minute in her mother's company without having a stand-up row. She ought to drop back to the gallery and collect some accounts, but she felt too irritated. She knew Penelope was suspicious about her sudden appointment, but it had been better to get away from her before they'd had a massive blow-up.

By the time she turned the corner and was heading towards Cashel Square, the scent of cherry blossom from gardens and the gentle warming of the sun's rays had eased her exasperation. Her mother had always been a bit of a fusspot. Drama was her middle name, and she was in her element when there was a crisis. Many years before, Lexie had suggested she go into event management.

'I wouldn't have the remotest idea of how to run a company like that, Lexie.'

'Of course you would, Mum. The business part might be a challenge in the beginning but we'd all help. You were born to organise the world. Why not get paid for it?'

Weddings, funerals, birthdays, christenings, Penelope wanted to be in the middle of them all. When an elderly neighbour of her parents slipped away, Lexie's comments were justified.

'I'd swear a light goes on in Mum's eye when someone dies,' Lexie had joked to Sam.

'God forgive you, that's a terrible thing to say.' He laughed.

'Not because the poor soul has passed on,' Lexie was quick to point out. 'Purely because she knows there's a funeral to organise. Just you watch. She'll be down at that house pulling priests out of her hat while writing the death notice and phoning the caterer with her free hand.'

Lexie knew her mum would love nothing more than to organise a fortieth birthday party. It'd keep her going for the whole summer. But the idea made her cringe.

Still, she'd say it to Sam over a drink before dinner and get his slant on it.

The cat came trotting to Lexie as she neared her house. 'Hello, Tiddly-widdly,' she said, scooping him up and burying her nose in his soft stripy fur. 'How's Mr Marmalade boy today, then?' Tiddles responded by blinking sweetly and nudging her chin with his nose. 'Thank you, furry boy. A lovely cat kiss for me!'

Her mobile phone rang. 'Dad! How was golf?'

'Lovely, thanks,' he said. 'Although it was actually too hot! We're never satisfied with the weather in this country, are we? How was lunch? Did you girls set the world to rights?'

'Oh, it was fine,' Lexie said. 'Mum was in one of her teacher-style moods. She's pushing to give me a birthday party.'

'Ah, she means well, love. It's not every day your baby turns forty! Have you any idea how old that makes me feel?'

'You and me both.' Lexie grinned. 'Which is why I don't want to highlight it.'

'You do whatever you like. It's your birthday after all.'

'Thanks, Dad. I'll let you go.'

'Talk to you soon, love.'

Several letters were protruding from the flap of the black cast iron post-box. Lexie balanced Tiddles on one shoulder and yanked them free. As she opened the front door and kicked off her shoes, Tiddles wriggled down and ran to his dish in the kitchen, miaowing.

'All right, boy, I'll feed you now,' she said, as she threw the letters on to the kitchen table.

Her phone rang again. Groaning, Lexie answered it.

'Hello, Dee,' she said. 'How are you on this fine sunny day?'

'Not great. Have you seen Amélie at all?'

'Yes!' Lexie said. 'She called in to the gallery a couple of hours ago with some of the girls. She said they were going for ice-cream. Isn't she answering her phone?'

'No, she's not,' Dee said tightly. 'And she's meant to be at home studying. I went to the supermarket and left her in her room surrounded by books. I assumed she was still there and just went up to give her a snack but she's gone.'

'Oh, I see,' Lexie said, biting her lip. 'Well, I'll keep an eye out for her, and if I spot her, I'll get her to call you.'

'Thanks,' Dee said. 'She went out to meet her friends last night and the deal was that she'd stay put and do some study this afternoon and evening.'

'I'm sure she'll be home soon,' Lexie said. 'I can't say I blame her. It's so sunny and warm out. Maybe she's just having a little break before knuckling down.'

'I'll believe that when it happens. I wish I had your faith,' said Dee. 'Thanks anyway. Chat to you soon, Lexie.'

Lexie sent a quick text to Amélie telling her to get herself home pronto.

Sighing, she called Maia.

'Hey,' her friend answered. 'I'm about to see a new client who's headed for a really nasty and messy divorce. I can't talk for long. How's life?'

'Crap,' Lexie said. 'I've just had the most frustrating lunch with my mother.'

'Is there any other type?'

'No, I guess not. She's pushing for me to have a fortieth party and now she wants me to have a baby.'

'Great!' Maia said. 'Well, good luck with all that. When does she need the baby by? Is she going to mind it while you work?'

Lexie could feel her shoulders relaxing already. Maia always made her feel better.

'Speaking of birthdays, you haven't forgotten Calvin's party is on Sunday, have you?'

'No,' Lexie said. 'Sam and I will be there with knobs on. I got him the truck you said he wanted too.'

'You're a doll. Thanks. He'll be thrilled. He's got so into cars. Mind you, I'd say ninety per cent of that is Josh passing on his petrol-head obsession! Now that he's minding him full time, I see a massive change in Calvin.'

'Really?'

'Yeah, they were amazing with him at the crèche but he's come on in leaps and bounds since Josh has been with him all day.'

'How's Josh finding it?'

'Good so far. He's so chilled out, as you know, and as it's only for a year, two tops, I think he's allowing himself to really enjoy the time.'

'That's great, Maia. It's a massive load off your mind, I'm sure.'

'You've said it. Josh was getting increasingly frustrated with his job. His hours were being cut more and more. This way he's guaranteed work again once the company takeover is complete and now he gets to be with Calvin and take him to as much therapy as he can fit in.'

'I'm thrilled, honey,' Lexie said.

'I've got to go – my client's here,' Maia said. 'But don't worry about your mother. In all the time I've known you, you've never been interested in having a baby and you're not about to change now.'

Lexie froze: she'd had a sudden flashback to her year in France. Christophe. She tried to refocus on what Maia was saying.

'So, we'll see you Sunday and don't turn up in one of your hippie-dippy arty outfits. Bring that Prada bag your mother gave you for Christmas. The neighbours around here wouldn't get art unless you were wearing a bandeau dress fashioned from the original *Mona Lisa* canvas.'

'I'll wear what I want, you cheeky cow.' Lexie laughed. 'And if your *nouveau-riche* snobby neighbours don't like me they can piss off.'

'Attagirl, Lex, love you!' Maia hung up.

Lexie flicked on the kettle and grabbed the pile of post she'd flung on to the kitchen table. Among the usual bills and an Australian postmarked letter from Sam's parents, there a handwritten envelope with writing Lexie didn't recognise. She picked it up, slid her finger into the puckered end of the envelope and ripped it open.

Dear Home owner

Allow me to introduce myself. My name is Kathleen Williams (née Walsh). I emigrated from Ireland to America in 1947, when I was eight years old. My family settled in Florida, where I've lived until now.

I am writing to ask an unusual favour of you.

I used to live in your house! In fact, I was born in the back bedroom, the one to the right at the top of the stairs.

I have come to spend a summer in Ireland and I would very much like to see my old home. I know this is a big ask and I understand totally if you feel this would be too much of an intrusion.

I promise not to stay long, and will strive to cause as little disturbance as possible.

Yours

Kathleen Williams

Lexie noticed a further note, in more wobbly writing, at the bottom of the page.

PS I will be staying at the Caracove Arms Hotel for the next couple of days, should you wish to contact me there. Otherwise this is my US cell number ...

Lexie whistled. How fascinating! And this lady had been born in their bedroom! Without hesitating, she grabbed her mobile phone and typed a quick text to the number at the foot of the page.

Hello Kathleen, Lexie Collins here. I live at 3 Cashel Square. I just got your note & would love to meet you. I'm intrigued! I would be delighted for you to come and visit. All the best, Lexie

'What do you think about that, Tiddles?' she asked, as he circled around her ankles giving out. She spooned some food into his dish and made her way upstairs to change into some gardening clothes. The planted pots out the back needed attention and she wanted to water the flowerbeds. A text came through immediately.

> Dear Lexie, how kind of you to text me so promptly. I'm so delighted you weren't put out by my letter. Please let me know when would be convenient for me to call & I'll be there! Kathleen

Lexie grinned. Normally she would be nervous about corresponding with a complete stranger and wouldn't consider asking someone she'd never met to her home. But something told her Kathleen was legitimate.

> Hi K – if it were me I'd want to come right now! I'm here for the evening if you're free? L

Lexie threw her phone on to the bed as she pulled off her white dress. Opting for a plain T-shirt and her favourite pale blue jeans, she grinned as yet another text pinged through.

> Dear L – if you're certain, I could be with you in 30 minutes? K

> Dear K – I'll be here waiting! No need to give you directions! This is surreal! See you soon, L

Lexie felt a sudden flash of panic. She picked up her dress and brought it into the walk-in wardrobe. Trying to gauge the room with fresh eyes, she hoped Kathleen would like what they'd done with it. It had been the first to be done up properly and Lexie adored it. The bed was made and she was satisfied it was tidy. She walked across the landing to one of the spare rooms and peered in nervously. It was what Sam referred to affectionately as the skip. All the stuff they didn't use was packed into it. They really needed to bin the whole lot, but hadn't got around to it. Knowing she hadn't time to go through every room in the house, she ran downstairs and dashed from one room to another making sure it was presentable. If she'd had more notice, she would've run the vacuum cleaner over the rugs or mopped the kitchen floor.

She dialled Sam's mobile and quickly filled him in.

'Wow, that's interesting!' he agreed. 'I'm really busy in here today, unfortunately, or I would've ducked out early. If she's easy-going maybe she'll stay for dinner and I can meet her then.'

'I'll text and let you know how I'm getting on,' Lexie promised. 'Who knows? Maybe she's the decoy in a criminal gang. You might come home to find the house ransacked and my bloodied body lying lifeless at the bottom of the stairs.'

'Stop it! That's not even funny,' Sam said. 'Now that you mention it, make sure you look through the spyhole in the front door before you open it. Check that she really is an old lady.'

'Ah, but what if they use a cute little lady to lull victims into a false sense of security? The ninjas with swords could be lurking in the bay bushes, ready to slice me limb from limb.'

'You watch far too much Tarantino.' Sam laughed. 'I'll tell you what, send me a text if you're being murdered. I can ring Ernie from next door and he can shuffle in and beat them with his Zimmer frame.'

'Ah, you're all heart!'

'See you later, hon.'

Lexie took scissors from the drawer in the kitchen and made her way down the hall to the main back door. The one in the basement led to a small neat yard but, as it rarely got much sunlight, she and Sam didn't use it. The other led to the garden. They'd spent years getting it right. Lexie wasn't exactly green-fingered, but she knew her efforts made for a pretty place to sit.

Snipping at random, she gathered a gorgeous selection of Canterbury bells. She loved their tall upright stems and the wonderful colours, from white to cerise to vibrant violet. Bunching them into a tall plain glass vase, she placed them on the kitchen table. Rooting in the cupboard, she found some chocolate chip and fudge cookies. The décor was ultra modern and neutral, but Lexie liked to mix kitsch girly accessories to add splashes of colour: she selected a cough-medicine-pink cake stand and emptied the cookies on to it.

Just as she'd finished folding two flower-printed linen napkins, the doorbell sounded.

Dear Diary

If only I could find a time machine. My school life just isn't moving at the right pace for my social life. Hanging out with Elton and the guys has shown me what a waste of time school really is. Most of them left school at sixteen and they have their fingers on the pulse.

They were going through all the ways they can get money from the social. Who says you need an A in maths? This lot have it sussed. The flat is exactly the way they want it to be, and serves its purpose. One of them has his name on the lease and they all chip in. The landlord hardly ever pitches up so long as the rent goes to his account. The sofa was taking up valuable mattress space so they sold it. The way the system works is that whoever crashes first gets dibs on the bed. But that's, like, a total sham because none of them ever wants to be the first to fall.

Elton was teaching me how to play chords on the guitar. He says you can get by knowing three. He's managing so that must be true. They're the smartest guys I've met for a long time. It's like they take all the convoluted and messy stuff that life throws at us and totally edit out all the unnecessary parts. It's genius. If the rest of humanity got with the plot we'd all be so much happier. I reckon my mum needs to go on a retreat to the flat. She could do with relaxing on all sorts of things that don't matter. They do the sharing-is-caring thing so well. On alternating weeks one person takes a bag of dirty clothes to the launderette. Then they all help themselves to fresh stuff. That mightn't work so well for girls but, as Elton pointed out, there's more to life than cleaning and washing. Elvis didn't become the king of rock and roll by ironing shirts.

The only bogus thing that happened was that my mother kept calling and texting non-stop. I felt a bit guilty but I had to turn my phone off. I didn't want Elton to think I'm a mollycoddled baby. I'm going to allow this new ethos to absorb a bit further before putting it all to my parents. If I leave school now it would actually solve a lot.

(a) saving of school fees

(b) I can get a job pronto rather than years down the line

(c) I could move into the flat – they said they could do with a woman's touch. (Elton also said I'm the first girl they've ever considered allowing to live there. Apparently they liked the way I cleaned the bathroom and chipped the dried-on Pot Noodle off the plates even without being asked.)

I'll mull it all over for a bit longer but I reckon Mum and Dad will go for it as an idea. There'd be nothing to lose, right? Elton and I will be together until death do us part. So what's the difference if we start all that right now rather than next year?

Later.

Am

Chapter 5

KATHLEEN'S HANDS WERE SHAKING AS SHE WAITED outside number three. She figured Lexie might be a little surprised she'd arrived so promptly, but she couldn't help it. The second the text messages had come saying she could visit, she had started getting ready. She'd slept for a short time in the armchair, and although her eyes were still rather peppery, she was fuelled by excitement.

As the heavy panelled door opened, Kathleen peered eagerly inside.

'Hello, Kathleen. I'm Lexie,' the woman said, with a wide smile. 'Duh, well, obviously!' She thumped herself on the forehead with the heel of her hand. 'Come on in! How weird is this?'

'Hi, Lexie,' Kathleen answered. 'I can't tell you how grateful I am to be here.'

'It's such a pleasure to meet you!' Lexie said graciously. 'And you're so much younger-looking than I expected.'

'Actually, so are you!'

Both women laughed. Trepidation weighed heavily in the air.

'Thank you! I'm hurtling towards forty, which my mother seems very keen on reminding me lately, but I still feel as if I'm twenty-five!'

'I know what you mean,' Kathleen agreed. 'I'm seventy-four and I honestly feel my head stopped counting at forty-five …' She trailed off and inhaled deeply, closing her eyes.

'Are you all right?' Lexie asked.

'Oh, yes. It's – it's the strangest feeling being back,' Kathleen stuttered. 'The house still smells the same! It's a mixture of furniture polish and wood. It's wonderful! You keep it so beautifully, my dear. You should be very proud.'

'I am,' Lexie said. 'Sam – he's my husband – and I, we've poured our hearts and souls into this place. When we bought it in 1998 it was kind of ramshackle and nothing looked the way we knew it could. It's taken us years to reawaken its beauty.'

'Well, you've done a sterling job. If I'm totally honest, it was never this gorgeous when I lived here. The only thing I recognise for sure are these black-and-white floor tiles,' she said, patting them gently with her foot.

'We had them professionally cleaned,' Lexie said. 'Sam and I agreed they were worth restoring. There's still a lot of work to be done, but we knew when we bought the place that it would be an ongoing project. Some day we'll win the lotto and manage to finish every room.'

'Have you any children?' Kathleen asked, as she gazed up at the ceiling, then to the oak staircase.

'No, it's just the two of us. Unless you count Tiddles, our furry boy.'

'Well, I would absolutely count Tiddles.' Kathleen's eyes shone. 'I'm a kitty momma too. I've got a furry girl back home.'

'Tea or coffee?' Lexie offered.

'I'd love a cup of tea, now that you mention it,' Kathleen said.

'Do you prefer herbal or green or can I tempt you to a good old-fashioned Irish breakfast tea?' Lexie said.

'A cup of builder's tea, as my darling mother used to call it, would be lovely,' Kathleen said, with a glint in her eye.

As they went into the kitchen the older woman gasped. 'This is wonderful, Lexie!'

'I'm glad you like it.' Lexie beamed. 'It's the most recent work we've carried out and cost a small fortune. We're utterly smashed now, but it was worth forgoing a foreign holiday and cutting back on silly spending for a while. The porcelain flooring can be a bit of a menace to keep clean, but I *had* to have it. Come and sit down. I'll put the kettle on.'

Kathleen tucked her hands into the pockets of her linen trousers and walked to the window. 'Who maintains the park? It's like something from a fairy tale. It's perfectly manicured yet it's not stuffy.'

'We have a little rota going. Each house contributes in some way, whether it's to cut the grass, sand and varnish the wooden benches or to plant one of the beds. We all do our bit so it never becomes a chore.'

'How wonderful,' Kathleen said, as she gazed out.

As Lexie placed the teapot on the table, Kathleen turned to sit down, with glassy eyes. 'I can't thank you enough for allowing me to come here today. I don't think I anticipated quite how special this was going to feel. To be in a position to revisit my past like this is quite simply a gift.'

'That's fantastic,' Lexie said. 'I'm more than happy to be the facilitator.' She poured the tea and gestured for Kathleen to help herself to milk, sugar and a cookie. 'How long are you planning to spend in Ireland?'

'My return ticket is for September first,' Kathleen said. 'It sounds like quite a long spell when I say it now, but I know it's going to fly. There are so many places I want to see and things I want to do. I'd like to revisit some of the places I used to love as a child. I have a proper schedule drawn up in my mind. It's going to be joyous.'

'Where are you staying?' Lexie asked, and bit into a cookie.

'I'm at the hotel right now, as you're aware, but I'll go to a local letting agency first thing in the morning and try to find a suitable apartment.'

'Would you like to see the rest of the house?' Lexie offered. 'You can take your tea with you.'

'I'm longing to see every nook and cranny,' Kathleen admitted. 'I don't want you thinking I'm a nosy old woman, though – I'm trying to be polite!'

Lexie laughed. 'I'd be exactly the same in your shoes. I'm actually a little nervous of your reaction,' she divulged. 'I'd hate to upset you. You might think what we've done is horrendous.'

'I doubt that very much, Lexie. I'll tell you what – how about I promise not to explode and throw myself on the floor in a wild tantrum?'

'Deal!'

They took their cups and Lexie led the way. First stop was the living room, which housed the second bay window to the right of the front door.

'Oh, my goodness,' Kathleen exclaimed. 'This is to die for! I love the duck egg blue tones in here. The tiny birds in the curtain fabric are like an extension of the park. And the floorboards look better than I remember them.'

'They were quite stained, so we had them cleaned and treated. It's a wax finish. All the wood in the house was done. It was tedious but we feel it's worth it.'

'I'll say,' Kathleen agreed. 'The cream leather couches are divine. I'd never have thought of putting something so modern in here but they look great.'

'All the original chandeliers were gone when we bought the place, but we sourced some at auctions. Are they anything like the lights you had once upon a time?'

'This one is very similar, although I reckon it's a lot prettier. My mother would've loved it. Her crystal was her pride and joy.'

As they made their way into the hall, Lexie explained that they'd closed off the entrance to the basement. 'We thought we'd convert it and rent it out to help pay the mortgage. We've installed a kitchenette and bathroom, but the living area has no furniture and neither does the bedroom. I know it's a waste of space, really, but we never got around to finishing it.'

'Well, given the choice, I don't think I'd relish the thought of a stranger in my basement either,' Kathleen said.

Lexie continued, 'So the door you once knew is gone from here.'

'It always caused massive draughts if I recall,' Kathleen said. 'The small room at the back was our den. My mother used to chase us in here when visitors were in the living room.'

'That's a makeshift studio now,' Lexie said, showing her. 'Excuse the mess.'

'It's charming,' Kathleen said. 'So peaceful. I love this room. I always came here of my own accord. It's very serene and I can totally appreciate how you love to paint in here. What sort of art do you do?'

'I used to do very intricate portraits. They were my passion. But

I had an accident and shattered my wrist, which meant I couldn't paint the things I truly wanted to do – I was forced to change career too. So, this room only gets sporadic use now. I was advised by my physiotherapist to use the wrist and try to regain some of my former control, but it became intensely frustrating and used to put me in terrible form so I stopped.'

'What a pity,' Kathleen said.

Lexie didn't answer, but continued with the tour. 'The back door leads to the garden, as you know. Come on upstairs and we can sit outside once you've finished looking.'

'Thank you.'

Lexie went up the staircase and decided to show Kathleen the spare room first.

'Too much order without so much as a sniff of disarray always makes me suspicious of folks,' Kathleen said, peering into the dishevelled room.

'Yeah, that's like my parents' house. Every single thing has a place and woe betide anybody who doesn't conform,' Lexie said. As they walked towards the master bedroom, she hesitated. 'I'm a little nervous of your reaction to our room because this is where you were born,' she said. 'You'll remember there were two rooms on this side of the house?'

'Of course,' Kathleen said, as they paused outside the closed door.

'We've created a suite instead. So it's slightly different,' she said.

As they walked in, Kathleen's hands flew to her mouth. 'Oh, Lexie, it's fabulous!'

'It was a labour of love, for sure.' Lexie laughed. 'My best friend Maia teases me, saying our bedroom is the size of a football pitch. But we love it.'

'So you should. It's gorgeous.'

'There's a bathroom and dressing room too,' she said, leading the way.

'Oh I'm so envious!' Kathleen said. 'Every girl dreams of a walk-in closet, right?'

'I do adore it.'

'I'm sure everyone says this but you've such an eye for design.'

'Thank you. I suppose this place was my biggest canvas. I own an art gallery too.'

Lexie showed Kathleen the one remaining spare bedroom before the final large one. 'This is Amélie's room. She's my niece. She's seventeen and currently hates the entire world and all its inhabitants bar me!'

'Oh dear! Poor Amélie. I can't say I'd like to be a teenager again.'

'Me neither. I know I'm almost forty, but I still remember very clearly how awful it can feel.'

'I do too, actually. I thought everyone was against me. It's a confusing and lonely time. Lucky Amélie to have an auntie like you.'

The room was any teenager's paradise. The walls were cream but they and a corner of the ceiling were adorned with neon images.

'It's not exactly classical in style,' Kathleen said, bursting out laughing.

'Isn't it like walking into a migraine? The day Sam and I helped Amélie do this was just such fun. She wanted her room at home to look like this but my brother and his wife were having none of it. It was cheap as chips to do and Amélie adores it.'

'I'd say she does. No wonder she thinks you're cool.'

'Well, it took a bit of persuasion on Sam's part to get me on board. Ordinarily I love all things French and chic. I spent a year in France a long time ago, so I must have inadvertently carried back some of the décor with me.'

'That's the wonderful benefit of travel. We learn so much,' Kathleen said.

'Oh, yes!' Lexie was leading the way back down the stairs towards the garden. 'Come and sit for a while. I'm sure your brain needs time to catch up with your eyes. Can I get you a glass of lemonade or some wine perhaps?'

'I'd love a glass of wine if you're having one,' Kathleen said.

Lexie showed her to the garden and settled her on a comfy chair. 'I'll be back in a jiffy,' she promised.

'Take your time, dear.'

Kathleen's eyes darted from one corner of the garden to the next.

The dividing walls were the same, but none of the rest was. When she'd lived here there had been a lawn and that was about it. There weren't half as many cobbled areas and cleverly designed features. She loved what the couple had done with the house – she liked Lexie too. Kathleen was certain the place had never looked as good.

'Here we are,' Lexie said, reappearing with two glasses of wine and a little bowl of olives on a wooden tray.

'Thank you. This is a fantastic treat,' Kathleen said.

They clinked glasses and toasted: 'To number three Cashel Square!' Lexie said.

'To number three and her welcoming owner!' Kathleen responded. 'I appreciate your kindness more than you'll ever know.'

'The pleasure is all mine,' Lexie said. 'I hope we'll get to know one another while you're in Ireland. You're welcome here any time. I'd love to show you my gallery too. I think you'd enjoy browsing.'

'I know I would,' Kathleen said. 'Mm, this wine is delicious.'

'Glad you like it.' Lexie smiled. 'Another little throwback to my time *en France*,' she said, with a perfect accent.

'The artwork throughout the house is stunning, but I'm especially taken with the smallish painting at the top of the stairs. The one of a little girl with curly hair wearing a pale pink summer dress.'

'Really?' Lexie said, looking pleased. Kathleen cocked her head to the side. 'I painted it,' she said shyly. 'It's Amélie when she was three. I did it from memory, which is probably against the rules when making a portrait, but I felt inspired after she'd spent one of her many weekends here.'

'Well, it's delightful.'

'Thank you.' Lexie looked down. When she raised her head again, the light had gone from her eyes. 'I miss painting so much sometimes it's like a physical ache.' She took a sharp breath. 'Still, I'm fortunate to have the gallery to keep me occupied.'

'I can't wait to see it. I'm sure it's a treasure trove of fabulousness!'

They continued to chat and Lexie refilled their glasses, the early-evening sun adding to the warmth that was growing between them.

Chapter 6

THE SOUND OF SAM'S VOICE, COMING FROM INSIDE the house, made Lexie jump.

'We're out here, darling,' she called.

Kathleen got to her feet and wobbled slightly. 'Oh, my goodness, I'm acting like a drunken old fool.' Sam was much taller than she'd expected. In the couple of photos she'd seen around the house, he was either sitting or leaning against something. He reminded her of an auburn-haired version of Liam Neeson.

'Sam, this is Kathleen, the lady I told you about earlier.'

'I guessed as much,' he said, with a warm smile. Kathleen held her hand out for him to shake. Ignoring it, he hugged her, then kissed her on both cheeks. 'Lovely to meet you,' he said.

'The pleasure is all mine,' Kathleen answered. 'It's not every day I get hugs and kisses from gorgeous young men. Apologies for the staggering. I'm blaming the jet lag – it has nothing to do with the wine!'

Sam laughed and gestured for her to sit down again. 'When did you arrive in Ireland?' he asked, as he pulled Lexie into a hug. He kissed the top of her head and stroked her hair.

'Just today,' she said. 'I came straight from the airport, delivered my little note and my lovely taxi driver recommended the Caracove Arms Hotel, so I checked in there. Lexie texted me right away.'

'Great.' Sam nodded. 'She told me you lived here once. What do you think of it now? I hope you approve of what we've done with number three.'

'Gosh, how could I not? It's just stunning. As I said to Lexie, it's a damn sight better than when my family lived here.'

'Some day it'll all be shipshape and perfect.' Sam grinned. 'How long are you staying in Ireland?'

'For the whole summer basically,' she said. 'Florida is stifling at this time of year, so it's a relief to get out. I've been meaning to come home for aeons, but it never happened. The years seemed to roll by and there was always a reason not to make the trip.'

'I never asked, have you many family members here still?' Lexie asked.

'Sadly not.' Kathleen shook her head. 'Any family that remained here are long gone and my siblings are all in the States.'

'You've certainly got an American twang when you speak, but you're undeniably Irish still,' Sam commented.

'You've no idea how thrilled I am to hear that, dear.'

'My folks are in a similar situation,' Sam said. 'They moved to Sydney twenty years ago. To me they sound pretty Australian, but their friends all love their Irish accents.'

'It's funny what different people hear,' Kathleen mused.

'I'm going to grab a glass of wine and a top-up for you two,' Sam said. 'I hate to sound all caveman here, but I'm famished. Seeing as there's no sign of dinner on the go, how about I do my usual form of cooking?'

'Oh, please don't let me interrupt,' Kathleen said, attempting to get to her feet again.

'You're not interrupting and we'd love you to join us,' Lexie said. 'Sam's idea of cooking is to phone the local Chinese restaurant and have food delivered!'

'Ah, I see!' She grinned. 'You sound just like my husband, Jackson. He can manage on nibbles and itty-bitty food for so long but then he needs a proper feed.'

'Is he here with you?' Lexie asked.

'No, dear. Sadly not. He organised this junket for me as a little trip down Memory Lane. As he said, there's nothing more boring than reliving the past when you weren't there to begin with. It's like looking at other folks' holiday photos.'

'So you're here alone?' Sam asked.

'Yup!' Kathleen said. 'How grown-up is that?'

'Very,' Lexie agreed.

'I also have some unfinished business to attend to while I'm here,' Kathleen said. 'I won't bore you with the details right now.'

'Please stay and eat with us,' Lexie begged, changing the subject.

'I actually ate earlier,' Kathleen said. 'I got room service as soon as I arrived. I can never eat while flying – it makes me queasy. But I'm hungry again so I'd love to have something with you.'

'Most airline food is enough to make anyone ill,' Sam said. 'So that's settled. Will I order a selection of dishes and we can all share or do you have a preference?'

'I'd eat anything without a pulse, especially if it's being handed to me!' said Kathleen.

'You're going to fit in nicely around here!' Sam laughed.

The food arrived promptly, and although it had been warm in the garden, once the sun had gone down, it became chilly. Lexie lit the two large outdoor heaters, discreetly installed at either side of the veranda roof.

'Can you believe I've never sat under one of those?' Kathleen told them.

'Well, why would you?' Sam asked. 'I doubt many are sold in Florida.'

'It doesn't usually get cool enough. There aren't as many bugs here, though.'

'We get infestations of midges every now and again,' Lexie said, 'but for the most part bugs aren't an issue.'

As the couple continued to chat, Kathleen sighed happily. She'd left Orlando International Airport with a heavy heart. It was alien for her to be away from Jackson. For forty-four years, she'd barely left his side.

'You need the time to reminisce,' he'd said. 'It'll do your heart good to surround yourself with familiar places and forgotten memories. You won't need me there for that, Kathy. I'd only cramp your style.'

She swallowed hard. She didn't want to cry in front of her new friends.

'Is everything all right?' Lexie asked, concerned.

'Oh, yes, dear. Thank you. Don't mind me. I'm just thinking about Jackson. I've wittered on about this return visit for as long as I can recall. Our holidays were precious and Jackson's business always took precedence before he retired.'

'What did he work at?' Sam asked.

'He was a vet,' she said.

'Did you end up with all sorts of stray cats and dogs in your house?' Lexie asked.

'Not quite,' Kathleen said. 'Jackson was in charge of the animals at Disney's Animal Kingdom. His main speciality was the large cats.'

'I can see why he wouldn't bring Daddy Tiger home for the weekend,' Lexie said. They all laughed.

'They look cute but those boys would swallow any of us whole!' Kathleen said. 'His job meant we travelled a lot to Africa to exchange cubs with other conservation centres. As a result Europe wasn't on our horizon.'

'So Jackson's retirement meant you could come?' Lexie asked.

'Totally. Jackson got a lump sum when he finished up at work so he bought me the ticket. He insisted I should come before I was too old to enjoy it properly.'

'Well, I'm glad you did,' Lexie said warmly.

All three cleared away the foil containers and the plates. Kathleen yawned, suddenly exhausted again. 'I think I'm going to leave you guys now. You've been so sweet to me. I never dreamed I'd meet such warm and welcoming folks.'

'We're honoured that you came to see us,' Lexie said.

'Absolutely,' Sam reiterated. 'Call over any time you like. We'd be delighted to see you.'

'Neither of us likes to drink and drive,' Lexie explained, 'so I'll call you a cab. We use a local company, so they'll take care of you.'

'I can walk!' Kathleen argued.

'Indeed you cannot,' Sam said. 'We'd never forgive ourselves if anything happened to you.'

They sat in the living room to wait for the taxi. Kathleen got up to gaze out across the square. 'I told my taxi driver earlier on that Mrs Caddy, the lady who used to live over there in number eight, was a dragon! She used to mutter to herself and shoo us away if we came within earshot of her.'

'She sounds awful,' Lexie said. 'There's a family with three children there now. The eldest is Amélie's age.'

'I'm glad old Mrs Caddy's bad karma hasn't tainted the place.'

As the taxi pulled up outside, Kathleen gulped.

'Are you certain you're okay?' Lexie asked, standing up from the sofa and crossing the room.

'Yes, dear. Thank you.' In spite of all her best efforts, Kathleen felt tell-tale tears seeping down her cheeks. 'Oh, no! I'm so embarrassed. Forgive me. I don't know why I'm crying. You must think I'm a crazy old doll.'

'I don't think anything of the sort,' Lexie said kindly. 'You've had a long journey all by yourself and walked back into a place you hadn't seen for donkey's years. It's not surprising you're a bit out there.'

'Lexie's right,' Sam said. 'You've been on an emotional marathon in the last twelve hours.' He glanced at Lexie and hesitated. Then he went on, 'Listen, why don't you stay with us for a few days? Just until you find somewhere suitable to rent. What do you think, Lexie?'

'It's a brilliant idea. I hate the thought of you being in a hotel with nobody to talk to.'

'Oh, I couldn't impose. I've already pushed myself on you enough. You're a darling couple but I need to venture back to the hotel and try to get some sleep, if it's all the same to you.'

'How about we compromise?' Lexie said. 'Would you meet me for breakfast in the morning? There's a gorgeous café just beside the gallery. They don't do greasy-spoon stuff, it's more along the lines of smoothies and porridge with yummy toppings like fruit compôtes and lavender honey.'

'And their home-baked breads are to die for,' Sam added. 'Lexie and I go there most Sundays for brunch. We munch our way through eggs Benedict or scrambled eggs topped with smoked salmon.'

'Okay, okay!' Kathleen said, cheering up. 'I'm sold!'

'I've to open the gallery and I've a client booked in to view a painting at nine thirty. Why don't you call at the gallery any time after ten and we can have brunch?' Lexie suggested.

'If you're sure I won't be muscling in on your day,' Kathleen said.

'I'd be delighted,' Lexie said, placing a reassuring hand on her arm.

'I'll be chained to my desk, sadly, so it'll be a girls' only affair,' said Sam. 'But I've no doubt we'll be seeing a bit of one another over the next few weeks. In other words, don't be a stranger.'

'Don't be a stranger,' Kathleen repeated. 'I haven't heard that phrase for quite some time.'

Even though they'd only just met, it didn't seem odd for them to hug as Kathleen departed.

The taxi driver wasn't overly friendly, which suited Kathleen perfectly. She was utterly shattered. As she paid and made her way into the hotel, she was looking forward to slipping into her nightdress and climbing into bed.

A few minutes later she lay back on the pillows. She welcomed the background noise of other guests and the lurching of elevator as it shunted up and down. She wasn't used to being on her own. She turned off the bedside light, lay back and tried to relax. The darkness was too much, so she flicked the light back on and padded to the bathroom. She'd leave the light on in there with the door open a crack.

Scolding herself for being so childish, she picked up the information pack from the coffee table and pulled out a postcard.

My darling Jackson

As usual you're right. It's wonderful to be back in Ireland. I cannot express how awesome it was to walk into my old home once more.

The owners are the most gorgeous couple called Lexie and Sam. They've turned number three into a modern and stylish home. They've proved that Irish people are indeed the most welcoming in the world. I spent the evening with them and already I feel as if I've known them for ever.

Thank you for insisting I come here. Maybe now I'll finally stop 'wittering on about it', as you delicately put it!

I love you and miss you, but I won't waste this precious time. I can almost see you wagging a finger in my direction!

Your loving wife,

Kathy x x

Taking a deep breath, Kathleen climbed back into bed, closed her eyes and went over every detail of number three Cashel Square, Lexie and Sam. They seemed so content and together. She couldn't imagine a better family living in her former home. The work and love they'd poured into the renovations were astounding.

Yawning, Kathleen found herself looking forward to the next day. She was longing to see the gallery and explore her childhood haunts.

Chapter 7

'I HAVE TO SAY I'M PLEASANTLY SURPRISED BY Kathleen,' Sam said, as he and Lexie lay in bed. 'I wasn't too happy about you inviting a total stranger into our home, if I'm honest.'

'I had a good feeling about her,' Lexie said. 'In my defence I don't make a habit of it.'

'I know that.' He swatted her arm. 'It could've been dodgy all the same. She might've been a lunatic or just plain awful.'

'Well, she was neither,' Lexie yawned, 'so no harm done. In fact, I think she's going to be a lovely addition to our lives this summer. We could see her as a grown-up version of a foreign-exchange student.'

'That's one way of looking at it, I guess.' Sam seemed pensive.

'What?' Lexie asked, resting her head on her arm and staring at him.

'Let's play it by ear for a little while, but how would you feel about offering Kathleen the basement for the summer?'

'Perfect!' Lexie said immediately. 'It would be right somehow, wouldn't it?'

'Well, we did all the work, putting the kitchenette and bathroom in and it's never been used.'

'She'd need some basic furniture,' Lexie mused.

'We could take the bed from the spare-spare room, as opposed to Amélie's room,' he quipped, 'so all she'd need is a sofa and a small table and chairs.'

'We could pick those up easily enough.'

'See how you get on with her tomorrow,' said Sam. 'You could always suggest it, if it seems fitting.'

Lexie felt oddly excited as she drifted off to sleep. She'd warmed to Kathleen instantly. She had such an easy nature in contrast to her own mother, who was at the other end of the spectrum, constantly fussing and consumed by what everyone else might be thinking. Kathleen had a relaxed elegance to her style and seemed happy in her own skin. She was so independent and open to adventure too. Clearly she had a very close relationship with her husband, Jackson, yet she'd come all this way alone. Penelope barely went to the supermarket without Reggie and even then she'd have to nag him and give out.

Lexie was going to take Sam's advice and see how tomorrow panned out, but she hoped Kathleen would be open to the idea of staying in the basement flat. The other woman seemed more than capable of looking after herself, but Lexie felt slightly protective of her all the same. She could just see the two of them sharing glasses of wine and chatting.

They jumped at the sound of hammering on the front door.

'I'll go,' Sam said groggily, and looked at his watch. 'It's half eleven. Who on earth would call at this time?'

'It's not *that* late,' Lexie riposted. She and Sam really were very set in their ways.

Maia had been telling her for years what fuddy-duddies they were. 'Try having a colicky baby bawling in your ear for a year and tell me you're tired.'

'Why do you think we haven't gone there?' Lexie said. 'Sam and I like suiting ourselves and doing what we want, when we want.'

Lexie grabbed her dressing gown and shot downstairs after him. The flashing blue light was visible through the glass panel to the side of the door.

'Hello!' Sam sounded astonished.

'I presume this young lady belongs to you,' the police officer said.

'What's going on?' Lexie asked, joining Sam at the door.

'There was a complaint from a local resident,' the police officer continued. 'A group of youths, your young lady included, were playing loud music in Hawthorn Park and drinking.'

'I see,' Sam said.

'Now your daughter insists she wasn't drinking and we didn't find any alcohol on her person, so we've given her a talking-to and thought it best to deliver her home. Some of the lads she was with were very abusive and brandishing bottles, so they've been taken to the station.'

'I see,' Sam said again. 'That's appalling behaviour, and I can tell you, it's not what we expect from *our* daughter,' he said, narrowing his eyes at Amélie.

'We had no idea you were in the park,' Lexie said, glowering at her. 'We're not in the habit of allowing *our daughter* to hang about in public places at night, I can assure you.'

'I'm sorry I went without asking you, *Mum*,' Amélie said.

'Let this be a warning to you, Margaret,' the police officer said.

Lexie and Sam shot her a look of puzzlement. Amélie raised her eyebrows and willed them not to dob her in.

'We're very grateful to you for bringing her home safely,' Sam said. 'I can assure you this won't happen again. We'll make sure she realises the error of her ways.'

'See that you do,' he said. 'And I'd advise her to give that gang she's hanging around with a wide berth. Some of those lads are known to the police and not the type you want a girl like Margaret being associated with.'

'You're very good to let us know,' Sam reiterated. 'There'll be stern talks in this house.'

'Thanks again, Officer,' Lexie said, and shut the door.

Amélie ran into the living room ahead of them.

'So, *Margaret*,' Sam said, with his hands on his hips. 'What was going on?'

'I *had* to give a false name,' Amélie said. 'We weren't doing anything wrong. Some nosy old bag with no life rang and gave out because we were having fun.' She pouted.

'Do your parents know where you are?' Lexie asked. 'Your mum rang me this afternoon and said she couldn't find you.'

'Yeah, I know. I got your text,' said Amélie. 'I told her I was studying at Sarah's, then coming here to stay with you.'

'What?' Lexie said. 'Jeez, Amélie, are you trying to get us all into trouble?'

'No!' she said. 'Please don't get all aggro with me. I know it was really stupid but I've just started dating this guy Elton and he's really cool ...' Her eyes lit up. 'He's a musician and he's really into saving the planet.'

'That's super-cool, marvellous and totes amazing,' Sam said sarcastically. 'But Auntie Lexie and I are old and decrepit. Funnily enough, we hate being woken by the police to tell us that our non-existent daughter Margaret is acting the maggot in a public place.' He stood closer and sniffed her breath. 'And you *were* drinking. Not cool, little lady. Not cool. Much as you mightn't like to face it, you're under age. You could get into serious trouble. If Elton's so keen on saving things, he should start with his girlfriend. I'm sure you think he's the most amazing person ever created, but so far he's not impressing me.'

'I'm sorry, Sam. I messed up.' She swayed from side to side with her hands clasped at her chest.

'You'll end up in trouble, Amélie,' he warned again, softening. 'I'm going back to bed because, as I already said, I'm old and boring, and guess what? I like sleeping during the night.'

Amélie plonked herself on the sofa as Sam began to leave the room. 'Elton?' he said. 'What kind of a name is that?' He left Lexie to do the rest of the lecturing.

'What are you going to do?' Amélie asked, looking up at Lexie.

'I'm not going to beat you with the fireside poker or anything,' Lexie said, sighing deeply. 'But you've really dumped me in it now, haven't you?'

'I'm more sorry than you'll ever know, like E-V-E-R,' Amélie said dramatically.

'Did you buy booze with the money I gave you for ice-cream?' Lexie asked.

Amélie nodded. 'Sort of. That stupid old goat in the off-licence wouldn't serve me earlier. Said I had to have proper ID. I have this fake one but he said it didn't look authentic so one of the lads bought it for me.'

Lexie rubbed her temples. 'If your parents hear about this you'll never be allowed out again.'

'I know, and they're already on my case.'

'Your mum says you haven't done any work for your exams,' Lexie said. 'And apparently you disappeared while she went shopping today.'

'She wouldn't let me out!' Amélie yelled. 'It's like being in a bloody concentration camp at our house.'

'Hey!' Lexie shouted back. Then she took a deep breath, closed her eyes and tried to calm herself. 'You just landed in on me and Sam, used us as an alibi while lying to the police. Don't raise your voice at me! I'm on your side here. Don't blow it, Amélie.'

'Sorry.' She looked at the floor. 'I'm just trying to live my life. I didn't go out intending to cause you loads of hassle, I swear.'

'Let's just go to bed. You need to cop on, Amélie. The police were very nice to you this time, but take this as one strike too many,' Lexie said. 'You only get away with this kind of messing once. After that it's serious.'

'Are you telling Mum and Dad?' she asked.

'I'll talk to Sam and decide in the morning,' she said.

'If you don't tell them, I promise you nothing like this will happen again. I'll go home tomorrow and study for fourteen hours. Straight up.'

'How about you go home and even do an hour of work? That would be a vast improvement.'

Amélie hugged her and Lexie tried not to wince at the smell. 'Don't drink that vile cider any more either. It'll pickle your insides and your brain. It stinks.'

'It's cheap.' Amélie shrugged.

Lexie took a deep breath. 'The other thing I'd like you to think about is this new guy Elton.'

'Oh, you'd love him! He's totally mint.'

'So far he doesn't sound it. Hanging out in parks and drinking cheap booze paid for by your under-age girlfriend? You can do better, honey.'

'We only went to the park because it was a nice evening. And there were too many of us to fit in the bedsit ...'

'Amélie. When you're in a hole, learn when to stop digging.'

Amélie looked like she wanted to argue, but didn't dare. They switched off the lights and went upstairs to their rooms.

Lexie climbed in beside Sam, who was pretending he was asleep.

'What'll we do?' she asked.

'I dunno.' He sighed. 'If we tell your brother and Dee, they'll have a total meltdown. She'll be grounded until she's forty.'

'I know,' Lexie said. 'But don't we have a parental duty or whatever it's called?'

'Well, we're not actually her parents,' Sam pointed out. 'Our daughter is called Margaret, apparently.'

They giggled quietly. 'Shush,' Lexie said. 'Whatever you do, don't let her hear us laughing. I'd say she nearly died when the police arrived.'

'I have to hand it to her, though, she can think on her feet. She was dead right not to go back to her own house in the squad car. She's not that stupid.'

Chapter 8

'TWO DAYS IN A ROW OF SUNSHINE!' LEXIE SAID TO SAM, as he bit into his toasted brioche the next morning.

'Hm,' he mumbled. 'Let's hope it holds out for the weekend. I'd like to get a bit of work done in the garden. Any sign of Sleeping Beauty up there?'

'She's having a shower and going home to study for the rest of her life.' Lexie grinned.

'How long do you reckon that'll last? Until lunchtime?'

'If we're lucky. I'm thinking we won't tell Dee and Billy about the shenanigans last night. What do you reckon?'

'It's your call because it's your family, but I don't really see what good telling them would do. There'd just be out-and-out war.'

'She seems really sorry this morning,' Lexie said.

'Yeah – sorry she got caught.' Sam smiled. 'Let's leave it so.'

'We were teenagers once,' Lexie said. 'She got a fright and it might make her think twice before she behaves like that again.'

'Or she has a taste for drinking in parks now and she'll be off again tonight.' As Sam stooped to kiss her goodbye, he paused. 'I forgot to mention it last night, but your mother called me yesterday.'

'Really?' Lexie looked mildly surprised. 'What did she want?'

'For me to cajole you into having a fortieth birthday bash at the yacht club.'

'I meant to discuss it with you, but it went out of my mind when Kathleen came,' she said. 'I hate the idea. I couldn't think of anything worse than having to be on display like a prize turkey, with my mother's cronies clucking around me.'

'Then there'd be the added hassle of forcing our friends to come along, make small talk and smile politely.'

'I told Mum straight up that I abhor the idea. But she's so enthralled with it, I don't reckon she heard me,' Lexie said.

'Oh, she heard you all right,' Sam said. 'She was very cross with you, actually. Apparently you were, and I quote, "less than gracious about the generous offer".'

'Oh, bloody hell, what is she like? Seriously! She's so stubborn at times. It gets on my wick.'

'And we don't know anyone else like that, do we?' Sam said, fixing her with a stare.

She rolled her eyes. 'The only reason I'm remotely considering it is because I know it'll make Mum ecstatic and keep her off my back for the summer. She'll drive poor Dad nuts too. It might be a mercy call for his sake, if nothing else.'

'I see your point, but don't be bullied into it if you really don't like the idea,' Sam said. 'This is like Groundhog Day from our wedding. Will you ever forget the fracas when we announced we weren't going to a church or a hotel?'

'The final nail in the coffin was my refusal to wear a meringue and a pair of curtains on my head!' Lexie giggled. 'Poor Mum, I have to feel sorry for her. She has only one daughter and I'm pretty dreadful. I give her no girly fix at all, do I?'

'Ah, stop now,' Sam said. 'Don't start tearing yourself apart. Just because you don't always do things Penelope's way it doesn't mean you're awful.'

Lexie stood and hugged him. They kissed briefly and he reluctantly left for work. Lexie wanted to tell him about the baby comments but she knew it wasn't the right time. She was still smarting after her mother's parting words.

It seemed as if the sands of time had run out with regard to Penelope's patience on that subject. Lexie knew she needed to have a very frank and open discussion with Sam. They'd agreed very soon after they'd met that children were not on the agenda.

'I have the maternal instincts of a marble slab,' Lexie had confessed one night, Dutch courage fuelled with a few glasses of wine.

'As in you're a cold, hard cow?' Sam had teased.

'Not in every way.' She had become oddly serious all of a sudden. 'But I don't ever see myself as one of those women who doesn't mind a small person wiping their hands on her linen trousers. I'd resent being woken during the night and I don't have an overwhelming urge to give birth to a mini-me.'

After she'd spouted her true feelings, Lexie had sat with her eyes screwed shut, praying that Sam wasn't going to spew his wine in horror and tell her she was a witch.

'Wowzers,' he'd said. 'I feel as if you've read my mind. Bar the linen trousers, naturally. If I ever start wearing those you'll know there's something very wrong with me.'

'Why?'

'I'm a redhead, Lexie. Milk-bottle white skin doesn't go with loafers and no socks, topped off with linen trousers.' They laughed.

She had sidled over to him and gazed into his eyes, longing to read his soul. 'Are you certain you're with me on the childfree-future plan?'

'Lex, when my brother had his kids I had to feign interest after the first couple of conversations. Each to their own and all that, but I'm beyond relieved you're happy to proceed with just you and me.'

'We'll have the best life together, right?' she'd said, feeling as if a weight had been lifted from her shoulders.

'You'd better believe it,' Sam had replied, kissing her.

Lexie couldn't have loved Sam more at that moment. She'd managed to exorcise her biggest inner demon without having to go into that episode in France. He'd simply accepted her wishes without question. She'd always known it, but right there and then, Lexie knew she and Sam were most certainly soul mates.

Over time, as each of their friends had babies, they had grown more certain of their joint decision.

When Calvin had been born, Maia and Josh had been rocked to the core. 'This is the worst day of my life,' Maia had cried, from her hospital bed, almost four years before. 'None of my scans showed any defects,' she said to Lexie. 'How can this have happened to us?' She sobbed, terrified and heartbroken. 'Apparently he has all the classic signs. The facial features … The space between his big toe and second toe is larger than usual …'

'I never knew that was a sign,' Lexie said, trying to take it all in.

'Neither did I,' Maia said. 'And he has no crease in his palms.'

'Can they do a test or something? Maybe they have it wrong.' Lexie was flailing.

'They've taken bloods, but only to determine which type of Down's he has. There are three apparently.'

'Shit.' Lexie had sat on the bed with a thud. Then, as the nurse wheeled the tiny baby back into the room, she had peered into his cot. 'Oh, Maia, he's so beautiful.' She had burst into tears.

'I know,' Maia agreed. But as she curled her legs towards her chest she began to howl. 'But I wanted a perfect child. God forgive me, Lexie.'

Lexie had hugged Maia for the longest time, stroking her hair. There was nothing she could say. All she could do was be there. 'Can I hold him?' she asked eventually.

'Sure,' Maia said, eyeballing the little bundle.

Lexie had scooped him out of the cot and nuzzled his little face. 'He's so soft and sweet.'

'It's so fucking unfair, Lexie,' Maia said, thumping the bed. 'This was meant to be the happiest day of our lives …'

Lexie held the baby and let her friend vent.

'How do I announce this? Do I send a text saying, "Hey, all, guess what, bit of a pisser, but …"?'

'Jesus, no!' Lexie said, appalled.

'What, then?' Maia asked, as tears poured onto her hospital gown. 'You're the arty, creative one. Come up with a line that sounds better. While you're at it, come up with something that makes me feel like I don't want to kill myself.'

That time had been awful. They had all gone through a sort of grieving process. Maia had slowly come to terms with the fact that her little boy was not what she and Josh had expected. The hospital confirmed he had Trisomy 21, which meant he had one extra copy of chromosome 21 in his make-up.

'Apparently ninety-five per cent of babies born with DS have this type,' Maia said. 'Look at me using initials like I know it all,' she said bitterly. 'The good news is that he doesn't have a heart defect. That's lucky, according to the doctors.'

'Great,' Lexie said encouragingly.

'Yeah? Why don't I feel the luck, then, Lex?'

'Because you're in a tail spin right now, honey, that's why,' Lexie said honestly. 'The dream you had originally is not coming true. You have a new one, though,' she added carefully.

'More like a really terrible nightmare,' Maia said, as anger washed over her yet again.

Lexie and Sam had spent as much time at the hospital as they could during the days following Calvin's birth. Sam and Josh had never been that close. They knew one another, but only through their wives. Their relationship altered massively at that time.

'We really appreciate the support you guys are showing us,' Josh said. 'It's such a shock. So many of our friends are avoiding us like the plague right now. Thanks for sticking around.'

'Hey, we'll be here to help in any way we can,' Sam said, banging Josh on the back.

'Of course,' Lexie reiterated. 'If you make us godparents, not that we're fishing,' she raised an eyebrow, 'we'll get him the coolest stuff!'

'Godparents you are,' Maia said, sighing heavily. She looked to Josh and he immediately nodded in agreement. 'Thanks, guys,' she said, as fresh tears sprang. 'Jesus, I've turned into a leaky mess. This being-a-mummy thing isn't what I expected, in any shape or form.'

'What about this little trouper?' Sam asked. 'Have you thought of a name yet? He's nearly four days old.'

'Yeah, we chatted about it last night as a matter of fact,' Josh said. 'Maia wants him to have a really cool one.'

Maia had grinned through her tears. 'Josh is too polite to repeat what I actually said.' Taking a deep breath, she continued, 'I vowed he wasn't having a boring or run-of-the-mill name. He's going to have tonnes of challenges during his life, so he's going to meet them head on,' she said, taking Josh's hand. 'And he's going to be Elvis or Dahl or Zack. The cool kids have names like that, right?'

Lexie had been unable to hide her concern. 'For the love of God, Maia, don't call the poor child Elvis! I know this is a rotten time and you're both stressed to the hilt but, as his godmother, I won't stand for it. Give him a cool name by all means. But not a downright stupid one.'

For the first time in days Maia had laughed. Belly-laughed with snot involved. 'Lex, you're a tonic. Even though I'm going through the worst moments of my life, I need a kick in the arse. No better woman to administer it! What does everyone think of Calvin?'

'That's gorgeous,' Lexie said, stroking the baby's cheek. 'It suits him. It's rock-star enough without being farcical.'

As the months had rolled by Maia and Josh had adjusted to parenthood, just the same as any new family. The initial shock had dissipated and they took to their new role like ducks to water.

Baby Calvin was as cute as a button and Lexie, for one, was besotted with him. Her phone was full of photos of him and Maia often teased her by opening her eyes wide and doing rocking motions with her arms. 'What's that for?' Lexie asked.

'I'm rocking and being the bunny-boiler in that movie *The Hand that Rocks the Cradle*. Get your own baby and stop grabbing mine all the time.'

'I don't want my own. I just adore snuggle-time with Calvin,' she said.

The comment had made her think, though. That evening she'd asked Sam what his thoughts were. 'Do you still feel happy that it's just you and me?'

He hesitated. Then, holding her gaze, he answered, 'I don't have a burning desire to be a father this second. Is that awful of me?'

'Hey, that's perfect. I feel the exact same way.' She sighed. 'Maia and Josh are amazing parents and I take my hat off to them … but there's so much to consider. What happens when Calvin grows up? What if they can't be there for him? He's strong as an ox so far, thank goodness, but how about long-term? What if he becomes ill? What happens when they die?'

'Jesus, Lexie,' Sam said. 'Those things are relevant no matter what. That's the choice people make by becoming a parent full stop.'

'I *know*. That's my whole point. That's why I don't see myself being a mother any time soon. I don't think I can make that commitment. And, for the record, Calvin's condition has nothing to do with my opinion.'

She wasn't being completely honest, she mused. Calvin's condition had made her think far more deeply about the prospect of parenthood. In fact, the idea of him being left alone without Maia and Josh *or* herself and Sam freaked the hell out of her. But it might come to pass. She and Maia had talked it over, strictly between themselves.

They'd gone for a meal, just the two of them. Josh and Sam had stayed in for a lads' night while minding baby Calvin. Maia had ordered a bottle of delicious yet very strong red wine, and they'd moved on to Irish coffee followed by gin and tonic. 'I'm feeling lashed,' she said, giggling. 'I'm going to be so hung-over tomorrow. It's not worth it with a small child. I'm an idiot.'

'Ah, sod it, don't beat yourself up,' Lexie said. 'You need to let loose every now and again.'

They clinked glasses and the question came out of Lexie's mouth before she could stop it. 'What's going to happen to Calvin when we're all dead?'

'I can't bear to imagine that scenario,' Maia admitted. 'There are wonderful care centres and we'll have to go down that route at some stage. But right now I'm trying to block it out.'

'I don't blame you,' Lexie said. 'Obviously if you get cancer and die any time soon, or get hit by a truck, I'll be there one thousand per cent, right?'

'Thanks, doll,' Maia said, grasping her hand.

'Not that I'm organising your funeral or wishing you dead.'

'I know,' Maia said. 'But thanks for saying it. Millions wouldn't.'

'Millions aren't you and me, Maia.'

Over the years, friends had made the odd comment about Lexie and Sam's lack of children. But as time passed less was said. Even Maia avoided the subject. Lexie knew time was marching on, though, and her mother was on a mission to become a grandmother again. It was only a matter of time before she started bringing up the subject with Sam as well. Damn her, Lexie thought angrily, as again she remembered her year in France. She'd been as gutsy and naïve as Amélie was right now. She'd thought she was invincible and that the world was there to show her a good time.

The art college had helped her find a part-time waitressing job to subsidise her year away. The on-campus digs weren't exactly palatial but she'd settled in immediately and adored being immersed in her new life in Bordeaux.

Maia had visited for a week and gone home pea-green with envy. 'I have to go back to my slog of a course in law while you swan around here absorbing culture, alcohol and the admiring gazes of delicious Frenchmen.'

Everything had been just perfect until Christophe had crashed into her life and jeopardised everything.

Lexie's moments of daydreaming and reflecting on the past came to a shuddering halt as Amélie thudded down the stairs, fresh-faced and dewy in a stripy T-shirt dress. 'I found this in your wardrobe. Okay if I borrow it? My clothes stink of cider.'

'Nice. I get to wash those, do I?' Lexie said.

'Would you?'

'Go on then. Put them in the wash basket.'

'I already did.'

'Listen, Sam and I have agreed we're not telling Dee and Billy about your little stunt with the cops last night,' she began.

'Oh, thank you, Auntie Lexie,' she cried, throwing her arms around her aunt's neck.

'As long as you realise you get one strike of this kind, okay? Do anything like that again and we'll have to tell your folks. I'm really in two minds about this, so don't make me regret having faith in you.'

'I won't. I'm so grateful. I promise I won't let you down.'

'Right you are,' Lexie said. 'Now get your butt home and knuckle down to some study today.'

'Totally,' Amélie said, grabbing her shoulder bag and skipping out of the door.

Lexie stood in the hall for a moment, second-guessing her decision. She knew Billy would tear her head off if he even suspected she was covering for Amélie. But she remembered so clearly what it had been like having a strict parent. Penelope hadn't allowed Lexie to go anywhere or do anything. If it hadn't been for her father, Lexie knew she wouldn't have gone to a single disco, let alone her year in France.

'Ah, let her go,' he'd said to Penelope. 'She needs to spread her wings. Where better to learn French than Bordeaux? And she'll get a whole different perspective on life while she's away.'

'I can't see how you think it's advisable for your only daughter to fly halfway across the world, stay in some flea-bitten digs and develop a drinking problem.'

'Who says I'm going to end up an alcoholic just because I live in France for a bit?' Lexie flared.

'Everyone knows French people think nothing of pouring wine for children, let alone students. It'll end in tears, mark my words.'

But in the end Reggie had won. Somehow he had managed to convince Penelope that Lexie would come home in one piece.

To this day Lexie had guarded the details of what had actually happened. She was about to turn forty and she'd still die of shame if her father knew what she'd done. Her mother was irritated enough by her, so she knew their already strained relationship would be in tatters if Penelope discovered the truth.

She sincerely hoped Amélie wasn't headed on a one-way road to ruination but, as Lexie was only too aware, young girls had to make their own choices and stand by them. That was life.

Chapter 9

THE GALLERY ALWAYS LOOKED INCREDIBLE IN THE sun. The floor-to-ceiling windows at the front meant the space was flooded with light even on duller days. A delivery truck was waiting outside when Lexie arrived.

'Sorry to keep you waiting,' she said. 'You should've called my mobile.'

'It's not a problem, love,' the driver said. 'I'm only here a short time. I'm heading back to the UK on the ferry, and I've an hour to kill.'

Lexie signed for the canvas prints and set to work displaying them. When she'd first opened, she'd been rather sanctimonious about mass-produced art. She'd vowed she'd never stock anything that wasn't an original. But business sense and her customers' demands had forced her to be more open-minded.

'Just because it's not your cup of tea doesn't mean it won't appeal to others,' Sam reasoned. 'Just look at how many of those creepy damaged fairy folk you sell!'

'They're fallen angels, not creepy fairies!' Lexie laughed. 'They're incredible pieces, Sam. Each one is handmade and they represent the tumultuous emotions people experience. The one we have in the hall is half skeleton and the rest of her face is normal. She depicts the truth that beauty is only skin deep.'

'If you say so,' Sam said. 'She just freaks me out and I try not to look at her, especially in the twilight when I've had a couple of glasses of wine.'

Lexie guessed the new prints would be more in line with what Sam preferred. They were bright and cheerful with nothing sinister or threatening about them.

The ping of the little bell over the door made her turn around. 'Good morning, Mrs Benson,' she said, smiling broadly. 'Isn't it a gorgeous day out there?'

'It certainly is, Lexie. How are you, dear?' The older woman tottered in and offered her cheek to be air-kissed.

'All the better for seeing you. How is little Mizzy?' she asked, patting the grey-muzzled pug that squinted at her from the woman's arms.

'She's finding the sun a bit of a trial. I've ordered her a pair of sunglasses but I don't know how she'll take to wearing them.'

Lexie knew it was more than her bank account was worth to smirk.

'What a marvellous idea! I never knew it was possible to buy shades for pets.'

'I thought it was inspired too. George had a fit when I told him. But he's always been jealous of Mizzy. Men are such babies.' Lexie nodded, hoping she looked sympathetic. If the truth were told, she thought George Benson ought to be canonised. His wife spent money like water and did nothing but give out about him. The only thing she loved more than herself was the dog and, much to Lexie's delight, art.

'Did my painting arrive, Lexie, dear?'

'It certainly did. I have it mounted on the display wall in the back so you can inspect it. As per usual, you're under no obligation to take it.'

'Thank you,' she said, walking towards the private viewing room to the rear of the gallery. 'I'll know the second I lay my eyes on it whether or not I want it.'

'Of course,' Lexie said. 'Come through and I'll fetch you a cup of tea. Would you like a scone?'

'Oh, no, thank you, dear. Just the cup of tea with my usual four sugars.'

'Of course.'

Lexie allowed Mrs Benson a few moments' grace before she joined her with the tea served just the way she liked it, in china cup and saucer. She grabbed a little bone-shaped dog treat from the box in the kitchenette to keep Mizzy happy. That had been one of Lexie's better ideas and impressed Mrs Benson no end.

'So how are you feeling about this one?' Lexie asked.

'It's perfect for the new extension!' Mrs Benson said, looking thrilled. Mizzy, now on the floor, took the biscuit from Lexie and snuffled to the corner to enjoy it.

'You're a terror spoiling Mizzy like that,' Mrs Benson said. 'Thank you for the tea.'

'My pleasure,' Lexie said.

'So what's the damage?' Mrs Benson wondered. 'I'm almost afraid to ask, seeing as the last one I bought by this artist was two and a half thousand.'

Lexie pulled an apologetic face. 'As it's so large, I'm afraid it's not cheap.'

'Go on, I'm prepared,' Mrs Benson said.

'The artist is asking twelve thousand euro,' she said. 'I'm willing to drop my commission from the usual twenty per cent to fifteen, seeing as it's you.'

'Done.'

Lexie couldn't hide her joy – she clapped and threw her hands into the air.

'I was expecting you to say fifteen thousand at least,' Mrs Benson confessed.

'Darn it! Can we rewind and start again?' Lexie giggled. 'I really appreciate the business,' she added sincerely. 'I hope you'll enjoy your gorgeous piece.'

'You know I will.'

'If I thought Sam would allow it, I'd have taken this for myself. When I opened the gallery I was like a toddler who couldn't bear to share. I wanted everything! It took several gentle reminders from Sam that I'm meant to be running a business here.'

'Well, I can sympathise. If I owned this place I'd have gone bankrupt years ago.'

Lexie processed the payment and arranged for the painting to be delivered. As she was showing Mrs Benson out, Kathleen arrived.

'Hello!' Lexie said brightly. 'How lovely to see you.'

'Hi, Lexie.'

Nodding in acknowledgement, Mrs Benson and Mizzy left.

'Thanks again and see you soon,' Lexie said, waving. Turning to Kathleen, she made a sweeping gesture with her arm. 'Welcome to Caracove Bay Gallery! Come in and browse.'

'Gosh, it's impressive,' Kathleen said. 'You'd fit nicely in downtown New York, never mind Caracove Bay.'

'Why, thank you, ma'am!' Lexie said, curtsying. 'I just need to listen to the messages on my answer machine. Are you all right to have a little look around?'

'Of course. I'm earlier than we'd agreed. I've been awake since five, so I decided to pop over now.'

'That's perfect. I'm sorry you didn't sleep, though. Jet lag is a nightmare, isn't it?'

'It'll pass,' Kathleen said easily. 'Don't let me interrupt. I'll be totally contented looking around.'

Lexie got through her calls and served a couple more customers before Kate, her assistant, arrived.

Lexie introduced her to Kathleen and grabbed her bag. 'We're popping next door for brunch if that's okay with you?' Lexie said. 'I'll keep my phone beside me so just text if it gets busy.'

'Sure,' Kate said. 'Enjoy.'

Lexie led the way to her favourite table, which boasted a view of the sea and the mountains.

'This is wonderful,' Kathleen said. 'And the smell of coffee mixed with freshly baked bread is divine.'

'As Sam said to you last night, we love coming here. It's one of my favourite places in the world.'

'What do you recommend?' Kathleen asked, as the waitress approached.

'Depending on how hungry you are, I'd go for scrambled eggs

with smoked salmon, or porridge with summer fruit compôte. I'm having the porridge,' she said.

'I'll join you,' said Kathleen closing her menu, with a flourish. 'And I'll have an Americano too, please.'

'Make that two,' Lexie said. 'I usually have two strong Nespresso coffees in the morning, but I only managed one today so I need my extra caffeine kick.' The two women smiled. 'Did you walk along the prom to get here?'

'Yes, and I cannot get over the changes.'

'The council spent a lot of money giving the seafront a face-lift. One of the few benefits of the Celtic Tiger,' Lexie said.

'I love the improvements to the park too. I sat in there for a spell. It may sound crazy to you, but I literally gulped in as much of the salty air as I could. It was as if my body recognised it and began to crave it.'

'Oh, I'd well believe it,' Lexie said. 'I don't think I could live inland, let alone in another country. I adore the sea air and miss it terribly even if I'm away on business for a few days.'

'So you've never had the wanderlust then?' Kathleen asked, as the porridge and coffee arrived.

'Well, as I told you last night, I spent a year in Bordeaux when I was nineteen,' Lexie said. 'Sam and I have travelled extensively too. We've been on safari in South Africa, island hopping in Thailand and to countless European destinations, but we've always been glad to return to Caracove Bay.'

'It's hardly surprising when you consider your home and business.'

'Well, we like it,' Lexie said.

'Do your parents live close by?' Kathleen asked.

'Um.' Lexie nodded, with a mouthful of porridge. 'Yup, they're in Blackrock, just ten minutes up the road. Dad's retired now so he plays golf and sails his boat. He's such an amazing man. You'll love him when you meet him. We're very close. He's always been my ally. Mum's a fusspot through and through. She was head girl at school and I don't think she ever stepped out of the role. She hangs out at both clubs, but isn't that interested in the actual activities.'

'That's fair enough,' Kathleen responded. 'Isn't it lovely for her to have the social outlet all the same?'

'She needs more to occupy her mind, if you ask me.' Lexie spoke without thinking. Flushing, she held up her hands. 'Sorry, that sounded rude. Mum and I get on fine. We're just different.'

'Have you always sparked off one another?'

'Mum likes to be very involved in everyone's lives. She seems to feel it's her God-given right to poke her nose into other people's business.'

'Some would say she's caring,' Kathleen said, raising an eyebrow.

'I know you must think I sound like a right cow, but it's hard to explain.'

'Try.' Kathleen smiled.

'Okay. I'm hitting forty in September,' Lexie said.

'Congratulations.'

'Thanks.' She smiled briefly. 'The thing is that I don't see the big issue with being forty. Mum wants me to have a party – well, she wants to organise one for me. I've said thanks but no. So she's been on to Sam and even texted me this morning about it.'

'Again, one might say she's just being kind and generous,' Kathleen said. 'I'm just being objective here.'

'That's why she's so darn annoying. She makes out as if all her actions are for the good of others, when she's actually suiting herself. I told her I'm not a big-bash type of gal and suggested she and Dad have one instead. Now she's sulking and went miaowing to Sam behind my back and made out I was dreadfully ungrateful.' Lexie's eyes shone with fury. 'She has a knack of making me look like the bad fairy while she's the poor put-upon princess who's been let down.'

Kathleen smiled. 'You have a very graphic way of describing things. I love that.' She paused, considering things. 'I understand what you're saying. Some women, particularly when they advance in years,' she fake-coughed, 'start to flail and feel they've less purpose in life. Maybe she just wants to know you still need her.'

Lexie rubbed her forehead. 'There's something else,' she admitted.

'Mum has started dropping hints about babies. The last few times I've met her, she's talked about Sam and me starting a family.'

'And that upsets you why?' Kathleen held her head to the side.

Lexie glanced over at her. They barely knew one another. She didn't want Kathleen to judge her. 'Well, the truth of the matter is that Sam and I don't want children. We were both clear on that from the very beginning.' She exhaled loudly.

'Have you told your mum?'

'Not as directly as I've just told you,' Lexie admitted. 'On the other hand, I've never told her I'd like a baby.'

'But won't you have to discuss it with her eventually? If both you and Sam agree, she'll have to accept it.'

Lexie smiled tightly. She hated having this conversation with anyone. It was private and personal and she realised, too late, that she probably shouldn't have mentioned it to Kathleen at all. 'Yes, I suppose.' She changed the subject. 'So have you thought about what you're going to do? You must be so excited, planning your summer.'

'It certainly is exciting. First things first,' Kathleen said, 'I'm going to call into an estate agent and hunt for an apartment. I'd prefer to leave the hotel, lovely as it is, sooner rather than later. It'll eat into my budget and I don't enjoy being cooped up in a single room.'

Lexie bit her lip. 'Please don't feel pressurised,' she began, 'but Sam came up with a suggestion last night and I'm with him all the way.'

'*Riiight* …'

'Would you like to camp in our basement for the summer? That way you have the security of having us nearby and you can slot back into Caracove Bay more easily.'

Tears welled in Kathleen's eyes and she dabbed at them with her napkin. 'Oh, Lexie, I don't know what to say … I … Gosh. Are you sure?'

'You don't have to answer right away,' Lexie added hurriedly. 'Go and have a look at what's available, if you wish, and let us know in your own time.'

'Blow me down with a feather,' Kathleen said. 'I'd adore to spend the summer at number three Cashel Square,' she said. 'It would be perfect. It's so close to the DART train and the sea and all the lovely amenities … Are you sure, dear?'

'Certain!' Lexie confirmed. 'Why don't you call round this evening and have a proper look at the basement?'

'I could organise that, I'm sure,' Kathleen said. 'Listen, you chat with Sam again, and I'll be over this evening. We can take it from there.'

'I wouldn't have said it if I didn't mean it,' Lexie insisted. Looking at her watch, she blew out her cheeks. 'Shoot! I've to run, I'm afraid.'

'Of course, go ahead. I know you're busy with work. Shall I pop over at around eight thirty? That'll give you both a chance to get home from work and have your dinner.'

'Why don't you join us?' Lexie asked. 'We can have a bite to eat and check out the basement.'

Kathleen hesitated. 'I …'

'Good! That's settled.' Lexie beamed. 'See you later. Can you make it by seven thirty so we're not all dying of hunger?'

'Sure.'

As Lexie began to root in her handbag for her wallet, Kathleen leaned over and put a hand on her arm. 'Brunch is on me. It's the least I can do.'

'Thank you, Kathleen,' Lexie said. 'That's very generous of you. Enjoy your day.'

As Lexie wandered back into the gallery, she knew she'd done the right thing in asking Kathleen to come and stay.

Hello, hi and how's it going!

You are now conversing with one half of Amelton! Like it? Love it!

Elton made it up — I'm not usually into the name-mash-up thing, but it's so catchy and most stuff sounds right when Elton says it.

Last night was such a blast. Elton and his mates ... OMG. What a riot. Not only is Elton going to save the world but he's lead singer with this really mint band. They're going be the next big thing. They've got tonnes of gigs coming up. Can't wait. Once school ends for the summer I'm going to be in charge of their social media, so I'll post up the venues on Facebook and Twitter.

We had a total buzz. It all kicked off in the bedsit, but a load of the guys pitched up and it was all a bit cramped so we skipped out of there to the park. Drinks (cider by the neck) and tunes (via Elton's new white iPhone).

Liamo plays drums in the band so he was using two sticks to bash out the beat on the back of the bench. If I wasn't completely committed to Amelton, I could possibly fancy Liamo. I might see if Lizzy wants to hook up with him. Take it from me, Liamo = hotto!

Elton was singing along to a backing track and he's got SUCH an amazing voice. I told him to do X Factor. He's thinking about it for next year but he says he needs to concentrate on getting the band going first.

X Factor can wait anyhow. Elton knows what he's doing. He's got a business plan. It's water-tight.

They're called Satan Goes to Church. I can't wait until they hit the top of the iTunes chart. Elton says we're going to travel the world and stay in hotel suites with Jacuzzis and mini-bars all the way. He reckons once they conquer Dublin, next stop is London, then New York. I actually hate flying but I'm sure I'll get over it, especially as we'll be rocking into first class.

Elton says we're going to be the new-age golden couple that the whole world just wants to BE.

The cops arrived last night, which was not cool. The lads all ran but Elton said he wasn't scared. We braved it and stayed.

I'm not sure it was the best plan, if I'm totally honest. He had ID and he's old enough to drink, but they still took him off to the station in a car because it's illegal to drink in public and cause a disturbance. I didn't cry until Elton was gone. But then I had to sit in the back of another cop car and they were asking me loads of questions. It was so bogus. I cried so much the lady cop said they'd bring me home. I lied about everything so they took me to Lexie's house. I am so stoked to have her and Sam. They are like THE coolest people EVER. I wish they were my parents. I knew it was a low blow to land in on them, but if I'd gone home Mum and Dad would've gone off the scale. Straight up, I'd say I'd be shipped off to boarding school for my final year.

They're always in bad form, even when I don't get caught doing stupid stuff.

Mum is like a black cloud all the time at the moment. Dad is all pale and looks like he needs about ten shots of Botox. They're barely speaking to each other. Either that or when I walk into the room they jump and act all weird.

They think I don't notice all the mad eyes they're giving one another — but I'm not thick. I would ask what the hell is going on, but I figure there's no point. If they can't be cool and let me in, then that's fine by me. I don't want to know anyway.

Roll on the end of these exams. Then I can hang out with Elton more and stay out of Mum's way. The constant sighing is head-wrecking.

GTG,

Amélie ♥

Chapter 10

KATHLEEN PAID THE BRUNCH BILL AND STROLLED out into the sunshine. The entire situation was surreal. This day last week, she was sweltering in the dense summer heat of Orlando. Now she was back to her roots and ready to embark on a summer of fun.

Jackson had insisted that a trip back to Ireland would work out for the best. He'd been so sure she'd benefit from revisiting her childhood haunts. 'You'll have the time of your life,' he said.

'But I don't know if I can do it without you,' she said.

'Of course you can. You have a knack of endearing yourself to others. You get under people's skin,' he said, tapping her nose and smiling. 'I bet you'll meet people on the plane over, never mind during the holiday. You're a charmer, darling. I'm not worried about you.'

Now she slung her bag over her shoulder and inhaled deeply. Lexie was like her fairy goddaughter. She couldn't have wished to meet a nicer girl.

She'd go and look in the window of the local letting agency to get an idea of the going rate for rents, just so she knew what to expect this evening. Budget wasn't really an issue, but she wanted to be certain Lexie and Sam were fairly paid.

Next stop, though, was the ticket office for the train. She'd heard about the electric rail system called the DART and was excited about using it. When she'd been a girl, the train was a real treat, only used if they were going on a day trip to somewhere like the zoo in Dublin. But this system seemed to have revolutionised inner-city travel, along with the LUAS trams.

The old station house looked exactly the same, as Kathleen approached. The pale granite frontage glittered in the sunlight as she walked through the Gothic-style wooden door that had been there when she was a child. However, the modern ticket-dispensing machines looked like unfriendly aliens, hovering menacingly at the side of the platform.

'Hello, love.' A man in a navy uniform, complete with cap, had addressed her.

'Hello,' Kathleen said. 'It's years since I've been here. Would you mind explaining how I go about printing a ticket, please?'

'No bother. Follow me,' he said, looking pleased. 'It's quiet enough at this time of the day. You're right to find your feet outside peak times. Some people get fiercely cranky if there's a hold-up in the queue.'

'I can imagine,' Kathleen said. 'I guess they're in a hurry to get to work.'

'I've no doubt they are,' the man agreed. 'But, as I always say, patience is a virtue. I've two teenagers at home and, believe me, they can blow things out of proportion. Take this morning. My daughter needed two euro to pay for something in school. Had her hand out to me like this,' he said, thrusting his upturned palm towards Kathleen. '"Do you think I'm going to spit the money out of my mouth?" I asked her. Well, she glared at me and stood tapping her foot! The Bank of Dad, that's me.'

Kathleen laughed as he rolled his eyes. Together they made their way to the ticket machine and he took her through the necessary steps. 'How long are you staying in Ireland?' he asked, as they posted cash in and waited for the change.

'A couple of months,' she said.

'Well, it was worth learning how to get your ticket so.'

'It certainly was,' she agreed. 'Thank you so much. I'm Kathleen by the way.'

'Fanta,' he said, offering his hand.

'Pardon?' Kathleen knew some Irish names sounded rather unusual, but she'd only ever heard of fizzy orange being called Fanta.

He pulled off his peaked cap, pointed to his hair and winked.

'No!' Kathleen said, laughing.

'Yup. Since the day I sprouted this mop of orange hair, I've been known far and wide as Fanta. On our wedding day my wife thought the priest had lost his marbles when he asked if she'd take Bernard's hand in marriage. She only knew me as Fanta.'

'Well, thank you for helping me and I might see you later.'

'Enjoy Howth, Kathleen. If you're looking for a bite to eat, try Fishy Dishy. They have the best mussels in white wine I've ever tasted.'

'I will, thank you, Fanta.' Kathleen smiled. She'd missed the slightly left-of-centre Irish sense of humour. The train pulled into the station and they moved forwards as it came to a halt and the doors opened.

'Grab yourself a nice window seat over the other side of the carriage and you'll enjoy the trip all the more.' Fanta waved her on to the train. 'There are plenty of changes around here, but the sea and the sky are still as lovely as ever.'

Kathleen took his advice and settled into her seat. She'd forgotten how the track snaked through tunnels around the mountains, so close to the sea she almost felt they might slide in. The colours were even more magnificent than she remembered. The sunlight bounced off the rippling navy water and the grey beaches curved in neat semi-circles; walkers with lolloping dogs added to the spectacle. The cliff-tops were coated with a thick, acid-green fuzzy grass carpet. The jagged rockfaces teemed with furiously busy snow-coloured seagulls scrambling for space on the crevices.

Although the train stopped at the various stations along the way, it never paused for long. Kathleen was almost disappointed when they pulled up at Howth. As she walked towards the village, she noted she wasn't the only tourist. A small group of Asians were snapping with cameras and speaking animatedly. Their language fascinated her. None of it sounded remotely like English.

Feeling a little naughty, she tagged along behind them, hoping they might lead her to an interesting sight. She wasn't disappointed. Moments later they were standing in front of a beautiful old castle. At first Kathleen hung back, thinking the group mightn't welcome her.

'You too?' asked a very smiley lady.

Kathleen attempted to protest, waving her hands and making uncharacteristic bowing movements. 'No! Thank you!' she stuttered.

'Please, lady,' said her new friend, gesturing for her to follow. Mortified, Kathleen shuffled over to the group. A man Kathleen reckoned was around her own age appeared at the castle's front door and made a quick welcome speech. The group huddled and made chirpy noises as their shiny dark heads bobbed up and down approvingly.

'Are you in charge?' the man asked, gazing over their heads to Kathleen.

'Eh, no,' she said. 'I'm embarrassed to say I just tagged along. But I stick out like a sore thumb, so I'm scuppered now.'

'Not to worry. Why don't you continue to tag along and I'll pretend I don't notice?' he said kindly. 'We don't open to the public that often, so you did the right thing in taking your chances.'

'Are you sure you don't mind?' she checked.

'Not a bit. You can keep me company as your penance for skulking.'

More sweeping arm movements and gesturing encouraged the group forward. Kathleen fell into step with the man, who was shunting from side to side as he walked.

'The same family have lived here for donkey's years,' he said. 'I'm a general dogsbody, but some of the family do cookery classes for pre-booked groups. That's why these people are here.'

'Oh, Jeez, I'll have to leave in that case,' Kathleen said. 'I'm so sorry for butting in. I'm just back from America for a holiday and I wasn't thinking.'

'Nonsense,' he said. 'Let me run it by the girls. I'm certain they'll be delighted to include you. What's your name?'

'It's Kathleen, Kathleen Williams.'

'Just a second. I'm Rodger, by the way, Let's pretend we're old pals, okay?' he said.

Before she could protest, Rodger had hurried over to two women and whispered something. They looked at Kathleen and smiled. One waved and called, 'Hello there. You're most welcome. Any friend of Rodger's is a friend of ours.'

'Thank you kindly,' Kathleen said.

Rodger gave her a quick nod and ambled away. The group filtered into the kitchen oohing and aahing as their cameras clicked and flashed.

'My goodness, we're being papped!' the woman said, and giggled.

'It's not often you see proper cameras these days,' Kathleen said. 'It's all phones now, isn't it?'

'Too true,' said the other woman, as she crossed the room to introduce herself.

Kathleen looked around the gorgeous old-style kitchen in awe. It was beautifully decorated in muted stone and cream tones. The large Aga that dominated the room was put to immediate use as the demonstration began.

Over the next hour Kathleen and the others learned how to bake old-fashioned brown soda bread, apple cake and rich fruity brack.

'We'll make a big pot of tea and you can all sit outside,' said Rodger, when he reappeared.

Kathleen leaned against a fence, drinking her tea and observing.

'Did you enjoy that then?' Rodger had joined her.

'It was wonderful. I bake all the time at home, but it's marvellous to see the traditional way of making brown bread. I can't wait to try it.'

'Are you staying in a hotel?' Rodger asked, and took a bite of brack.

'At the moment I am, but I'm planning on renting somewhere.' Kathleen told him all about number three Cashel Square and how kind Sam and Lexie were.

'They sound like decent people. I'm glad there are still some welcoming folk around. Ireland has the name for being friendly and I'd hate for that to be ruined.'

'I agree,' she said. 'It always gets my goat when people who don't know Ireland assume it's a land of boozers and leprechauns.'

'Is that a general assumption in your experience?'

'For some folk,' Kathleen admitted. 'I've always fallen between the cracks so to speak. When I was growing up I was known as "the Irish girl". As the years went by I guess I became more American, but to this day I'm continually asked where I'm from.'

'You have a distinct American twang, but you still have a lot of Irish in you!'

'Aw, you are sweet!' Kathleen said. 'I use plenty of Americanisms, I say trash instead of rubbish, trunk instead of car boot and I've heard myself saying awesome on more than one occasion!'

Rodger laughed, wincing. 'That hurt,' he said. 'I need a hip replacement but I'm resisting.'

'Why?' Kathleen asked, astonished.

'I'm not a fan of hospitals if the truth be told.'

'Well, I can't imagine anyone who is,' she said. 'But surely it'd be better to go through a bit more pain and come out the other end feeling … awesome?' She raised an eyebrow and smiled.

'Awesome sounds a far cry from where I am at the moment,' he admitted. 'I've been so stubborn about it but my doctor has told me I've to come to him when I'm ready.'

'Really? That doesn't sound like he's taking much of an interest in you. It's hardly professional either, if you don't mind me saying.'

'If I'm honest, it's more a case of him washing his hands of me until I do what he wants,' Rodger said.

'That's awful.' Kathleen tutted.

'I've been a naughty boy,' Rodger confessed. 'I had the operation scheduled and bottled it. The surgeon and his team were waiting and I let them down.'

'Ah. That's a different story, I guess. When was that?'

'Four months ago,' Rodger said.

There was a short silence between them.

'It's not such a terrible operation, you know,' Kathleen said.

'How do you know?'

'I had my left one done three years ago and the right one last year. I had an epidural and they gave me the coolest headphones. I listened to Vivaldi while they sawed me up. I felt like one of those glamorous magician's assistants.'

Rodger stared at her in astonishment. 'You don't limp or look remotely as if you're in pain.'

'I'm not.'

He sighed. 'You must think I'm a melodramatic old fool refusing to make myself better.'

'I don't think anything of the sort,' she said honestly. 'I wasn't exactly thrilled with the thought of surgery, but my husband Jackson was very black-and-white about it. There was no discussion and no option. I was frog-marched – well, frog-hobbled – right in there.'

Rodger looked instantly glum. 'My late wife Claudia would've been like your Jackson. The morning I was meant to be in having the operation I ended up at her graveside. I was almost waiting for a wagging finger to come down from the sky.'

'That was tough for you,' Kathleen said, her head tilted to the side.

'My two daughters are furious with me,' Rodger went on. 'I know they've written me off in a way. They were so intent on telling me what an idiot I was for refusing surgery that they overlooked the fact I was genuinely rigid with fear.'

'Poor you.'

'I can see their point,' he said gruffly, trying to make light of it. 'They're grieving for their mother and busy supporting their young families in these austere times. The last thing they need is some silly old fool being needlessly difficult and refusing to help himself.'

'I'm sure they don't think that way,' Kathleen said quietly.

The group all began to stand up. More bowing ensued and they gravitated back into the house via the side door.

Kathleen and Rodger fell into step with them. By the time they'd walked back through the main hall and down the front steps, Rodger was clearly in agony. Kathleen held out her hand to him. 'It was a pleasure to meet you, Rodger. I hope you feel better soon.'

'I will,' he said decisively. 'I'm going to contact my doctor as soon as I leave here and reschedule that surgery.'

'Good for you!' she said. 'I'm so proud of you.'

He laughed. 'You're more American than you think. Irish people don't express emotions quite like you just did.'

'Really?' Kathleen was mildly surprised. 'Can I take your number? I could give you a call and see how you're doing. Only if you'd like.'

'Now you're being totally American,' he told her. '"Can I take your number?" I love it! I feel like a teenager! Yes, of course you can have my number.' He rooted his mobile phone from his pocket. 'How about I send you a text and then you'll have my details?'

'Actually, I need to get an Irish phone. I've only got my American cell right now, so call out your number and I'll save it. As soon as I get a local phone I'll text.'

'Are all Americans so forward with the gentlemen?' Rodger asked.

Kathleen blushed furiously. 'Oh, gosh, I was just being sociable. I thought we could be friends, that's all. I hope you didn't think I was trying to pick you up.'

He burst out laughing. 'You look horrified at the thought!' he said. Then he took her hand and shook it. 'I'm just teasing you. I know you're a married woman and I understand perfectly that you're just being friendly. I'm always putting my foot in it and I've just done it again. Don't mind me.'

Kathleen felt relieved. She took his number and waved goodbye.

Twenty minutes later she relaxed on the train and thought of Jackson. He'd get such a laugh out of Rodger insinuating she might be trying to pick him up.

She'd met Jackson at a cousin's wedding. Kathleen was her bridesmaid and felt she might die of shame. The dresses were probably the height of fashion back in the seventies, but the thought of those canary yellow and brown patterned kaftans with gold braiding still made her feel nauseous. 'You can't be serious!' she'd said to her cousin, Maeve. 'We'll be like psychedelic picnic tables!'

'It's called fashion, Kathleen. Don't be so uptight. You'll be the envy of every girl and the desire of every man there.'

It appeared Maeve had had her finger on the pulse that day. All the guests oohed and aahed over the dresses, pronouncing them groovy, cool and far out. The only person who had seemed to share Kathleen's view was a friend of the groom.

Kathleen was perched in a corner, close to the bar, wishing she was anywhere else when he approached. 'If you're attempting to hide, you're wearing the wrong dress,' he teased.

'Oh, don't I know it,' Kathleen said. 'It's not my wedding, and I'm honoured to be a bridesmaid, but no matter what people say, I feel like a pair of hideous curtains on legs.'

He guffawed. 'You've got it down with that description, I've gotta hand it to you,' he said. 'My girlfriend insisted I wear this purple and orange tie and I think it's revolting.'

Kathleen remembered how her heart had sunk when Jackson had mentioned his girlfriend. She'd chatted to him for a few minutes longer, laughing and joking … He had been the first man to make her feel beautiful.

A tall, confident bottle blonde had strutted in their direction. Her bell-bottomed jumpsuit and sky-high platforms had made Kathleen's dress look dull. 'Jackson?' she shrilled. 'I've been looking for you. I've asked the DJ to play "American Pie". Come dance with me,' she said. 'Sorry to break up the party,' she said to Kathleen.

She hadn't spoken to Jackson again until the end of the night. Just as she was getting into her parents' car he had rushed over and tapped her on the arm. 'Can I call you? I'd love to take you on a date.'

'You have a girlfriend,' she answered, slamming the car door and nearly taking his nose off.

She had thought of him quite a lot in the weeks that followed, but he was out of bounds. No matter how much she liked him, he was another gal's guy. When he turned up at her front door one Friday night, Kathleen thought she might expire. 'Jackson! What are you doing here?' she asked.

'That's not the welcome I was hoping for,' he said, pulling his fingers through his jet-black oiled quiff. 'I'm a single man. I'd like to ask you out on a date.'

Kathleen's heart was doing flips in her chest. She knew if she let go of her grasp on the door she'd begin to tremble. 'I'll consider it,' she said. 'When were you thinking of?'

'How about now?' he answered. 'No time like the present, huh?'

'How did you find my house?' she asked coyly, playing for time.

'I asked your cousin Maeve,' he said proudly. 'I told her I was smitten with you and I needed to find you.'

Kathleen giggled. Jackson hopped from one foot to the other, jingling change in his trouser pocket. 'So, what do you say, Kathleen?' he asked. 'Will you come out with me?'

She couldn't think of anything she'd like more. Glancing over his shoulder she spied a shiny sky blue Buick parked at the kerb.

'I'll drive you wherever you want to go,' he added.

'I can't tonight,' she said evenly.

'Tomorrow, then,' he shot back.

Her smile was the only answer he required. 'I'll be back same time tomorrow. You won't regret it!' he had called over his shoulder as he ran to his car.

By the time the DART pulled up at Caracove Bay, Kathleen was feeling tired and emotional. She'd have given anything to have Jackson waiting for her in that Buick right now.

She got out of the train and began to walk towards the hotel. When she saw a newsagent, she grabbed a postcard from the stand outside, probably the cheesiest one available, and went inside to pay for it. Then she found a bench looking out to sea, sat down and fished a pen out of her bag.

My Dearest Jackson

Today was wonderful. I took a train to Howth by the sea. You would've laughed till you cried if you'd seen me. I tried to mingle with some gorgeous Japanese tourists. Yes, I got caught and made a total fool of myself for a change!

I met a lovely man by the name of Rodger. I'm guessing he's around our age. He was so kind and friendly that I asked for his number. I hope he didn't take it the wrong way. I forget that people do things differently around these parts. I think I may have put my foot in it. What's new? I love you and miss you. I wish you were here.

Your loving wife x x

Chapter 11

LEXIE'S FEET HURT. SHE'D HAD AN UNEXPECTEDLY BUSY day at the gallery. Still, she mused, she ought to know by now that sunshine brought people out in droves. As she locked the main door to the gallery she was just in time to catch Larry at the fishmonger's before he shut up shop too.

'Talk about cutting it fine!' she said, as he beckoned her in.

He flicked the lights back on and made his way around the counter. 'I've nothing out on display, Lexie. It's all in the cold room. What had you in mind?'

'What's good today?' she asked.

'Everything, of course,' he joked. 'I've a few queen scallops left, if you think Sam deserves a starter this evening.'

'Delicious! Have you enough for three? We've a guest joining us.'

'I'll have a look now. After that I've black sole, which I know you both adore.'

'Done!' Lexie said. 'I'll take a bunch of your asparagus and two lemons as well.'

'No bother,' he called, from inside the cold room. 'You're in luck.' He emerged smiling. 'I've exactly nine scallops left. Three each tossed in garlic butter with a bit of crusty bread and you'll be in seventh heaven!'

'You're a star,' Lexie said. 'We've a lovely American lady with us tonight. She used to live in our house when she was a child.'

'Is she single?' Larry asked, leaning over the counter hopefully.

'No!' Lexie giggled. 'You're incorrigible! Besides, I thought you were besotted with my mother, God help us all.'

'Ah, your mother is a fine woman,' he said, gazing into the middle distance. 'But so far that's a real case of unrequited love.'

'Well, you haven't seen my American lady yet.' Lexie laughed. 'But perhaps she mightn't be your type.'

'Lexie …' He paused and clasped his hands together around his rotund belly. 'Do you think I'd be fussy? As long as she's halfway mobile and has a strong pulse, that'll do me.'

Lexie paid him for the fish and veggies, then set off for home. Poor Larry had been openly hunting for a wife since the day she'd met him, twenty years before. Penelope barely tolerated him, which upset and embarrassed Lexie at times. 'He's crass and loud. I don't appreciate him waddling out from behind his counter and trying to kiss my hand,' Penelope complained.

'You take him too seriously, Mum,' Lexie said, with a grin. 'He's a decent old soul. Don't be offensive – please.'

'He might come in handy if I pop my clogs,' Reggie said.

'Reggie! I'm not finding this conversation amusing. Can we drop it?'

Tiddles was waiting on the doorstep when Lexie got home. He miaowed and rubbed against her legs furiously. 'That's a lovely furry welcome,' she said, scooping him up and nuzzling her nose into his furry head. 'You're looking very handsome in your stripy tights today.' She unlocked the door and brought him inside.

She'd only just put the fish in the fridge when Sam arrived in behind her.

'Hey!' she said, walking out to the hall to kiss him. 'You're earlier than usual.'

'I was at a meeting just outside town and made a management decision to bunk off early.'

'Good for you. I got yummy scallops and black sole from Larry for supper.'

'Excellent,' he said. 'Did he declare his undying love for Penelope again?' Sam loosened his tie.

'He was more interested in hearing about Kathleen. I'd say he'd be here now if I'd suggested it. I did point out that she's married, but you know Larry.'

'Speaking of which, what time are we expecting her?'

'I said around seven thirty,' Lexie said. 'You've loads of time – it's only just gone six.'

'Fantastic. Just what I wanted to hear,' he said, as he picked her up and kissed her firmly on the mouth. 'Is something wrong?' Moments later, Sam pulled back. 'You seem distracted.'

'I know. I'm sorry. It's just ...' Lexie hesitated. 'I need your reassurance on something.'

'Okay, shoot,' he said, mildly perplexed.

'My mother has invaded my thoughts,' she continued. 'Lately she's been probing about whether or not we're going to finally start a family.'

'Ah, I see,' Sam said, nodding. 'And what conclusion have you come to post-invasion?'

Lexie stared at him, trying desperately to read his mind.

'Hello?' he said, waving his hand in front of her face. 'I know we're compatible and soul-mates and all that, but I'm not a mentalist, Lexie!'

'I'm worried about saying the wrong thing,' she confessed.

'To me?' he said incredulously. 'Come on. I think you know me better than that.'

'I know neither of us wants babies, and that's what we always said, but I'm going to have to be really direct with my mother to get her off my back once and for all.'

'What kind of stuff is she saying?' Sam asked.

'Ah, the usual, that we'll regret it if we allow the window of opportunity to slip by. She keeps pointing out how much we both adore Amélie and Calvin, yadda yadda yadda. You know the drill.' Lexie waited but Sam didn't reply.

'Sam?' she stared at him. He averted his gaze. 'Sam, talk to me,' she said. 'You are still on the same page as me on this, right?'

'Sure,' he said eventually.

'So why don't I believe you all of a sudden?'

'I ...' He pulled his fingers through his hair and blew out air noisily. 'Maybe ...' He looked at her. 'Don't blow a gasket here, okay? But maybe your mother has a point, what with the window and time passing and all that ...'

His words hung in the air, like thick black smoke, chilling her to the bone.

'How about we mull it over for the next week?' he suggested, and smiled.

'What?' She burst out laughing.

'I'm being deadly serious here, Lexie,' he said. She realised his smile was nervous. 'I'd like you to spend the next week being aware of children and babies as you go about your business.'

'You're cracked, do you know that?'

'Maybe,' he conceded, 'but this could be a very useful exercise for us both. Let's take the week to observe children and look at whether or not we feel we'd like one of our own.'

'Can we go to Argos and buy one on sale or return?'

'You're not taking me seriously,' he said, with an astonishing sadness in his voice.

'Give me a break, Sam. This is bananas!'

'Can you indulge me, please?' he begged. 'I need this exercise so I can make up my mind too.'

'Okay, your wish is my command,' she said, holding up her hands in defeat.

Lexie felt sick. At that moment Sam might as well have told her he'd been having an affair, she felt so slighted. They'd agreed! This issue was set in stone, as far as she was concerned. Why in the name of God was he suddenly back-pedalling?

'We can say what we feel to one another, right?' Sam was asking anxiously.

'Pardon?' she asked, playing for time as she attempted to hide her shock.

'We can have a discussion and explore this thought process together, can't we?'

'Of course,' she said, forcing a smile. 'Sure we can. And don't forget we've got Calvin's party on Sunday. There'll be lots of children there. We could go the whole hog and imagine it's our child's party, if you like.'

'Are you angry with me?' Sam said.

'No!' she said, sounding a little high-pitched. 'I'm just trying to get into the swing of the experiment, that's all.'

'Good for you,' he said, clearly relaxing. 'I was chatting to Josh earlier and he said Maia's going all out. I think she's having a game of Freak the Neighbours, actually. She's pretty much booked an entire fun fair for the day.'

'I know,' Lexie said, with a genuine smile at the thought of her best friend's plans. 'When Maia decides she's doing something, she goes for it hammer and tongs.'

'Okay, I'm having a shower,' Sam said, heading upstairs. 'Then I'll go down to the basement and make sure it's okay to show Kathleen.'

Sam normally enjoyed singing very loudly in the shower. He knew he was tone deaf, but Lexie would either come in and join him, just to shut him up, or bellow up the stairs that he ought to be muzzled.

Today he wasn't in the mood for acting like a goon.

This baby-talk was a bit odd. He could see that Lexie was uncomfortable with it. But he was fairly certain she was only being so negative because of her mother. The two women rubbed each other up the wrong way. Always had. Sam simply wanted to be sure she wasn't denying both of them the opportunity to become parents just to spite Penelope.

Lexie knew she needed to prepare dinner but she was rooted to the spot, lost in her own astonished thoughts. What was going on in Sam's head? Had her mother got to him? Had he been brainwashed by his friends?

She glanced towards the stairs and noticed the silence. Sam wasn't murdering some poor song in the shower. Clearly he was on the fence with all this. Spooked. That was it. All she had to do was bide her time and they'd have a frank discussion about the fact that neither of them had changed their minds and that would be that.

As she began to prepare dinner Lexie forced herself to partake in Sam's proposed game. She owed him that. She needed to ensure she was being honest when they had the defining chat.

She looked down at her flat, toned tummy. Would she welcome stretch marks and a bulging belly? Would she love a baby the way she was expected to? Would she have the patience to nurture and teach a tiny person all the things he or she needed to know? What if the baby had something wrong with it? She thought back to the days following Calvin's birth. Maia was amazing now – she adored Calvin and said he was her saviour – but Lexie couldn't help remembering how devastating it had been in the beginning. So many conflicting thoughts zoomed around her head she almost felt nauseous by the time Sam appeared in his favourite Hollister shorts and T-shirt. Lexie had boiled tiny new potatoes, mixed them with mayonnaise and garlicky French dressing and sliced some thin ribbons of cucumber into a separate bowl.

'I'm keeping it very simple,' she said. 'I don't want Kathleen to think we're too formal. If she's to consider staying in the basement, I'd like her to feel at home.'

'Good plan, Lex,' he said, showing no sign of his pre-shower tension. 'I'm going down to have a scout around. Call me when she arrives.' He went out through the front door.

They'd once been able to access the basement via the back of the staircase, but it had been blocked off for years.

Lexie marvelled at how easily Sam could drop an emotional grenade, compartmentalise it and carry on as normal. She, however, needed to look less like a rabbit in the headlights, with Kathleen on the way, so she put a CD into the stereo and hummed along to Carole King. Her music therapy worked: she became so engrossed in singing the haunting tune, ironically called 'It's Too Late', that she didn't notice Kathleen arriving.

'Hello?' Kathleen called. 'I hope I'm not barging in. The door was on the latch and I rang the bell twice.'

'Sorry,' Lexie cried. 'I was having a Carole moment!'

'So I heard.' Kathleen gave her a box of handmade chocolates.

'Ooh, delicious! Thank you, Kathleen, you shouldn't have.' She kissed the older woman on both cheeks and ushered her into the kitchen. She was genuinely happy to see Kathleen because she liked her a lot, but Lexie couldn't help feeling relieved that she was there: the strange atmosphere between herself and Sam might dissipate. 'Wine?'

'Yes, please,' she said. 'Is Sam still at work?'

'He's down in the basement. Let's bring him a glass of wine and you can have a look around.'

'I'd love to.' Kathleen smiled.

Moments later they joined Sam, who was fiddling with a light bulb.

'Hey, Kathleen,' he said, jumping off a chair. 'There are a few things that might need fixing if you decide to move in.'

'Hi, Sam,' she said. 'I can't see many things myself, and it's so much brighter than I was expecting.'

'We painted it all cream and added those glass double doors leading onto the yard to optimise the natural light,' Lexie explained, as she handed Sam a glass of wine. 'But, as you can see, it's just an empty shell.'

The living area was open plan, with the original flagstones and fireplace. A compact yet perfectly functional kitchenette at one end led to a corridor.

'There's a large bedroom and shower room, which I'd suggest you use, and a small box room if you have visitors,' Sam said. 'You'll need a bed, sofa and dining set. These chairs are from the yard outside. I reckon you might like something less industrial.'

Kathleen wandered around, wide-eyed. 'It was such a dingy damp space when I was a girl. My mother didn't allow us down here much. It smelt of mildew and was infested with spiders.'

'It was fairly rank when we moved in, wasn't it?' Lexie said to Sam.

'Yeah – and it was full of boxes for about three years!' Sam said. 'I had a week off work at some point and decided to sort it out. I hired a skip and cleared it.'

'We got it to this point with the intention of renting it but never went any further,' Lexie explained. 'Come out and we'll show you the little yard. It leads to the main part of the garden via stone steps, but it's quiet and private if you don't feel like socialising with the riff-raff upstairs.'

'It's gorgeous!' Kathleen exclaimed. 'I could plant some pretty flowers in those containers if you were agreeable.'

'Are you saying you'd like to move in, then?' Sam grinned.

'Well, if you both still think you could cope with me,' she said tentatively.

'Of course we could. I just hope you don't mind us practising our clog dancing in the upstairs hall,' said Sam.

'Or our cage fighting in the back garden,' Lexie added.

'Not one jot, assuming you have no objections to me taking up the drums,' she quipped. 'How about we start by saying I'll rent the place for a month? If we feel it's not as easy as we hope, I'll be out of your hair. No hard feelings.'

'That sounds perfect,' Lexie said.

'Fine by me,' Sam added.

'I took the liberty of sniffing around the estate agents in Caracove Bay earlier. Would one thousand euro a month sound like a fair rate?' Kathleen asked.

'That sounds totally exorbitant,' Lexie said. 'I don't think we need anything like that, do you?' she asked Sam.

'No way. I'll tell you what,' Sam suggested. 'How about you help out with purchasing some furniture – say, a sofa, sofa-bed and dining set in IKEA – and we'll leave it at that?'

'You're going to choose a three-thousand-euro sofa now, aren't you?' Kathleen teased.

'At least!' Sam laughed. 'One made from cow hide and gold bars!'

He locked the basement, then ceremoniously handed Kathleen the keys. 'How about we make a trip to IKEA this weekend?' he said.

'If you're happy to be stuck with me, that'd be great,' Kathleen said.

'That sounds like a song!' Sam joked. 'I'd be delighted to be stuck with you.'

'Let's mosey up to the kitchen so we can get some food,' Lexie said. 'I'm in the danger zone where I'll decide I can't be bothered cooking in favour of another glass of *vino*!'

'Oh, I know how you feel,' Kathleen said. 'I can't tell you how many times that's happened to Jackson and me. The thing about my husband is that he's never been remotely militant. He's a real roll-with-the-punches type. So if I can't be bothered to cook, we have a toasted sandwich.'

'Well, I'm not Jackson,' Sam said. 'I'm starving and I happen to know there's some gorgeous food waiting to be enjoyed.'

The other two positioned themselves at the table while Lexie tossed the scallops in foamy garlic butter.

'To a summer of fun and new friends,' Sam toasted, as Lexie delivered the starters.

'I'll drink to that,' Kathleen said.

'To summer at Caracove Bay,' Lexie added. Her smile matched Kathleen's but underneath she was feeling more than a little uneasy.

Dear Diary

I'm so stunned I can barely write. I feel like a stranger in my own home. I was all ready to have a shower and do some study for the exams when a mega-row kicked off downstairs. Mum was mumbling at first, then Dad lost the plot totally. I mean epic style.

I know I shouldn't have listened in but I was drawn to the stairs and then I crept down to the hallway. Mum would've killed me if she'd known I was earwigging. She has a real thing about it.

I wish I'd listened to her warning about hearing stuff you might not like and all that ...

Dad was stressing about money and saying he can't magic cash out of his arse. That made me laugh. Then Mum started crying and said none of it — what ever 'it' might be — was her fault. Then came the thing I wish I'd never heard.

Mum said she wished things were different. That from the word go their marriage had been 'engineered by our bloody mothers'.

Dad totally exploded then and said, 'For the millionth time, Dee, you told me you were on the pill. It was eighteen years ago. So what? My mother and your holier-than-thou parents marched us up the aisle. Millions of other couples were cajoled into getting married quickly because they were pregnant. Big swing. Get over yourself, will you?'

I feel violated. Like I've been assaulted. Mum and Dad have never been all touchy-feely with one another, but I thought that was just them. They're hardly wild and wacky, let's face it. But I always assumed they at least loved each other. More than that, I thought they loved me.

I figured that was why they're so down on me all the time. I thought they were just worried and wanted me to be safe.

'We want you to be the best person you can be.' That's a real Mum one-liner.

'We want you to make us and yourself proud.' That's a Dad special.

I stupidly reckoned they had my best interests at heart. But now it's all so obvious. How could I have been such a dope? They never wanted me in the first place. I was a horrible mistake between two kids who were only planning on fooling around and calling it a day. But instead of them having fun and walking away and possibly finding true soul-mates, I imprisoned them in a jaded relationship for life.

I feel like I want to vomit. All the tutting and disappointed shaking of heads makes sense now. I see it all clearly. Crystal clear.

I don't know what to do or where to go. Should I confront them and tell them I heard their dirty secret? Tell them they can get divorced and I'll drop out of school and get a job in a bar in Turkey? Let them know they're free to learn to live again now that I'm old enough to fend for myself?

I sat and stared in the mirror just now. I look the same as always, but I'm not. I wasn't wanted and I've ruined my parents' lives.

A thought has struck me. Grandma, Granddad, Auntie Lex and Uncle Sam must know about this. They're all in on it. They know that I'm the reason my parents are miserable.

I bet that's why Auntie Lex and Uncle Sam don't have kids. They're happy. They can't keep their hands off each other. I hear them sometimes at night. They love each other. No doubt in my mind about that. I'll bet they saw the crap existence my parents have and wisely decided they're not falling into that trap.

I wish I was dead.

Elton has just texted. He can't meet me today after all. He's going to size up some professional equipment for Satan Goes to Church.

I'm glad. I couldn't be all cool and cutesy right now and I don't know him well enough to tell him what I've heard. I need to get away, though. I have to think about how I'm going to handle this. It's a vile feeling to know I wasn't wanted.

Amélie

Chapter 12

THE FOLLOWING SATURDAY AFTERNOON, KATHLEEN found herself walking towards the pier. She'd checked out of the Caracove Arms and had had a busy morning with Sam in IKEA. She had sensibly left him and his friend Jeremy assembling the furniture they'd bought but had suddenly been overcome with tiredness and a need to be on her own. It was incredibly windy and rather chilly, so she walked to the other side of the pier and leaned against the great stone wall. The sun shone down and the salt-doused air tickled her face, making her inhale deeply. Closing her eyes, she listened to the seagulls calling over the lapping waves. Remembering she had a pair of sunglasses in her bag, she unhooked it from across her body and pulled them out. As she put them on, she spotted a man walking a small dog. They were too far away for details but his gait was so like Jackson's that she gasped. She shielded her eyes with her hand and squinted. She missed Jackson dreadfully. The initial excitement was most certainly still with her, but in the back of her mind, she was genuinely worried as to whether she'd manage this whole trip on her own.

'Life is precious, darling. Opportunities don't come knocking every day. Embrace the good things and tuck them away in a little pocket of your mind, ready to be revisited when you're feeling blue.'

Sobs invaded her. She crouched down, willing herself to be quiet. When the tears finally stopped, she searched for a handkerchief and dabbed her eyes and cheeks.

Grateful that few people were about, she stood up again and, uncertain what she wanted to do or where she wanted to go, she meandered towards the town and Lexie's gallery. Perhaps she'd offer

Lexie and Kate a whipped ice-cream or a cappuccino. She picked up speed and arrived at the gallery in time to bump into Lexie.

'Hi,' Lexie said. 'I was hoping to find you. Kate is happy to stay here on her own for the rest of the afternoon, so I'm escaping.'

'How lovely,' Kathleen said.

'How was this morning? Did you find what you needed?'

'Yes,' Kathleen said. 'Sam was just marvellous. He's such a darling man, so patient and easy-going. Unlike Jackson, he's actually good at shopping.' Out of nowhere, the tears burned once more.

'Oh, Kathleen,' Lexie said gently, 'are you missing him terribly?'

She nodded miserably. 'I'm meant to be having the trip of a lifetime and I'm trying. Really I am ... But I don't know what's come over me today ...'

'Hey, it's totally understandable! You don't have to explain anything to me. I'd be a basket case without Sam. Tell you what, why don't we go home now, I'll put on the kettle and you call Jackson?'

'What I'd give to do that,' Kathleen said. Fresh tears fell as she tried to regain her composure.

Lexie glanced at her watch. 'It's early morning in the States but I'm sure he won't mind.'

'He wouldn't at all,' Kathleen said sadly. 'But I can't call him, Lexie.'

'Why not?'

'Because my darling Jackson died last month.'

Chapter 13

LEXIE TOOK KATHLEEN'S ARM AND LED HER BACK to number three Cashel Square. They could hear Sam and his friend Jeremy laughing and chatting in the basement. 'They're happy down there. Let's go into the kitchen upstairs and have a chat,' Lexie said.

She made a pot of tea and perched on a chair opposite Kathleen.

'I'm sorry for making a scene just now. You poor girl! You were in such good form and I had to ruin it all for you by sobbing on the sidewalk. Ugh! I'm so ashamed.'

'Kathleen, please! I can't believe you didn't tell us before that Jackson had died.'

'Oh, honey, I'm sorry. I probably should have said something when we first met, but this was our plan, you see.'

'Go on,' Lexie said.

'We knew he was dying. He had a brain tumour. It had been there for years. He did so well for so long. The doctors were wonderful,' she said. 'But the mountain got too high for Jackson to climb. He became quite frantic towards the end. He was in such pain but he was so panicked about leaving me alone.'

'Oh, Kathleen,' Lexie said, and tears of sympathy poured down her own cheeks.

'Then he came up with the idea that I should take a vacation here when the time came. He asked me to bring him a laptop and he booked my flights online. It was the last transaction on his credit card before he passed away.'

'He sounds like a wonderful man, Kathleen.'

'Oh, he was,' she said. 'He was my world. I knew it was going to be incredibly hard without him, but I never dreamed it would be quite so empty. That's how I feel most of the time, Lexie – empty. It's like a huge part of me is missing.'

'Well, it is,' Lexie said quietly. 'Jackson was your other half and it must be unbearable that he's gone.'

Kathleen took a deep, shuddering breath. 'He said I should come home and revisit my childhood. He wanted me to have a purpose. An agenda. Something to do while I was learning how to live without him.'

'He was a clever and wise man.'

'Yes, dear, he was. He also knew I wouldn't want to assume the role of grieving widow floating around in a black cloak for the rest of my days. So he thought coming here for a few months would exempt me from all of that too.'

'Wow,' Lexie said.

'The day before he slipped into a deep coma, he wagged his finger at me and told me I wasn't to waste the time I had left. He warned me that he'd come and haunt me if I did.' She forced a watery smile.

'Oh, Kathleen, you poor love.' Lexie hugged her and sniffled. 'I'm sorry, I'm not very good at this. I'm not helping matters much, am I?'

'You're making me feel a lot less silly. It's good to see you have as much mascara inking your cheeks as I do!'

'Glad I'm of some service.' Lexie patted her hand and grinned sheepishly.

'I'm so delighted to be in Ireland again,' Kathleen said. 'I know for a fact it's easier than being in our home without him. It's good, also, to avoid the pitying stares of friends who love and miss him too. They're all so dear to me and I know some of them were totally mystified by my decision to fly away from it all. But Jackson knew me better than I know myself. He made the right call.'

A long pause ensued as both women were caught up in their own thoughts.

'He gave me tasks to do while I'm here,' Kathleen added.

'What sort of tasks?'

'He asked me what my three favourite memories of Ireland were,' she said, smiling. 'The first was salty chips on the beach after a sea swim, with a grey sky above and wind whipping my cheeks.'

'That happens on most Irish summer days,' Lexie said.

'The second was going with my family to Dublin Zoo.'

'I'd say nearly every Irish man, woman and child does that at some point in their lives,' Lexie said.

'The third was a picnic at the lakes of Glendalough, including tea from a jam jar.'

'Tea from a jam jar?' Lexie said in surprise. 'I never had that!'

'Oh, it's gorgeous,' Kathleen said. 'Especially if it's cold and miserable out. My mother used to pack the jars in tea towels and we'd savour every drop.'

'They're wonderful memories, Kathleen,' Lexie said.

'I promised Jackson I would revisit them all. That pleased him no end, but he had to have the last say, so he added one other "task". I've to look up an old friend. I have no remaining family here, so he set me the challenge of finding someone from my past.'

'He really thought long and hard about what you should do to keep your mind active.'

'That was Jackson all over.' She grinned.

'Well, I'm here to help with the friend-finding if you need me. And if you'd like company along the way with the three other tasks – and you may not – I'd be honoured to join you.'

'Would you?' Kathleen's eyes lit up.

'Oh, I'd adore it,' Lexie said, wiping her tears away. 'You just let me know when and I'll be there.'

'Thank you, dear,' she said, patting Lexie's cheek. 'You're an awesome girl. I'm blessed to have found you. I know Jackson sent me to you. And please don't start treating me like a widow. That's why I ran from all the folk I know.' Kathleen paused. 'If Jackson and I had been blessed with a daughter I would've wanted her to be just like you.'

'Oh,' was all Lexie could manage before she dissolved into tears again.

'We longed for children, you see,' Kathleen said. 'For years we hoped we'd be blessed with a son or daughter. I used to dream of how they'd look. Our son would have Jackson's height. He was six-four with treacle-dark hair and always wore an impeccably pruned thin moustache and goatee beard. I've never been a fan of beards per se, but Jackson's suited him just fine.'

'He sounds so distinguished,' Lexie said.

'Oh, he was. And such a gentleman. He was old school, you know? Believed in holding doors open for ladies and pulling out my chair before we sat to dine. He treated me like I peed port wine!'

'Oh, dear Lord, that's not a phrase I'd expect to hear from you.' Lexie giggled.

'It was one of Jackson's favourites. He had a way with words too. He used to say, "Love was invented for me and you."'

'That's so sweet.'

Kathleen twisted a handkerchief in her hands and peered up at Lexie tentatively. 'If I tell you something will you promise to keep it to yourself?'

'Of course.'

'Jackson made me a promise the day before he died. Once he knew I'd come home to Ireland, he told me he'd look after me and be here with me.'

'And I've no doubt he's with you each and every second of the day,' Lexie said.

'Well, I hope so,' Kathleen said. 'He said he'd do something else. While I was keeping my side of the bargain and doing my three jobs, he'd do another thing too ...'

Lexie was willing her to go on.

'He instructed me to look for a rainbow on my birthday, his birthday and our wedding anniversary. He says it'll show me that he's not actually gone. That he's simply moved away from the pain and sickness. That although I can't see him, he hasn't left me.'

'Oh, my God, that's so beautiful,' Lexie said. 'Sorry.' She flapped a hand in front of her face. 'I'm blubbing again.'

'My birthday is next week.'

'No!'

'Certainly is. And Jackson's is in July. Our anniversary is August. Summer used to be our time for celebrations and getting together with friends.'

'Sam and I will make sure you still have some form of merriment. It won't be the same, but having said that, nothing ever will be again. We'll try to help you make the best of things.'

Just then Sam and Jeremy appeared, chatting loudly and totally oblivious to the mood in the kitchen.

'The basement's much more homely now,' Sam announced.

'The bed and wardrobe are in place too,' Jeremy added. 'We had to take them apart but they're all assembled again.'

'Thank you, both,' Kathleen said, standing up from the table. If the men noticed she'd been crying, they didn't show it. 'Let's go and take a look,' she said. Lexie squeezed her arm, and Kathleen winked to let her know she was okay.

The basement was transformed. The furniture, colourful rugs and accessories Kathleen had chosen were perfect.

Lexie whistled. 'Wow! You should go into interior designing. This is so fresh and bright. I love the lime-green and cream accents. Nicely chosen, guys.'

The men decided to leave them to it, so Lexie and Kathleen were alone again. 'I'll help you make your bed,' Lexie offered.

'Thank you for being so thoughtful,' Kathleen said. 'I need to say something to you.'

'What is it?'

'I'm a little nervous now. I can't help feeling I shouldn't have told you about Jackson's promise with the rainbows. It probably won't happen and I don't want you to think badly of him. No matter what, he loved me.'

'Kathleen, you don't need to say that! I can tell from the way you talk about him that you were both so much in love,' she said. 'You don't ever have to justify your love or his for you.'

'Thank you.' Kathleen looked well and truly exhausted. 'I think I might take a nap, if that's all right with you?'

'It's your home for the summer. You do exactly as you please.

I'll help you fix up your bed and I'm out of here. Sam and I will be around and about, so pop up if you feel like it. I've to go to the supermarket at some stage, so I'm guessing you'd like to get some provisions too.'

'That'd be great, thank you.'

They swiftly made the bed and parted company. Lexie strode up the stairs to join Sam and Jeremy, who were having a cool drink in the garden.

She plonked herself into the soft cushion of the basket-weave garden chair.

'I'm out of here unfortunately,' Jeremy said, glancing at his watch. 'Hannah will kill me if I'm not home soon. We're off to the park for a late picnic lunch.'

'Give my love to Hannah and baby Aoife,' Lexie said. 'How are they?'

'Great, thanks!' Jeremy said. 'Aoife is probably a little too young to go on the swings or anything like that, but we're dying to do family stuff, so we'll bring her playmat and hopefully she'll enjoy the sounds of the other kids. And who knows?' Jeremy continued, with a glint in his eye. 'Maybe she'll have a little friend to play with at some point.'

Lexie accepted a glass of juice from Sam and looked up at Jeremy. 'Don't tell me Hannah's expecting again!'

'Eh, no,' Jeremy said, blushing. 'I meant you guys. Sorry. None of my business and I should know better than to make throwaway remarks like that. Forgive me.'

'Don't sweat it, mate,' Sam said easily, and clapped him on the back. 'Enjoy the afternoon with the girls. Let's all get together soon. If this weather keeps up we'll be able to use the barbecue. We want to have Maia, Josh and Calvin around as well. Let's make a day of it soon.'

By the time Sam had shown Jeremy out and rejoined her, Lexie was deep in thought.

'You okay?' he asked, sitting beside her.

'Yeah,' she said, with a heavy sigh.

'You don't seem it. Did Jeremy's blunder upset you?'

'No,' she fibbed. 'I didn't give it a second thought.'

'Are you sure?'

'Yes, Sam,' she snapped. There was an uncomfortable silence as Sam stood and sipped from his glass. He sat on the armchair opposite her. She looked at him guiltily. 'Sorry. I didn't mean to bite your head off. I'm a bit stressed today. Poor Kathleen is having a tough time too.' She sighed.

'Why *poor* Kathleen all of a sudden?'

'You know her husband Jackson? He's dead.'

'*Whaat?*' Sam was clearly shocked.

'Yup. He died last month. That's the main reason Kathleen came over here.'

'Ah, God love her,' Sam said. 'When did she tell you?'

'Earlier on. I met her as I was coming out of the gallery. She was having a weepy moment, the poor love.'

'Ah dear. That's awful. How come she decided to fly all the way over here, then?'

'Jackson organised it for her just before he died. Thought it would be easier for her to be away from their home and all the grief.'

'I can see his reckoning, but she's a brave lady to travel alone, isn't she?' Sam said.

'I know. I definitely think it was Fate that we asked her to stay in the basement. I'm so glad we did now.'

They drank their juice, and Lexie sank into the chair relishing the warm glow of the sunshine. She was just drifting off when Sam's voice jarred her: 'Even Jeremy's passing comment now,' he said.

'Mm,' Lexie agreed.

'You know the way we're meant to be mulling over the baby idea?'

'Mm?'

'Can we chat now?'

'I'm busy dribbling,' she said.

Sam walked over to her. He launched himself at her and sat awkwardly on her lap, making her squeal. 'Ugh, you weigh a ton. You're going to squash me to death!'

'Well, I have your attention,' he said, shifting his weight so she could find a more comfortable position.

'So what are you thinking?' she asked, squinting into the sunlight. 'Honestly?'

'Duh, of course. What's the point in discussing this if you're not brutally honest?'

'Okay. Well, I'm kind of leaning towards the idea that it might be nice to have a little Lexie or Sam to fill this garden with laughter.'

'What?' Lexie said, wriggling free of his arms.

'Would the prospect be so abhorrent to you?'

'Sam, we agreed a long time ago that we wouldn't have children. You said you felt the same way I did. I have the maternal instincts of marble, remember?' Lexie said. 'We have a great life. We have Amélie on loan whenever we need her. We have Calvin as our godson. Mother Nature's biological clock simply isn't ticking loudly inside me. I don't think we should have a baby just because society, my mother, lovely Jeremy or anyone else thinks it's a foregone conclusion.'

'But you agreed that we both needed to think about it,' Sam pointed out. 'Reconsider before the window of opportunity passes us by.'

'Well, I have, and I'm sticking by my original decision,' Lexie retorted crossly.

'Take it easy, Lex. Why are you getting so hot-headed about this?'

'I'm not,' she shouted.

'Eh, yes, you are. What's going on?' he asked, staring at her intently. 'I feel like I'm hitting some sort of a raw nerve here. In fact I'm sure of it,' he said. 'Lexie, is there something you're not telling me?'

'Nope,' she said. 'I'm just feeling a bit let down by you. I thought we'd agreed. You and I, not anyone else. So where is this all coming from?'

'It's not coming from anywhere in particular, Lexie. I've just been thinking a lot about it lately.' He grabbed her hands. 'I've seen you with Calvin. I know Maia is like your soul sister and all that, but you turn to jelly when you're in Calvin's company. Why not? He's a special little guy in every sense of the word.'

'I just love his sunny nature and he's always happy to see me, that's all,' Lexie said defensively. 'That doesn't mean I want a baby too.'

'Whoa there,' Sam said, as his smile faded. 'You're acting as if having a baby sounds like a life sentence. It doesn't have to be that way.'

'Doesn't it?' she seethed. 'Since when are you the new Supernanny?'

He looked like she'd slapped him across the face. Blinking, he dropped her hands, stood up and walked towards the house. Then he turned back.

'I don't understand why you're being so aggressive about this, Lexie. It was meant to be an open discussion between two adults. Not a mud-slinging fight.'

Sam went to the kitchen and poured himself a stiff gin and tonic. He took a gulp, and the fizz burned his nostrils. Sure he was bringing up the whole baby thing because of all the comments. But it couldn't be ignored. Everywhere he looked, his friends were having babies. It was the done thing, whether Lexie chose to acknowledge it or not.

He'd honestly thought she'd be her usual level-headed self, take his idea on board and think it through. Nothing could have prepared him for the boiling fury he'd unleashed in his wife. This was a side of Lexie he hadn't known existed.

At the end of the day he couldn't force her to have a baby. But that had never been his intention. It was her body and she was entitled to choose whether or not she wanted to grow a baby inside it. But he was immeasurably shocked by her reaction. He'd never before felt they were anything but equals in the marriage. Now he felt as if a line had been drawn in the sand. From where he was standing, Lexie appeared to hold all the cards and all he could do was wait.

He hated feeling as if he were at his own wife's mercy. But that was how it was. Swallowing hard, he realised that if Lexie had made up her mind she never wanted a baby, there was damn all he could do about it.

Chapter 14

KATHLEEN DREW THE CURTAINS AND CLIMBED INTO her new bed. Nothing felt familiar yet. The new smells and sounds alerted her tired senses. She knew she'd feel better if she could sleep for a short while. Her body was worn out but her mind was on overdrive. Shards of light seeped through the curtains reminding her it was mid-afternoon. She stretched her arms up and folded them behind her head.

'If you're here with me, Jackson, help, please! I'm struggling, darling. It's so hard without you. I'm trying my best. I hope you're proud of me, but it's getting harder not easier.'

She stared up at the ceiling. The presence of a single spider in the corner cast her back to the summer before they'd immigrated to America. Her best friend at the time, Betty Clarke, had come to tea. 'Can we play ghosts in the basement, Ma?' Kathleen had asked.

'Only if you're very careful. The dinner will be ready in a few minutes so see to it that you're back up here. I don't want to have to come shouting for you. I've enough to do with all the packing.'

Kathleen and Betty had huddled together holding hands, each making the other more nervous. A candle lit the way, the flickers adding to their fear.

'Do you think there are dead bodies down here?' Betty asked, breathing heavily.

'Tonnes,' Kathleen said.

She wondered what had become of Betty Clarke. They'd promised to write to one another and stay friends that way. It had worked for a while, but once they'd hit the teenage years the letters had ebbed, then stopped altogether.

Kathleen made a mental note to try to look her up. Betty might be the friend from the past who would tick Jackson's box.

She must have fallen asleep, because she woke with a start. It took her a moment to realise where she was. Swinging her legs out of the bed, she padded towards the main living area. The sun was still shining so she made a cup of tea and brought it to the little yard out back.

'Hi there,' a voice said, from the main garden. 'You must be Kathleen.'

A strikingly pretty girl with cascading golden hair and flawlessly tanned skin was looking down at her. In a simple white lacy cotton dress and navy Converse runner boots, she oozed confidence.

'Yes – and you must be Amélie!' she responded.

'Auntie Lexie told you about me, eh?'

'Of course. She talks about you plenty. I've seen photos of you around the house upstairs too.'

'Can I jump down?'

'I'd love you to.' Kathleen smiled. 'Come and see what I've done with the basement. I hope you like it.'

Amélie bounced over the small granite wall and landed in the yard with a thud, having ignored the steps. 'Hey, this is great. Did Auntie Lexie pick all the stuff?'

'I did, with the help of your uncle.'

'I'm well impressed,' Amélie said. 'I'm going to see if I can move in here soon.'

'Good plan, but you might need to finish school first and do some boring stuff, like going to college or getting a job.'

Amélie shrugged her shoulders and waved her hand to show she wasn't in the market for considering any of those things right now. 'I've got some stuff going on at home and I might be getting out of there sooner rather than later.'

'I'm sorry to hear that,' Kathleen said evenly. 'I found being a teenager really tough, if it helps.'

'It's nothing to do with my age,' she said. 'It's kind of complicated. Would you mind if I don't go into it right now?'

'Of course. It's no biggie. I'm afraid I'm not very good with kids. I never had any, you see.'

'Why not?' Amélie asked.

'My husband and I wanted them so badly, but it never happened.'

'You might be better off. Kids aren't all they're cracked up to be. I'm one and all I seem to do is annoy everyone.'

'I'm sure that's not true. Your aunt and uncle are so proud of you and they totally adore you. They think you're pretty awesome.'

'I love the way you say "awesome".' Amélie grinned. 'It's … awesome!'

'Thanks,' Kathleen said, handing her a cup of tea.

'You would've been the coolest mum. For what it's worth, I think God has a lot to answer for at times. He gives some total saddo wasters like junkies and murderers a baby and doesn't let really sound people like you be a mother. That's just bogus.'

'Who knows why things happen the way they do?' Kathleen said. 'It's a funny old world, isn't it?'

'How long are you staying here for?' Amélie asked, as she followed Kathleen back out to the garden.

'Three months,' Kathleen told her. 'My husband gave me the ticket as a present before he died.'

'Oh, bummer. When did he die?'

'Last month.'

'That sucks. Were you married for yonks or was he, like, your third husband?'

'We were married for yonks,' Kathleen said, chuckling. 'I haven't heard that word for a while.'

'My mum hates it. Tells me to speak properly.' Amélie sighed. 'I'm really sorry about your husband. What was his name?'

'Jackson.'

'Yup, it would be,' Amélie said, slapping her thigh. 'Such a mint-bomb name.'

'Mint-bomb?'

'Uh, deadly – amazeballs, then higher than that in the cool stakes comes mint or mint-bomb,' said Amélie, moving her hands upwards to demonstrate.

Kathleen laughed. 'He was totally mint-bomb, so gorgeous when we first met. He was tall, dark and handsome. Just like a fairytale prince.'

Amélie sat and pondered briefly. 'I'm seeing this guy at the moment. Among other things, it's causing rows with my folks. They hate him.'

'Why?'

'My dad says he's too old for me and has no direction. He's starting a band. It's sort of meant to be kept under wraps but I'll tell you,' she said, pausing for effect. 'It's called Satan Goes to Church and it's going to be totally amazing.'

'Do your parents know about the band?' Kathleen asked.

'Uh-huh.' Amélie nodded. 'Dad says he's a waster and will never amount to anything. He's so narrow-minded. As far as he's concerned any potential boyfriend should be a fully fledged accountant wearing brown cords and a tweed jacket.'

'How old is he?'

'Elton's twenty.'

Kathleen pulled a 'yikes' face. 'I know you're gonna hate me for this, but he *is* kind of old for you, although three years will seem like nothing when you're older. But, right now, this guy is out of school and you're still there. You're at different stages, that's all.'

'I know, but none of that matters when two people love each other, right?'

'Yeah, it would be wonderful if the world worked that way, but sadly it doesn't most of the time. I can see your point and I can also understand that your folks want to protect their little girl.'

'Oh, they don't want to protect me,' Amélie said emphatically. 'They just want to ruin my life.'

Before Kathleen could answer, a voice interrupted them. 'There you are! Hello, Kathleen! I'm glad you two have met,' Lexie said. 'Amélie, Dee was just on the phone, and said you're not answering her texts and calls yet again.'

'I'll ring her later,' Amélie said crossly.

'I think she'd appreciate if you called her right now,' Lexie told her. 'She's concerned because you're not studying and she said you skipped out of the house without telling her again.'

'Who cares? She certainly doesn't,' Amélie scoffed. 'I'm the one doing the exams. If I end up sitting there and can't even write my own name, so what?'

'It might be a bit embarrassing if you can't answer any of the questions, don't you think?' Kathleen said, choosing to ignore Amélie's rising irritation.

'I hate the school system here,' Amélie said. 'If you're not a swotty Goody Two Shoes nobody wants to know.'

'I agree that the school system sucks,' Kathleen said, surprising both Lexie and Amélie. 'It's all about academics and how many points you can clock up. It has no bearing on the type of person you might be. Take medicine, for example. The grades needed to apply are sky high, yet some doctors are totally unable to have a conversation with a patient.'

'That's what I think,' Amélie said, visibly cheering.

'But,' Kathleen said, holding her hand up, 'it's the only system you've got. So bend it to your advantage. Work your ass off and use school as a stepping stone to do whatever you like. I know you don't *get* the reason why you have to learn some of the subjects, but use this as a tool to show the world you're smart. It's your ticket to life.'

'I've never thought of it like that,' Amélie mused.

'It's a good way of putting it,' Lexie said. 'Use the exams as ammunition to show everyone how great you are. After you leave school you don't ever have to study maps or learn French verbs, unless you choose to.'

'Believe me I won't!' Amélie said. 'Does that mean I have to study?' Amélie raised an eyebrow and looked at Kathleen.

'If you want to show the world what you're made of,' Lexie reiterated.

'I suppose,' she said reluctantly. 'Anyway, I'm going to zip off and meet Elton. I need to give him something and then I'll shoot on home.'

'Okay, but don't be too long. Your mum is genuinely worried,' Lexie said.

'I won't!' Amélie said, smiling now. 'You two are great. I might have to come and live here.'

'Well, you'll have holidays in a few weeks and you know you're welcome any time,' Lexie said.

Lexie walked her niece to the front door of the main house as Kathleen rinsed the teacups. Amélie was a great kid. Feisty and, no doubt, capable of causing many sparks to fly, but she was smart and knew her own mind.

Lexie appeared in the garden and called down, 'I'm going to the supermarket now, would you like to come?'

'I'd love to,' Kathleen said. 'I'll lock up, grab my purse and meet you out front.' She felt so much better. She wasn't sure if it was the sleep or the chat with Amélie. Either way, the desolation and sense of doom had shifted considerably. She was very excited about going to the supermarket and stocking up.

Lexie had the car running by the time she made her way outside. 'I love these Fiat 500s,' Kathleen said, lowering herself in. 'The baby blue colour is just precious – and look at your co-ordinating leather seats!'

'Isn't it just the cutest thing you've ever sat in?'

'Sure is!'

'Amélie thinks you're mint-bomb by the way.' Lexie grinned.

'Wow, that's a serious compliment! She's a great kid. I couldn't say it to her, but I'd hate to be that age again. It's so tough, isn't it?'

'Yes, it is,' Lexie agreed. 'My brother and his wife are possibly too close to her, but I can't help feeling they forget the difficulties of being a teenager at times.'

'I reckon they're doing a pretty good job, though. She's so friendly and well able to articulate her thoughts. Some of my friends back home have grandkids and they barely grunt, let alone have full-blown conversations.'

'Sam and I adore her. She's our part-time daughter and it's wonderful to be able to dip in and out of her life.'

'Amazing that she wants you to,' Kathleen pointed out.

'I don't take her for granted. We're so lucky to have both Amélie and my best friend Maia's boy Calvin in our lives. It's like the best of all worlds if you ask me.' Lexie fell into her own thoughts. Sam wasn't speaking to her. He'd gone up to their room and hadn't come down. She called up the stairs to say she was going out, but he didn't answer.

There was a companionable silence as the women drove towards the large grocery store on the outskirts of town.

'Do you regret the fact you didn't adopt, seeing as you and Jackson couldn't have kids?' Lexie asked, as they approached the centre.

'Ooh, that's a deep question.'

'Sorry – don't answer if you don't want to. It's just that Sam and I are at a sort of crossroads right now,' Lexie explained. 'As I told you, my mother is piling on the pressure, but now it seems that it's coming from every angle, comments left, right and centre, and we know it's make-your-mind-up time. I was so certain I knew my own mind, but what if my choice alienates Sam irrevocably?'

'All I can say, dear, is don't rush anything. Give yourself some time. You and Sam are a wonderful couple. I'm certain you'll make the right choice.'

As they walked into the supermarket, Lexie wished she had Kathleen's faith.

Dear Diary

I hate my parents. I hate them for lying to me. But most of all I hate the fact they're miserable and it's all my fault.

Elton is one of the only people who loves me for who I am. He's always happy to see me and makes me realise just how much my parents hate and resent me.

No matter what I do they're not happy. Mum is nothing but a moan on legs. Her mouth is constantly flapping and it's all bad stuff. I can't remember the last time she laughed.

Dad is worse. He goes around like a semi-dead corpse with a grey face and angry eyes.

I'm considering my options, but I reckon I'll have to take drastic action soon.

Ciao for now

A ☹

Chapter 15

THE FOLLOWING SUNDAY, LEXIE AND SAM WERE IN bed. The plan had been to have a sleep-on and rise in time for brunch at around midday before moseying over to Maia and Josh's for Calvin's party.

'It was like sleeping beside a jackhammer last night – you were all over the place.' Sam groaned.

'Was I? Sorry. I'm just upset about this baby thing.' She propped herself on her elbow and stared down at him. 'Sam, I don't think I've changed my mind. I'm sorry, but I still feel the same way I always have.' She lay down again.

'I see.' His words hung in the air. He didn't stomp off or sigh heavily or look at her as if he hated her.

But she couldn't relax: she was lying as stiff as a board, her arms flat on the duvet.

'Jeez, now you look like you're waiting to be embalmed,' Sam said.

'In a way I am,' she said. 'I've decided I'm going to call over to my mother and tell her she won't be adding to her grandchild quota through me.'

'Why do you need to tell her now?' Sam asked. 'Besides, I thought we were thinking it over still.'

'Sam, I don't want a baby. Not now and not next year or the year after. At least if I'm clear with my mother, she might stop hassling me about it and we can forget about the whole thing.'

'What about me?' he asked, clearly pained. 'Don't I have a say?'

'Well, unless there's been an amazing advance in medical science it's my body that has to grow the baby and give birth to it.'

'Well, obviously,' Sam said. 'Naturally you'd have to do the pregnancy and birth. But we could work it out with regards to childcare. Look at Josh and Maia. They're doing brilliantly with their routine.'

'That's different,' Lexie said, flicking her hand. 'Josh chose to be there to help with Calvin. But the situation isn't the same. If Calvin wasn't special needs he'd be in a crèche and Maia would be tearing around like a blue-arsed fly, juggling.'

'Lexie, you've got that whole situation wrong. Josh said he wanted to take the time off. I reckon he'd have done so regardless. That's what parents do.'

'Yeah, well, I don't want to be a parent, Sam. And in case you're having some sort of an attack of amnesia, you agreed with me until now.'

'I simply want you to reconsider,' he said. 'Explore our options.'

'No, Sam,' she said, through her teeth. 'It sounds like you want to move the goalposts all of a sudden. That's a different thing altogether.'

Flinging back the duvet, she jumped out of bed and walked briskly to the shower. Scrubbing her hair vigorously, she hoped the citrus-smelling shampoo might give her a much-needed lift.

While Lexie was in the shower, Sam lay in bed, anger growing inside him. Why did Lexie get to call the shots? Why would she not even consider what he might want?

She was like a woman possessed. And for the first time since they'd met, Sam felt totally at odds with her.

By the time Sam had showered, Lexie was downstairs, had fed Tiddles and texted Maia to say they'd see her later.

'Do you want to forget about going out for breakfast?' he asked.

'No,' she said. 'It's Sunday and that's what we do. It's part of our routine, something we enjoy as a couple. Something we happen to agree upon. So let's roll with it by all means.'

Sam was staring at her, looking hurt. 'Should we knock on

Kathleen's door and see if she wants to come too?' he asked, after a moment.

'It's a bit of a dodgy one, isn't it? I don't want her to feel she has to join us all the time, but I don't want her to feel lonely either.'

'I'll ask her,' he called, over his shoulder, as he made for the front door. Secretly he was crossing his fingers that she'd join them. For the first time in their relationship he didn't want to be alone with Lexie.

Sam spotted Kathleen as soon as he walked down the front steps towards the basement.

'Morning, Sam,' she said, as she opened her door.

'Hi! How's it going? Listen, Lex and I are off to the local café for some breakfast. You're more than welcome to join us but if you'd rather do your own thing that's cool too. We're conscious of not being pushy neighbours so feel free to pass if you'd rather a bit of R and R. We just want you to know that you're automatically included any time. Just pitch in if the mood takes you, yeah?'

'Thank you, Sam,' Kathleen said, and her eyes twinkled. 'You're so like Jackson at times it's scary. He, too, was a no-nonsense type of fellow. I hear ya and I'd be delighted to join you both this morning. For the record, I'm not going to become your shadow this summer either. I don't want you thinking I'm Grandma in the basement who has to be hauled everywhere as a duty call.'

'Spot on!' Sam said, saluting. He reversed up the small steps and stood at the foot of the main ones where Lexie was waiting. 'Kathleen's coming, and we've dispelled the awkwardness with regards to inviting or not inviting. She's not a needy ageing grandma and doesn't expect to be treated as such.'

'Jeepers, Sam,' she hissed. 'Don't be so familiar. Poor Kathleen is having a hard time right now and she's still a guest, so to speak.'

'Chill out, Lex, before you give yourself an ulcer,' he whispered. 'You're really starting to over-think things. If you're not careful you're going to overtake Penelope on the nag-o-meter.'

'That's not funny,' she said quietly, glancing to see if Kathleen was on the way.

'It wasn't meant to be,' Sam said, thoroughly fed up with her attitude.

She seethed. 'Are you for real? I'm only trying—'

'Hi, Kathleen,' Sam said cheerfully, as Kathleen appeared at the top of the steps. 'Ready to rock and roll?'

'Certainly am!' she responded. 'Morning, Lexie, how are you today?'

'Good, thanks,' Lexie said, forcing a smile. 'How about you? Did you get any sleep?'

'Some,' Kathleen said. 'Truthfully, I was a bit at sixes and sevens. But that's to be expected. I need to get to know my surroundings and I'll be just fine.'

As they walked to the café Sam did most of the talking and led the way. It wasn't quite as sunny as the previous few days but it was still warm.

'I love the soft salty sea air,' Kathleen said. 'The difference in the clarity after Orlando is so stark. I feel like my lungs have been lying dormant all these years.'

'It's good for the soul around here,' said Sam. 'Especially when the weather is fine. Speaking of which, you seem to have brought the sun with you. Already we've had more sun in the past few days than for the last two years combined.'

'Well, it's funny you should say that because my memories of Ireland all involve sunshine and being outdoors,' Kathleen said. 'Then I've met Irish people over the years who tell me the weather here involves four seasons in one day with plenty of rain in between.'

'Ah, you're wearing the rose-tinted spectacles of childhood,' Sam said. 'I have those same thoughts from when I was little. Us Irish are great at getting on with it and doing stuff no matter what the weather. Even if it's chilly and windy we put on a Puffa coat over our swimsuits and go to the beach.'

'Yes!' Kathleen said, animated. 'Or we go for a picnic and end up wrapping ourselves in the picnic blanket rather than sitting on it.'

'Too true!' Sam laughed. 'I can remember eating hot chips doused in vinegar from newspaper with numb fingers after a sea swim. We were so cold my mother would wrap us tightly in a towel and sit us on the sand. We looked like a row of little caterpillars in cocoons.'

'How sweet!' Kathleen said. 'I was actually telling Lexie about my little agenda while I'm here,' she said. 'One of my jobs is to do just that, sit on the beach and have chips.'

'Well, if you need company, I'm your man.'

The café was full to the gills, so the trio stood at the door, waiting for a table to become free.

'I'd love to try it,' Lexie said, breaking her silence.

'Didn't you do any of those things as a child?' Sam asked.

'With my mother? Are you joking? She was obsessed with cleanliness,' Lexie explained to Kathleen. 'She'd probably have all sorts of theories about eating on a beach. She'd try and convince you there'd be germs and, God forbid, we might get our clothes dirty. My brother was allowed to get muddy if he was playing sports, but I was treated like a china doll.'

'We'll have to fix that,' Kathleen said. 'I'll make sure you have chips on the beach, tea from a jam jar and a whole host of other rough-and-tumble activities while I'm here.'

'It has to be freezing cold and preferably raining or it won't be as good,' Sam pointed out.

Kathleen laughed and nodded fervently in agreement.

'You two are crazy,' Lexie snapped, as the waitress came to tell them they had a table.

Once they'd all been seated, Kathleen glanced at Lexie. 'What's up, Lexie?' she asked.

'Mm?' She looked up and tried to focus on the others.

'You seem totally distracted. Are you feeling okay?'

'Yeah, I'm sorry. I keep thinking about my mother and the faces she's going to pull when I meet her next.'

'Lexie has made a decision that I think is none of Penelope or anyone else's business, including mine, as it happens,' Sam said, clanking the cutlery in annoyance. 'But Lexie thinks she owes it to the world to make some sort of announcement.'

'Do I want to hear this?' Kathleen asked.

'Well, you've been dragged in now,' Lexie said, glowering at Sam. 'We've made up our minds not to have a baby.'

'Correction. Lexie has decided we aren't having a baby,' Sam said.

'And I want to tell my mother about our decision, let her have a hissy fit and move on. It'll be short, sharp and so over.' Lexie allowed her forehead to thud onto the table.

Sam rolled his eyes. 'Meanwhile you're going to drag yourself around like a wounded animal and head-butt the table, making our fellow diners think you're on day release from the local nuthouse.'

'Yup,' Lexie said, into the table.

Kathleen caught his eye and he looked away.

'Why don't you do us all a favour and go over to your parents and get this over with right now?' Sam asked. 'It's like sitting beside a live electric cable.'

'Sorry,' she said, biting her lip. 'I'll have some food first and go.'

'Great,' Sam said.

The food was delicious but Kathleen and Sam were pretty much left to make idle chit-chat as Lexie alternated between chewing slowly and staring into space.

'Just go, Lexie,' Sam said eventually.

'Right.' A smile flickered across her face. 'Will you two be okay?'

'Do you actually care?' Sam asked.

'Sam ... I ...' Lexie looked embarrassed.

'Just go if you're going,' he said, dismissing her.

'See you later, Kathleen. We're going to my friend Maia's son's party so we'll be gone for the afternoon.'

'Enjoy,' Kathleen said, smiling warmly.

'Thank you,' she said, but she was staring at Sam. 'Sam, you're not helping matters. I have to get my mother off my back, okay?'

'Lexie,' he said evenly. 'You do whatever makes you happy.'

As the door to the café closed, Sam muttered, 'I'm so sorry about bringing you into the middle of this mess, Kathleen. I'm embarrassed you've had to witness this. Lexie and I never normally fight. We usually back one another, no matter what.'

'But this time it's different?'

'Yeah,' he said gruffly. 'This time it's kind of serious.'

Chapter 16

LEXIE GOT HOME IN RECORD TIME. INSTEAD OF going back into the house and delaying things, she unlocked her car and drove straight over to her parents' house. It was only ten minutes from Cashel Square but at that moment it seemed an entire universe away. Every traffic light was red and the Sunday drivers were out in force, ambling in the middle of the road as if they hadn't a care in the world.

As their beautiful Georgian home, Woodview, came into sight Lexie could feel butterflies in her tummy.

Turning off the ignition, she was planning to go over a little speech when her father appeared. 'Hello, love,' he said, looking thrilled. 'This is a nice surprise! I've just finished clipping the hedge at the back. You've timed it perfectly – Mum's making me a cup of tea.'

'Oh, right,' Lexie said. Hugging her dad, she suddenly felt incredibly nervous. She didn't want to dash his hopes.

'How's Sam?' he asked.

'Great! I need to have a bit of a chat with you and Mum,' she said. To her horror, her voice was wobbling.

'Is everything all right with you, love?' Reggie asked.

'Yeah. Dad, I need you to back me up now. Promise?'

'Of course. I'll always have your back, you know that, love.'

'Thanks.'

'Penelope! It's Lexie! Isn't this a lovely surprise?'

'Hello, dear,' her mother said, offering her cheek to be kissed. 'To what do we owe the pleasure of your company?' She raised an eyebrow, then stood with her hands clasped, expectant.

'I need to have a bit of a talk with you both,' Lexie said. Her mouth was dry. She felt as if she was sixteen again and about to tell her parents she'd done something awful, like taking drugs or shop-lifting.

'You look a little off colour,' Penelope said. 'Come and sit down, pet, and tell us your news.'

'Well, there's a couple of things. First, we've rented the basement to a wonderful American lady called Kathleen.'

'Lovely,' Reggie said. 'What brought that on? Are you and Sam strapped for cash?'

'No, Dad, it's a long story. She used to live in our house. She called in to visit and we clicked.'

'Are you certain she is who she says?' Penelope asked, wildly suspicious.

'Yes, Mum. She's hardly going to make it all up,' Lexie said. Why did her mother always have to assume the worst?

'What's the other thing?' Reggie asked.

There was fission in the air and their eyes were on Lexie.

'Well, the thing is … Sam and I—'

'Oh, Lexie, that's wonderful news!' Penelope exploded. Dabbing at her eyes with one of her perpetual hankies from her sleeve, she fanned her hand before her face and tried not to cry.

'Ah, look at you!' Reggie said. 'You're such a softie.' Turning to Lexie, he cupped her face in his hands. 'Congratulations, sweetheart! We never wanted to say anything, but your mother and I have been praying that you and Sam will be blessed with a baby. Your life is going to be so wonderfully enhanced by this. There's no honour like being a parent. There's no love like the unconditional type a baby induces.'

Lexie burst into tears.

'Ah, now,' Penelope said. 'Don't get upset, my precious girl. It's your hormones. This happens. It's normal, though,' she said. 'In fact, it shows the pregnancy hormone is good and strong in your body. That's fantastic.'

As she sat opposite with her hand placed on top of Lexie's, Penelope was evidently and unabashedly thrilled.

For her part, Lexie was tongue-tied. She had no idea how she was going to rain on this parade. How on earth could she dash their hopes and tell them the real reason she'd called in?

Tuning back into the conversation she listened, horrified, as her mother poured out all the inner thoughts she'd clearly been burying for so long: 'I've actually cried myself to sleep, I was so heartbroken that you and Sam hadn't been blessed with a child.'

'She has too,' Reggie confirmed. 'She only wants you to have what we had, you understand.'

Lexie felt as if she was going to vomit.

'I still have your christening robe. Of course, Amélie wore it, but Dee kindly had it cleaned and gave it back. Just imagine, your flesh and blood is going to wear it too!'

'And now that I'm practically retired I'll be delighted to take the little 'un for a walk in the pram any time you need a moment,' Reggie said.

'You never did that for our children,' Penelope said, pouting.

'I was at work, Penelope. Morning, noon and night, I was slaving away to keep you in the style you were accustomed to. Can you imagine if I'd told you there was no money for a holiday or that you'd to cut back on the groceries?'

'All right Reggie,' she said, sniffing and shifting in her seat. 'I don't suppose I can complain.'

'The other thing is,' Penelope turned to Lexie and lowered her voice to a whisper, 'Dee is faultless as a daughter-in-law and I adore her, but it's not the same as your own daughter having a baby. She does things the way her mother taught her. And that's only right. But you'd be more like me. So it'll be marvellous in every way.'

'But I—' Lexie began.

'The other thing is,' Penelope went on, 'I never wanted to revisit the whole sorry situation, but it was a veritable nightmare for me when Amélie came along.'

'Pardon?' Lexie looked stunned.

'Well, all that business with Dee and Billy not being married. It was awful. I couldn't tell anyone at the golf club or the yacht club that we were about to be grandparents. I had to hide it, rush into organising their wedding and then pretend the child was premature.'

'It was very stressful for your mother,' Reggie confirmed.

'But that's preposterous!' Lexie said. 'I knew Dee was pregnant and so did everyone at the wedding. She had a bump, for crying out loud!'

'She was only four months gone. I told my friends she'd simply put on weight with the stress of the wedding. Comfort eating was what I said.'

'Who cares if they were married or not?' Lexie exclaimed.

'I did,' Penelope said, eyes like steel. 'Lexie, it was almost eighteen years ago. You may not remember the attitudes people had then, but I do. We wouldn't have been able to show our faces at the golf club. It may have been accepted by some, but not *our* circle.'

'Oh, I remember the attitudes only too well,' Lexie said. 'But I think the worst one was yours. You played a very dicey game marching Dee and Billy up the aisle. It was pure luck their marriage stood the test of time.'

'Nonsense.' Penelope sniffed. 'It's stood the test of time because they knew it was the right thing to do. People these days are too quick to throw in the towel and walk away. If they have a hard five minutes, they yelp, "Divorce!"'

Lexie's head dropped into her hands. 'Mum,' she said, through gritted teeth, 'I don't know anyone who gets divorced for the fun of it. People do try to make things work. Sometimes that's not enough. Couples grow apart, circumstances change and often there's no other way for them to find happiness unless they call it a day.'

'I don't agree,' her mother said, with her nose in the air.

Lexie thought she was going to cry she was so angry. She caught her father's eye and he winked.

'So when is the baby due?' Penelope asked.

'What?' Lexie said. Her brain was numb. She couldn't think of a single thing to say.

'Ah, she's all in a muddle, bless her,' said Reggie. 'All that negative talk about something that happened years ago is not what Lexie needs right now, love. Let's stop with the upsetting and argumentative talk, eh?'

'I'm merely explaining to Lexie why I'm so pleased about her news. We can finally rejoice in this pregnancy. I've waited my whole life for this moment. If you two think that's wrong of me, then I apologise. But I'm going to be able to hold my head up and tell our friends we're going to be grandparents!'

'You already are grandparents!' Lexie flared. 'Or do you not tell your narrow-minded fossil friends that Amélie is your granddaughter?'

'Let's calm down, please, pet,' Reggie soothed. 'This isn't good for you or the baby. Mum didn't mean to upset you like this. I think it's just the emotion of your news that's bringing buried hurt to the fore. Am I right, Penelope?' he said, eyeballing her.

'Yes, Reggie,' she said, dabbing her eyes and looking like an injured small furry animal.

'Mum, I'm sorry to be such a killjoy but I need to go home and have a lie-down.' Lexie felt faint. She started to cry. 'I need to go home to Sam.' As she ran out of the door she glanced back at her parents, who were waving like two goons, looking all sympathetic.

'Drive carefully, won't you? Be aware you're carrying two precious cargoes at once now!' her father shouted.

Terrified to stay a second longer, Lexie started the car and zoomed away. Her knuckles were white as she gripped the steering wheel. When she screeched to a halt outside the house, she made it as far as the front door.

Sam was waiting there for her and caught her in his arms. 'Hey! What happened, babe?' he asked, as she buried her face in his chest. 'Did they freak out and say awful things?' The previous animosity that had hung between them was wiped out.

'No,' she managed. 'The opposite. Before I could even say all the stuff I'd rehearsed, they put two and two together and came up with five.'

'Huh?'

'They think I'm pregnant, Sam.'

'They what? How? What did you say?'

'They went off on a tangent. It was horrendous. I couldn't interject and tell them they had it all wrong. I hadn't the heart to say I was there to tell them the opposite.'

'Oh, Lex.'

'They're so happy, Sam. I've never seen them so delirious. Then my mum was talking about christening robes, and Dad took over, saying we were in for a treat with all the unconditional love thing ...' Puffing out her cheeks, she tried desperately to control herself. 'I feel such a fraud.'

'Hey, it's not your fault,' Sam soothed.

'Yes, it is!' she shrieked. 'I should've stopped them in their tracks. I should have pushed my chair back, stood up and told the truth. But I didn't. I sat there like a lettuce and now they think they're going to be grandparents again.'

Sam blanched. 'Did you manage to tell them to keep it to themselves?'

'I didn't even *tell* them anything in the first place. It's all a bloody shambles.'

Sam scratched his head. For once he didn't seem to have a solution.

'Maybe you could phone them tomorrow and say you lost it,' he said eventually.

'What?' Lexie was horrified. 'I can't do that to them. That's two lies instead of one. Then what do we do? Pretend to be shattered and smile bravely and say things like "Ah, well, it was God's will. We can try again"?'

'You're shouting,' Sam stated.

'What do you expect, you making suggestions like that?'

'Fine, it was stupid. I'm just trying to help.'

'Well, don't!' she yelled. 'I'm doing really well making a total pig's arse of everything without any help from you or anyone else.'

'Well ...' Sam hesitated, '... what if we were to try and make a baby for real? We could work out the logistics at a later stage, but if you got pregnant really quickly your folks would be so delighted it wouldn't matter.'

'Are you clinically insane?' she shouted. 'No way, Sam.'

Lexie ran up the stairs. Their room didn't seem like the right place to seethe, so she went to the spare room.

She sat on the floor, staring at the space where the bed used to be. Since it had been moved to the basement, the need to sort the room was even more apparent.

'Can I come in?' Sam said, minutes later, knocking on the door.

'Yeah,' she said sheepishly.

'How're you doing?'

'Oh, God, Sam! I'm sitting here trying to see if my body clock is ticking. But the truth of the matter is that I don't think I have one. It would be so much easier if I was longing for a baby, but it's such a big deal when my heart isn't in it.'

Sam sighed sadly. 'I think the best policy is to let this sit with your folks until tomorrow. It's time to go to Calvin's party now.' She nodded. 'Lexie, I've been feeling you're slipping away from me lately. I'm starting to think we both want different things.'

'No, Sam,' she cried. 'I want you. I want us. I want things to stay the same as they've always been.'

'But what if I don't?'

Lexie hoped to God her face didn't betray her shock as she looked him in the eye. Instinctively she hugged him tightly and waited for the moment to pass. As she inhaled his familiar scent and rubbed her cheek against the soft fabric of his T-shirt, she felt sure she could take on the universe, if Sam was with her.

Lexie knew in her heart of hearts that she didn't want a baby. But seeing Sam so tortured, and knowing how much it meant to her parents, she was beginning to question things. Her mind flicked back to France. Shaking her head, she forced herself to block the images. She couldn't afford to look back. She wondered what the future held. Should she go against everything *she* had decided in order to make others happy or was it okay to follow her heart? Lexie longed for a crystal ball to glance at the future. She had no idea which direction her life was about to take, and that scared her beyond belief.

Chapter 17

ON THE WAY TO MAIA'S HOUSE SAM HIT THE SPEED limit. Lexie would normally have called him Jenson Button and told him to slow down, but the atmosphere was too strained.

'Have you remembered Calvin's present?' Sam broke the silence.

'Of course,' she said. 'I got him the truck with the small cars to go on the back. The one he wanted.'

When they pulled up at Maia and Josh's detached five-bedroom mock-Victorian new build, Lexie gasped. 'Oh hell, what has Maia done?'

A massive inflatable assault course was poking its head above the roof from the back garden. The front porch was festooned with helium foil balloons, and a clown on stilts was welcoming people while blowing bubbles.

'This is insane, even for Maia.' Sam slammed the car door and marched inside with Calvin's present under his arm.

'Sam! Sam!' Calvin said, running forward with his arms out. Lexie's anger totally dissolved as she watched her husband hugging the little boy.

'For me?' Calvin asked, pointing at the gift.

'All for you,' Sam said. 'Happy birthday, Calvin. You're a big boy now!'

'It's my burr-day,' he said, clapping.

'Sure is, dude,' Sam said, and helped him unwrap the truck.

Calvin reacted brilliantly when he saw his present – Josh appeared in the hallway just in time to see his son jumping up and down with delight.

'Hey, Sam, how's it going? Hi, Lex. Maia's in the kitchen.'

'Look, Daddy,' Calvin said, clapping some more and pointing. 'It's my burr-day.'

'Wowzers, Calvin,' Josh said, bringing his hands to his mouth dramatically. 'Lucky you!' He held his hand out and Calvin went to high-five him.

'Good job, Calvin!' Sam said. 'When did you learn to do that?' Calvin clapped again.

Lexie hugged and kissed Calvin before striding to the kitchen to find Maia.

'Hello!' Maia tottered over to her on six-inch heels.

'Where are you off to?' Lexie said, looking her friend up and down. 'Are we all moving on to a nightclub or something? Look at the get-up on you, Mrs Sex Kitten.'

Maia whispered, in Lexie's ear, 'All the neighbours are coming so we're having the works, hence my rocking it in my Louboutins, skinny jeans, and showing my painfully worked-on abs.'

'You're a basket case,' Lexie said, laughing.

'Whatever,' Maia said. 'Right! Get ready to show off. Here's Lauren from down the road. She thinks she's the cat's whiskers, and her son is a little shit. He pushed Calvin over when they were playing on the green last week. Josh says it was an accident. I know he did it on purpose.'

Lexie watched Maia saunter out of the kitchen towards the other woman with saccharine greetings.

'The place looks astonishing,' said Lauren. 'I'm amazed you went to so much trouble for Calvin. I mean, he's only four, and would he understand any of it anyway?'

'Pardon?' Maia towered over her and stood with a hand on her hip.

'Oh, I mean, it's all just lovely …' The other woman was plainly scared.

Within half an hour all of the children had arrived. A puppet show had begun and some of the kids had had their faces painted.

'Will I bring Calvin to the face-painter's table?' Lexie asked Maia.

'Jesus, no!' she hissed. 'He'll go ballistic if you put anything near his head or face. I only booked the woman because Lauren said she couldn't be got. She's the in-thing at the moment. She does balloon animals and magic tricks too.'

'Well, Calvin loves animals,' Lexie said positively.

'Yeah, and he adores the bouncy castle. Did you see his trampoline? We got it for him as his present.'

'Cool,' Lexie said.

'I'm going to do two hundred bounces on it every day – it's meant to be amazing for your pelvic floor. Nobody wants to be weeing down their leg by the age of forty-five, eh?'

Lexie helped herself to a glass of bubbly from a table set up in the garden and handed one to Maia. They sipped as the children rushed to the front garden to get an ice-cream from the truck that had just pulled up.

At the opposite end of the back garden, Sam was chatting and laughing loudly with a group of fathers as they tossed burgers on the barbecue. Lexie tried to catch his eye but he was studiously ignoring her.

She guzzled the rest of her drink, then topped it up.

Three hours later the younger children and parents had gone home. Lexie had polished off the entire bottle of champagne.

'Christ almighty, thank goodness that awful Lauren woman is gone,' Maia said, peeling her shoes off. 'I know these shoes are a fashion must-have but possibly not for a children's party. I should have worn my trusty Crocs.'

'You look amazing, though,' Lexie said. 'I'd say she hates you. She's about two foot shorter than you and has very bulgy eyes.'

'Ha.' Maia laughed. 'I stood on her son's toe too. I apologised profusely and made a song and dance of how awful I am, but I managed to hold his gaze. He won't push Calvin again.'

'Way to go, Mummy Tiger,' Lexie said. 'You're evil.'

'If anyone messes with my boy, they mess with me,' she said. 'Now fill up my glass before I fall over.'

'Eh, I've kind of drunk it all.' Lexie grimaced.

'Not to worry, there's plenty more in the fridge,' Maia said, walking gingerly to the kitchen. 'Are you going to tell me what the hell is going on?' she called. 'You and Sam have been edging around one another like opposing gang members all afternoon. Has he shagged his secretary or something?'

'No!' Lexie said. 'And be careful or he'll hear you.'

'They're all busy finishing off the barbecue,' Maia said. 'So,' she prompted, 'have you shagged Larry from the fish shop, then?'

'Ugh, no!' Lexie grinned.

'What, then?'

'Is it that obvious?'

Maia came back into the sitting room, flopped onto the sofa and set about opening a fresh bottle of bubbly. 'I know you too well. Spit it out. Tell Maia.'

Over the next half-hour Lexie offloaded the whole baby saga in hushed tones. Calvin bobbed in and out with a little boy called Simon. But the men remained in the garden.

'Well,' Maia said, glancing around to make sure Josh wasn't within earshot, 'there's a similar hassle going down in this house.'

'Really?' Lexie asked.

Maia nodded. 'Josh wants us to have a brother or sister for Calvin.'

'And you don't?'

Maia shook her head. 'It's been a long road, Lex,' she said. 'Don't get me wrong, I wouldn't change Calvin for anything in the world. He's my soldier and I love every hair on his little head, but it's not easy. This isn't fun all the time. I know being a parent to any child is tough, but I'm terrified of having another.'

'In case it has Down's too?'

'I guess. But there's the guilt. What if the new child resents us for bringing him or her into the world and feels he or she has to look after Calvin in years to come?'

'Then you make provision. You said you were going to do that anyway,' Lexie said.

'Yes, and we will. It makes things more complex, though, and there are far more considerations.'

'But?' Lexie encouraged.

'But there's nothing like the feeling of having your own child. I'd love Calvin to have a sibling. It would bring him on and show him a whole different aspect to our home life.'

'Whatever you decide I'll support you,' Lexie said, hugging her.

'Thanks, honey,' she said. 'You and Sam were so amazing to us when Calvin came along. We'll never forget that. Josh and I still marvel at how lucky we were to have you guys. We've shed so many friends since Calvin's diagnosis … On the flip-side we've met new people who are wonderful and we couldn't live without them. It's been eye-opening for sure.'

Lexie was silent. She had only ever kept one secret from Maia. Christophe. She needed to get it off her chest. But it wasn't the right time. It never seemed like the right time to tell anyone what she'd done. Instead she filled her in on the awful mishap with her parents that morning.

'Cripes! You really know how to mess up big-style.' Maia grinned.

'Thanks for the support,' Lexie said, sticking out her bottom lip. 'I'd be offended but I'm mildly anaesthetised with champagne. I'm exhausted by being in the wrong all the time.'

'Hey, who says you're wrong?' Maia asked. 'You're entitled to your feelings and opinion. It's just damn hard when nobody appears to agree with you.'

'Do you understand why I feel this way?' Lexie beseeched her.

'Lex, that's an impossible one for me to answer because I'm a mother. I wanted a baby and I've got Calvin. All I can say is that you need to listen to your heart. A baby isn't the same as a goldfish or a kitten so you're either in or out. You've said you'll support me and, believe me, I'll be there for you too. All the way. No matter what you decide. That goes without saying, right?'

'I know, but it's still good to hear. Thanks, Maia.'

'Hey, guys.' Sam popped his head around the door. 'I'm splitting, Lex. Stay longer if you wish but I need to get some stuff ready for work tomorrow. Thanks for an amazing afternoon,' he said to Maia.

'I'll come now,' Lexie said. 'I just need to run to the bathroom.' She stood up, swaying slightly. As she stumbled towards the door, Maia teased her: 'You lush! Just look at her – drunk at a child's birthday party. Disgraceful carry-on!'

As Lexie wove her way towards the toilet, Maia said, 'You okay, Mr Sam?'

'I'll get there,' he said. 'We're just having a bit of an odd time. No doubt Lexie's filled you in.' Both knew there was no point in pretending they didn't know the score.

'I hope you get it sorted one way or the other soon,' Maia said. 'You're great together, you guys.'

'I know,' Sam said. 'At least, we used to be.' He kissed Maia's cheek and waved out of the door to Josh, then headed for the car.

'Where's he gone?' Lexie asked, blinking in the evening sunlight.

'Out to the car,' Maia said. 'He's hurting right now, Lex,' she said. 'You guys need to chat.'

'Yeah, pot calling the kettle black,' Lexie said.

'I'll talk to Josh. But make sure you don't overlook Sam's feelings, doll. He's a good guy and he loves you.'

In spite of Maia's warning, there was very little chat as Sam drove home. Lexie was at a loss as to what to say, so she pretended to be asleep. As she closed her eyes she wished she could fast-forward her life five years. At least by then this would have been resolved.

The reality that Sam might not be a part of her life by then hit her like a tonne of bricks. Opening one eye, she peered across at him. Then she clamped a hand over her mouth to stifle a sob.

'Are you about to puke?' Sam asked, as the car wobbled on the road.

'No,' she managed. 'I'm fine. I was just having a moment.'

They stared straight ahead again. There were no appropriate words right now.

Chapter 18

KATHLEEN BRACED HERSELF AS SHE PLUGGED IN THE laptop. It had been sitting in its box since the day Jackson had handed it to her. 'When you're ready, open this and click on the little icon I've named "from me to you",' he'd said, from his hospital bed.

'Oh, Jackson, I don't think I can cope with any of this,' she'd said miserably. Grinding her tears away, she'd tried with every fibre of her being to hold it all together. 'I don't want to be without you. I can't work a computer and I don't want to see messages that will break my heart.'

He'd lain back on the starched white pillows and looked at her lovingly. Wordlessly he held up his hand. She took it. 'I wish things could be different, darling. But we both know I've been living on borrowed time for so long now. I'm tired. I wish I could take you with me. I hate the thought of you being lonely and sad. But I have no regrets, Kathleen.'

'I've loved you every minute of every day since we met,' she said. 'I'll learn to live without you. But I'll have to let *this* Kathleen die with you. *This* Kathleen,' she said, thumping her chest, 'belongs with you alone. I'll have to reinvent myself.' She smiled feebly.

That was how the idea had sparked for her to travel.

'You'll meet people who never knew you before,' Jackson told her. 'You can be whoever you want. You can even invent a whole other life. Imagine! You could say you're a retired circus performer.' She burst out laughing, grasping for a tissue to blow her nose. 'Or how about an actress? Even better you could say you're a brain surgeon! We both know enough about matters of the brain – I've been carrying this damn tumour around for so long.'

'That's a point, sweetie,' she said. 'Oh, Jackson, you're a tonic.'

'Tell me you can do it,' Jackson said. He was still smiling but Kathleen saw desperation in his gorgeous eyes.

'I'd rather not, but of course I can and will carry on,' she vowed.

The following morning when she had arrived at the hospital, Jackson was animated. 'One of the nurses helped me. I booked this on-line and they printed it.' He had handed her the envelope with her tickets to Ireland.

'I don't know what to say.' Kathleen had looked at the tickets and back at him. 'You've booked the flight for May thirtieth. That's a few weeks away.'

'Yes,' he said calmly.

'But we don't know when ...' Kathleen trailed off. 'Was it wise to pinpoint a date, love?'

Jackson didn't speak. Instead he patted the bed, signalling for her to lie beside him. They often did that. She'd cuddle into him, then flick on the TV and they'd watch a movie together. Putting the envelope with the tickets on his bedside locker, she kicked off her shoes, curled onto her side and nestled into him.

'Do you remember our wedding day?' he asked.

'Of course I do.'

'You know I promised to love you for the rest of my life?' he asked.

'Yes, Jackson, and I said I'd love you for all of mine.'

'We did good, didn't we?'

'We sure did.' She smiled.

'I'll visit you in your dreams and I'll be certain to let you know I'm with you. I will always love you.'

'And I will always love you too. Thank you for being you. I can just imagine you up there on a cloud with that mischievous smile on your lips, plotting how you're gonna make yourself known to me!'

Jackson's deep laugh hadn't filled the room.

Kathleen had moved her head from the crook of his arm. As soon as she had gazed up at him she'd known he'd left her.

Before that day, Kathleen had never been so close to a dead body. She'd always thought she'd find it terrifying. At funerals in the past she'd shuffled past the corpse, avoiding looking at it for any length of time. But right at that moment there was no fear. Her Jackson could never be anything but wonderful. Kathleen had allowed herself a few stolen moments longer with the light of her life, before pressing the bell and alerting the nursing staff to his death.

As soon as the outside world learned of his passing, Kathleen knew their time as husband and wife was well and truly up. A whirlwind had ensued as she had thought it would. There were umpteen papers to sign, arrangements to make and people to inform. A river of sympathy had flooded towards her, and Kathleen embraced it, thanking their extended family and friends for their kindness.

She had truly reached saturation point with the whole business by the time the trip to Ireland came around.

'You were right again, Jackson. Thank you for having such foresight,' she'd said to the ceiling, as she packed to travel. She still looked to the sky each time she spoke to him. 'I don't even know if you're up there, Jackson, but it seems somehow right to talk to you this way.'

Now that she was ensconced in her basement apartment in number three Cashel Square, she felt it was time to click on the icon Jackson had made. The laptop sprang to life, playing a short jingly tune. A lovely pattern of a rainbow spread across the screen.

Kathleen smiled. Jackson had remembered how much she adored rainbows. Already, tears were trickling down her cheeks as she focused on the screen and found the little icon he had told her about. With trembling fingers she fumbled before she managed to click on the correct one.

Instantly it flashed on the screen before bursting into life.

As if by magic Jackson's face appeared.

'Oh, darling!' Kathleen exclaimed, as her hands shot to her mouth.

'Hello, Kathleen. How're ya doing, my sweet?' he said. She reached out to touch the screen, hoping against hope that she might be sucked in to join him.

'Hi, honey,' she whispered.

'I hope by now you're in Ireland. Knowing you as I do, I'd say you're bawling like a baby right now.' He grinned and paused. 'Don't you stay sad for too long, ya hear?' He wagged a finger. 'I'm still all around you and I'll be waiting until we meet again. Meanwhile I'm going to send you three rainbows just like I promised. One on your birthday at the end of June. A second on my birthday in July, and the third on our wedding anniversary in August. Keep an open mind and search for your rainbows. I love you, Kathleen. Don't forget me and have a wonderful time.' He leaned forward and blew a kiss into the camera. The colours of the rainbow crept across the screen, then faded into a blur.

Dropping her head onto the table, Kathleen cried until her entire body ached, her nose burned and her throat throbbed.

Unable to stop herself, she clicked on the icon again.

By that night she'd watched the footage so many times she knew it off by heart. She even let it play while she cooked the dinner, taking comfort from the sound of Jackson's voice in the room with her once more. If she closed her eyes and ignored the content, she could almost convince herself he was back with her again.

That night she slept soundly for the first time since he'd gone.

Chapter 19

LEXIE HAD AN AWFUL SKIN-CRAWLING ALCOHOL-fuelled sleep. At the party all she had eaten was a small piece of birthday cake, which had been an alarming shade of aqua and slightly gritty, so it was no wonder she had post-alcohol fear right now. Sam had slept with his back to her and was still clutching the duvet tightly, like a startled koala. She knew they had to talk. She'd have to talk to her parents too. She was pretty much banking on having no friends by lunchtime. Feeling desolate, she padded down to the kitchen to distract her addled mind with Facebook and make a cuppa. She'd forgotten the special feeling a champagne hangover gave her. Her entire head felt as if it was bound tightly with bubble-wrap and sealed with strong brown tape. A sudden banging on the front door startled her. She glanced at the oversized mounted wall clock and looked out of the window in dismay. Relieved there were no flashing blue lights or squad cars, she wondered who on earth could be calling at six o'clock on a Monday morning. Suddenly worrying it might be Kathleen, feeling distressed, she hurried to open the door.

'Oh, thank God you're up!' Amélie huffed, bustling past her at the speed of light.

'Amélie, what on earth are you doing?' She followed her into the kitchen. 'Do you know what time it is?'

'Sorry.' She looked at the floor for a few seconds before her shoulders began to shake.

'Hey,' Lexie said, taking the girl in her arms. 'What's happened? Aren't you meant to be starting your exams this morning?'

'I am,' she said. 'That's the problem. I haven't done a tap, Lexie. I've been so caught up with Elton and all the messing with my supposed friend Suri. It's been such a disaster.'

'What's Suri got to do with Elton?' Lexie asked. 'Do your mum and dad know you're here?'

'No way! They were asleep and I snuck out of the house. I thought they might be happier if I wasn't there when they woke up.'

Lexie grabbed the house phone from its stand on the sideboard.

'Please!' Amélie begged. 'Don't call them. Not yet.'

Lexie bit her lip. She knew her brother and his wife would be frantic to find Amélie's bed empty, but figured five minutes wouldn't hurt. Besides, she'd probably be the first person they'd call.

'Right, let's talk – but I'll have to tell your folks where you are sooner or later, okay?'

Amélie shrugged her shoulders. Lexie gave a warning look, so she relented and nodded.

'So …' she took a deep breath '… I met Elton late last night. I left the house once Mum and Dad were asleep, yeah?'

'Not cool, honey,' Lexie said. Her niece was really distressed, so she held her hands up and puckered her lips inwards to show she wasn't going to say another word.

'I really love Elton, Auntie Lexie. I thought he loved me too, but I landed at his bedsit and he was there with Suri.' Her face crumpled, as she covered it with her hands. 'I feel such an idiot,' she sobbed.

'I know this isn't what you want to hear right now,' Lexie said, tucking some hair behind Amélie's ear. 'But he's a total creep. Suri isn't blameless in all of this but Elton shouldn't have taken up with your friend. The whole thing stinks and you've *got* to try and be strong. Your exams start today – you can't afford to let this dweeb ruin your chances of doing well.'

''Kay,' she said, sniffing. 'If he's such a moron,' she shuddered, 'and I know you're right, why do I feel like I want to die of a broken heart?'

'Because you love him. We can't help whom we fall in love with, honey. I had some pretty tricky boyfriends before I met Sam. I knew they weren't right for me, but it didn't stop me falling for them.'

Amélie stared at Lexie. 'Thank you for believing that I love him,' she said. 'I told Mum about it last night. I was so upset and I needed to talk. I didn't tell her I'd gone out or anything. But I went into her room and asked her to come and chat to me. It was really late, and I know she was asleep, but she made a face like she was sniffing sweaty trainers and told me I was far too young to know what love was. She said I was trying to find yet another feeble excuse to avoid doing my exams. Then she pointed out that she didn't appreciate me waking her at that hour.'

Amélie was so stricken that Lexie's heart went out to her. 'Your mum's a good person but I think what's happened here is that things have got a bit out of hand. You're both sort of fractious with one another. So it might be best if you just call a truce until after your exams.' Lexie felt a heel doling out advice to Amélie. She knew she ought to say, 'Hey, don't sweat it, Amélie, we all mess up. I do it all the time. In fact, you'll get better at it the older you are. I have.' Instead, she attempted to keep her expression neutral and pretend she was in a position to counsel her.

'I'm a disappointment. Who can blame her for being so pissed off with me? I can't do anything right.' Amélie burst into tears.

Amelie desperately wanted to tell Lexie about her parents' argument. But she couldn't bring herself to say the words. She was genuinely upset about the break-up with Elton but most of the tears were down to shame from what she'd overheard. 'I know Mum and Dad would be so much happier if they had a daughter they could be proud of.'

'Hey, that's rubbish and you well know it,' Lexie said. 'They *are* proud of you, darling. We all are. It's really, really tough being a teenager, Amélie. I know. I was one.' Amélie looked up at her with such a sad, tear-stained face that Lexie pulled her closer. 'I found the stage you're at right now to be the most difficult in my life. There's so much happening with school friends, boyfriends, family, hormones, you name it. It's a minefield.'

'When will it get better, Auntie Lex?'

'Oh, my poor girl,' she said.

Tears prickled in her eyes too. Lexie knew she couldn't say what she really thought, which was that it never gets better, that the problems evolve and often get a hell of a lot worse. Instead she said what Amélie needed to hear in the most honest way she could. 'I wish I could do something to make it all seem better. But life can be full of ups and downs, honey. That's the way it goes.'

'I'll bet your life is pretty perfect at this stage.' She sniffed. 'You and Sam have it all sussed. You have this cool house, money to buy anything you like. You never have to worry about phone credit or feel broken-hearted because some moron's gone off with your supposed friend. And, to top it all, you have the one thing that can't break your heart – your gallery. You're so right to have that place at the top of your list. It can't dump on you. And you know the person you share a house with truly wants you there.'

Lexie paused. Should she tell her niece that her life was on the edge of a cliff and that the only people who were actually talking to her, apart from Amélie, were Kathleen and Maia?

'Amélie, when you're my age, there's a whole host of other stuff that'll make you want to cry at times. Yes, I have plenty of credit for my phone and a great house and, of course, I have Sam.' She balked for a second. She sincerely *hoped* she had Sam. 'But I work hard for all those things. Sam and I work hard to stay connected. None of it comes easily. That's just not the way of the world, Amélie. I guess what I'm trying to tell you is that life isn't easy for anyone. We all have stuff to deal with that we hate.'

'Great,' she said sadly. 'So all I have to look forward to is a bigger pile of poo than the one I'm wading through right now.'

Lexie grinned in spite of her heavy heart. 'Give me a hug,' she said. 'There are two ways of looking at life, Amélie. You can take the life-is-shit-and-then-you-die view, or you can go with the when-life-hands-you-lemons-make-lemonade approach. It's up to you. Bad stuff will always happen. That's a guarantee, sadly. But you'll survive, my pet. You'll survive because you're a clever, strong and wonderful girl. Don't ever let anyone tell you anything different.'

'Thanks,' Amélie said, sounding less stricken. 'Maybe one day I'll turn out to be as perfect as you.' She grinned. 'Or, at worst, a lemon.'

Lexie laughed. 'Just be yourself, darling. Do you want to go up to your room and have an hour's sleep? I'll wake you for your exam.'

'No, thanks. I'll go home, have a shower and get ready for school.'

'Okay. If that's what you want.'

'It is.'

'Right, let me grab my coat. I'll run you over in the car.'

Silence prevailed because Lexie had purposely turned the radio off. Every couple of seconds she glanced at Amélie. She was pale and anxious. They pulled up outside her house and Lexie killed the engine. 'You're in luck. Only the en-suite light is on in Billy and Dee's bathroom. If you go in now they won't have to know you ran away. Go on in, sweetie, and good luck today. You're a clever girl. Try to keep your wits about you. You'll be fine.'

'Thanks for everything,' Amélie said, leaning over to hug her.

'Text me later if you think of it and let me know how the exams went.'

Amélie shut the car door as quietly as she could and scurried into the house.

As Lexie drove the short distance home, the feeling that something awful lay ahead returned ten-fold. And she couldn't block a comment Amélie had made. Her niece honestly thought the gallery was her one true love. Did everybody think she was that cold and emotionless? Did Sam think she loved her business more than him? Did her parents too?

As she remembered her parents' glee of the day before, which had been in stark contrast to the look of hurt and disappointment Sam had given her, she understood why Amélie thought running away would be a good option. With a sinking feeling, she let herself back into number three Cashel Square and headed for the shower.

Sam stirred as she appeared in their room wrapped in a towel with wet hair. 'Where did you go?' he asked, stretching.

'I had an early-morning visit from a distressed Amélie.'

'What's up? Where is she?'

'I dropped her home a while ago. She was having a bit of a meltdown. Boy trouble mixed with exam nerves and a bit of my-parents-are-aliens thrown in.'

'Ah,' Sam said, nodding. 'Poor kid.'

'I felt so bad for her,' Lexie said, gripping the edge of the bath towel. 'But I also felt like a complete fraud giving her advice. My own life is such a mess I'm hardly role-model material.'

'She doesn't know that. At least she feels she can talk to you,' Sam said, throwing the covers back and getting out of bed. He didn't hug, kiss or even touch her as he walked into the bathroom. Lexie stood frozen to the spot. Sam had never been like that before. Normally he'd hug her, reassure her that she wasn't a mess and tell her he loved her. There was silence from the shower again.

Lexie was still standing in the same spot wrapped in the damp towel with her hair dripping down her back when Sam emerged from the bathroom with a towel around his middle.

'Why are you standing there shivering? I thought you were going to your parents' this morning.'

'I am,' she said. 'I wanted to ask if you'd come with me.'

He paused. 'Right, then. Let's go and get it over with.'

'I'll get in touch with Kate and make sure she can open up the gallery,' she added.

Sam felt awful. He'd known something was going on with Lexie for the past few weeks, maybe even months. He'd never felt removed from her before now. He'd thought they had a really special relationship and could talk about anything. His mates often said stuff about their wives or girlfriends. Derogatory stuff, about how naggy or moody they were. He'd always had a laugh with them about it and, in retrospect, had probably been a bit of a smug git about his marriage. 'You should be with someone like Lexie,' he'd say, amid groans. It was a running joke with the lads that he and Lex were the perfect couple.

He could talk to Josh about this bad patch. They'd really bonded after little Calvin was born. But Sam wasn't sure he wanted to bare his soul and admit to the cracks that seemed to be forming in his life. He'd never envisaged feeling lonely when Lexie was at his side. But that was exactly how he'd felt lately.

He knew he was going back on his word. He *had* said he'd be happy without kids. But that was years ago. They'd been at a different point in life then. They'd just got married, bought the house and then Lexie had had to rejig her career. Meanwhile he had been busy establishing his own space in the business world. At the time he hadn't been able to think about children. They'd never spoken about it as a couple, but he was certain Lexie had been as rocked by the shock of Calvin having Down's as he had.

Now, with hindsight and knowing that gorgeous little boy, who was bursting with personality and ready to take on the world, Sam could see the happiness he brought Maia and Josh. Things had changed. He and Lexie had built their life together – business was going well and they had a beautiful ready-made family home.

He missed his parents and brother. He couldn't possibly go on Skype and tell his folks that he was terrified his marriage was over. How would he put into words that he wasn't sure whether or not he could stay with Lexie if she wouldn't give him a child?

Why didn't she long to have a baby? Why didn't she see those gorgeous children yesterday and think she'd love to have one of their own flesh and blood, with either pigtails or a cute little spiked haircut? Sam sat on the end of their bed and stared into space. At that moment, he felt as if he were living in a different universe from his wife.

Chapter 20

LEXIE MADE BREAKFAST AND PUT ON A WASH, THEN phoned Kate. Thankfully, she was obliging as usual and agreed to do the morning shift instead of her usual Monday afternoon. The ducks were in a row. All she needed now was Sam.

Fear crept through her as he appeared downstairs. She rushed to the kitchen table with a basket of toast and his freshly made coffee. 'Okay, now … We'll have a bite to eat and see what time we're at. I need to get to my parents' house as quickly as possible.'

'Are you sure I should be there for this chat?' he asked. 'I wasn't there when the confusion began and, to be perfectly honest, I can't say whether or not I can back you up on it.' Sam paused. 'I never thought I'd hear myself saying it, but I think I agree with your mother on this one …' There was a silence. 'I actually don't think I can do this today …'

'Please, Sam,' she begged. 'I need you with me. We can talk later about our future plans. Maybe we will have a baby some day,' she said, in panic. 'Who knows? But right now I feel like the bad fairy coming in to ruin everyone's happiness.'

'If that's how you feel, maybe you should think deeply about whether or not you're making the right decision. Often when things don't sit well it's because they're wrong.'

Her voice was barely above a whisper. 'I don't think I've made the wrong decision about not having a baby.'

'Right,' he said, grabbing his briefcase. 'I'll accompany you to your parents' house because you've asked me to. I can't call the office and say I'm not coming in because we've a lot on this morning so I'll have to be quick. Let's go.'

As they sat in his car, Sam put on the morning news and drove without uttering a single syllable.

Lexie sat like a poker in the passenger seat, feeling increasingly nervous as they approached her childhood home.

'Ready?' Sam said, as he turned off the ignition and opened his door.

'No, but let's do it.'

Lexie used her key to open the front door. Her parents were at the breakfast table as they entered the kitchen.

'Well, hello there, you two!' Penelope shrilled. 'Two visits in one week? We're honoured.'

'Good morning, folks. Sorry to barge in on you while you're enjoying your breakfast,' said Sam.

'Not at all, come and join us,' Reggie said, getting up. 'Congratulations, Sam. Penelope and I couldn't be happier.' He pumped Sam's hand up and down and banged him on the back.

Sam looked at Lexie. She widened her eyes.

'Eh, this is more than a little awkward,' Sam began. 'There's been a misunderstanding.'

'Oh, really?' Penelope said, still smiling. 'Sit down, both of you. All that hovering around makes me nervous!'

'Mum, when I called in yesterday—'

'Oh, you made us happier than we've felt for years!' Penelope interrupted.

'You really did,' Reggie confirmed, leaning across the table to pat his beaming wife's hand.

'Mum!' Lexie said loudly. 'Sorry.' She squeezed her eyes shut and took a deep breath. 'I didn't mean to shout. But I need you to listen to me. You got the wrong end of the stick yesterday.' She looked at Sam for back-up.

'Lexie's not pregnant,' Sam said.

There was silence as Reggie and Penelope looked at each other, then at Lexie and Sam. Sam's eyes were on the floor.

'Why did you tell us you were, then? How could you let us believe you were having a baby?'

'I didn't, Mum. You put two and two together and came up with five.'

'So why didn't you put us straight? You shouldn't have left this house without clearing it up,' Reggie said. He was clearly gutted.

'Oh, Dad, I'm so sorry.' Lexie's voice cracked and she began to cry.

Meanwhile, Sam sat observing the scene with dismay. His immediate reaction was to put his arm around her and tell her it was all going to be fine. But when he tried to lift it, it felt like lead. He didn't want to comfort her. The terrible part of him was actually pleased she was so upset.

'I don't understand,' Penelope said, choked. 'What were you trying to tell us?'

'I … We … I don't want children. I thought it would be better to tell you so you're not wondering any longer,' Lexie managed.

'But that's preposterous!' Penelope barked. 'What do you mean you don't want children? What happy couple doesn't want a baby?'

'Are you two separating?' Reggie asked. 'Is that it?'

'No. Not at all,' Lexie said, albeit slightly hesitantly.

'Then why don't you want to enrich your life by starting a family?' Reggie asked. 'I don't understand.'

'Dad, we're happy the way we are,' Lexie said. 'Other people choose to have a family but it isn't compulsory.'

'Have you tried and it didn't work? You could get help. Lots of couples have fertility treatment. Dad and I can help if it's a money issue.'

'No, Mum,' Lexie said, sighing. 'It's none of those things. We simply don't want children.'

Penelope and Reggie stared at them in astonishment.

'I feel like I don't know you recently,' Penelope said to Lexie.

'Mum! That's a terrible thing to say,' Lexie cried.

'And what you've both just said isn't?'

'This is getting us nowhere,' Sam interjected. 'I think we should go now. Lexie was adamant she wanted to tell you both about her choice. We've done that now. I need to get to work.'

'I see,' Reggie said gruffly. 'Sam, you're not saying much.'

Sam looked him directly in the eye.

'You just said *her* choice. Are we correct in presuming that this is your choice too, Sam?'

The words hung in the air and Lexie shifted in her seat. 'Sam?' she said weakly. 'Did you hear what Dad said?'

'Yes,' he said, sounding strangled. 'I did hear you, Reggie, and I'm struggling with how I should answer.' They all waited. 'I'm not actually sure how I feel at the moment so, if it's all the same with you, I'd rather not discuss it now.'

Reggie nodded. 'Sorry. I had to ask.'

Sam stood up and walked swiftly from the room.

Lexie was staring at both her parents.

'Thank you for calling in,' Reggie said, standing up.

'Dad!' Lexie pleaded. 'We don't want to fall out with you. Please ...'

'Look at how well you get on with Amélie,' Penelope said.

'Yes, but we only see her in snippets,' Lexie said. 'We get the good parts and her poor parents get the day-to-day difficult bits.'

'What about Calvin? You adore him,' Penelope said. 'You're always buying him clothes and toys and showing me pictures of him. How do you not want a child, Lexie? What's wrong with you? Was your childhood so dreadful that you don't want to replicate it?'

'What about when you're old?' Reggie added. 'Who will look after you?'

'Sam and I will look after each other or we'll go to a nice retirement home,' Lexie said. 'Besides, we wouldn't have a baby just so it could grow up to be a free geriatric nurse.' Lexie was shaking from head to toe. She couldn't believe how dreadful she felt. It seemed everyone, including the people she loved most, was starting to view her as a monster. Was she a hideous person? Did she have some sort of dreadful emotional affliction?

She was sick with guilt at upsetting her parents and making Sam so cross. But Lexie was certain of one thing. She still didn't want to have a baby.

She didn't attempt to hug either of her parents. Instead she grabbed her bag and rushed to the front door. Sam had already started the car. His face was stern as he stared directly ahead, gripping the steering wheel.

'Please!' Penelope had run after her. 'Reconsider, Lexie. Don't do this. You're missing out on so much. You don't know what it's like to hold a baby when it's just born. It's magical. At least, that's what I imagine,' Penelope said, as she began to sob.

'What are you talking about, Mum?' Lexie was astonished.

'I missed out with both you and Billy. He was a Caesarean delivery and I lost so much blood they had to operate on me and take him to the special-care unit.'

'I didn't know, Mum. That's tough,' Lexie whispered.

'You were premature. Because I'd been so sick with Billy they told me my body mightn't manage another pregnancy. But I wanted you so badly I risked everything for a second child.'

'I nearly lost Penelope. I thought I was facing the challenge of raising two babies alone,' Reggie said. 'It was a terrible time.'

'You were six weeks old by the time I got out of hospital,' Penelope said. 'Your father was wonderful. He knew how to change nappies, make bottles and co-ordinate Billy's little meals.'

'I found it seriously difficult at first,' he admitted, 'but once I got into my stride I was fine. People were so kind. Everyone, including me, was convinced Penelope would die.'

'Oh, Dad, it must've been hell for you,' Lexie said, leaning against the wall. 'And you, Mum. Stuck in a hospital away from your family.'

'By the time I was well enough to take over from your dad, I felt like an intruder in my own home.' Penelope's face crumpled and she began to cry.

'Mum!' Lexie said, crying too. 'I'm so sorry. I had no idea.'

'You cried when I tried to pick you up,' Penelope said. 'You sat in your bouncy chair and eyeballed me, terrified of your own mother. The only time you smiled for the first week was when Reggie came home from work.'

'Why didn't you tell me any of this before?' Lexie thought back to all those times when her mother had lost her reason if she sat on a wall, dirtied her clothes or messed in the garden. She had a thing about washing hands, and it wasn't unheard of for Penelope to disinfect the front doorstep.

'I only wanted the best for you,' Penelope said tearfully. 'But the more I tried to reach you, the more you pushed me away.'

'That's not fair, Mum,' Lexie said. 'You can't blame me for not wanting to sit quietly while my friends played in the park. Or for rebelling when you wanted me dressed in frills ninety per cent of my childhood and threatened to send me to my room if I got dirty.'

'Was I that bad?' Penelope asked sadly.

'Yes, Mum. You were.'

'And when Billy got Dee pregnant, her parents called here and read the Riot Act,' Reggie recalled. 'They ranted and raved and called our Billy every name under the sun. They even tried to insinuate he'd taken advantage of their daughter.'

'What?' Lexie scoffed. 'Are they crazy?'

'No, just old-fashioned and deeply religious. They were rocked to the core that their daughter was pregnant out of wedlock.'

'They were older having Dee, so they were practically a different generation from us,' Penelope said.

'They begged us not to tell a soul about the pregnancy. Billy and Dee got married and you know the rest.'

Lexie stood at the front door and tried to take it all in. She felt so sorry for her mother. It didn't excuse her cracked behaviour during Lexie's childhood but it explained it to a point.

'I know I've been pushing you to have a baby, Lexie,' Penelope said, 'but I didn't mean any harm. I only want you to be happy. I want you to have a little person who looks up to you and whom you can adore.'

'I hate to sound awful, but I need to get to work and so does Sam,' Lexie said. 'I know there's probably years of upset to be chatted about but it's good that we've made a start. Getting things out in the open has to be healthy.'

'I agree,' said Reggie, immediately. 'Once we all talk we'll be just fine. We love you so much, darling, and it was very wrong of us to try to bamboozle you into doing something so important for our gain. We're sorry, aren't we, Penelope?'

Lexie glanced at her mother. After a moment Penelope nodded. They all hugged and said they'd see each other soon.

Lexie sat into the car and Sam drove like a bat out of Hell.

'How are you feeling?' Lexie asked him.

'I needed all that drama like a hole in the head,' Sam said.

Lexie explained what her parents had just told her. 'I actually feel sorry for Mum,' she said. 'Clearly she's so uptight because of all that pent-up emotion. If it happened now, she'd be offered counselling. Back then, people were just turfed out of hospitals and left to fend for themselves.'

Sam didn't answer.

'Do you not agree?' Lexie ventured.

'I've never been a fan of all this bullshit counselling stuff. I can't help thinking that dredging over things again and again is worse than facing up to stuff and bloody well getting on with it.'

Lexie had never known Sam could be so cold. How could he not empathise with her mum and dad?

Sam turned the radio up and drove on.

Lexie got out of the car around the corner from their house and Sam sped off towards the office. For the first time she hadn't leaned across to kiss him.

Dear Diary

I'm sitting outside the exam hall and, instead of doing some last-minute cramming, I'm numb. Now that I know the truth, everything is so clear. I've been so dumb for so long. I don't know how I didn't cop on.

The situation at home is rank. Mum and Dad are being all bright and breezy when they see me, but they don't fool me any longer. I know they can't bear to be in the same room as one another.

They're doing all this tight smiling and slow blinking and forced chatting. I can't believe I never realised how little enjoyment they get out of life and each other. I'm puzzled as to why they've stayed together for so long.

Maybe it's because Mum is very into the Catholic thing. She goes to mass every Sunday without fail. She says it gives her great solace. She doesn't make me go now that I'm older. Dad stopped going a long time ago. My grandparents were staunchly religious. I do know that. The photo of them on our sideboard at home shows Holy Mary statues on the mantelpiece behind them. So I guess it's in her psyche to be like them. That could be why she's still with Dad. Perhaps she feels it's her duty to soldier on until the bitter end, as man and wife, come what may.

I nearly lost it just now. We were having breakfast and Mum was sipping a cup of tea and looking like she was swallowing poison. Dad was trying. He made her toast and she pushed it away, saying she couldn't stomach it.

I feel trapped. Like I'm in a bubble of misery with no way out. The bell has gone. I've to go and sit in the exam hall now and attempt to concentrate on some random questions in Irish. Like this is going to serve any kind of purpose. None of this stuff has any bearing on life. Why don't the schools have classes that teach teenagers how to cope when they realise they're a mistake?

Amélie

Chapter 21

KATHLEEN RUSHED TO THE WINDOW WHEN SHE heard Sam's car pull up outside. Peeping through the blinds, she saw Lexie waving and walking towards the house. Unthinkingly, she moved to her own door and opened it.

'Kathleen,' Lexie said. 'Good morning.'

'Hello, Lexie. How are you today?'

'Great,' Lexie said, and burst into heaving sobs.

'Oh dear,' Kathleen said, alarmed. 'Can I make you a cup of tea?'

Lexie nodded and made her way into the basement.

Kathleen set to work filling the kettle and finding cups. Guessing Lexie would speak when she felt able to, she gave her time to gather herself.

By the time she'd set a pot of tea and two cups on the table, Lexie had told her the bones of what had happened.

'Oh, gosh, that's a terrible mix-up for everyone concerned.'

'That's one way of putting it,' Lexie said miserably. 'I feel like everyone is upset with me. My mother glared at me as if I'd just murdered and cooked her first-born child. My father was shattered.'

Lexie went on to tell Kathleen about Penelope's difficult births, Dee's parents and all the heartache her mother had suffered. 'I feel so guilty, Kathleen. I can't believe I rejected my mother like that. She could've died and then I wouldn't even let her pick me up.'

'You were only a tot,' Kathleen admonished. 'You did nothing wrong. Who's to say you would ever have been close? You're not alike in personality, and that all happened a very long time ago. There's been ample opportunity to make amends. You and your dad are close and that's wonderful. Not something to regret. Maybe now she's got it off her chest your mum will be able to accept the relationship you guys have and build on it. Looking back is a bad plan a lot of the time. We need to learn to embrace the present.'

'You're right.' Lexie sighed. 'I can't change my actions as a baby. I didn't act out of malice. I was only six weeks old, for crying out loud.' She shook her head. 'But my mother still managed to make me feel as if it was all my fault. That's her speciality, you know.'

'As I said, maybe this is a positive turning point for you two. Now that everything is out in the open, perhaps you guys can forge a fresh new path together.'

'Yeah,' Lexie said, unconvinced and exhausted. 'Who knows?'

Kathleen sat back and clasped her hands. 'Honey, you haven't really mentioned Sam in any of this. How's he taking it?'

Lexie's shoulders shook and deep sorrowful sobs took over.

'Let it go, girl,' Kathleen said, as she stood up and went to stroke her hunched back.

'It's been awful, Kathleen,' Lexie eventually managed. 'I think he hates me now. He's changed his mind and says he wants a baby. If I don't have one I'm afraid he'll leave … But if I do have a baby, I'd only be doing it to please him.'

'You can't make a massive decision like that for somebody else, Lexie. It's all very raw right now. People are letting go of emotions that have caused untold friction for years. Don't try to fix it all in one morning.' She sat beside Lexie. 'If I know one thing about problems, dear, it's this. They'll still be there, waiting to be resolved, tomorrow. Don't feel you need to solve them all right this minute.'

'Thanks, Kathleen,' she said, as she blew her nose. 'You're right. Even if I wanted to sort this entire mess right now, it's not going to work.'

'I'd like to share something with you,' Kathleen said. She fetched the laptop, opened it and clicked on Jackson's icon.

Lexie was barely breathing as she watched. When it ended she threw her arms around Kathleen. 'I'm so sorry, Kathleen. Here am I ranting and raving about something that will be resolved in time and you've been faced with such a momentous event. Seeing Jackson like that makes me so sad for you. He was such a handsome and vibrant man.'

'And he was so ill. But he was still beautiful, wasn't he?'

'Gorgeous. Oh, Kathleen, you must miss him so much.'

'Yes, dear, I do.' She smiled calmly. 'But it's an awesome message, right?'

'Totally,' Lexie said, still sniffling. 'I hope the rainbows happen for you. I'd say you're counting the days until your birthday now.'

'I'd be lying if I said I wasn't,' Kathleen said. 'But I'm terrified too. What if he can't keep any of his promises? I'll feel like I've lost him all over again.'

'I'm sure he'll make them happen,' Lexie said firmly.

Kathleen closed the laptop. 'When you look at me, all alone with no children to keep me company in the winter of my life, does it make you question your choice *not* to have any?'

'My mother made that point too,' Lexie admitted. 'I had no idea this would open such a can of worms. Why is it such a taboo *not* to want children?'

'I guess we're all pretty conditioned into believing we should.'

'Especially since all the fertility treatments,' Lexie mused. 'So many people spend so much time, energy and money striving to conceive. I just happen to be bucking that trend.'

'As is your right, honey,' Kathleen said.

'I can't believe we've known one another such a short time,' Lexie said. 'You're so easy to talk to. I feel like I can say anything to you.'

'Thank you.' Kathleen's eyes crinkled into a smile. 'I feel the same way. I have an idea,' she said, sitting forward in her chair and patting Lexie's hand. 'Why don't we plan a day out? When's your next day off?'

'I'm going to look at a potential new artist's work in Wicklow tomorrow,' she said. 'She's in the wilds of Glendalough, the back end of nowhere. Would you like to come with me and we could have lunch?'

'Better still I'll pack a picnic. You can help me fulfil one of my promises to Jackson.'

'Oh, dear Lord, forgive me! I wasn't thinking straight. Of course! I'd be honoured to share the experience with you.'

'That's settled, then. Bring a jacket in case it's chilly and we'll find a fairy tree or magical meadow for our dining room.'

'You're on,' Lexie said. 'I'm going to head straight down to the gallery now. I asked Kate to do the morning shift, but I don't like leaving her for too long. Especially now I'll be gone all day tomorrow. I need to sort some paperwork too.'

'You run along and leave the catering to me,' Kathleen said.

'Are you sure?' Lexie asked.

'Certainly. I'll enjoy shopping and cooking. There's nothing like having a bit of purpose again. In fact, you're doing me a great favour.'

'Well, if you put it like that …' Lexie smiled. 'A bit of Wicklow air is probably just what we both need to clear our heads.'

As Lexie meandered to the gallery she felt less hopeless than before. If she could have avoided upsetting her parents, things would have been so much easier. But what was done was done and they'd all move on from it in time. As Kathleen had wisely pointed out, perhaps this misunderstanding was just the catalyst they needed to alter their relationship for the better.

The rift she'd caused between her and Sam was a different matter. Her head throbbed from crying and the thought of what lay ahead for them as a couple. Lexie had never felt more trapped by the idea of having a baby. But equally she'd never been so scared that Sam was going to walk away.

An hour later, Lexie was up to her tonsils in the gallery and feeling so grateful to have her job. The people to-ing and fro-ing meant she had to stop wallowing and put on a brave face. She was actually very good at pretending things were tickety-boo.

She was busily measuring one of the wall spaces so she could mount an abstract oil painting when her mobile phone rang. Figuring she'd call the person back, she stayed on the step-ladder and continued to make pencil marks.

'Can you pass me a hook, please, Kate?' she called. The system

Sam had designed for her walls worked brilliantly. He'd tacked up rows of brackets so she could click hooks in wherever she needed them. As Kate was walking towards her, the gallery landline rang.

'I'll grab that,' she called. 'Caracove Bay Gallery, Kate speaking … Oh, hello, Penelope … Yes, just a moment, please.'

Kate walked over with the cordless handset. 'She says it'll only take a second.'

Lexie climbed down from the ladder and gingerly took the phone. Kate had no idea what had happened. Lexie had never discussed private business with her colleague. 'Hello, Mum.'

'Lexie, I know you think you've made your mind up,' Penelope said, launching straight into a big speech, 'but can you answer me this?' She paused for dramatic effect. 'What if you were to discover you were pregnant? What would you do then? Would you have an abortion? Or would you feel too guilty to kill your baby?'

'Mum,' Lexie hissed into the phone, 'it's neither the time nor the place for what-if conundrums. Besides, there's no way I can answer such an off-the-wall hypothetical question.'

'Just think about it,' Penelope begged.

'Why?' Lexie was running out of patience.

'Because I know your mothering instinct is in there somewhere. You simply need to ignite it. Dad and I agree that you're just scared. That's all right, Lexie. Every woman worries whether or not she'll make a good mother. It's fear of the unknown.'

'Mum …'

'I know the thought of the pregnancy and birth are more than a little daunting. But it's only a few months and then a very hard day's work. But look at the prize at the end of the process! Dad has a suggestion. Hold on. I'll put him on.'

'Mum!' Lexie shouted. 'Mum? Hello?'

'Hello, darling, it's me, Dad.'

'Hello, Dad,' Lexie said, rubbing her forehead roughly. Her temples were throbbing and she wanted to scream.

'I'd like to pay for you and Sam to have a holiday. That lodger you have in your basement could feed Tiddles and keep an eye on things.

We were thinking if you went off on a lovely cruise you might relax and see things from a different perspective.'

'You mean from your perspective?' Lexie asked.

'Ah, Lexie, please,' Reggie said, sounding exasperated. 'Mum and I are simply trying to safeguard your future happiness. We cannot comprehend why you've taken this figary and decided to … rebel or behave in this … strange and quite frankly cold manner.'

'Thank you for the kind offer, Dad. Sam and I don't need to float around on a boat for a week right now. We've made a decision and, in case you haven't noticed, I'm a grown adult,' Lexie said, resisting the urge to yell at him. 'I'm in work, as you well know, so I'm putting the phone down now.' She replaced the handset on its stand in slow motion. She was terrified of snapping and firing it against the nearest wall. Kate was pretending to be busy at the other side of the gallery, but Lexie knew she'd overheard the whole conversation. 'Sorry about that,' she said, forcing a smile. 'Let's get this picture hung and you can shoot off. It's nearly lunchtime.'

'Is everything okay, Lexie?'

'Oh, yes, fine. Thank you for asking,' she said firmly. 'My mother has decided Sam and I should go on a cruise. All to do with my milestone birthday coming up.'

'Ooh, I had no idea!' Kate said, excited. 'Are you thinking of doing a party too?'

'No,' Lexie said immediately. 'Sam and I aren't into that sort of thing. We'd rather have a meal out somewhere special. Or we might even go to Venice or Barcelona. Something along those lines anyway. But definitely no cruises.'

'If they really need to buy a cruise for somebody, I'll go,' Kate quipped.

'Ha!' Lexie laughed. 'I'll mention that to them. You should split now, Kate.' She hoped Kate would take the hint and end the conversation there. Luckily she did.

Once she was alone in the gallery, Lexie sank into the chair behind the cash desk. The holiday idea mightn't be a bad one, she mused. If nothing else, she and Sam would get some quality time together. They usually travelled in September. They preferred the temperatures in Europe at that time of year and there were fewer people about as the children were back at school.

Lexie grabbed the computer mouse and clicked onto the internet. Shaking her head, she was astonished by the astronomical prices for mediocre destinations during the peak season. There was no way she would pay over the odds just to appease her parents. She phoned Sam. 'Hey. I've had a call from my parents. They want to buy us a cruise so we can have some quality time together in the hope that we'll realise we actually want children after all.' She forced a chuckle. There was silence. 'Sam?'

'Are you serious?' Sam asked.

'Yup.' She laughed drily again.

'Wow,' he said, whistling. 'I'm astonished.'

'Aren't they being totally ridiculous? I'll phone my mother back and tell her to hump off. They're poking their noses in and being out of order. Glad you agree.'

'Lexie,' Sam said. 'I'm astonished at you. Not your parents.'

'Pardon?' Her blood went cold.

'Reggie and Penelope are trying to help. They're devastated by what happened yesterday. You've shattered them. Don't you see that?'

'But, Sam ... We used to be on the same page ... I'm flailing at the moment...'

'Lexie, we're not even featuring in the same story right now. I'll call your folks and tell them I appreciate the offer but I don't want to go on a cruise with you at the moment. I couldn't stomach it.'

Sam slammed down the phone. Grabbing his keys, he strode to the car park and started his car. His brakes screeched as he swerved to miss his secretary, Rea, trundling into the underground car park. He stopped, jumped out and ran to her. 'I'm so sorry, Rea. Are you all right?'

'Ooh, yes,' she said, looking pale. 'You're in a hurry. I thought my number was up just now.'

'I'll come back up to the office with you and make you a cup of tea. That was a near one,' he said. Rea didn't argue – she seemed truly shaken.

As they travelled up in the lift, she was juggling several files.

'They're not from here, are they?' Sam observed.

'They're to do with my volunteer work,' she said, blushing. 'I'm not going to use office hours to deal with any of it,' she was quick to add.

'I wasn't suggesting you would.' Sam grinned. 'What is it, if you don't mind me asking?'

Rea had worked as his secretary for almost two years and Sam had never thought to ask her anything personal. She was incredibly efficient and almost shrew-like in appearance and manner. He knew she was unmarried, had no children and lived in an apartment not far from Caracove Bay. But that was it. She dressed conservatively in a skirt suit, was never late and was yet to call in sick. On the couple of occasions Lexie had met her, she'd said she looked like a real 'auld one'. 'That set-looking hairdo and sensible style! You'd almost mistake her for a nun.'

'I don't care what she looks like. She's the most organised assistant I've ever had. Besides, I'd like to see how you'd react if I spent my days being attended to by a sexy young thing in a mini skirt, plastered in makeup, who misses every second Monday morning because she's dying of a hangover.'

Now Sam was ashamed to admit he'd never stopped to chat to poor Rea at all.

'This is to do with the Samaritans,' she said. 'I've worked with them for twenty years. It's very rewarding.'

'Wow! I had no idea,' Sam said, impressed.

'Things are very difficult for people at the moment. Recessions always weigh heavily on relationships and family life. Our lines never stop ringing.'

'What sort of stuff do people call you about? Without being specific,' he added.

'All sorts,' she said. 'Marriage issues, money, addiction, abuse, you name it.'

Sam cocked his head to one side. He knew he would be stepping over the mark, but he suddenly wanted to ask Rea what he should do about Lexie.

'Not that you'd need any support, Sam,' Rea added. 'You and Lexie seem to be rock solid.'

'You'd think,' Sam retorted bitterly.

Rea looked at him in surprise. 'Sam?'

'Actually, we've been going through one or two things ourselves lately.' To his horror, he felt his throat constrict. He gulped.

'Sam, do you want to talk?'

And all of a sudden Sam found himself confiding in her. 'I hate counselling,' he said sheepishly, as he finished. 'I have a bit of a thing about it. I'm always telling Lexie I think it's for egomaniacs who have an insatiable desire to talk about themselves.'

Rea smiled. 'Sometimes even the most perfect people need to talk. I'm not the right person to continue with. It wouldn't be ethical as you're my boss. But I know someone who I think could help you.'

'Leave it with me,' Sam said. 'Thanks for listening just now. I hope I haven't put you in an awkward position. It's just that I thought Lexie and I could work through anything, but now it feels like we're on completely different sides – and I'm not sure how we're going to get past it.'

'Not at all, Sam. I'm glad you felt you could tell me. And, for the record, what was just said between these four walls won't be shared with anyone else. I'm good at keeping things to myself.'

Chapter 22

THIS TIME IT WOULD BE SO POIGNANT. KATHLEEN'S first without her beloved. It would fulfil one of her promises.

Still, she mused, if tomorrow proved a success maybe she and Lexie might enjoy many more over the next few months.

The following afternoon Kathleen walked to the supermarket. She was delighted to have a picnic to plan. Jackson had been like a child on Christmas Eve when she suggested one.

The familiarity of picking up the ingredients for her favourite meat loaf put a pep in her step. She'd go all out and do a chocolate biscuit cake too. Experience had taught her that loaf-shaped delicacies were the easiest to transport: they could stay in their tins and be cut into neat slices in the wilderness. Spying a stand with special-offer sparkling wine, Kathleen took a bottle, with the plastic long-stemmed glasses the shop was selling.

Salad leaves and a bottle of mustard dressing would give them one of their five a day, along with some added crunch. Luckily the supermarket had an impressive baking section so she picked up two loaf tins.

Her heart went out to Lexie. She was a lovely young woman. But she could tell from a mile away that Sam was struggling dreadfully. Kathleen sincerely hoped they would find common ground. She'd hate to see their marriage fall apart.

After Kathleen had arranged for the shopping to be delivered to number three later that afternoon, she decided to go for a walk along the beach. As soon as she hit the promenade she was pleased she'd come. The old-fashioned bandstand was filled with what looked like an old folks' choir. A gaggle of white-headed ladies and gentlemen were singing their hearts out while swaying in time to the music.

'Not bad, are they?'

Kathleen turned to see Fanta from the DART station smiling at her.

'Hello, Fanta. Fancy meeting you here.'

'So,' he grinned, 'do you come here often? This is my wife, Deirdre,' he said, introducing a small round lady holding an enormous ice-cream.

'Hello, love,' she said.

'Kathleen here is the lady I told you about,' Fanta said. 'She's the one who's back for a visit from America. I helped her use the ticket machine.'

'Fanta told me all about you,' Deirdre said. 'He loves to fill me in on the stories from his work.'

'I'd say you meet all sorts.' Kathleen smiled.

'Indeed I do.'

'Who are the choir?' Kathleen asked.

'They're a local over-sixties crowd. I wouldn't be seen dead with them,' Fanta said, shuddering.

'Why ever not?' Kathleen asked.

'And announce to the world I'm that old? You must be joking. While I still have my own hair and teeth I'm not acting as if I'm just passing time before they put me in a pine box six foot under.'

Kathleen laughed. 'I'm sure they're attempting to prove they're still very much alive and well. The ones who are filling in days before they pass on wouldn't be out here in the elements singing and smiling.'

'Whatever you say, love,' Fanta said. 'I'm still only thirty-five in here,' he said, pointing to his head.

'Men just never want to grow up, never mind grow old,' Deirdre said, tugging his arm. 'Let's leave Kathleen to her walk. Nice to meet you, Kathleen. Enjoy your holiday and be sure to let Fanta know if you need help with the ticket machine any other day.'

'I will, thank you,' Kathleen said. She stayed and listened to the choir for a little longer before continuing. Perhaps it was the sea breeze but her eyes began to water a little, blurring her vision: when she squinted at a man walking in the distance she could pretend he was Jackson. Unlike the time before when she'd felt she'd die of a broken heart, the game now comforted her.

'It's like you're still here with me,' she said quietly. 'The man right at the end of the pier is you, Jackson. You got antsy waiting by the bandstand and walked on ahead, telling me you'd see me in a few minutes.'

Passers-by must have picked up on her happy expression as they smiled back and some even saluted her.

By the time she'd done the four-mile round trip, Kathleen felt oddly euphoric. 'I enjoyed our walk, Jackson,' she muttered into her chest. 'It was wonderful to feel as if you were with me again. I'll invite you again the next time. I love you.'

She joined the queue at one of the many ice-cream vans that were dotted along the coast road and paid for a ninety-nine.

'Would you like pink and green sauce?' the man asked.

'Yes, please,' Kathleen said, with a grin. She was astonished by the lurid syrup that was promptly drizzled on top. Jackson would have had something to say about that, she mused. He'd had a thing about foods that were unnatural colours. Just the sight of a Slushie machine was enough to set him off on one of his rants.

'How can people buy a drink that's electric blue? What naturally occurring food is that shade? Am I the only one who thinks this is totally insane?'

As she licked the instantly dripping soft ice-cream and accepted her change, a little giggle escaped her. She moved away from the crowd so she could continue her chat with Jackson.

'I can't say there are many advantages to you being gone, my darling, but at least I can consume this neon green sauce in peace!'

By the time she arrived back at Cashel Square, Kathleen felt better than she had in weeks.

The prospect of the picnic with Lexie the following day sustained her happy mood as she let herself back into the basement. Opening the laptop, she listened to Jackson's message as she cooked for the picnic, then swept and mopped the kitchen floor.

From the corner of her eye, she spotted a small pile of books tucked onto the outside windowsill. Opening the window she carefully pulled them inside. There was a note from Lexie.

I thought you might enjoy these. Hope you haven't read them all! Love Lex

Kathleen was touched as she turned the Maeve Binchy books over in her hands. She'd read one, but not the other two. Delighted, she selected one, curled up on the sofa and lost herself in the story.

When she looked up, it was bedtime. Kathleen stretched and padded over to the kettle to make a cup of valerian tea. Lots of people had told her it was marvellous for helping with sleep. She pulled the little bag from its paper pouch, sniffed it and reeled. It smelt pungent, like cat pee. When she poured the water over it, the aroma filled the air. It was so awful and made her wrinkle her nose to such an extent that she felt quite giddy.

'Jackson, this stuff takes the biscuit. Even you with your healthy eating obsession would have trouble stomaching it.'

Oddly, it didn't taste quite as bad as it smelt. In fact, Kathleen was pleasantly surprised. It was mildly grassy, and if she held her nose she knew she could finish it.

Eager to get back to her book, she washed her face and brushed her teeth in record time. The bedroom smelt of the tea, which was steaming in the mug on her bedside locker. Now that she'd got into bed she felt far too lazy to get up and pour it down the sink. The only way to get rid of it was to down it in one, so she sat propped up against her pillows and knocked it back.

She managed a few more chapters before her body began to relax. As she drifted off to sleep, Kathleen wasn't sure if it was the sea air, her make-believe walk and chat with Jackson or the valerian tea, but she felt wonderfully peaceful.

Dear Diary

I've done it. I've left home. The exams were a total head-wreck so I decided to cut my losses and go.

I know he'll probably hate me for the rest of my life — well, more than he already does — but I took Dad's credit card from his wallet last night, booked my ticket on-line and here I am.

It's not a plane to somewhere exotic, but a ferry to France.

It was cheaper than flying and I figured the crossing would give me more time to figure out what I'm going to do when I get there.

I have sixty-two euro in cash (borrowed yesterday from Grandma's purse) and some food from the fridge. If I'm frugal and do my best to find a job as soon as I get there, I'll survive.

I've brought my French book from school and I'll use the journey to swot. If nothing else, this will put all those hours of verbs and vocab to good use.

I wish I could write about my exhilaration and excitement. But I'm terrified. My hands are shaking as I write this. I felt alone at home, but that was only the tip of the iceberg.

I don't regret going, though. I know it'll be bogus for the first while but I'll settle. I can do this.

It's for the best.

I considered ending it all. I even found tablets in the cabinet in Grandpa's bathroom yesterday. But I don't want to die. I just want to find a place where I feel happy. Somewhere I know I'm not a constant reminder of the life I've forced my parents to live.

Maybe my departure will afford them the freedom to finally go their separate ways.

There's a group of kids, a bit older than me, sitting across from me. They've got a guitar and look like they're going backpacking or to work for the summer. I'm going to chat to them and see if I can get some ideas of where to look for work.

Dear Diary, you are my one and only friend right now. So I'll keep you posted.

Amélie

Chapter 23

THAT EVENING WHEN SAM ARRIVED HOME HE announced that he had to go to New York for a couple of days.

'Why the sudden departure?' she asked.

'These trips come up. It's hardly unusual.' He paused. 'Sorry,' he relented. 'But I've to see a potential customer. I'm leaving here at three thirty in the morning, so I'll go into Amélie's room. I don't want to disturb you.'

'You won't disturb me,' she said. 'Stay in our bed.'

'No. It's for the best,' Sam said, as he left the room. He felt like his heart was being ripped out of his chest. If truth be told, he'd volunteered to go that afternoon when one of his colleagues had come down with a stomach bug. He could do with the space to think and decide what he wanted from the rest of his life. The veil of sorrow that had shrouded his previous happiness was stifling him.

Lexie felt like she'd been thumped in the stomach as he disappeared to pack a bag and sealed himself into Amélie's room. She barely slept and heard Sam leave at around three. Eventually she dozed for a couple of hours and woke the next morning to the drumming of rain on the paving stones and a grey woolly sky.

Hauling her weary bones into the shower, Lexie tried to convince herself that the rough patch she and Sam were experiencing wasn't a big deal.

In the past, she'd always found that yesterday's problems seemed insignificant by the following morning. Usually a fresh day brought a new, calmer outlook. Today that theory wasn't working and it wasn't ideal weather for a picnic either.

Needing comfort, Lexie pulled a container of ready-to-roll croissants out of the fridge. Once the oven was hot enough she popped the little curls of dough inside. She made coffee while the croissants puffed into delicious flaky crescents. When they were ready, she tipped them into a round basket, brought them to the table and found a jar of homemade jam. In spite of the delicious smell, she managed to eat only a single bite.

Kathleen appeared, balancing a cardboard box and dressed in an oversized full-length spinach green raincoat. 'Good morning!' she cried. 'It's a tad wet out there,' she put the box on the hall table, 'but that won't dampen our spirits, right?' She looked so excited and hopeful Lexie hadn't the heart to say she'd rather not go.

'Have you made lots of things?' Lexie asked, peering into the already soggy box.

'Just a few fail-safes that Jackson and I enjoyed over the years. I hope I'll convert you to outdoor dining today.'

'You're so good,' Lexie said, hugging her briefly. 'Give me five minutes to grab my rain gear and a couple of blankets and we'll head off. The pictures I'm collecting are small oils, so they should fit into the back seat of the car. This box will just about squeeze into the boot. Poor Bluebell will be bulging at the seams!'

'Is that your car's name?' Kathleen laughed.

'Certainly is. Baby Bluebell is her full title. Bluebell to her friends.' Lexie vowed she wouldn't spoil the day by acting as if her world was ending.

A short time later they were zooming along the N11 motorway towards Glendalough. Taking its name from the Irish for 'the valley of the two lakes', the famous tourist attraction boasted magnificent walks. It was also home to a monastic tower and a visitors' centre.

'It's still the way I remember it,' Kathleen exclaimed, as the vista came into sight.

'Luckily some things remain the same in this world,' Lexie said. 'The artist's house should be just after the main car park. She's apparently renting a painter's cottage to maximise her inspiration and utilise the solace of the area.'

'What a wonderful idea.'

'Isn't it? Fingers crossed the work is as remarkable as it appeared in the emailed photographs.'

The artist, a Scandinavian woman by the name of Agata, welcomed them in. Lexie introduced herself and Kathleen.

'I'm delighted to meet you,' said Agata. 'I have heard so much about your gallery and I think it would be the most wonderful place to showcase my work.'

She led them to an open-plan room with floor-to-ceiling windows. Lexie couldn't help admiring the young woman's lean, almost athletic figure and shock of pale straw hair. 'This is my daughter, Britta.' Agata scooped a miniature version of herself, with the same flaxen hair and pale blue eyes, out of a cute wooden playpen.

Dressed in a navy-and-white-striped jersey dress, the child's honey skin made her look like a little catalogue model.

'She's gorgeous,' Lexie said, crouching on her hunkers. 'Hey, Britta, aren't you a little dote?'

'It's just the two of you, I take it?' she said, as she straightened.

'It's better that way,' Agata stated. 'Let's get to the crux of your visit. Come and have a proper look at my work. I know you liked what you saw on the computer but a photo doesn't provide the same impact.' She stood aside and motioned for Lexie to examine the four paintings. Framed in rustic wooden boxes, the twelve-inch-square pieces were a series involving the same goblin-type creature in each scene. The detail of his surroundings was breathtaking.

'Wow! I love the way you've made the leaves and shrubs seem as if they've been photographed and your little character is nestled in each picture so clearly. He seems lifelike.'

'He's alive to me.' Agata shrugged. 'He's been in my head for many years and it's only now I am managing to share him with the rest of the world. Maybe it's since Britta's birth, but I suddenly felt compelled to unleash him.'

'Does he have a name?' Kathleen asked.

'Kara spelled with a K,' said Agata. 'It's Swedish for "dear".'

'How wonderful,' Lexie exclaimed. 'He'll fit in beautifully at the gallery. Cara spelled with a C means "friend" in Irish.'

'How wonderfully apt indeed,' Agata agreed. 'So does this mean you're interested in buying my work?'

'It certainly does,' Lexie said.

'While you ladies crunch numbers, could I possibly sneak into your garden?' Kathleen asked.

'Sure,' Agata said, sliding the large glass door open.

The views drew Kathleen to the boundary hedge. As she neared the edge of the property, she stumbled. 'Ouch,' she muttered, as her ankle turned. A crunching noise from her hip made her wince.

All of a sudden, Rodger sprang to her mind. She'd promised to text the lovely man she'd met in Howth and had totally forgotten. Fishing for her phone, she scrolled through her contacts. She'd transferred all her old numbers to the Irish cell she'd bought. Unsure about calling him directly, she opted to text him instead. That way she figured he could ignore her if he preferred.

> Hello Rodger, Kathleen the skulking American here! I'm in Glendalough and suddenly thought of you. How are you? Did you manage to speak to your doc again? You have my number now. Call or text if you'd like to chat or have a coffee some time. No strings attached. Kathleen.

She hit send and shoved her phone back into her pocket. She hoped Rodger was doing okay. He'd seemed so genuine when they'd met.

'I'm just about ready to leave,' Lexie said, poking her head outside.

'Sure. I'm coming this second,' Kathleen answered. Butterflies rose in her tummy as she thought of the picnic. 'Come too, Jackson,' she whispered. 'It's going to be great.'

They stacked the bubble-wrapped pictures carefully on the back seat of the car, then waved to Agata and baby Britta.

'These will sell like hot cakes,' Lexie said. 'They're small enough for all sorts of buyers. The bigger pictures are often more impressive but few people have the wall space to show them off. This kind of thing is accessible for everyone. The mythical stuff is brilliant too as it appeals to all ages.'

'Will Agata do more if you want them?' Kathleen asked.

'Totally. I said I'd let her know how they're selling and we can take it from there. She's very talented. Art is sort of like writing.'

'How do you mean?' Kathleen wrinkled her brow.

'Well, I've often heard authors say that easy-to-read books are the hardest to write. The same goes for pictures. If they're to appeal to many, it means they're expertly done. Otherwise people only see the flaws.'

'Ah, I get it,' Kathleen said, nodding.

Lexie pulled up at the practically deserted car park. 'Looks like we're one of the only carloads of loonies willing to go walking in the lashing rain,' she said. A large part of her wished Kathleen would pronounce the weather too inclement and suggest they eat in the car. The view would still be magnificent and they'd be dry.

'That makes it all the more magical for us,' Kathleen said, opening her door and pulling up her hood.

'Yay!' Lexie said, injecting as much gusto as she could into her voice.

Kathleen giggled. 'You're so bad at hiding how you feel, Lexie. I know you think I'm a mad old bat dragging you out in the rain, but it'll be worth it. Besides, I promised Jackson.'

Kathleen was like a sixteen-year-old as she yanked the box out of the boot and marched towards the high path. 'Come on, slowpoke,' she teased. 'Keep up!'

Lexie locked the car and trudged on. The rain was coming in driving sideways sheets, soaking them from every angle. 'If it wasn't so nippy I'd nearly opt for doing this in my swimsuit,' Lexie said. 'Where are you taking us?'

'Just on another little bit,' Kathleen said. 'Nearly there. I want to get up a tiny bit higher and we'll find a spot.'

Lexie certainly managed to forget her woes as the freezing rain continued to hammer down. 'I'm going to die of hypothermia in a minute,' she moaned. 'I'm never going on a date with Bear Grylls I can tell you.'

'Who?' Kathleen asked.

'He's a survival explorer from the television,' Lexie said.

'Ooh, I like the sound of him,' Kathleen said. 'Anyway, no need to drop dead. We're here.' She glanced back at Lexie with sheer delight on her face. 'Burrow in there and we'll find a patch of dry ground. It's so many years since I've been here, but it's astonishing how childhood haunts stay in my memory. Unlike Caracove Bay, this place has changed very little. That's the beauty of nature, isn't it?' she said, clearly thrilled. 'We have the world at our feet from up here. Just look at the lake! The raindrops make it look like it's bubbling.'

Lexie tucked her chin to her chest and headed into the undergrowth. Astonishingly it was bone dry and quite silent. 'Wow,' she said. 'It's so serene in here.'

'Isn't it? It's as if the entire world has been covered in a soft mossy carpet and a pause button has been pressed.'

'Yes!'

'Now,' Kathleen's eyes twinkled, 'here you are. This is your entrée.' She handed Lexie what looked like a roll of tea towels. It was heavier than she had anticipated.

'Unravel it carefully,' Kathleen instructed.

Lexie broke into an instant smile when she found a jam jar with still warm liquid inside. 'Tea in a jam jar!' she squeaked. She popped the lid off and drank some, closing her eyes to savour the sweetness. 'Oh, that is seriously delicious. Hand on heart, I've never tasted tea quite like it.'

'Mixed with numb fingers, a sniffly nose and a view so spectacular, it's pretty special, isn't it?'

Kathleen slid out the meat loaf, inverted the tin and placed it on top. 'This serves as a little table so I can slice it,' she said. Two small plastic tubs each filled with green salad came next. 'Can you shake up the dressing and drizzle a little on each pile of leaves?'

Lexie grinned as she watched Kathleen in action.

Moments later they were perched side by side on the rug tucking into their lunch.

'What do you think so far?' Kathleen asked. 'Is this or is this not the most scenic vista you've enjoyed for a while?'

'Mm,' Lexie said, struggling to eat slowly. 'It's a stunning view and the food is so tasty. Wow, you're a fabulous cook.'

'Thank you. But you know what they say? Hunger is the best sauce! It's the whole al-fresco experience. Clean air and lots of chlorophyll are a sure-fire reason to believe that Heaven exists. Just look at that winding path. Isn't it like a painting?'

'Certainly is,' Lexie agreed. 'I can understand why some folk choose to be hermits. I wouldn't worry about ironing or vacuuming or paying bills if I lived up here.'

'True, but it might get a little less awesome at night or in the depths of winter.' She smiled.

'It's nice to fantasise, though,' Lexie said. 'How does life get so damn serious, Kathleen? It's kind of complex, isn't it? When you stow away in the crook of Nature's arm like this, all the issues we battle with every day seem sort of futile, don't they?'

'Totally. I know the world has to evolve and we have such amazing inventions from computers to medical science. But somewhere along the way I can't help feeling we've all lost the true meaning of living,' Kathleen said. 'Now that Jackson is gone, I've had to look at *my* world with fresh eyes. I'm going to have to sift through all the debris, figure out which parts truly matter and piece together a new jigsaw to call my own.'

'Sam and I will help you in any way we can,' Lexie said.

'Thank you, sweetie. You've already helped me more than you'll ever know,' Kathleen said, as she clambered to her feet. 'Now, are you ready for my world-famous chocolate-biscuit cake? Do you think you can handle it?'

'Bring it on!'

'Ooh, I forgot the sparkling wine!' Kathleen said. 'Let's have it with dessert.'

'Gorgeous!' Lexie said. 'I'll have a tiny glass, though. Otherwise we'll end up in a very scenic ditch on the way home.'

'So you'll have a nice fat doorstep of chocolate-biscuit cake with your bubbly – added soakage – followed by a long walk in the rain.'

'Well, if I'm still alive after all that, I'll be happy to drive home.'

Lexie lay back on the picnic rug while Kathleen served the dessert. She didn't interfere: the older woman was thoroughly enjoying being back in her comfort zone as Queen Picnic Provider. Instead she stared up at the green canopy above. The gnarled trunks and splaying branches made wonderful patterns against the grey sky.

'Isn't it mesmerising to absorb nature?' Lexie mused. 'Look how all the tiny branches are twisting and weaving, creating a lattice way up high.'

'I'm so thrilled you see it too,' Kathleen observed. 'She *gets* it, Jackson,' she shouted to the sky, laughing.

They ate the wickedly dense cake and sipped the bubbly while deciding where to walk. On Kathleen's advice they left the picnic things in their den and marched off. 'If it gets stolen we'll survive, but there's no point lugging it with us.'

The rain had lifted only to be replaced by a muggy mist, which made the place even more magical. The chat stopped as their stride increased. Before long they were right at the top of the trail. Looking down on the glassy lakes, not another soul in sight, they stood, hands on hips, and smiled.

'I feel as if we're on the top of the world looking down!' Kathleen said.

'That's because we are!' Lexie said, bending over to catch her breath. 'I'm so unfit it's a joke.'

'Well, we were walking rather quickly up a very steep incline.'

'You're perfectly fine, though. I need to get myself in shape,' Lexie said.

'Well, you're getting old, I guess,' Kathleen said, laughing.

They rested for a bit. Once she could muster the energy, Lexie stood up. 'Come on, follow me quickly or I'll fall asleep there and never wake up. If you ever want to rejoin civilisation it's now or never!'

They plodded back to the picnic spot and retrieved the box before continuing to the car park. As they drove away from Glendalough the rain fell in such heavy sideways sheets it became difficult to drive.

'Poor little Bluebell is going to drown,' Lexie said, patting the dashboard protectively.

'This certainly is a good old-fashioned soaking,' Kathleen agreed. By the time they pulled up outside number three Cashel Square tiny rivers were running down the sides of the footpaths.

'So much for the summer sun!' Lexie said, bracing herself to get out of the car.

'Do you want to leave the art work here until the rain stops?' Kathleen asked.

'No, I'd be afraid something might happen,' Lexie said, twisting herself around to grab her treasures from the back seat. 'You wouldn't run on ahead and open the front door, would you?'

'Sure thing, honey,' Kathleen said. 'One, two, three— Ooh,' she screeched, as she made a dash for it.

As soon as the door was open Lexie followed her. 'That is crazy madness,' she puffed. 'Tea? It won't be quite as divine as the stuff from the jam jar, but I'll do my best.'

Moments later Kathleen held up her full mug, preparing for a toast. 'Thank you for sharing my first memory,' she said. 'I feared it would be horribly sad and leave me feeling desolate. But it's given me a new lease of life. To friendship.'

'To friendship,' Lexie repeated, clinking mugs.

Chapter 24

KATHLEEN WOKE TO THE SOUND OF A PHONE ringing. Sitting bolt upright in bed she gazed around in confusion, trying to figure out where the noise was coming from. Unaccustomed to the sound of her new cell, it took her a few moments to establish what she was hearing.

'Hello?' she said, diving at it just in time. She didn't see who was calling.

'Ah, hello,' said a man's voice.

Kathleen inhaled sharply. She didn't recognise the tone and was about to hang up when he continued: 'It's me, Rodger.'

'Hello there!' Kathleen said, relieved. 'How are you?'

'Ah, not too bad. You'll be delighted to know I'm in St Mark's hospital,' he said, laughing.

'Oh, no, poor you. Of course I'm not delighted,' Kathleen said. 'Would I be right in assuming you … Did you have your surgery?'

'Yesterday,' he confirmed. 'That's why I didn't answer your kind text then.'

'Well done, sir,' Kathleen said. 'How's the pain today?'

'Not as bad as I'd anticipated,' he said. 'I'm taking a whole host of tablets, though.'

'Good. That's what they're for.'

'I feel it's a bit of a cop-out all the same. I'll try to cut down on the painkillers tomorrow.'

'Your body won't heal if you're in pain. Besides, there are no medals for being a martyr.'

'That's true.' He chuckled. 'You're a breath of fresh air, Kathleen. I'm glad I called.'

'Would you like a visitor?' she asked spontaneously.

'Uh …'

'Oh, shoot. You don't have to say yes. I'm doing it again, being too pushy. Forget I said anything.'

'I'd love you to visit if you have the time,' Rodger said. 'To be honest, it would be great to see someone who doesn't look at me as if I'm a nuisance. My children say they're glad I finally had the surgery but I feel as if I should be bounding around playing soccer in the corridor to show I'm totally fixed.'

'I'm sure they don't expect that.'

'You're probably right,' Rodger agreed. 'I can't help feeling I'm a burden on them all the same.'

'I've no plans today,' Kathleen ventured. 'Shall I pop in?'

'That'd be great. They aren't strict with visiting hours in this section of the hospital, so any time would suit me. I'm not going anywhere.'

'I'll be there in about two hours. How's that?'

'I look forward to it.'

Kathleen hung up, invigorated. She was thrilled to have a purpose. She'd walk to the village and buy some fruit before getting the DART to the hospital.

The ritual was oddly comforting. She'd grown so accustomed to visiting Jackson in hospital over the years that she was enjoying the chance to make herself useful again.

By the time she arrived at the stop near the hospital, the rain was coming down in spits. Beneath her small umbrella, she made quick progress. Rodger had texted his exact location, so she followed the signs and found his room easily. She'd already knocked on the door before she had time to think.

'Come in!' Rodger called.

Feeling suddenly shy, Kathleen's heart thumped as she strode in. All too late, she realised she was in a private room with a near-stranger, who happened to be a man in bed.

Rooted to the spot, she loitered in the doorway. 'Oh, I didn't think …' She wanted to back away and run.

'Excuse the state of me,' he said easily. 'They don't go in for black tie around here.' His warm smile urged her into the room. 'Take a pew,' he instructed, pointing to an armchair upholstered in a sea-green shade similar to the floor.

'I could lie and tell you how wonderful you look,' she ventured, 'but that used to annoy my Jackson more than anything. He'd almost blend in with the sheets, looking like Casper the ghost, and folk would tell him how great he looked.'

'Why was he in hospital?' Rodger asked.

'He had a brain tumour,' Kathleen said, and proceeded to tell him everything.

'Oh, Kathleen, I'm ever so sorry,' he said. 'I wittered on about how much I miss Claudia and didn't give you the opportunity to tell me about Jackson.'

'That's not your fault. When we met I was feeling so raw that I was pretending he was still alive. It's me who should apologise to you.'

'I understand,' Rodger said. 'I almost wish I'd thought of doing the same thing after Claudia went. It might have eased the pain somewhat.'

Kathleen shook her head. 'It didn't work. The pain is there, no matter what.'

'Death does that to a person,' Rodger agreed. 'It's so final. So harsh and so difficult to comprehend.'

Kathleen smiled and nodded. Rodger's face was coated with a dusting of ashen stubble. His hair was matted on one side and he was dishevelled, no longer the dapper gentleman she'd first encountered. She didn't know him well enough to touch him, but a part of her itched to shave him and brush his hair. She was a dab hand at both. It used to cheer up Jackson no end.

'So what has the surgical team said to you? Are they pleased with how the operation went?'

'By all accounts it was fairly straightforward. As they'd suspected, I needed a full replacement rather than that coating-the-joint business some people get away with.'

'Better to go the whole hog, I say.' Kathleen grinned. 'You'll have a busy time getting your strength back. But if you do what the physiotherapist tells you, it'll be just dandy. Look at me! I'm what you might call "Here's one we made earlier." I'm the hip-replacement poster girl!'

Rodger laughed. A brief knock at the door was followed by a whoosh of air.

'Daddy!' An attractive woman in her thirties burst in. 'Oh … I … Sorry, I didn't realise you had company. Hello. I'm Bee. And you are?' She raised an eyebrow and stood with her hands on her hips.

'Hello,' Kathleen said, standing up to offer her hand. 'I'm Kathleen. Pleased to meet you, Bee.'

'You're American,' Bee said, with mild distaste.

'Not entirely,' Kathleen said. 'I was born here and raised in Orlando.'

'She didn't leave Ireland until she was eight,' Rodger added.

'Well remembered! I'm impressed,' Kathleen said.

'I came because I thought you might appreciate a visitor. I had no idea you'd be entertaining. I've a hundred and one things to do,' Bee said, sighing dramatically, 'so I'll push off.'

'Please don't go on my account,' Kathleen said. 'I'll go find a coffee shop. You sit with your father for a spell.'

'Thank you for trying to organise my time, Kathleen, but, as I said, I'm busy. 'Bye, Daddy.'

''Bye, love. Thanks for coming,' Rodger said hurriedly, as the door banged shut.

There was an awkward silence. Kathleen looked at the floor. 'I'm sorry if I've upset your daughter. I hope she didn't think there was anything untoward going on.'

'Bee was well named,' Rodger said. 'She's constantly buzzing around in a frenzy, acting as if she wants to sting the world.'

Kathleen smiled, but she was sad for Rodger. His daughter was a rude little madam. She should realise her father was feeling sore and vulnerable and act accordingly.

'She's been very distant since Claudia died. The girls were like a little threesome. They loved their shopping trips and doing all the usual girly stuff. Aisling, our eldest, has coped with her mother's death better. But I guess Bee has found it difficult. She's the baby of the family so it's very tough for her.'

Kathleen decided to keep her thoughts to herself. She didn't know anything about Bee or her life. It wasn't fair to judge her from one brief encounter. She changed the subject. 'Did you and Claudia talk much about the future? You know – the time after she was gone?'

'No,' Rodger said sadly. 'We didn't know she was going to die. It was a heart attack and she'd had no previous sickness to speak of. Why?'

'Jackson and I knew he didn't have long – he'd been ill for years – so we had plenty of those talks. They were terribly sad in the beginning, but over time we got better at expressing our wishes to one another.'

'That's pretty heavy,' Rodger said.

'I guess,' Kathleen said, holding her head to the side and pondering. 'He gave me three tasks to do while I'm here.' She explained about the picnic and how she had the other two still to finish.

'I'd happily accompany you to Dublin Zoo. Claudia and I used to go often with the children – we had a yearly membership once upon a time.'

'Well, I'd be honoured to do that with you. As soon as you're well enough,' Kathleen said.

'Now there's a challenge,' he said. 'Tell me about Jackson's video.'

'He had the last word.' She smiled. 'He promised me three rainbows.'

Rodger listened intently. 'How wonderful. That's commonly known as ADC,' he said matter-of-factly.

'It is? So you don't think I'm crazy to hope that he may be able to send me these rainbows?'

'Oh, no. After-death communication is a phenomenon that's been around for centuries. Some believe it's God's way of reassuring us that our loved ones are back with Him. Others believe it's their loved one sending them a direct message.'

'I've never heard of it,' Kathleen said. 'I was almost afraid to tell anyone in case it's all a load of baloney.'

'The most common forms of communication from beyond are via butterflies and rainbows.'

'Really?'

'Oh, yes,' Rodger said. 'I read plenty about it just after Claudia passed away. So many people have reported seeing butterflies in the most unusual places. They say they get a strong feeling that it's a message, rather than a regular butterfly flitting about.'

'So you reckon Jackson may be able to deliver on his promises?'

'I firmly believe he will.' Rodger hesitated. 'Seeing as you've shared your message with me, can I tell you something?'

'Sure you can.'

'I talk to Claudia most days. In fact most hours of most days.' He chuckled shyly. 'But I've asked her over and over to send me a butterfly.'

'I'm sure one will come,' Kathleen said.

'I hope so. It's been nine months, though. Still, I must be patient, eh?'

They chatted a while longer, and although Kathleen felt she could talk about Jackson, and how it felt to be a widow for another five hours, she could see that Rodger was tired. 'I'll leave you now. You've been through a lot. You need to rest.'

'I'm sorry. I wish we could talk for longer, but my body is telling me I need a nap.'

'I understand. I could come visit again, if you like,' she offered.

'I'm only here for another two days, all going well,' he said. 'After that I'll be back in Howth. I reckon it's way too far for you to travel. A day trip every once in a while is one thing, but I couldn't ask you to come just to see me.'

'Why not? Because I'm so busy?' She grinned. 'I'll happily come on the DART. But let's not pre-empt things. You mightn't want some mad old Yank barging in on you at home.'

'You've been a bit of a trial if the truth be known,' Rodger deadpanned. Kathleen burst out laughing and leaned forward to clasp his hand.

'I've enjoyed our chat. It's good to be able to talk to someone who understands how I feel.'

'Ditto,' he said. 'Thanks for the visit. I'll be in touch. We need to arrange our visit to the zoo.'

'Absolutely – and we need to talk rainbows and butterflies again.'

'Sounds good.'

Kathleen left the hospital and gazed upwards. The rain was falling so lightly that the drops were being blown about in little wisps. As she caught the train back to Caracove Bay, she could barely contain her excitement. The second she got home she wanted to watch Jackson's message again. Rodger's knowledge of ADC had renewed her faith in her husband's promise.

Chapter 25

LEXIE WAS ABOUT TO FINISH HANGING AGATA'S pictures at the gallery when Dee burst through the door. 'Is Amélie with you?' she asked, clearly frantic.

'No,' Lexie said. 'What's happened?'

'She wasn't in her bed this morning. Billy's at work and I was so cross I drove to your house to have a showdown with her. She's been ducking out and suiting herself all the time lately.'

'I know she's been very down,' Lexie said carefully.

'Lexie,' Dee said. 'I've had it with her. Don't try to stick up for her either. I know the two of you have this bond, but it's about time she learned some respect.' She rushed to the door.

'Where are you going?' Lexie asked, following her.

'To the school to make sure she's sitting her exams.'

As the door banged shut after Dee, Lexie grabbed her mobile and dialled her niece's number. It went directly to voicemail. 'Hey, Amélie, only me. Just want to see how you are. Your mum was here looking for you. I presume you're in your exam. Call me when you get a chance, yeah? Love you.'

The gallery was busy for the rest of the morning. Agata's stuff was causing even more of a stir than Lexie had predicted. She decided to call Agata and commission more. 'I reckon the ones you gave me will be gone by week's end.'

'I'm thrilled,' Agata said. 'I have many more completed works.'

'Why on earth didn't you show me?' Lexie was amazed.

'I didn't want to cheapen the ones you were getting. I've been squirrelling pictures into bubble-wrapped resting beds for months. I have quite a collection.'

'I'm delighted to hear that,' Lexie said. 'Why don't we do an exhibition of your work? Would you be interested in coming to host an evening at the gallery? I've done it many times before. Some artists love the idea and look forward to the excitement while others shy away from the limelight. Please do whatever you're comfortable with.'

'You are sweet,' Agata said. 'I'd love it. There's only one slight hitch. I'd have to bring Britta too. Would that be a problem?'

'Not at all,' Lexie assured her. 'We could make it an afternoon event – say, four o'clock, so it's not too late for her.'

'That sounds brilliant. I'd feel odd doing it without her. She inspired the creation of Kara. I began painting him soon after discovering I was pregnant. I wanted to make some pictures to decorate the nursery. I suffered insomnia during the pregnancy so I had plenty of time to spill my creative juices.'

'Well, that's to all our advantage. Kara is wonderful. I'm flicking through my diary here,' Lexie said. 'How would Thursday week suit you? We tend to do late-night opening in conjunction with the other shops in Caracove. If we start the exhibition at four it would probably wind up around seven.'

'That would be fine. Britta could sleep on the way home.'

Within the hour Lexie had phoned her contacts at the local newspaper and one national publication. Both agreed to send a reporter and photographer.

The phone rang.

'Caracove Bay Gallery, Lexie speaking.'

'Hello.' Penelope sounded strained. 'I don't suppose you had young Amélie in your house last night, did you?'

'No,' Lexie said. 'Dee was here earlier but we all assumed she was in school.' Panic crept over her.

'The school called Dee a while ago to ask about Amélie,' Penelope said.

'Oh, Jesus,' Lexie said. 'Where's Dee now?'

'She and Billy are going home to look for clues in her room. Did she tell you anything over the last few days that may be important now?' Penelope asked.

'Like what?' Lexie said.

'I don't know. That she was thinking of going anywhere. With a boy or anything?'

'No, in fact she's just split with a guy. Dee knows about him … What's his name again? Uh – Elton. I'll go over to their house now and help them look.'

'No. Dee asked if you'd check your house and also with your lodger to see if she knows anything. Odds are Amélie's just taken off to skip an exam. It's maths today, which Billy says she hates.'

Lexie hung up, tears burning, and quickly explained the situation to Kate. 'If she comes in, please call me and don't let her leave,' Lexie begged.

She dialled Sam's number and left a message – he was in a different time zone.

Lexie was sweating by the time she reached Cashel Square. There was no sign of Kathleen in the basement, so she ran into the main house and up the stairs to Amélie's room. Dashing from one side to the other, she looked for something suspicious. Nothing seemed out of place. The bathroom threw up no clues either, so she dialled Dee's number.

'Lexie?' Dee answered. 'Any news?'

'No. I was hoping you'd have found her by now. There's no sign of anything unusual here, I'm afraid.'

'Well, your father just called and he says there's money missing from Penelope's purse.'

'How much?'

'Sixty euro.'

'Well, she can't have gone far on that,' Lexie said. 'Can I call over?'

'Sure. See you shortly.'

Lexie knew she shouldn't jump to conclusions, but she had a really bad feeling about this. Amélie hadn't been herself for a while. She'd noticed and made a mental note to talk to her, but she'd put it all down to boy trouble. As she drove to her brother's house, she prayed that Amélie was safe. Her heart dropped when she spotted a police car parked outside.

She found Dee, looking very pale, at the kitchen table, giving a description of her daughter.

'Any word?' Lexie asked.

'No,' Dee said. 'But we found her mobile phone in her room switched off. She never goes anywhere without it.'

'Oh, God, do you think she's been taken?'

'No, nothing like that,' Billy said, walking in behind her. 'She used my credit card to book a ferry ticket to France. I've just found the transaction on-line.'

'France?' Lexie was pale now too. 'Why would she want to go there?'

'We've no clue,' Dee said. 'But the officers here have been very helpful. A girl matching Amélie's description was sighted on last night's sailing.'

'What are we waiting for?' Lexie asked. 'Let's book flights and follow her.'

'It's not that simple,' Dee said, wringing her hands.

'Why not?' Lexie asked. 'We know she's in France, so let's go!'

It was decided that Dee should stay behind. 'In case she sees sense and comes home of her own accord. This often happens with kids her age.'

'She's seventeen,' Lexie pointed out, 'not twelve. I'd say she's planned this for the long haul. She's not the type of girl to bugger off on a whim, change her mind and dawdle home with a stick of rock for everyone in the audience.'

That made Dee cry and bury her face in her hands. Lexie knew the poor woman needed some support, so she rang her parents, filled them in and asked them to come and keep Dee sane.

'We're on our way. Leave Dee to me,' Penelope said. In spite of the dreadful situation, Lexie couldn't help smiling inside. Her mother was over the moon with the drama. She'd be in that kitchen making tea, sandwiches and apple tarts to beat the band. Lexie had once thought her favourite drama was funerals, but now she knew Penelope came alive with missing teenagers too.

Sam phoned from America and was stunned to hear that his wife and brother-in-law were on their way to France.

'Where are you going?'

'To Brest Bretagne airport. It's just over fifty kilometres from there to Roscoff where she landed.'

'And what are you going to do? Trawl the streets in the hope that she's sitting at a café sipping a beer in the sun?'

'Sam, this isn't a time for jokes. If anything happens to Amélie, I'll die.' She hung up.

By the time they touched down in Brittany, Billy and Lexie were frantic. They called Dee and were beyond relieved to discover the local police had found Amélie.

'She's at a hostel and knows you're on the way to find her,' Dee said.

'She won't run away again, will she?' Lexie asked.

'No,' Dee said. 'She's terrified and was relieved we'd all missed her.'

'How could she think we wouldn't?' Lexie asked.

'I don't know,' Dee said. 'But something has put the idea into her head that we'd all be better off without her.'

Lexie texted Sam with an update. Remembering Kathleen, she sent her a quick text too so that she knew what was happening.

Amélie knew she was headed for the lecture of a lifetime. She couldn't begin to imagine how angry her father was going to be. She had a whole list of misdemeanours to her name now. Stealing, skipping exams, running away and causing a fuss. No doubt her mother was applying to boarding schools right this second. She was relieved Auntie Lexie was with her dad. She'd stick up for her. She was sorry she hadn't told her she was going. She'd considered it, but knew she'd only try to change her mind.

France wasn't what she'd imagined. She'd been there when she was little, but to Paris, a far cry from this back-end-of-nowhere place she'd ended up in. The group on the boat had been total dicks. They were college students with a bag of weed, barely any money and no prospects. They would've let her tag along if she could have got an InterRail ticket. They were friendly but two of them had tried to hit on her and were insistent she go out on deck with them to smoke joints.

'I'm not into it,' she'd said.

'But this is deadly stuff, home-grown.'

'Nah, you're all right, thanks.' As soon as they docked, she'd made excuses and split. Her vision of pretty little roadside cafés with chic waitresses and gorgeous men was nowhere to be seen. The bereft fishing village offered nothing but a stopgap for weary travellers. She hadn't the funds to go anywhere, so she'd found a room at a dingy hostel and hoped for a miracle.

After a couple of hours, she knew the situation was futile, so she made her way to the tiny police station, racked her brains and surprised herself with how much French she actually knew.

The officer she spoke to wasn't overly friendly, but he agreed to allow her to call her parents. She'd felt like a heel when her mum sobbed down the phone. Amélie was genuinely surprised by how upset she sounded. She was astonished to learn that Lexie and her father were already on the way to find her. 'What? All the way to France?'

'Of course,' Dee said, sniffling. 'We'd go to the end of the world to find you, darling.'

'Oh,' was all Amélie could manage.

It was really late by the time Lexie and Billy pulled up in a taxi. Amélie spotted them and ran outside.

'Amélie!' Billy pulled her into his arms. 'Thank God you're safe.'

'I'm so sorry, Daddy,' she said, bursting into tears.

'It's okay. It'll all be okay now that you're safe,' he said.

'Auntie Lexie,' she said.

'Sweetheart.' Her aunt hugged her tightly. 'God, you frightened the living daylights out of us all.'

'I can't believe you're both here,' she said.

'I can't believe we are either,' Lexie said, glancing around the dank police station. In flawless French she thanked the cop for keeping Amélie there.

'Wowzers, sis,' Billy said. 'Impressive. I totally forgot you spent some time here way back when.'

'I don't get to use my French that often, so thanks for providing me with the opportunity,' she said to Amélie, drily.

The taxi was waiting outside, so they all got in and Lexie instructed the driver to take them to the airport. 'There's a bog-standard hotel nearby. We'll spend the night there and get the first flight possible tomorrow,' she added, in English.

Once the flurry of phone calls was over, there was veritable silence in the cab. Billy held Amélie's hand as if he meant never to let her out of his sight again.

Once they'd checked into the hotel and Amélie had showered, they ordered food from room service. Billy was in the room next door, so Lexie knocked on the wall and he came in. 'Feeling a little better?' he asked Amélie.

She nodded, looking far younger than her seventeen years.

'Why did you do it, love?' he asked.

Amélie looked from one face to the other and hesitated.

'You need to try to talk,' Lexie coaxed. 'This must be really serious if you felt you couldn't stay. But I promise, whatever it is, I'll help you if I can.'

Once she began to talk, Amélie couldn't stop. Billy was stunned to learn Amélie had overheard him and Dee arguing. 'But you got the wrong end of the stick,' he assured her.

'So you and Mum didn't get married because of me?'

'Well, technically we did,' he said. 'But we've stayed together because we love each other.'

'It doesn't appear that way,' she said. 'You seem to hate each other most of the time. You never show affection, you argue, you snap at one another. I never hear you laughing. I'm not stupid, Dad.'

'I know you're not,' he said. 'And I can see why you think Mum and I aren't happy. Things aren't easy right now. That's for sure. But it's nothing to do with how we feel about each other.'

'What is it, then?'

'We're struggling financially. Mum was told she has another five weeks at her job and then she's being made redundant. I've had to accept a wage cut and it's hard to make ends meet right now.'

'Oh,' Amélie said. 'I see.'

'There's another matter that we need to discuss,' Billy said, as there was a knock at the door and a man called out in French that he had their food.

'Let's sit down together and have a proper chat with Mum when we get back,' he said.

'Okay,' Amélie agreed.

They wolfed the steak sandwiches and fries.

'Well, I don't know about you two,' Lexie said. 'But it's four in the morning and I'm bushed. Let's get some sleep. Once we're home, there'll be plenty of time to work things through.'

Billy hugged his daughter and went next door.

It was eleven o'clock the following night before they finally touched down in Dublin. Amélie looked pale and thin, and most certainly not the better for her trip. They found Lexie's car and she drove them home.

'Call me tomorrow,' she said, waving to them.

Alone at last, Lexie allowed the tears to fall. It was so long since she'd heard French accents and even dipped her toe into French life. All the smells, sounds and tastes she had encountered made her long-ago stay there seem like yesterday. As she pulled up outside her home, she wondered how she'd managed to crawl back from the depths of despair she'd experienced in France and end up here.

As she walked into the empty house, she took a deep breath. The time had come to tell Sam what had gone on so many years before.

Chapter 26

WHEN LEXIE WOKE THE NEXT MORNING RAIN WAS pelting the windows. She'd call Amélie a little later and check in on her. Meanwhile, she knew she needed to speak to Sam. Dialling his mobile number, she prayed he'd have the phone switched on.

'Hello?' he answered groggily.

'Hey, it's me,' she said.

'Lexie, it's two o'clock in the morning,' he said. 'I'm only in bed an hour. The dinner presentation went on and on.'

'Sam, I need to tell you something.'

There was a silence.

'Why do I feel nervous all of a sudden?' he asked.

'I need to tell you something I've kept from you. This thing with Amélie and the baby business—' Lexie broke off, a sob catching in her throat. 'Nobody knows,' she continued. 'Not even Maia.'

'Right,' he said. 'Go on.'

'When I went to France years ago, I was in the university.'

'I know. You told me.'

'I worked in a café to make extra money. It was meant to be a few hours a week but Christophe, the boss, took a shine to me.' She hesitated. 'My hours were gradually increased until I was at the café more than college.'

'Right.'

'I didn't know he was married when we started going out. His wife never came near the café and he didn't speak about her.'

'Obviously,' Sam said.

'Yeah.' She smiled momentarily. 'I thought I was living the dream. He was quite a bit older than me.'

'How much older?'

195

'He was forty-five.'

'Okay,' Sam said. 'I hate to sound narrow-minded, but weren't there any young studs around campus?'

'There were,' Lexie said. 'But I only had eyes for Christophe. He was typically French. You know, sallow skin, dark hair and eyes ... Full of "bof" and "*Je t'aime*" ... I was flattered he liked me.'

'Go on.'

'We'd been together a few months when he told me he was married. I thought I'd die of shame and a broken heart. I'd honestly thought we'd be together for ever. To discover he wasn't mine to have was a slap in the face. I couldn't believe he'd lied to me.'

'What prompted him to tell you then? Was he planning on leaving his wife for you?'

'No,' she said. 'He simply thought it was time to let me know. He was astonished when I cried and ranted and raved. He actually laughed at me.'

'Why?' Sam asked.

'He said it was the French way, the done thing, and that all French women accepted it.'

'So what did you do?'

'I broke up with him immediately and said I never wanted to see him again, naturally.' She hugged herself and sighed at the painful memory. 'He mocked me and said I'd be back, and when I came, he'd be waiting. He blew me a kiss and carried on with his work, as if nothing had happened.'

'Nice,' Sam said sarcastically.

Lexie closed her eyes and took a deep breath. 'Two weeks later I discovered I was pregnant. I was shattered. I knew I couldn't talk to my parents. Mum ... Well, we both know what Mum would've done. And Dad, darling Dad, would've been shattered.'

'Why didn't you tell Maia?'

'I didn't want to burden her and, besides, I needed to deal with the situation there and then. So I had an abortion,' she stated. 'I went to Paris alone, found a clinic and had the job done. Afterwards I stayed in a hostel for two nights until I felt well enough to return to college.'

'You stayed after that?' Sam said incredulously.

'What else could I have done? Arrive home early and say I was homesick?'

'Well, yeah!'

'It was better to stay,' Lexie said. 'I didn't know that many people my own age because I'd been hanging out with Christophe so much.'

'So what did you do?'

'I decided to wipe the slate clean and start again. I vowed that I would bury the whole affair and the pregnancy, never to be revisited. Nobody knew and I honestly thought I could hide it for ever.'

'But didn't your college friends notice you were acting strangely? Surely there was one person who copped on.'

'Sam, I was a different person back then. I've never been a gang-of-friends type, you know that. To this day I have Maia and my family. My other friends flit in and out of my life, but I don't do big girls' nights out. Never did. So, when I surfaced again at the university, a lot of my peers thought I was new. I made a few friends and got through the course.'

'That must've been so lonely for you,' Sam said. His voice had softened for the first time in days.

'I mulled it over in my head for a long time, Sam. I went through all the possibilities in my mind from adoption to my eventual choice. I knew I didn't want a child. It wasn't the right time and it would've altered the path of my life entirely.'

'Do you have any regrets?' Sam asked.

She sighed heavily. 'Honestly? No. I felt dreadful guilt for the longest time. Guilt on every level … For the affair with a married man. For lying to my parents and family and for having the abortion. I'm so sad in my heart when I think of that time. My life would've been far simpler if I'd never been in that situation. I wouldn't wish it on any girl. I was terrified but I made the right choice for me.'

'Why have you never spoken about it?' he asked.

'I couldn't bear to be judged by people. It was my mess, my mistake and my decision. At the end of the day, it's not something I'm proud of.' Squeezing her eyes shut, she asked Sam, 'Do you hate me for what I did?'

'No,' he answered. 'Of course not. I just wish you'd told me sooner. I wish you'd felt you could trust me, Lex. I thought we shared everything.'

'But it's in the past, Sam. It's done. Gone. What was the point in highlighting it?'

'Why did you tell me now, then?' he asked.

'Because I've just been to France … Because the baby question mark has been hanging over our heads recently … Because I somehow felt it was the right time.'

'Is that why you don't want a child?' he asked. 'Would it take you back to that awful time and make you feel trapped again?'

'Maybe there's an element of truth in that,' she said. 'But mostly I'm happy the way I am. Sam, I don't regret having that abortion. I don't look at kids who would be that age now and wish I had one. I just don't.'

There was a long pause.

'Thanks for telling me, Lex.' There was another silence. 'I'd better get some rest. But I'll talk to you soon.'

They hung up and Sam lay alone in his hotel bed. He wasn't angry with Lexie for having the abortion. But he was deeply bothered that she'd never told him. He knew it was probably the wrong way to think, but he couldn't help asking himself what else she might be concealing. Over the past few weeks she'd never once considered telling him. He'd known she was acting oddly but he hadn't been able to put his finger on why.

At least now he knew. Or did he?

For the first time since they'd met, seventeen years before, Sam wondered how well he actually knew his wife.

Dear Diary

I know I should be feeling like the luckiest girl in the world right now. I'm so grateful that Dad and Auntie Lex came to find me. I was totally delighted to see them. But I can't help feeling the reason I left hasn't changed.

Mum looked like she'd been beaten up when I got home. Her eyes are dull and she seems to have lost whatever zest for life used to be there. The guilt is humungous. How am I meant to shoulder it? What do I say or do to make my existence better? Dad says all the hassle is nothing to do with me and that it's purely down to finances ... But I don't believe him. I know deep down that I am the reason they're so unhappily bound together, it's a massive pressure. I honestly thought that if I wasn't there, they'd be free. But clearly that's not the answer.

I wish I knew what they're hiding from me. Because there is something bogus going on.

Amélie

Chapter 27

LEXIE FELT UNSETTLED AFTER HER VISIT TO FRANCE and telling Sam what had happened to her there. As she climbed out of bed, found fresh clothes and showered, she felt almost as awful as she had all those years ago. Instead of being cathartic, talking about it was like picking a scab.

She phoned Maia. 'Can I call over?' she asked.

'I'm on the way to work, so by all means come to my office,' Maia said. 'I've a meeting at nine, though, so hurry. Is everything okay, doll?'

'I'll explain when I get there.'

Lexie zoomed over, shot into a parking space right outside the door and took the stairs two at a time.

'That was quick. Did you jump every light between here and your place?'

'Probably,' she said, throwing herself onto one of Maia's leather chairs.

'What's the biggie?' Maia asked.

Lexie told Maia everything. 'Sam and I are seriously walking the plank right now too,' she finished.

'I can't believe you had to go through all of that on your own, hon.' Maia paused. 'But would having a baby be so awful?'

'Jeez, not you too. Maia, I thought you of all people would understand that I have a right to make a choice. You agreed with me at Calvin's party. You understood that women should be allowed to say no.'

Maia looked at the floor.

'What?' Lexie said.

'I'm pregnant again,' Maia whispered. 'I don't want anyone to know yet. I only found out last night. I decided to throw caution to the wind and hope for the best,' she added sheepishly. 'I never thought it'd happen so quickly. But here I am, up the duff.'

'Wow,' Lexie said.

'I'm sorry to tell you, with everything you're going through, but we're really happy.'

'Oh, Maia,' she said, jumping to her feet. 'I'm thrilled for you and Josh. I hope everything works out.'

'Well, I'm doing just fine. So sod it!' She grinned. 'I may as well enjoy it. I plan on eating all the wrong foods, doing as little as possible and milking this pregnancy to the hilt. I got Josh to go to the Spar at midnight last night just to buy me some Chocolate Fingers.'

'You didn't.'

Maia burst out laughing. 'I know I'm a right bitch, and he's too good for me. But I can't help it. I love pushing people to the limit!'

'And I love you for it,' Lexie said, hugging her. 'Right, that's enough dirty linen aired for one day. I've got a gallery to open.'

'You and Sam will be fine, Lex,' Maia said, suddenly serious. 'He idolises you. It'll be cool.'

'Thanks,' she said. She had to rush away so that Maia wouldn't see her tears. In spite of her friend's kind words Lexie still felt incredibly lonely. She drove to the seafront and got out. The rain was still falling and the onshore winds were howling. It suited Lexie perfectly.

She decided to walk to the pier, hoping the salty sea-laden gusts might lift her mood.

She was so caught up in her own thoughts that she marched straight past Kathleen. 'Have we fallen out?' Kathleen called, through the wild winds.

'Kathleen! I'm sorry. I was miles away.'

'So it seems. Is everything all right, honey?' Kathleen was struggling to hold the hood of her coat.

'I don't want to be negative every time we meet,' Lexie said. 'I'm afraid you got me at a stage when my life appears to be crashing down around my ears.'

'I can handle that. Want to share your thoughts?' Kathleen asked.

As usual she was stoic as Lexie told her everything. She made all the right noises at all the right times. As the story unfolded Kathleen tucked her arm into Lexie's. 'I thought I'd feel somehow ... I dunno ... free! I always figured hiding stuff was meant to be heavy on the soul,' Lexie said, 'but now I feel so much worse.'

'It's hardly surprising,' Kathleen said. 'Sometimes buried emotion becomes like a possession. It's almost like there's a bit of control there because you're guarding it and not letting anyone else in. When I arrived in Caracove Bay I made up my mind that I wasn't going to tell anyone Jackson was gone. That way I could fool myself into thinking he was waiting at home. I could pretend I was still the same person I'd always been.'

'Weren't you going to tell me?' Lexie asked.

'Nope,' Kathleen said, smiling. 'But you came upon me while I was having a moment of sadness and I knew it was right to tell you.'

'Did you feel better that I knew? I hope you did,' Lexie said. 'I was so glad you'd shared it with me. Don't get me wrong, I was and still am shocked and saddened that Jackson is gone, but I would hate to think of you shouldering that load alone.'

'Thank you, dear. Can you now take the words you just said and apply them to your own confession?'

Lexie nodded. 'Am I a bad person, Kathleen?'

'No, dear. You're a wonderful, kind and caring person. You did what you felt was right for you and your life. We all make choices – that's what life is about.'

'I didn't want a child. I was young, naïve, and I knew it was wrong for me.'

'Then you absolutely made the correct choice. May I ask you something?'

'Sure.'

'Your decision to not have children now, with Sam ...' Kathleen closed her eyes for a moment. 'Are you not having children to punish yourself for the past, or do you know for sure that you don't want to be a mother?'

Lexie thought about it for a moment before she answered. 'I don't want to be a mother,' she said. 'I know that goes against the grain for many women, but I can't help the way I feel.'

'No, you can't,' Kathleen agreed. 'And I think you know your own mind, dear. My goodness, you are a strong lady!'

The two women chatted for a long while. By the time they reached the pier, they were both soaked and needed a coffee.

'Thank you for listening and being so rock solid,' Lexie said, as they walked in the direction of a coffee shop. 'All I've done is talk about myself. Any news with you?'

'Yes, as a matter of fact,' Kathleen said, and a smile spread across her face.

Lexie listened intently as Kathleen told her about Rodger and his theories on after-death communication. 'I can't help feeling a bit freaked out by it all,' she admitted.

'If it was Sam, God forbid, you wouldn't find it scary, surely.'

'If it were Sam I think I'd go out of my mind,' said Lexie, honestly.

'Well, Rodger has been begging his late wife Claudia to send him a butterfly ever since she passed away. He's holding out hope, bless him.'

'I hate to sound like a total cynic,' Lexie said, 'but won't he just pin the next butterfly he sees on Claudia?'

'I guess he might, but I don't see what harm it can do to carry a little hope in one's heart.'

'Of course,' Lexie agreed immediately, hoping she hadn't offended Kathleen. Lexie wasn't much of a fantasist. As far as she was concerned death was final. Fleetingly, she wondered how she'd cope without Sam. More to the point, she sincerely hoped she wouldn't have to try any time soon. 'Hey, on a more positive note,' she said, 'I spoke to Agata earlier. She's going to have an afternoon exhibition in the gallery on Thursday week. I'm sending the invites out as soon as I get back. You'll come, won't you?'

'I wouldn't miss it,' Kathleen said.

'You could invite your new boyfriend, Rodger,' Lexie teased.

'Ha! I don't know if he'd be too pleased to be called that. His daughter certainly wouldn't find it funny. Jeez, she stormed into his hospital room like a fireball. To say she's highly strung is putting it mildly.'

'Is she a troubled teenager?' Lexie asked. 'Maybe she and Amélie could link up.'

'She's a grown woman and mother of two,' Kathleen said.

'All the more reason to invite Rodger. With a daughter like that he could do with some level-headed and kind friends.'

Kathleen fell silent for a while. Eventually she divulged, 'The day of the exhibition is my birthday.'

'Really? We'll have to celebrate afterwards then.'

'Oh, I don't want to steal Agata's thunder. Please don't make a big deal of it.'

'As you wish,' Lexie said. 'I know how it feels when people ignore your requests and do what *they* want. Let's see how you feel closer to the time. Maybe a small group of us could go for a meal after the exhibition ends.'

'Perhaps.'

As they meandered back towards the gallery, Lexie remembered Jackson's message. Feeling suddenly nervous for her friend, she said a silent prayer that the rainbow would come. She couldn't bear to think how disappointed Kathleen would be if nothing happened.

Chapter 28

LATER THAT EVENING LEXIE WAS LYING ON THE SOFA with a glass of wine, listening to a CD, when she heard a brief rap on the door followed by the unmistakable sound of Amélie bursting in. 'Auntie Lexie?'

'In here, Amélie,' she called, swinging her legs around so she could sit upright.

'Hey,' Amélie said. She swooped and kissed Lexie, then sat beside her and sighed. 'Oh, it's *sooo* lovely here. Quiet and peaceful with nobody miaowing in my ear. Can I stay tonight?'

'If Mum and Dad say so, of course. How are things today?'

'Strained,' Amélie said. 'We had a bit of a chat this morning … Well Dad lectured, Mum looked like she was sitting on a spike, and we all agreed we need to put everything behind us and move forward.'

'What about school? Are you going back?'

'The exams are almost over, so Dad is speaking to the headmaster and I've promised to knuckle down in September.'

Lexie felt so sorry for her niece. 'Would you like to talk about what's going on?' she asked.

'I'm not able to talk about it yet,' Amélie said. 'But I'd really like to stay here for a while if I can.'

'You know your room is there whenever you like.'

'I mean I'd like to move in for a couple of months,' Amélie said. 'I can't pay you any rent, but I could work at the gallery instead. Do a kind of barter system.'

Amélie's face lit up so much that Lexie thought her heart might break. Even though she and Sam needed to sort through a lot, she couldn't say no to her niece. She thought of her situation in France. Granted she had been a little older than Amélie at the time, but Lexie would've given her right arm then to have someone on her side, someone she'd felt she could trust. 'If that's what you really want, I can talk to Billy.'

'Let me call him now,' she said.

The conversation went a lot better than Lexie had expected. It seemed Billy and Dee needed a break from Amélie as much as she did from them. Billy was actually relieved his daughter would have a purpose during her summer holidays. 'Tell her we love her and that we'll be over in the morning to have a chat, okay?'

'Will do. 'Bye for now,' Lexie said, hanging up and going back to Amélie. 'All sorted,' she announced cheerfully.

'Seriously?'

'Seriously.'

'Auntie Lex, you're a legend. Thank you,' Amélie said, throwing her arms around Lexie's neck. You'd make the best mum in the world, you know. Why can't mine be more like you? You listen when I talk, but underneath it all you're only really interested in the stuff you like. You don't pretend to be someone you're not,' she said.

'Thanks.' Lexie smiled. 'I try to stay true to myself.'

'You're *all* about the gallery. The art and your business come first with you and everything else just kind of slots in around it. That's so cool.'

While Lexie nodded she felt cold inside. She didn't want Amélie to know how hurt she was, but she'd just been given a glimpse of what her niece and Lord knows how many others really thought of her.

'Just for the record, I care about Sam and you and my family more than the gallery,' Lexie said, trying to keep her voice even. 'And my friends. All those people are more important than the gallery.'

'Yeah, right!' Amélie scoffed. 'Listen, it's me you're talking to. I'm totally down with the way you've got things sussed. There's no wasting time with babies and all that stuff. Just because your friends are into the typical wife garbage doesn't mean you should be.' Amélie blew out air and flopped her arms out in a T shape. 'I'm going to suit myself just like you when I grow up. Believe me, I cannot wait.'

Amélie excused herself and went up to her room for a shower, leaving Lexie feeling winded. Is that what her parents had been trying to tell her? Were they using the softly-softly approach to hint to her that she was cold or callous?

Panic washed over her and her chest hurt. She wanted to stand up and go outside for air, but her legs had stopped working. She tried to call Amélie but her throat constricted and the room began to spin.

'Lexie?' She heard Amélie but couldn't see her. 'Lexie!' Before she knew it Amélie had grabbed her shoulders and started to shake her. It was gentle at first but when it yielded no response the shaking became more violent. 'Lexie! Answer me! What's wrong with you?'

'I … I … Oh dear …' Lexie's eyes hurt, as if someone was shining a really strong torch in her face.

'What's going on?' Amélie was looking at her as if she were crazy.

'I have the most awful migraine,' she said. 'It's obviously affecting my speech. That can happen when it's a really bad one,' she explained. 'I need to lie down for a bit.'

'Can I get you anything?' Amélie asked.

'No thanks, hon. I'll be fine in a while.'

'Let's go upstairs. I'll be in my room right across the landing, so you just yell if you need something.'

'I will, thank you,' Lexie managed.

She shut her door and leaned against it. Once the tears began to fall, she couldn't stop them. Sliding down onto the floor, Lexie grabbed two handfuls of her hair at either side of her temples and tugged hard. The pain was mildly comforting.

She'd never felt so confused in her entire life. Several weeks ago, she had been blissfully happy. She loved Sam. Sam loved her. They had enjoyed their life both socially and at work. She hadn't realised she was existing in a universe that most others viewed with scorn. She'd thought her parents were being invasive and narrow-minded. She'd genuinely assumed she had a choice about what she did with her life. But now everyone, including Maia and Amélie, seemed alien to her.

She still had a choice all right. But at what cost?

She shook her head. The truth was meant to emanate from the mouths of babes. How accurate that was turning out to be.

Lexie knew Amélie hadn't meant to hurt her. She understood that her niece had merely been shooting her mouth off. But her words were like shards of broken glass viciously bursting the bubble of happiness she'd been so comfortably living in.

Chapter 29

SAM WAS DUE INTO THE OFFICE THAT AFTERNOON but on his way back from the airport he decided to call in at the house. He wanted to grab his iPad and a fresh shirt. Knowing Lexie would be at the gallery, he let himself in, went into the kitchen and flicked on the kettle. Then he switched on the sound system and made himself some coffee.

He was sitting at the kitchen table in a world of his own when Amélie came in. 'Hey!' she shouted, over the loud music. 'How's it going?'

Sam jumped. 'Oh, hey!'

'Sam,' Amélie looked a little uncomfortable, 'did Auntie Lexie tell you?'

'Tell me what?' Sam said.

'That I'm staying here?'

'Sure, you great big goon!' Sam said. 'When have I ever minded you being here?'

'Uh, that's so great,' Amélie said, visibly relaxing. 'It's just slightly different me staying here the odd time and moving in for a few weeks, that's all.' She turned away from him to get some cereal out of a cupboard.

Sam's jaw hit the floor. Moving in? He gulped his coffee, scalding himself.

'Where is your Aunt Lexie now?' he asked casually.

'She's gone to work. She was feeling really dodgy earlier but I presume she's fine now.'

'I see. I've to dash, Amélie. Only a flying visit, busy-busy. See you later,' he said, rushing up the stairs. As he ripped off his shirt and found a fresh one, he wanted to thump the wall. How could Lexie invite Amélie to live with them and not consult him? Pulling on his shirt and grabbing his iPad, he dashed out of the house and leaped into his car. So they weren't having kids, but it was fine to take on someone else's messed-up runaway teen?

He punched the speed-dial button on his hands-free.

'Caracove Bay Gallery,' Lexie said, answering the phone.

'Hey, it's me,' Sam said.

'Hi,' Lexie said. 'Are you on your way back to the office?'

'I was just at home to change and bumped into our new foster child.'

'I was going to tell you later,' Lexie said. 'You were too busy travelling and all that last night so I didn't mention it then.'

'Uh-huh,' Sam said. 'And you didn't consider waiting and *asking* me if it might suit me?' he fumed.

'Are you annoyed?' Lexie asked.

'Lexie, how could you take this on without speaking to me?'

'I thought you liked Amélie. I don't understand why you're so annoyed.'

'If I moved someone in without consulting you, it would be all cool, would it?'

'Sam, I—'

'Lexie, do you know what? This is a pointless conversation because it's done.' He hung up.

He rubbed his temples and revved agitatedly as the traffic lights went red. Somehow, in the last couple of days, the girl he loved and thought he knew better than anyone in the world had become a stranger.

Amélie knew she needed to have a very frank conversation with her parents but she couldn't face speaking to them. Instead she'd decided to write them a letter – and had written several during the night. Each time she read them back, though, they seemed wrong. The latest attempt would have to do.

Dear Mum and Dad

First, I'm sorry for putting you through so much heartache. I know things have been weird between us for a while now. But I am sorting it all out in my own head.

I need some space if possible. Can you let me sit and stew for a few days? Then we can all sit down and have a calm and grown-up chat. There are some issues that I am working through. I don't want you to worry. I won't do anything else stupid. I promise.

Things will work out for the best once we have a bit of breathing space from one another.

See you in a week.

Amélie x

She folded it and stuffed it into her pocket. Her parents would probably arrive at Lexie's house fairly early so there was no time to waste. She reached her home in record time and slipped the note under the front door. She felt like a small child playing knick-knacks – ringing doorbells and running away.

Satisfied that she'd bought herself some time, Amélie made her way to the gallery. She'd promised Lexie she'd help and she wanted to keep her word.

Chapter 30

THE FOLLOWING WEEK FLEW BY. LEXIE AND SAM were like ships passing in the night. Amélie's presence at the house meant they had very little alone time, which seemed to suit them. They were sleeping in the same bed, but Lexie certainly didn't reach for Sam and he seemed to have assumed a new sleeping position on his back where he successfully ignored her.

Kathleen and Amélie became semi-permanent fixtures at the gallery. They were a marvellous help with setting up Agata's exhibition. 'I can't thank you two enough for all the amazing work you've done,' Lexie said one afternoon, as she treated them to an ice-cream.

'Uh, the pleasure is all mine,' Kathleen said. 'I've loved learning about the entire process. I'd thought I was too old to deliver flyers. I used to do a paper round many moons ago and it reminded me of that.'

'I'm really into it as well,' Amélie said. 'Why can't school be as fun as this? I understand the number system here now. Mark-ups and profit and all that. It made zero sense when the business teacher rattled on about it. But this is so exciting! I'll probably scream if you put red sold stickers on the paintings tomorrow,' she said.

Lexie laughed. 'Now you know why I love my business,' she said. Her smile faded as she remembered how Amélie had assumed the gallery was all she cared about.

'I'm definitely running my own business when I'm older,' Amélie continued.

'You've done an awesome job,' Kathleen said quietly. 'What is it they say? Lead by example? Looks like you've got a future entrepreneur on your hands here.'

Sam pulled up outside in a borrowed van. 'I need one pair of hands to help me collect the last of the paintings,' he called, rolling the window down.

'I'll go,' Kathleen volunteered. Lexie waved to him but didn't go out to talk, instead busying herself with a pile of fairy lights, which had turned themselves into a tangled mess.

Things were polite between them, but they certainly weren't on the same page. Lexie was convinced it was because she'd told Sam about the abortion. Every time she thought of her confession she cursed herself. The secret had been safe, locked away in the recesses of her mind. She'd held it there for years. Why had she ruined everything by dredging it up now?

Sam was feeling quiet. Kathleen was such easy company, though, that he didn't feel uncomfortable turning on a music station.

'I love country-and-western songs,' she mused. 'They make me grateful I don't live the lives they talk about.'

Sam grinned. He loved Kathleen's take on the world.

He knew Lexie was busy right now. The exhibition was a big spinner for her and she was trying to help Amélie through her crisis. But he felt like an outsider in his wife's world and wasn't enjoying it.

Only this morning he'd been sitting in his office at his desk staring into space when Rea had arrived with a bunch of documents needing a signature. 'Is everything okay with you, Sam?' she'd asked.

'No,' he'd stated. 'It's not. I'm in a kind of no man's land right now. Maybe it's a mid-life crisis or maybe I'm hitting a stage when I need to do something new. But my emotions seem to have numbed.'

He'd said way more than he'd intended. In fact he'd voiced stuff he hadn't even *thought*.

'I see,' Rea said calmly. 'Would you like to chat?'

'I would, but it's not ethical if I talk to you, is it? Not if we work together.'

'No, but as I said before, I know someone who is excellent,' she said. 'Would you like me to make a phone call?'

Sam nodded.

She walked from the room and buzzed him what felt like seconds later. 'No time like the present. John can see you in twenty minutes if you're up for it.'

'Are you serious?'

'Yes.'

'Okay. I'll do it. Thanks, Rea.'

She knocked on his door and passed him a Post-it note with John's name and address neatly written out.

Moments later, as he'd sat in the slightly musty-smelling prefab, Sam wasn't sure whether he wanted to laugh or cry. How on earth had he ended up sitting on a horrible brown plastic chair chatting to a randomer about his marriage problems?

The session had gone better than he'd ever expected. John hadn't told him what to do or what to say. Nothing like that. But he'd made him talk about how he felt. About Lexie. The baby issue. Work. Amélie. And loads of other stuff ...

Kathleen looked relaxed as they sped through the countryside. 'This area is unspeakably beautiful, isn't it?' she mused.

'Yeah, pretty majestic, all right,' he agreed. 'I can see why Agata wanted to come here and paint.'

Soon they were pulling up in front of Agata's cottage where she and Britta were waiting outside. 'Hello, you two!' Kathleen said. 'This is Lexie's Sam.'

'Hello,' Agata said. 'Thanks for coming to move the rest of my things.'

'No bother,' Sam said. 'Show me where the paintings are and I'll get them loaded up.'

'She's a little sweetie,' Kathleen said, nodding to Britta. 'You must be so proud of her. Is her father involved at all?'

'I used a sperm donor,' Agata said matter-of-factly.

'Bet you wish you hadn't asked,' Sam whispered to Kathleen, as he shot out of the cottage with a painting.

'Aren't you going to ask why I used a sperm donor?' Agata asked, as she plucked Britta out of her playpen.

'Lord, no! That's none of my business.'

'It's not a secret,' Agata said. 'I was living with a wonderful man. We'd been dating for eight years, sharing a place for five. We'd talked about starting a family. He was as enthusiastic as me. But I sensed he'd changed.'

'In what way?'

'I couldn't put my finger on it, but I knew he wasn't quite the same. I followed him one Saturday afternoon. He told me he was going to the gym but he led me to a café instead. I watched from a distance as he hugged and passionately kissed my longest-standing friend.'

'That's harsh,' Kathleen said. 'A double whammy, you poor love.'

'It was like being punched in the gut, that's for sure,' Agata agreed. 'But it was better to know. At least I had confirmation that my hunch was right. Instinct is a powerful thing, Kathleen. Anyway, I decided I couldn't let their selfishness ruin my life.'

'Had I been in your shoes, I would have gone barmy,' Kathleen said. 'I wouldn't have known which end was up, let alone how to go about fixing things.'

'Well, I've always been practical. Yes, I'm artistic, but I'd like to think I'm not stupid.'

Kathleen smiled. 'You're about as far from stupid as it's possible to be.'

As she packed some things into a shoulder bag, Agata continued to chat. 'So what about you? Do you have children and grandchildren?'

'Neither, sadly,' she said. 'My late husband and I longed for a family but it wasn't to be.'

'Sorry about that.' Agata held her gaze. 'I've just said all the wrong things. If I hurt you just now, talking about having Britta, I apologise.' Then she said suddenly, 'I have an idea. My parents are dead ten years. So Britta has no grandparents. Perhaps you could step into the breach while you're in Ireland.'

Kathleen was speechless. Then she recovered herself. 'But we barely know one another ... I ... Gosh, that sounds so rude. I'm stunned.'

'I don't know you well, that's true. But I told you just now that I trust my instinct. It's never let me down. I get a good feeling from you. Besides, if you turn out to be a total crazy lady I can always lie and tell you I'm returning to Sweden.'

'You don't strike me as a liar.'

'Ah, there's always a first time for everything!'

They laughed again and Kathleen held out her arms to Britta. The little girl went to her and grinned, showing her new teeth.

They went to the car and secured Britta in her baby seat.

'I'll go on ahead with the van,' Sam said. 'Why don't you travel with the girls?' he said to Kathleen. 'This old thing is a bit of a bone-shaker.'

'All right,' Kathleen answered. 'We'll see you at the gallery anon.'

Sam waved and drove on.

'He's such a darling man,' Kathleen said. 'He and Lexie are a wonderful couple. Fate led me to them.'

As they followed Sam in the car, Kathleen told Agata all about her childhood and how number three Cashel Square was playing a starring role in the new chapter of her life.

Travelling along Wicklow's scenic roads, with miles of unspoilt greenery on either side, Kathleen had a momentary out-of-body experience. A month ago she had been experiencing the worst gut-wrenching pain imaginable. She had been doubtful as to whether or not she'd even make it through a day, let alone a week, without Jackson. Now she was part of a whole new world, with people who had welcomed her into their lives.

By the time they drew up outside the gallery little Britta was asleep.

'I'll wait in the car with her until she wakes,' Kathleen offered.

'Are you sure?' Agata asked.

'Certain. That's the type of thing a grandma does. I should know,' she said, winking.

'I really appreciate this,' Agata said.

'I'll bring her to you as soon as she wakes.'

Agata smiled and leaned across to hug Kathleen.

As she watched Agata rush inside the gallery, Kathleen thought about the young woman's situation. It couldn't be easy for her living in such a remote area alone with a small baby, yet clearly Agata couldn't have been happier. She hoped the exhibition would be a success. The paintings were brilliant and eye-catching, and Kathleen was rooting equally for Agata and Lexie. They deserved to make a big splash tomorrow night. As she turned to gaze at the sleeping cherub in the back seat, Kathleen took a deep breath. 'There's a lot riding on tomorrow, little one,' she whispered. 'Your mummy needs it to go well. Lexie does too. And as for me? I'm wishing for a rainbow.'

Chapter 31

ON THURSDAY LEXIE WAS UP EARLIER THAN USUAL. Instead of having her normal leisurely breakfast, she filled a coffee flask to go. Breakfasts at number three simply weren't the same any more. Thoughts of her abortion, her parents' disappointment and how she'd hurt them pricked her conscience. Sam's resentment was almost palpable but Amélie's comment distressed her most of all. Did everyone she knew agree that she simply didn't care about much outside her job?

Relieved that the exhibition was taking up so much extra time, Lexie took a deep breath, fixed a smile on her face and skipped down the steps to knock on Kathleen's door.

'Good morning,' Kathleen called. 'It's lovely and bright. Just what we need to draw the punters in.'

'Happy birthday!' Lexie said, kissing her cheek and handing her a card.

'Thank you, sweetie,' Kathleen said. 'Shall I open it?'

'Of course!'

The card, which Lexie had made, had an old black-and-white photo of number three Cashel Square stuck to the front.

Happy birthday Kathleen,
With love and best wishes from
Number three, Sam and Lexie!
PS Your gift is your choice of a picture from today's exhibition!

Kathleen hugged her and dabbed her eyes. 'Thank you, darling girl. You're so kind and thoughtful.'

'I know today must be hard without Jackson, but I hope you'll enjoy your birthday as best you can.'

They walked to the gallery, chatting about the last-minute jobs that needed doing.

'I'll pick up the canapés from Ramona at the café just before four. There's no point in fetching them too early – we've nowhere to put them and I'm always nervous of food around the art work.'

'Did you stick to sushi or have you opted for hot things too?' Kathleen asked.

'It's all sushi but Ramona will do a good variety of both vegetarian and fish. Deep-fried things are asking for trouble. Grease doesn't mix well with paintings or ceramics. All I need is for someone to leave paw prints on one of the pieces and it'd be ruined.'

Lexie also had a large stack of brownies coming – she'd asked Ramona to stud them with birthday candles – but she kept that to herself.

'Where's Amélie?' Kathleen asked, as they arrived at the gallery.

'I left her sleeping. She went out with some friends last night and didn't get home until late. I figured she wouldn't thank me for hauling her out of bed at the crack of dawn.' Lexie smiled.

'My friend Rodger called last night. He'd love to come today and he's waiting to hear if beastly Bee can give him a ride.'

'Fingers crossed for that,' Lexie said.

'It would be nice for him. I hope the long journey to and from Howth with that crotchety daughter of his won't wear him out.'

'She sounds ghastly,' Lexie said, pulling a face.

By nine o'clock Agata and Britta had arrived. Lexie watched as Kathleen held her arms out to the baby. 'Hello, sweet child.' She nuzzled the little girl's soft, downy hair.

'She has a card for you,' Agata said with a grin.

Kathleen handed the baby to Agata and fumbled the envelope open excitedly. 'Look what it says on the front!' Kathleen said, eyes shining.

Happy birthday to a wonderful grandmother

'Huh?' Lexie was perplexed. 'Am I missing a beat here?'

'We agreed I'm going to be Britta's grandma while I'm in Ireland. There was a vacancy for the role.'

'I see,' Lexie said, raising her eyebrows. She caught herself muttering under her breath as her reflection showed a furrowed brow and cross expression. Again she thought of Amélie's comment. Forcing a smile, she vowed to stop being so tetchy. She'd caught Kate glancing at her questioningly from time to time too. She needed to keep herself in check a bit.

The morning flew by. Little Britta got a bit fed up especially when it became clear that she couldn't pull herself up using the various tables displaying ceramics.

'Don't do that, honey!' Lexie swooped to scoop her up. 'I'm terrified something might land on top of her,' she said apologetically, to Agata. 'It's not really a great place for a little demolition demon.'

'I'll take her to the promenade,' Kathleen offered. 'I can push the buggy to the water's edge and, if you've no objection, Agata, I could let her paddle for a bit.'

'She'd love that, thank you,' Agata said.

As Lexie, Kate and Agata hung the paintings and made sure the gallery was welcoming, Amélie arrived.

'You look gorgeous,' Agata said. 'I love that bright blue on you.'

'Yeah, it really suits you,' Lexie said, with a smirk. 'Funnily enough, the dress is very like one I paid a king's ransom for and haven't even worn yet.'

'Ooh, sorry!' Amélie said. 'I didn't have anything smart. I thought you'd be happier if I borrowed something rather than turning up looking like a scarecrow.'

'You look great. I won't ever be able to wear that dress now, because I'll look ancient and wobbly in it after you,' Lexie quipped.

'You heard her,' Amélie joked. 'She pretty much said I can keep it! So, what do you need me to do?'

'Would you go and see if Ramona needs some help with the canapés?' Lexie asked.

'Sure. I'll catch you all in a while,' Amélie said.

As she walked out of the door, Agata watched with her head tilted. 'She's a great girl, isn't she? You've a lovely relationship, you two.'

'I'm lucky to have her in my life. She's going through a bit of a hard time right now, so she's staying with Sam and me for a while,' Lexie said.

'I'm sure she'll be fine. She has lots of support and she knows you love her.'

Four o'clock came before they knew it. Like a floodgate opening, the gallery door seemed to swing non-stop. Kate was brilliant, handing out information leaflets. As Kathleen returned with Britta, Sam appeared with Amélie and a man in a wheelchair came into view.

'That poor fellow seems to be struggling. There's a slight incline on the footpath, which wouldn't be noticeable to us when we're walking,' Sam explained, and rushed out to his aid.

'It's my friend Rodger,' Kathleen exclaimed, balancing a chirping Britta on her hip as she followed suit.

Lexie watched through the window as Kathleen swooped to hug the man before ushering him along, Sam helping.

'Here we are,' Kathleen announced. 'Everyone, this is Rodger!'

'You're so welcome. Kathleen told us all about you. I'm Lexie. That's Sam behind you, this is Amélie, our esteemed artist, Agata, and her daughter, Britta.'

'Hello,' Rodger said, saluting and waving. 'Apologies for the grand entrance just now. My daughter was kind enough to give me a lift but, as she pointed out, it was beyond her level of patience to drive around the maze of one-way streets to get here.'

Kathleen pinched Lexie and glanced sideways.

'Well, you're here now,' Sam said, attempting to smooth things over.

'Indeed,' Rodger said. 'I'm insisting on getting the DART home and I can flag a taxi from the station. So at least there won't be any further unnecessary trauma.'

'We'll drop you to Caracove Bay station whenever you want to go,' Sam promised. 'But for now you're just the gentleman I need to test the sparkling wine. Are you up to it?'

'I don't need to be asked twice,' Rodger said.

As Rodger moved towards the drinks table, Amélie turned to Lexie. 'What kind of a sadist is his daughter?' she hissed. 'The poor man just had surgery and can barely move. He seems so sweet too. She seriously needs to get a life. Stupid witch.'

'It seems pretty cruel to have dumped him with any distance to travel,' Lexie agreed. 'But we can't judge her if we don't know the situation.'

'Yes, we can,' Amélie spat. 'What a mean cow! If someone did that to me I'd never forgive them.'

'Be careful,' Lexie hissed. 'We don't want Rodger to hear us.'

'Why are you being so holier-than-thou all of a sudden?' Amélie asked. 'You're acting all antsy full stop. What's up?'

'Oh, nothing,' she lied, glancing at Sam. 'I hope tonight is a success for Agata, that's all.'

Agata was proudly showing Rodger some of her work. With one hand on her hip, she was gesturing wildly and giggling.

'Well, she's having a whale of a time, if you ask me,' Amélie said. 'So chill. Enjoy it. It isn't like you to be so uptight. That's usually my mother's job. What've you done?' she asked, narrowing her eyes.

'I love the way you jump to all sorts of conclusions about me.'

'Sorry,' she said sheepishly. 'But you've got to admit you're acting kind of spooked.'

'I'm just in work mode, honey. That's all. Now, can you please help my stress levels and feed the growing crowd?'

'Sure thing,' Amélie said, grabbing a tray and mingling.

Lexie wanted to feel her usual relaxed and happy self but too many demons were addling her mind.

Much to everyone's delight, punters continued to pour through the doors. Before long the gallery was buzzing as people enjoyed the wine, sushi and art.

'I'm going to make a little speech,' Lexie whispered, as she led Agata towards the desk by the elbow. 'Would you like to say a few words too?'

'I'd be delighted,' Agata said. 'I've nothing prepared but that's okay, isn't it?'

Lexie nodded, then clambered on to a chair and clapped her hands high above her head. 'Good afternoon, folks,' she shouted, as shushing dominoed around the room. 'Sorry to interrupt but I want to say a few words before handing you over to the star of the show.'

Met by a sea of smiling faces, Lexie told everyone how she'd stumbled across Agata's work and how honoured she was to find such a talent. 'Little did I know it, but Agata had quite a collection of completed work she'd been carefully squirrelling away. Now I know how Ali Baba must've felt when he shouted, "Open, Sesame," and the cave wall drew back revealing hidden treasure!' The crowd applauded as Lexie jumped down and Agata took to the chair.

'This is simply wonderful. I am so grateful that you all made it here this afternoon. I especially want to thank Grandma Kathleen for being so fabulous with my darling Britta.' There was another round of applause as Kathleen jiggled little Britta and helped her wave at her mummy. 'But none of this would have happened without the strength of Lexie's belief in me. Lexie, you have an incredible gallery here and I know we all agree that you give your heart and soul to this place. I for one am so very grateful.'

The claps and cheers as Agata got down and hugged Lexie should have lifted her heart. She knew it was a moment she ought to have seized and enjoyed. But she felt dead inside: everyone saw the gallery as her one true love. Her heart and soul.

Just then Maia wove her way through the crowded room towards her, clasped her hand and kissed her cheek. 'Hi, doll, sorry I missed the very beginning of your speech. I came as soon as I could. Work was insane today. It's going really well in here,' she congratulated her. 'Kate is flat out and loads of the pictures have red "sold" stickers on them. If things keep going the way they are, we can book a lovely holiday in the Caribbean. Just imagine us, a girly break ... I'd love it.'

'Am I cold and selfish, Maia?' Lexie asked, out of the blue, searching her face for honesty.

'Pardon?' Maia nearly choked on her sparkling water. 'Where on earth did that come from? Aren't you enjoying the buzz? This is a resounding success, Lex. What's with the Mopey Mabel stuff?'

'Nothing,' she said. 'Forget I said it. I need to do something,' she said, rushing to the tiny storeroom. Moments later she emerged with a large tray of brownies dotted with lit birthday candles. An impromptu rendition of 'Happy Birthday' began and people craned their necks to see who the brownies were heading for.

Kathleen looked astonished and baby Britta ecstatic as the tray stopped in front of them. 'You monkey,' Kathleen murmured to Lexie. 'I could die of mortification. But I'm also very touched. Thank you.'

Lexie winked at her and waited until Kathleen had helped herself to the first brownie before taking off around the room with the tray.

'Do you want me to do that?' Sam offered, as he trailed her.

'Great. I'd better go and give Kate a hand. She's not an octopus after all.'

'Looks like your baby is going to throw a nice bundle of cash in our direction tonight,' Sam added, glancing around.

'This place is my business. Not my baby. I don't refer to your job as your child. Just because I'm a successful woman, why should people automatically assume I'm a cold, hard machine?'

'Hey!' Sam caught her wrist as she turned to walk off. 'It was a joke. I was attempting to speak to you in a light tone, seeing as we've barely said two words to one another for weeks now. Forget I said anything.'

He started to walk away but she called him back. 'Sam, I'm sorry. It's just ... It's disconcerting to realise that people in general view me with veritable disdain and think I'm pretty much bereft of emotion.'

'Lexie! Nobody thinks that of you,' Sam said, with a furrowed brow. 'You're extremely uptight at the moment. Try to relax and enjoy the evening. You've worked hard and today you should pat yourself on the back. You should be enjoying the buzz. After all, this is what you wanted, isn't it?'

'No, Sam, it isn't. I wanted to be happy with you. I wanted to be an artist. I wanted to live a tranquil life where I could be who I am and not feel as if I need to apologise for that,' she flared. 'But clearly it's not going to happen. None of it.'

Thankfully, as it turned out, someone needed her assistance to buy a painting, so Lexie was able to bury her head in her work for a while. Over the next couple of hours, she knew Sam was trying to catch her eye. But she made certain she was in the centre of the action and hadn't time to stop.

As the crowd began to thin, she looked at her watch. 'It's almost nine o'clock.' She was astonished.

'Yes, and it's all gone so well,' Kathleen said. 'Sam has kindly gone to the DART station with Rodger. He'd got quite sore. He hadn't meant to stay so late, but he enjoyed it thoroughly and said to thank you.'

'I'm sorry I didn't have a chance to speak to him properly. He seems a lovely man.'

'I'm sure he understands. You were busy, dear. Besides, he said he'd gladly come to Caracove again. He got on very nicely with your parents too.'

'Oh, good,' Lexie said.

'Rodger and I are going to take a trip to the zoo soon.'

'That's great,' Lexie said. 'I'm going to show the remainder of the guests the door and shut up shop. Otherwise I'll be here all night.'

Lexie collected glasses, making it obvious the exhibition was over, and within twenty minutes the place was deserted, bar family, Kathleen, Agata and Britta. The baby was rubbing her eyes and resting her head on her mummy's shoulder. Plugging her thumb into her mouth, she fought to stay awake.

'I'd better get this little lady home,' Agata said. 'Thank you so much for everything. I've had such a wonderful time. I have two new commissions too. I can't believe it!'

'You deserve it all,' Lexie said. 'Let me help you out to the car.'

Kathleen came too. As soon as Britta was in her car seat, she turned her head to the side and closed her eyes.

'She'll sleep the whole way back,' Agata said, with a smile.

'None of us will be far behind her,' Kathleen said, stifling a yawn.

'I'll call you tomorrow and we can discuss the money,' Lexie told Agata. 'Well done, and thanks again for being so fantastic. The customers loved meeting you and chatting about your upcoming work.'

They hugged and Lexie excused herself, leaving the other women to say goodbye. She waved her parents off too, then noticed Sam had arrived back and was sweeping the floor.

'Amélie is waiting outside for Kathleen and she'll walk home with her. I said we'd be along shortly,' he said.

'Right,' Lexie said tiredly.

'Will I mop the floor now or would you rather leave it until tomorrow?'

'No, you go on, thanks. I'll do it. I don't want to come in and face it first thing.'

'I'll do it for you,' Sam said. 'I don't mind.'

'Actually, Sam, I'd be better left to do it. I need a bit of breathing space.'

'I'll see you at home, then. I'll accompany Kathleen and Amélie. Are you sure you don't want me to wait and walk with you?'

'No. Thanks, but no.'

She watched through the window as Sam held his arms out for Kathleen and Amélie to link and they departed, chatting animatedly.

As soon as she knew she was alone, Lexie threw the mop at the back wall. Sitting on the floor, she savoured the silence.

Chapter 32

KATHLEEN WAS DOING HER LEVEL BEST TO APPEAR fine but as they approached Cashel Square all she could do was look at the sky. She checked her watch twice during the short walk home. It was almost ten o'clock. The light was fading and she knew that, unless some sort of miracle happened, the chance of a rainbow appearing right now was highly unlikely.

She forced her eyes downwards and concentrated on the cracks in the ground as they walked. She convinced herself that if she avoided the big ones, the rainbow might appear.

'Is everything all right?' Sam asked her, as they reached the house.

'Oh, yes, dear, I'm just tired,' she lied. 'It's been a long and lovely day.'

'I was thinking you might come up to the living room and have a nightcap with us,' Sam said. 'But if you feel you've had enough ...'

'I appreciate the offer, dear, but I'd rather go to my bed if it's all the same to you.'

'Of course,' he said. 'I'll be up for a while so if you change your mind, knock on the door and I'll be delighted with the company.'

'Will do.' Kathleen kissed his cheek. 'Nighty-night, Amélie, love,' she said. As they waved to her, she did her best not to run like a scalded cat down the steps to the basement door. As soon as she got inside it was as if a dam had burst. Her shoulders shook and she wanted to climb into the back of the closet and hide behind the clothes the way she used to as a small child.

Instead, she half staggered, half ran to the bedroom, managing to shed her coat and shoes in time to collapse on the bed. Burying her face in the pillows, she let loose. A well of tears she'd thought had long since dried up poured forth.

'Jackson, how could you disappoint me like that?' she shouted into the mattress. Then, afraid Sam might hear her and think she was in trouble, Kathleen forced herself to regain control. Flinging herself wildly off the bed, she strode into the dining area and found the laptop.

Forcing it open she clicked on the usual icon and hit play. As the speech she knew so well began, she walked back to the confines of the bedroom clutching the machine. Through gritted teeth, she growled, 'Why did you build my hopes and shatter me like this, Jackson? You left me once and that was bad enough. Now I feel as if the only taste you've left in my world is one of bitter disappointment. You've destroyed me.'

For a split second she considered throwing the laptop at the wall. The sound of it smashing and crashing to the floor might have been satisfying – for a moment. But Kathleen knew that was all it would be – momentary. She'd never been violent or destructive and she knew that seeing her laptop shattered would traumatise her further.

She padded into the bathroom and turned on the shower. Perhaps if she lathered her body in a fresh-smelling shower gel, she'd feel less awful. Knowing she wasn't going to sleep much, she took her time patting her skin dry and applying body lotion. By the time she had cleansed, toned and moisturised her face and brushed her teeth, she needed to lie down again.

Her anger was gone. A slight hangover had started to pulsate at her temples. The sparkling wine that had been such a wonderful idea earlier was now causing heartburn and making her feel ill. All that remained as she slid between the cool sheets was a dreadful sense of emptiness. Determined not to cry again, she flattened her bedspread and rearranged her pillows. She flicked on the bedside radio, turned off her light and lay back, hoping she might be able to relax.

Just as she forced her eyes to close, a soothing late-night DJ's voice came over the airwaves: 'I haven't played this song for many years, but for some reason it came to mind the second I woke this morning. It's an old favourite of mine and I sincerely hope you will enjoy it too.'

Kathleen felt as if she was floating above the bed as the dulcet tones of Judy Garland filled the room. The instant the lyrics of 'Somewhere over the Rainbow' began, Kathleen knew it was a sign. 'Oh, Jackson,' she cried. 'You kept your promise, darling.' This time as the tears coursed down her cheeks, Kathleen was grinning like a Cheshire cat.

As the song finished, she blew a kiss skywards. 'Good night, sweetheart, and thank you for my birthday rainbow.'

It was after ten when Kathleen woke the following morning. Glancing at the radio, she tucked her hands behind her head and smiled.

'Jackson, I'm so glad I didn't break the laptop last night. I would've felt like such an old fool.' She sighed happily and lost herself in thoughts of her late husband.

As she climbed out of bed, she couldn't wait to tell Lexie all about her first rainbow from Jackson.

There was no sound above as she put on the kettle for a cup of tea. Figuring Sam and Lexie had gone to work, she planned to have breakfast, then stroll to the gallery.

Chapter 33

LEXIE WAS SITTING CROSS-LEGGED ON THE PURPLE spongy yoga mat she'd fished out from under the stairs. She'd bought it ages ago, with a pair of stretchy yoga pants, a matching singlet and a zip-up hoody. She'd signed up to a course at the local gym, fully intending to become a regular. The thought of a bronzed, toned midriff had enthused her.

She'd done really well for the first three weeks. But as soon as she'd allowed herself to miss one, that had been it. The spell was broken and she knew the gear would just add to the pile marked 'waste of wad' on the ledger in her mind.

Sam had slipped out to work this morning after hesitating several times, then tiptoeing over to her side of the bed. 'Lex?' he whispered. She didn't answer. She could hear him and knew he was anxious, but she didn't put him out of his misery.

As soon as he closed the bedroom door gently, her eyes had snapped open. She stared at the wall, wondering why she was being so awful. She knew she ought to call him and wish him a good day. But she didn't do it. The front door banged and she sat up in bed, pondering.

Yoga. That would solve it. She'd try to soothe herself with yoga. She'd never felt like this before. It was weird. She couldn't put her finger on it. She was angry but not in a shouty-screamy way. It was more a deep, simmering fury that was dangerously inking its way through each and every fibre of her body leaving a trail of poisonous negativity in its wake.

The deep breathing exercises were a waste of time so she walked purposefully into the bathroom and leaned on the heels of her hands at the edge of the basin. She examined her face in the mirror. She arched her eyebrows as high as they'd go, then scrunched them down, making as many wrinkles as she could. Relaxing her face, she brushed her teeth. The deep line between her eyes appeared again. Blowing out loudly, she wondered if she should think about getting Botox. Lexie wasn't sure if she liked the idea. Maia was addicted to it, but she'd resisted so far.

'If you had a four-year-old keeping you awake and making you feel fifty years old, you'd be getting regular shots too,' Maia told her. 'Keep the wrinkles at bay, Lex. Once they set in you're headed for Prune City.'

As she pulled on a layered Indian cotton blue-grey maxi dress and twisted her hair into a pretty knot at the back of her head, Lexie suspected that no amount of Botox would help with the tugging sense of foreboding that had wormed its way into her heart.

Her mobile phone rang, flashing up Kate's name.

'Hiya!' Lexie said, injecting as much cheer into her tone as she could.

'Lexie?' Kate sounded alarmed. 'Where are you? I've just arrived at the gallery and it's still locked up.'

'Sorry about that,' she said. 'I'll be along soon. Can you open up and get started? A few things have come up and I didn't have a chance to call you.'

'Oh, sure,' Kate said, sounding relieved. 'Take your time. I was just having a mild heart attack there. I had a terrible feeling you'd told me to open up and I'd forgotten.'

'No, all my fault. No hassle. I'm sure the world will keep turning if the gallery isn't open on time,' Lexie said.

'Eh … Is … is everything okay?'

'Certainly is. I'm on my way. I'm about half an hour away,' she lied, 'so I'll see you soon. I'd better get going.'

Lexie grabbed a pair of sandals from her wardrobe and a long blue-grey cardigan to match the dress, then walked woodenly down the stairs. Raising her eyes to Heaven, she picked up Sam's breakfast things and put them into the dishwasher.

A wave of anger washed over her. Stabbing at her phone, she texted him.

Would it be 2 much trouble 2 put your stuff in the dishwasher?
Are you quadriplegic all of a sudden???

She hit send and made coffee. Her phone beeped.

What's eating you? If it's that much hassle leave them and I'll do
it when I get home.

Lexie balled her fists. As if he'd clear away the stuff that night! Why
hadn't he just done it earlier? Who did he think she was – a servant?

She made some coffee. Then, rooting in the cupboard, she found
a packet of foil-wrapped chocolate-covered marshmallow biscuits.
Ripping it open, she ate one after another. She barely chewed. There
was an odd sense of satisfaction in boycotting multigrain toast in
favour of unhealthy fattening fodder.

Before long there was a small pile of wrappers in front of her.
Draining her coffee, she scrunched them up, flung them into the bin
and grabbed her bag and phone. She'd go for a quick walk around
the block before heading to the gallery. Her phone beeped. It was
Sam again.

You ok????

Feeling a bit mean, she answered, albeit abruptly.

All fine. I'm busy.

Sam threw his phone on to his desk. What was with Lexie? He'd
done his best to support her last night. He'd walked Kathleen and
Amélie home, then grabbed a half-bottle of bubbly and waited for
her in the living room. He'd hoped a glass of champagne and some
soothing music might ease their addled minds.

He'd had another session with John yesterday. He'd told Sam to try
to woo Lexie. That often gave a couple a fresh start. He was nowhere

near the mood for being nice to her after her snappy behaviour at the exhibition, but he'd tried all the same.

He had been ready for a bit of romance and loving when she'd crashed through the front door, poked her head into the living room, announced she had a 'pain in her face with today' and strode upstairs.

He was so peeved that he'd popped the cork on the champagne and guzzled it anyway. The fizz had clawed at his throat and made him cough roughly. Such a fine drink wasn't designed to be glugged to drown sorrows. It was meant for sipping with smiles.

When he'd made his way upstairs he'd found her cocooned in the duvet with a pillow over her head. She didn't speak, so he didn't bother attempting to cajole her.

He'd probably stay late at the office tonight, Sam thought, or call Josh to see if he could meet for a beer. Whatever happened, he wasn't going home to that house full of female hormones.

It was sunny and bright outside and the scent of blossoms should have cheered her but Lexie couldn't shake her irritation.

'Good morning! I wasn't expecting to see you at this time.'

'Hi, Kathleen,' Lexie said, forcing a smile.

'Sorry to be the one to point it out to you,' Kathleen said, 'but you've got chocolate on the front of your dress.'

'Oh, bloody hell ...'

'Sorry, dear, but I hate nothing more than discovering these things. I never understand why folk don't alert me. I suspect you'd rather not go around for the morning looking like you've been on a date with Willy Wonka.'

Lexie dropped to the bottom step and sighed.

'Hey.' Kathleen rushed to her side. 'I'm so sorry if I upset you.'

'Ah, it's not you,' Lexie said. 'I'm having the worst time, Kathleen. I ... I don't know *who* I am any more.'

'What's brought this on?' Kathleen asked.

'I just feel like I'm drowning. I keep having dawning realisations that I'm this awful sort of person. That I'm selfish and crass and totally obsessed with my job and nothing else.'

'Whoa there, cowgirl!' Kathleen said, holding up her hand. 'Who told you that?'

'Nobody – everybody … I don't know. I'm snapping at people left, right and centre and I want to run away. I'm not fit company for anyone right now. Maybe if I went off for a few days it would make things better.'

'Maybe,' Kathleen said carefully. 'But it might just make you feel even more alone and upset. Why don't you come down to the basement and we can have a cup of tea?'

'Or a pint of gin?' Lexie suggested, with a wry smile.

'I don't think I've got any, but I have wine. Would that do? You could drink it by the neck and smash the bottle against the wall out back.'

Lexie grinned. Standing up, she followed her friend. 'I feel a bit sick too. I just ate an entire box of chocolate marshmallows.'

'That's very good for you every now and again,' Kathleen said. 'I'll make you some peppermint tea – it'll cut through the chocolate.'

Lexie pulled out a kitchen chair and watched Kathleen fill the kettle. 'Can I tell you about my rainbow?' Kathleen asked.

'Oh, dear Lord! Your birthday rainbow. Kathleen, I'm so sorry! How could I have forgotten? You must think I'm the worst friend. Tell me! What happened? Did it appear?'

'Yes!' she said, with a glint in her eye. 'But not in the form I'd been expecting.'

Lexie sat up straight and listened as Kathleen filled her in. As the older woman described the lows and wonderful final high of her day, guilt washed over her again. How could she behave in such a juvenile and self-centred way? Here was poor Kathleen, thousands of miles away from her home and in the throes of grief, yet she could still find a reason to smile.

'You amaze me, Kathleen,' she said. 'You're going through this massive trauma and you're so upbeat and positive. I'm trying to cope with a totally measly issue in comparison and I'm so awful at it. I don't know how to be *me* any more,' she said miserably. 'I can't help feeling I'm always in the wrong somehow.'

'What makes you think that?'

'I've upset everyone over the last few days. I raised my parents' hopes and dashed them again. Amélie thinks my one true love is my gallery. Sam is looking at me as if I'm a murderer ...'

She pushed the chair back and began to pace the room. Kathleen stayed where she was and made no comment.

'I'm starting to think this is Mother Nature's way of telling me I should have a child after all. What else am I doing on this earth? Maybe if I had a baby the indescribable sense of failure that's infecting my psyche would go away. Maybe then I'd be more socially acceptable.'

Kathleen remained silent. Lexie continued to pace.

'I always thought that other women became obsessed with the desire to have a child because they felt they couldn't go on a second longer without having a little bundle to hold.'

Kathleen nodded.

'But now I'm wondering if body clocks tick in different ways for us all. Maybe I'm feeling it this way ... Maybe it's manifesting itself by producing a hopeless sense of uselessness. If I were someone's mother, would that give me more of a purpose in life?'

'I don't know what to say, Lexie. I can't tell you how to feel or promise you this awful hurt you're experiencing right now will go away if you become a mother.'

'But you said you felt it. That for years there was an emptiness inside,' Lexie said.

'Yes, darling, I did. But only because I had that longing you mentioned. I'd watch babies in strollers and imagine for a split second that they were mine. I used to wake at night crying for the baby that I never got to hold. It was a want that was physical as well as emotional.'

Lexie exhaled loudly. 'I'm sorry for making you think about all that,' she said. 'I'm doing it again, you see. Everybody I come in contact with ends up sad. I'm like a disgusting slug leaving a slime trail behind me.'

'Hardly.' Kathleen smiled. 'You haven't made me sad again either. That sadness never goes away, Lexie. I reckon I'll mourn the children I never had until the day I die.'

'That's heavy,' Lexie said.

'Isn't it?' Kathleen wrinkled her nose. 'But it's the truth.'

'How come you aren't in the depths of depression? How do you manage to keep going? You're so calm and sweet-natured and cheerful. How do you do that?'

'Thank you, dear. But the simple answer is that I know I'm blessed. I may not have children of my own, but I've known true love with my Jackson. I have many wonderful people in my life. I've had plenty of adventures and I know there are still some to come. Life is full of hope and expectation, Lexie. Sometimes we just need to delve a little below the surface to find it.'

'Right now I think I need a hammer and shovel to help me,' Lexie admitted.

'You'll get there, darling girl. Just take your time. Be patient with yourself. You have all the time in the world. You're very young.'

'I'm nearly forty!'

'I repeat, you're very young!'

Lexie grinned. She watched Kathleen as she crossed the room to put the empty tea mugs in the sink. When she reached seventy-five would she be as content as Kathleen if her life continued the way it was going? Somehow she doubted it. In fact, Lexie had a terrible feeling she'd peaked and, unless she did something drastic, her life would be on a downhill slide from here on in.

'I'd better get to work,' Lexie said. 'Thanks for sharing your amazing rainbow story. If you're free later, come and choose your birthday picture.'

'I'll try. It might be another day, though. I think I'm going to pop to the library and use their local records to look up an old pal.'

'Really? Who?'

'Betty Clarke. She was my best friend as a child.'

'Aha!' Lexie twigged. 'You're on your mission to find someone from the past, just like Jackson instructed. Am I right?'

'I feel ready to do it now. Lord only knows if Betty is still around or what became of her. But she's someone I've always wondered about. I missed her dreadfully when we emigrated. You know what it's like when you're a kid? Your friends are so important.'

'Indeed I do. Maia and I are like sisters. I would've been heartbroken if we'd been separated. Where did Betty live when you left?' Lexie asked.

'Literally around the corner,' Kathleen said. 'In one of the cottages on the road just behind the gallery.'

'Those houses have looked exactly the same since I've lived around here. Would it be worth knocking on her door to see if anyone knows of her whereabouts? Who knows? Maybe she still lives there.'

'Gosh, that'd be something, wouldn't it?' Kathleen said. 'I never thought of that.'

'I'll be in the gallery all afternoon. If you're at a loose end, call in, okay?'

'I will, thank you, Lexie.'

As she walked towards the promenade, Lexie tried to imagine what it might feel like to wheel a pram. Gulping in sea air, she worked on convincing herself that becoming a mother was the answer to all her problems. Her phone rang.

'Hi, Maia,' she said.

'Ugh,' she answered. 'I'm as sick as a dog. Holy shit, Lex, I think my body's attempting to turn itself inside-out. If I puke once more I swear my intestine is going to shoot out my nostril.'

'Nice,' Lexie said. 'Where are you? It sounds noisy.'

'I'm on the side of the motorway. I had to get out of the car. I've filled the space between the seats with vomit so I've rung the AA to come and rescue me.'

'They won't take your car unless you've broken down, surely,' Lexie said. 'I'll come. Wait there.'

'No, it's cool,' Maia said. 'I had a pocket-knife in the glove box so I slashed a tyre. The AA will drag me to a garage and Josh is going to rescue me.'

Lexie grinned. 'You're a total nutcase. How did you even think of slashing your own tyre?'

'Hormones. Crazy bat-shit pregnancy things zooming round my body. Anyway, I was calling to say that you're not a cold bitch. I love you and I'm worried you're losing the plot. If you feel like topping yourself or any other insane notion, call me, okay?'

Lexie started laughing. Really loudly, with snorts.

'What's so bloody funny?' Maia yelled, as a whooshing sound passed her.

'You're on the side of a motorway puking and slashing your tyres and you're giving me advice on being a Mad Mary?'

As Maia joined the laughter, Lexie felt a tiny spark of hope spring to life, somewhere deep in the recesses of her mind.

Chapter 34

KATHLEEN HUMMED AS SHE WASHED THE MUGS. Poor Lexie was certainly at a major crossroads in her life. She was young enough to start a family yet old enough to decide she didn't want one.

'You know, Jackson, it's taken me seventy-five years to see it, but there's no such thing as perfect,' she said, to the closed laptop. 'If that tumour hadn't claimed you, things would have been perfect. Having said that, I'm beginning to notice a pattern here, my darling. There'll always be a flaw or a snag or an "if only", won't there? Is that just human nature, d'ya reckon? Does it all go away when we die? Is that what Paradise really means? That we no longer feel we're missing out on one thing or another?'

Of course Jackson didn't answer. But Kathleen had grown used to their one-sided conversations. The silence didn't tug at her heart quite as much as before. Jackson's physical absence wasn't quite as shocking now that she'd realised she could get through a day, a week and even a month without him. She felt an odd sense of pride that she was surviving on her own.

'I'd still give everything I own to have you back, my love,' she said, as she gathered her things to go out. 'I'd sell my soul to the devil for five minutes with you. But I'm still here and I've got to do this living thing while I have the chance. You know me better than I know myself, honey. Bless you for giving me this mission.'

Bolstered, she set her sights on searching for Betty Clarke.

Lexie had had a point when she'd suggested Kathleen should start at Betty's old home and work from there.

Moments later, she felt like a little girl again as she pushed open the small waist-height black iron gate at Betty's childhood house.

The place was very neat and tidy. The small garden left and right of the narrow cobbled path that led to the front door was so immaculately kept it made the place look almost like a doll's house.

Mrs Clarke might have been green-fingered but Kathleen didn't remember the garden being so neatly manicured or so many pretty plants in window boxes.

She knocked on the door, stood back and waited. The sound of a small yappy dog burst forth from the back room. Kathleen squinted and tried to look in through the mottled glass panel in the door. She could see a smudge of white bounding up and down excitedly.

A dark-haired man who looked to be in his late thirties opened the door with a white terrier in his arms. 'Hello there,' he said, smiling.

'Hi,' Kathleen said. 'My name is Kathleen and I was wondering if you could help me. It's a long shot, but I'm trying to trace an old friend, Betty Clarke. Would you happen to know anything about her?'

The man's eyes lit up. 'I certainly do,' he said. 'She's my mother. I think you'd better come in.'

'Oh, my!' Kathleen said in shock. 'I guess I didn't expect to get any information on her. This is a wonderful turn-up for the books.'

The man stood back and beckoned her in. The layout had completely changed since Kathleen had last been there. The old façade was literally all that remained of Betty's childhood home. The downstairs was now one bright, open space, with a metal spiral staircase leading to the upper floor.

'This looks awesome,' Kathleen said.

'Thanks. I'm Ben, by the way. Mum doesn't really share your opinion but, as I've pointed out to her on numerous occasions, it's not her house any longer.'

'Where does she live now?'

'Connemara in the wild west!' he joked. 'She's been there for the last five years since Dad died.'

'I see,' Kathleen said, trying to take it all in.

'I've two older sisters, both of whom live in Connemara with their kiddies. Hence the draw for Mum. She minds Ruth's two while she works part time.'

'Good for Betty.'

'She's a fantastic gran and I know the little ones have kept her going since my father passed away.'

'I can imagine.'

'She still comes to stay with George, my partner, and me from time to time,' Ben said. 'But she hates the minimalist look we've injected into this old place.'

'That's a pity,' Kathleen said. 'I guess it must be kind of tough on her to see her old home torn apart, though.' She gazed around. 'I have to tell you, Ben, you've done a wonderful job on the place.'

'Ah, I can't really take the credit. It's all down to George. He's an architect and has a great eye.'

'Clearly,' Kathleen agreed. 'Would you give your mother my cell number? I'd dearly love to speak with her and possibly arrange to meet her.'

'Why don't I call her now?' Ben suggested.

'Oh, gosh. That might put her on the spot?'

'Well, had she been here when you knocked she would've been put on the same spot. There's no difference. Besides, I've got a strong suspicion she's going to be thrilled to hear from you, Kathleen.'

Before she could argue, Ben had hit speed-dial on his phone. 'Mum, how's it going? Great … Yes, Mum, everything's fine. Hold the line, I've got a surprise for you.'

Ben handed her the phone and did a little excited dance. Biting her lip, Kathleen's throat was suddenly dry. 'Hello,' she ventured.

'Hello?' the voice at the other end answered.

'Betty, this is Kathleen Williams, née Walsh.'

There was a short pause.

'Well, I'll be damned!' Betty said. 'What a fantastic blast from the past! Oh, my, I'm delighted to hear your voice, lovie. How on earth have you ended up in Ben's house?'

'It's a long story, but I'm staying in the locality for the remainder of the summer and I was wondering if you might like to see me?'

All of a sudden Kathleen felt incredibly vulnerable. This was a person she'd played with as a small child. Who was to say they'd have anything at all in common as adults? They mightn't have two words to say to one another.

'I'd love to, Kathleen,' Betty answered immediately.

'You would?'

'Of course, girl! Now, we need to work out the logistics. I mind my daughter Ruth's children while she works. Two boys aged three and one. Unfortunately they wouldn't fare too well in a car all the way to Dublin.'

'Why don't I come to you?' Kathleen said, as excitement sparked. 'I'm just a party of one and I've all the time in the world. If you tell me where you are, I could find a hotel and we could meet in the evening, if that's easier for you.'

'Well, now, wouldn't that be lovely?'

'Let's do it,' Kathleen said. 'I can find out from Ben where to go and the rest is easy. He mentioned you're in Connemara, right?'

'Yes – it's so beautiful here, Kathleen. I think you'll love it.'

'I know I will. How would you feel about me coming tomorrow? We could have dinner together at my hotel. Would that work for you?'

'There's a fabulous country-house hotel close to me owned by a dear friend. Ben knows the details. I don't think you'd get better.'

'Perfect. I'll give them a call.'

'Do indeed. Ben will give you my mobile number,' she said.

'I'll text you later once I have my accommodation organised.'

'Terrific!' Betty said. 'And thank you so much for calling me. I'm really looking forward to seeing you again.'

'Me too, Betty. 'Bye for now.' Kathleen handed the phone back to Ben.

She left twenty minutes later with the country-house hotel booked, including dinner for two, and her train ticket reserved.

Kathleen walked to the promenade where she perched on a weathered paint-peeling bench and gazed out at the ebbing and swelling, glistening aqua mass before her.

'I've done it, Jackson,' she said out loud. 'I brazenly knocked on her door. I'd never have done something like that if you hadn't set me that task.'

Although it wasn't cold, Kathleen suddenly felt chilled. Standing up, she decided to walk into the village and try to buy a small suitcase. The enormous one she'd arrived with was too cumbersome to take to Connemara.

A few minutes later, a pretty leather-goods shop caught her eye. Although knowing she should probably go to a chain store or somewhere with less luxurious stock, Kathleen decided to have a quick look. One bag caught her eye instantly. 'How much is this, please?'

'Ah, you've good taste!' said the assistant. 'It's a hundred and twenty euro. It's small enough to be used as cabin baggage and it weighs practically nothing. Although it's rather expensive, it's a good one.'

'I'm sure it's fabulously functional,' Kathleen said, 'but it's the zebra print that's selling it to me.'

'It's gorgeous all right,' the woman agreed.

'I probably shouldn't, but I'm going to take it,' Kathleen said, with a giggle. 'It'll make me smile every time I use it.'

'Good for you! Will I pack it for you?'

'Gosh, no! I want to wheel it.' Kathleen laughed.

She paid and left pulling the bag behind her. Needing to share her fabulous new purchase with someone, she decided to pay Lexie a visit.

'Oh, seriously! I've seen it all now,' Lexie exclaimed. 'You're a scream!'

'Don't you just love it?' Kathleen asked.

'It's the hot pink click-up handle and wheels that do it for me.'

'You're too arty and tasteful to appreciate this fully,' Kathleen said, with a snigger. 'Personally, I'm in love with it.'

'You won't lose it too easily and you won't be mugged with it as nobody else would even *steal* that bag it's so awful,' Lexie continued. 'In fact, I've come around to thinking it's probably a fantastic buy.'

'You're jealous!' Kathleen laughed.

'Where are you planning on taking it?'

'Don't look so worried, I'm not asking you to accompany it,' Kathleen joked. 'I went looking for my friend Betty and guess what?'

'You've found her?'

'Yes, ma'am, I certainly have. It turns out her son Ben is residing in her house with his partner, and Betty has moved to Connemara to be near her grandchildren. I'm going there on the train and staying in a country house.'

'Good for you! When are you going?'

'Tomorrow! I'm so excited.'

They chatted for a little while longer, but there were quite a few customers milling around the gallery. 'I'm going to leave you to it,' Kathleen said. 'I may not see you tomorrow, but I'll catch you when I get back.'

'How long are you staying?'

'Two nights, possibly more. Who knows? I'm a lady of leisure and my own boss, so anything could happen.'

'Would you text me when you arrive so I know you're safe?' Lexie asked. 'I don't want to fuss, but I'll worry if I don't know you're all right.'

'Bless you, darlin',' Kathleen said, kissing her. 'I'll be delighted to know someone's thinking about me and it'll spare me that awful lurching sensation when I'm standing in my single room as I realise I have nobody to share the moment with.'

Lexie rubbed her arm affectionately. 'You'll always have me from now on.'

'Thank you, dear.'

Kathleen left her and, pulling her new suitcase, headed for Cashel Square. 'Look at me now, Jackson,' she said. 'I think I've finally lost the plot. I'm dragging an empty wheelie-bag, which looks like one of your former patients styled by Barbie, and talking to the sky.' Giggling, she noted she was also laughing at her own jokes.

Chapter 35

THINGS COULDN'T HAVE BEEN BETTER AT THE gallery, business-wise. In fact, Lexie could barely believe the jump in figures from the same time last year. She knew everyone was very keen to point out that they were still in a recession, but it didn't seem to apply to her gallery.

Her mobile rang and Sam's name popped up. 'Hi,' she said evenly.

'How are you feeling?'

'I'm fine.'

'O-kay,' he said, sounding unconvinced. 'Listen, I've to go to London for three days. I know it's short notice but I only found out this minute. Why don't you come with me? We could do with a break away from everything.'

'When are you going?'

'Tomorrow evening. I've two flights held at the travel agent's. I can put mine through the company along with the accommodation, so it'll only cost us the price of your flight. What do you say?'

'I don't think so, Sam,' she said. 'I can't leave Kate in the gallery at such short notice and there'd be nobody to mind Tiddles.'

'Can't Kathleen feed him?'

'She's going to Connemara to visit an old friend she looked up.'

'Then we'll ask Ernie and Mary in number two, like always.'

'I can't leave my business at the height of the busiest season without prior arrangement. Kate is going to a wedding on Saturday too.'

'Couldn't you close the shop for one weekend?' Sam sounded tired.

'Sam, there are so many shops closing for ever right now, and I don't need my customers thinking I've gone belly-up. All it takes is for a few people to see the shutters down and assume I've gone.

Word spreads, especially when it's bad news. People mightn't come back.'

'It was just a thought,' he said. 'Don't worry about it. I'll see you at home later.'

'Sam, you're making me feel as if I'm being difficult here. You wouldn't close your entire computer firm for three days and jet off for a break.' There was a pause. 'Furthermore, I wouldn't ask you to. Please afford me the same consideration.'

'Lexie, I'm not my own boss. So your scenario is out of the question. But if you asked me to beg for some time off so we could spend some much-needed time together, I'd at least try.'

Lexie hung up, feeling torn. Was she being unreasonable? She hadn't much time to contemplate it as Amélie burst in like a lightning bolt. 'I've just come from Grandma's house,' Amélie spat. 'She told me what you did to her and Granddad last week. How could you upset them like that? I admired you and looked up to you. But obviously I had you *all* wrong.'

'Amélie—'

'Don't speak,' she said. 'According to Grandma, you couldn't think of anything worse than having a child of your own. Well, I'm here to let you know that I won't be bothering you any more. I won't invade your privacy and wreck your buzz by landing in on top of you. I'll take all my stuff out of your precious house and you won't see me again.'

'Amélie, wait! I don't want to be a mum but that doesn't mean I don't love being an auntie. I adore you and I thought you knew that.'

Amélie was striding up and down balling and unfurling her fists. Lexie could almost *see* the anger emanating from her.

'I used to think you loved me. I adored the fact I have a room in your house. I saw you as my ally when Mum and Dad were getting on my wick. But now I realise you hate kids, hate being disturbed and probably resent me for bursting in on top of your *perfect* life. You're not the person I thought you were, Lexie.'

'Amélie!' Lexie cried, rushing towards her.

But Amélie had fled.

Lexie grabbed the landline phone and stabbed at the buttons with anger-fuelled speed.

'Hello?'

'Mum! What did you say to Amélie?'

'Oh, Lexie, it's you.' She sounded dismissive.

'What did you say to her?'

'I told her the truth, that's all,' Penelope said.

'Expand,' Lexie fumed.

'Amélie popped in. She's feeling blue right now. I asked her why she ran away. Nothing seemed to be getting through to her about how precious she is and how much she means to your father and me. So I told her how heartbroken I am right now. I felt we could relate to one another. We're both sensitive creatures, Amélie and I.'

'What did you say to her, Mum?' Lexie shouted.

'Don't shout, Lexie. It's coarse and unladylike. Not to mention horribly aggressive.'

'Cut the shit, Mum,' Lexie said.

'Well, that's just charming. Foul language too.'

'Mum, tell me what you said before I hang up.'

'I only told her the truth, Lexie. How you practically ripped our hearts out when you called with Sam to tell us that not only were you not pregnant, as you'd led us to believe, but you were never having children and couldn't think of anything worse.'

'I never said that and you know it,' Lexie exploded.

'Didn't you?' Penelope asked. 'I thought you said you had enough going on in your life and children were superfluous to requirements.'

'Oh, my God, Mum, that is so unfair. You're really twisting this.'

'Am I?' Penelope shot back. 'So are you phoning to tell me you've changed your mind? Are you finally going to admit that you're wrong and you regret your selfishness?'

'Are you for real?' Lexie asked. She could feel the tears coming. Her stomach was churning. Fearing she might say something she'd regret, she hung up. Crumpling forwards onto her desk, she sobbed.

A group of six tourists walked into the gallery.

Lexie tucked her head under the desk, blew her nose, fished a small makeup compact from her bag and did her best to patch up her blotchy face. As she surfaced she realised the group were waiting for her beside one of Agata's larger paintings. 'Can I help you?' she asked.

'How much, if you please?' a man asked.

Lexie smiled through her pain and went into sales mode. Thankfully, their enthusiasm and apparent obliviousness to her misery spurred her on. She knew she was winning when they agreed to take the painting. Her mood was levered further when they chose two more. As soon as the payment had gone through, she took their details. 'I'll have them shipped immediately so they should arrive within two weeks,' she explained. Knowing her customers might not understand, she plucked a diary from her bag and began to point at dates.

They nodded, looking delighted.

By the time they left, Kate had arrived.

'That was a great sale,' Lexie said enthusiastically. 'Agata's largest one is gone too. I must give her a quick call. She'll be thrilled.'

'Eh, before you do, can I have a word?' Kate asked.

'Sure. Is everything all right?' Lexie asked. Her smile faded as she noticed how drawn and pale Kate looked.

'Everything's fine. It's just …' Kate looked her straight in the eye. 'You know your parents were suggesting you go on a cruise?'

'Yeah.'

'Well, I took out a Credit Union loan and I'm going travelling for a year. If I don't do it now I never will.'

'Wow,' Lexie said. 'I admire your impulsiveness.'

'I know you're probably a bit miffed with me, Lexie. I know the gallery is your main priority so I'll do my best to help you find a new assistant.'

'Don't worry about me. And please don't think I'm more concerned about the gallery than I am about you.' Luckily the landline rang, so she went to answer it. After that she needed to go to the bank, so she skipped around the corner.

'Hello there, Lexie,' said Larry from the fishmonger's. 'I'm headed for the bank, not that there's a massive wad of cash in my man bag.' He chuckled.

'I'd never have pictured you with a man bag, Larry,' Lexie managed.

'It's not really my style, is it?' He grinned. 'Or so I thought. I didn't want to say this in front of the other customers in the shop earlier but I met a lovely lady at Caracove Bay bingo hall a few weeks back. She went on holiday to Turkey and brought this for me as a present.'

'Swanky!' Lexie giggled, as he paraded around in a circle. 'So is this a special lady in your life?' she asked.

'I'm afraid to jinx it all, but I think so,' Larry said shyly.

'That's wonderful. I'm thrilled for you,' she said. 'Good for you, Larry.'

'I'm biding my time on this one,' he confided. 'I'm going to wine and dine her a little bit longer before I pop the question.'

'Wow! You really are smitten.'

'Ah, I'm not sixteen any more, Lexie, and Pauline isn't either, so what's the point in hanging around?'

'There isn't any,' Lexie said. 'You gotta grab life by the horns, Larry.'

'Too true!' he said, and trundled on past. It was the most hysterical sight, Larry in his white shop coat with the smart black satchel-style man bag hanging off one shoulder. His overweight waddle made it swing precariously as he headed for the bank.

Instantly Lexie thought to call Sam and fill him in. He'd love to hear Larry's good news. Her smile faded as she remembered Sam's irritation. Sighing, she waited a moment, not wanting Larry to notice her sudden sadness. Once she knew he was inside going about his business, she followed on into the bank and lodged her money.

Lexie felt as if a weight had landed on her shoulders, one that was becoming too much to bear. Her once simple and happy life had been tossed into disarray. As she walked back to the gallery it occurred to her that she had the power to change it. She just wasn't sure if her idea was the right one.

Kate was dealing with a customer but she glanced over her shoulder and waved. Lexie put the paying-in book away, let herself into the small back office and closed the door.

Dialling Sam's number, she hoped he'd pick up.

'Hello,' he answered, sounding hassled.

'Hi,' she said, a lot more forlornly than she'd intended. She cleared her throat and tried again. 'Hi, I've gone through things here and I really can't up sticks and leave. I'm sorry. But we need to talk this evening before you go.'

'I understand. It's fine. I know I was being a bit unreasonable earlier on. I'm just stressed and I hate this feeling of strain between us lately. I wanted to smooth things over, that's all.'

'I know, Sam, and I love you for it,' she said. 'I'll talk to you this evening. I'll pop into Larry and get us some fresh fish and we'll have a nice supper before you go away.'

'That sounds like a plan.'

Lexie had butterflies in her tummy as she hung up. She was well aware that her marriage was hanging in the balance right now. She was incredibly nervous of how Sam was going to react. She felt cold inside. This was the first time the warm cocooned feeling of their marriage had left her feeling so exposed and Lexie hated it.

Chapter 36

KATHLEEN WAS DELIGHTED WITH HER PLANS. SHE'D been to Connemara as a child but all she could recall were the vast mountain expanses and never-ending fields. Her sense of purpose was invigorating. When her phone rang, she answered cheerfully. 'Hello, Agata!'

'You sound happy,' said the younger woman. 'Do share the good mood!'

'I'm off for a little break in the west to visit an old pal,' Kathleen said.

'How lovely for you. As it happens I was calling to ask you a massive favour.'

'Sure,' Kathleen said.

'I need to get some art materials and visit a few places in Dublin city. I was wondering if by any chance Britta and I could stay at your apartment for a night?'

'Of course you can!' Kathleen said. 'I'd be delighted. You can come and use the place while I'm gone, or if you wanted me to mind Britta, I can be home by Monday.'

'Well, I had thought of coming on Sunday, spending the night and going into the city centre early on Monday morning.'

'Well, why don't you do that and spend Monday night with me too? That way we can have some dinner and share our news.'

'That sounds like a lovely idea,' Agata said. 'You don't think Lexie will mind me staying there with Britta, do you?'

'I shouldn't think so, dear. Besides, it's my place for the moment. Britta won't bother Sam and Lexie.'

'All right, then,' Agata said. They chatted for a while longer as

Kathleen explained about Betty and how long it had been since they'd seen one another.

By the time they said goodbye, Kathleen was even more excited about her little trip.

'I won't be coming home to an empty house now, Jackson,' she said. 'I know I can tell you things all the time, but it'll be great to have a two-way conversation for a change.'

It occurred to her as she was packing her suitcase that she hadn't heard from Rodger, so she called him. 'How are you today?'

'Better, thank you,' he said. 'I'm finding each day easier. I certainly need to move around. Sitting seems to be the worst thing. I have to remember to mobilise the hip as often as possible.'

'I feel your pain, Rodger, but you're doing exactly the right thing.'

She filled him in on her trip and promised to call him when she returned.

'Maybe you'd come to Howth on the DART again towards the end of the week when Agata and Britta have gone. We could have lunch together, if you'd like.'

'That would be wonderful, and it's my turn to come in your direction,' Kathleen said.

'Can I ask you to do something for me?' Rodger said.

'Sure, what is it?'

'Any time Claudia went away, she sent me a postcard. You know the sort, a cheesy one with idyllic pictures of the area. I haven't had any since she passed away. My children think they're a waste of time and money so I don't bother asking them.'

'Rodger, I'd love to write you a postcard!' Kathleen said. 'Text me your address.'

He laughed. 'We're mixing it up, as my son would say. A bit of old-world with the new. I'll gladly text you my address. Thanks for saying you'll do that. I'll look forward to getting something that isn't a bill or a begging letter.'

By early evening Kathleen was nicely tired. She'd given the already clean apartment another quick once-over to make sure it was shipshape for her guests. She was glad she'd had the foresight to buy the sofa-bed. She'd told Agata on the phone that she was most welcome to stay in her bed, but the younger woman had insisted she'd be happier in the spare box room.

'I'll bring my own duvet and I have Britta's travel cot. That way you don't need to fuss about changing sheets. Such a waste of time, if you ask me.'

Remembering she hadn't told Lexie about her visitors, Kathleen decided to pop upstairs and fill her in. She rang the bell and waited patiently. Seconds later Lexie pulled the door open. Kathleen had to stop herself gasping. Lexie looked drawn and exhausted.

'Hello, honey,' she said. 'I won't disturb you.'

'Please, come in,' Lexie encouraged her, standing back to make way.

'I don't want to appear rude, but I've a few things to do and I'm aiming for an early night,' Kathleen said firmly. 'I just want to let you know that Agata and Britta are spending the night on Sunday. I won't be here, so I was wondering if you might give them my key. I'll post it in your letterbox when I leave in the morning.'

'Sure,' Lexie said. 'It's kind of you to invite them.'

'You're not annoyed, are you?' Kathleen asked, anxious that Lexie might think she was taking liberties.

'Of course not. I'm delighted you and Agata have struck up such a lovely friendship.'

'It is lovely,' Kathleen agreed. 'I'll be home on Monday. They're going to spend that night with me too.' Kathleen wriggled her shoulders in glee. 'I'm sure she and Britta won't disturb you.'

'That's brilliant,' Lexie said. 'As it turns out, Sam is going to London for a few days so I'm more than happy to have the company downstairs. In fact, I might see if the girls will join me for an early supper.'

'Good plan,' Kathleen said, relieved that Lexie wasn't cross. 'I didn't know Sam was going away.'

'Neither did I,' Lexie said, rubbing her temples. 'It was a spur-of-the-moment thing.'

'I see. Well, I'll let you get on with making your dinner. Something smells divine.'

'Fish pie. It's Sam's favourite.'

'Yum,' Kathleen said. 'I'll see you when I return. Enjoy your evening.'

Lexie had just put the finishing touches to the table when Sam arrived home.

'I'm in here,' she called from the kitchen. 'Dinner's just ready.' She poured him a glass of wine.

'Hi,' he said, tossing his jacket over the back of a chair. 'Cheers.' He clinked glasses with her and tasted the wine. 'Delicious. Is that fish pie I can smell?'

'Certainly is,' she said. She knew her voice sounded ever so slightly too high. Her smile was probably too bright and she'd already had more than enough wine, considering she'd barely eaten all day. 'Sit down and I'll get it out of the oven.'

Before Sam could even loosen his tie and stretch out his legs, she'd banged the pie onto a mat and was digging a serving spoon into it. 'This is lovely,' she said loudly. 'Amélie is at the cinema and won't be home until later. She hates me, but that's fine. I'm sure she'll get over it.'

Sam put his hand on hers. 'Chill, Lex,' he said.

'Pardon? Uh, yes … Of course … I'm fine. I'm actually starving, that's all. I haven't eaten much today so I'm at that stage where I can barely talk I'm so hungry.'

She began to tuck into her pie, blowing on the steaming fish and attempting to eat.

'What's going on, Lexie?' Sam asked, ignoring the food and clasping his hands at the side of the table.

'What do you mean?'

'You're like a cat on a hot tin roof. You're so wound up I'm afraid you're going to self-combust there.'

She put down her knife and fork and closed her eyes for a moment. 'I think we need to reassess things, Sam,' she said. 'I'm not happy.'

'I know that,' he said sadly. 'In case you hadn't noticed, neither am I.'

'I've been doing a lot of soul-searching lately,' she said. 'I think we've been too rash. Well, I have … I've come to the conclusion that we should probably have a baby after all.'

'I see,' Sam said calmly. He didn't move a muscle. He simply stared directly at her and waited.

'Is that all you have to say?' she asked. 'What do you think? Are you happy or sad about it? Do you think it's a good plan? What?'

'I'm not surprised you're saying it,' he said. 'In fact, I thought this might be coming.'

'And what do you think?'

'That you're knee-jerk reacting. You've had a face full from your mother and me. I think you've slipped into panic mode and you don't know what you want any more.'

'There's a grain of truth in what you're saying. My mother has shaken me. There's no denying that. But maybe that's a good thing. Maybe she's right. I need to realise I'm on the cusp of being too old to change my mind.'

Sam took a slow sip of wine and put down his glass gently. Looking out of the window, he swallowed and remained silent.

'Sam, talk to me,' she said, throwing her chair back and standing up.

He stared up at her. 'Sam, please!' she yelled.

He didn't budge. He still didn't speak.

Hurt and humiliated, Lexie stormed out of the room and upstairs where she threw herself face down onto their bed.

Back downstairs, Sam sat in silence, staring out at the beautifully manicured park with the pretty flowerbeds. Tiddles was sitting on the windowsill taking it all in too. Momentarily Sam envied the cat. Oh, for a life of eating, sleeping and purring like Tiddles, he mused.

He'd arranged to meet Josh for beers this evening, but when

Lexie had phoned and said she needed to talk, he'd cancelled. Yet again he wished he wasn't at home. He'd felt like that a lot lately. He used to rush home but now he'd do anything to avoid being there. He'd put himself forward for all the foreign trips at work. Most of the others had children and were angling for time off, never mind junkets abroad, so he knew he'd be away quite a bit for the foreseeable future.

The trip to London would be stressful, hot and rushed. But anything would be better than the walking-on-eggshells existence he had here right now. He filled his glass and took it to the living room. He knew he ought to follow Lexie upstairs and try to tease out what on earth they should do to 'fix' the rest of their lives so they could live happily ever after. But he simply hadn't the energy. Kicking the living-room door shut, he sat on the sofa and stared into space. He knew Lexie better than anyone. He wanted a baby. But he was certain she didn't. If he went ahead and said they should have one, who knows what sort of a mess they'd end up in down the line? At least this way, if they split, no small people would be hurt in the process.

By the time she'd calmed down, Lexie felt as if she'd aged by ten years. Her head hurt, her tummy grumbled and she was stiff and chilly. There was still no sign of Sam. Normally when they'd had a barney, he'd been hot on her heels, ready to fix the situation. Now he was nowhere to be seen.

Not sure what to do, Lexie tumbled off the bed and staggered into the bathroom. Peeling off her clothes, she climbed into the shower and turned the heat up to an almost scalding temperature. As the water cascaded down her back and the room fogged up, the bathroom door opened. Sam walked in, closed the toilet lid and sat down heavily, his head in his hands.

Lexie turned the water off but remained inside the cubicle. 'What should we do, Sam?' she asked, unable to hide the pain in her voice.

'For the first time in my life, I actually don't have the first idea of what's right,' he said. 'I don't know if I have the answer to eternal happiness in the world, Lexie. But I know one thing for certain. If we don't start communicating a little better we're going to drift apart. If you honestly want a baby, that's fine. But I need to know that you're suggesting we become parents because *we* think it's right, not because of some deep-seated guilt.'

'That's not my reason for changing my mind,' Lexie said, emerging from the shower. Sam handed her a towel, which she wrapped around her damp body.

'Amélie thinks I'm an ogre. Maia is pregnant again and it's as if I'm on an island now.'

Sam listened silently.

'Look at Agata. She's an incredibly talented and imaginative artist. She'll go from strength to strength. Her work is ingenious. Little Britta is the light of her life.' Sam seemed deep in thought. 'Maia is a total ball-buster and one of the most successful lawyers around, yet she and Josh seem to cope flawlessly with Calvin ... Then I see Kathleen. She's such a warm and wise lady. From the moment I met her I was drawn to her.' Lexie sighed. 'But she's pretty much alone in this world now that Jackson's died.'

'She seems to be doing just fine,' Sam said.

'Yes, she's coping. But she's told me that she longed for a child. For years it was all she wanted. But it didn't happen and now she's like a lovely sparkling bouncy ball that hops from one situation to the next all alone.'

'Lexie, no matter what happens in life, we all end up on our own. For some it's all day, for others it's only an hour a day. But when push comes to shove, the only person who can make us happy is ourselves.'

Lexie fell silent again. She wanted to hide from Sam and the rest of the world.

'Let's think this over while we're apart,' Sam said.

Lexie hugged him. 'The main reason I want to have a baby is because I don't want to lose you,' she said, burying her face in his neck.

He held her and stared directly ahead.

'Those were the words I've longed to hear. But now that you're saying them I feel as if I've hoodwinked you into saying them.' Still holding her close, he stroked her hair. 'Let's have another shot at eating dinner, yeah?' he suggested. 'Then I'm going to have to pack and get to bed. I've a cruel start tomorrow. My taxi is arriving at four thirty in the morning because I'm on the red-eye to London.'

She nodded, looking miserable.

As she watched Sam go back down to reheat the fish pie, Lexie pulled on her dressing-gown and slippers. She combed her hair and studied her pale, drawn face in the mirror. Anything had to be better than this, she mused. Perhaps body clocks ticked in different ways and hers was showing its colours by slowly dismantling her entire life.

Dear Diary

I want to start again. I've had enough of being a rebel. Running away is too scary. I honestly thought I was going to be raped or murdered in France.

I feel so awful for shouting at Auntie Lex. I was so angry after being with Grandma, but now that I've had time to cool down, I realise I was too harsh on her. Grandma has always been a drama queen. It takes one to know one, right? Mum is always saying I'm just like her. That used to annoy me and I figured she was making it up. But I'm starting to see that there could be a teeny-tiny grain of truth in it.

I'm freaked about Lex and Sam. They're arguing all the time. I never noticed them being like this before, but maybe this is just the way it goes when you're married. Unless I meet a guy who is damn close to perfect and begs me to be his wife, I'm staying single. This marriage thing stinks.

Uncle Sam is going away again so I'll be by Auntie Lexie's side tomorrow and I'll tell her how awful I feel for being such a witch to her. She needs someone on her side. After all, she was right there with me when I needed her in France.

She's been so good to me. Nobody else I know would lie to the police and drag their butt across the sea to rescue me. She's the coolest and most sound person on the planet and I need to cut her some serious slack.

I'm going to a party tomorrow night. It's with some new people I met through the girls at school. It's in a flat so we can do what we like apparently. I'll have a couple of beers and then I'm getting my shit together. I want to make people proud of me. I'm going to get shedloads of points in my exams next year and go to business school. Working at the gallery has shown me what's out there. Helping organise the exhibition with Agata was mint, seeing it all come together and how the crowd flocked in and were awestruck by what we'd done. It was the bomb.

After the party tomorrow night I'll start organising my life.

And that's a promise.

Ciao

Amélie

Chapter 37

KATHLEEN RUSHED OUT TO THE TAXI JUST BEFORE six the next morning. 'That's not exactly a granny bag,' the driver commented.

'It's my little nod to my inner craziness,' Kathleen explained.

'Ah, you're American,' the driver said, as if that explained everything.

'Not totally,' she corrected. As they hurtled towards the station, Kathleen explained her situation.

'So you haven't seen this old doll since you were a kid,' the man said. 'You see, that's the difference between men and women. I'd never in a million years think of looking for a long-lost friend. I'd just go to the local bar and meet new people there.'

'I guess that's one way of doing things,' Kathleen said. 'But I'm very excited about seeing Betty.'

By the time she had found the correct train and settled into a seat, Kathleen was hungry. Luckily she'd taken Ben's advice and booked a ticket that included a full Irish breakfast. Less than twenty minutes after she'd set off, a waitress appeared with the dining trolley.

The meal was rather like aeroplane food but the cappuccino was surprisingly good, as was the packet of fresh brown bread. The newspaper had a couple of colourful weekend supplements, so Kathleen was perfectly entertained.

As the train pulled up at the station the announcer on the Tannoy instructed the passengers to remove all personal items.

Moments later Kathleen was sitting in a seat at the front of a bus that was winging its way to the Connemara House Hotel. As they left the city behind them, she was cast into a near-trance as she gazed at the incredible scenery. 'It's so long since I've experienced this,' she said in awe. 'It's so much more beautiful than I remember.'

'I come here day in, day out, and I never take it for granted,' agreed the driver. 'Depending on the weather, the colours around the mountains can go from vibrant to misty and mysterious.'

Today the sun was lighting the mauves and soft greens of the mountain range with such clarity it looked almost like a Hollywood set. Huddles of scribbly white sheep dotted the landscape, like tiny Fuzzy Felt creatures that had been strategically placed to make the scene pretty. Apart from a few tourists, there were no cars on the road. No people rushing by. No noises or commotion.

'It's like we've stepped back in time,' Kathleen breathed, 'to before the world took off and we all thought we should be in a constant hurry.'

As they drew up at the country-house hotel, the last of the cerise blooms of the rhododendrons welcomed her. Stepping off the bus, Kathleen inhaled the pure air gratefully. She waited until the bus had driven away and then, sitting on a bench, she drank in the serenity of her new surroundings. Tiny birds twittered and flew daintily from one pale green leafy branch to the next. The Atlantic Ocean sparkled in the sunlight as seagulls glided back and forth, occasionally diving to catch food.

The cars parked to the left of the main house indicated that there must be other guests, but Kathleen couldn't hear any human life. The pretty tumbling lilac blooms of the wisteria that covered the entire frontage of the hotel scented the air with a delicate fragrance.

The building was quaint and charming with a large oak door that had been propped open with an iron boot scraper in the shape of a hedgehog. Old-fashioned white-painted sash windows added to the country-chic feel. Kathleen went inside, pulling her bag behind her.

The warm aromas of fresh bread and beeswax assailed her. The décor was a mix of antique and contemporary colours. The walls and floors were a neutral shade of honey and the brightly chequered armchairs, rugs and bowls of peonies added welcome splashes of colour.

'You're most welcome to our hotel,' a young woman in a navy skirt suit said.

'Thank you. It's beautiful,' Kathleen said, as she gazed around.

'I'm glad you like it. My name is Clara and I'm a member of the Fitzgerald family. We've lived here for the last three generations and we're proud to share our home.'

'How wonderful.' Kathleen gave her name.

'Can I offer you tea and scones? Your room is ready so I can ask my brother to take your bag up. But I'm guessing you'd like a little snack after your journey.'

'That sounds gorgeous,' Kathleen said. Clara showed her to a room that was dotted with soft golden sofas, plump cushions, and shiny wooden coffee tables.

'This is our drawing room and you're most welcome to sit here. Alternatively we have a gorgeous walled garden just to the right of the house. It's particularly lovely on a warm day like today. I've brand-new tables and chairs out there if you'd like to check it out.'

'I'd love to,' Kathleen said. 'I could do with a breath of fresh air after being cooped up on the train.'

'Good idea. Follow me.'

Kathleen was expecting it to be a little breezy and chilly, but as she sat on the decorative wrought-iron chair, with the pink and white gingham cushion, she felt as if she'd landed in Paradise. Clara returned with a wooden tray laden with delicious goodies.

'Wow! That looks almost too good to eat,' Kathleen said. 'Is all this for me?'

'Ah, they're only tiny,' Clara said. 'A mere mouthful in each one. I decided to bring you our afternoon tea selection. I thought you'd enjoy it.'

The tiny smoked-salmon sandwiches were interspersed with egg and cress and dainty cucumber ones. 'I'll leave this with you,' she said. Kathleen clapped her hands and giggled as Clara handed her a small brass handbell.

'Tinkle and I'll come trotting,' she promised.

Kathleen poured tea into the porcelain cup and took great pleasure in using the tiny silver tongs for the sugar lumps. She made great headway with the delicate sandwiches before polishing off the bite-sized scones and miniature butterfly buns.

A couple passed. 'Enjoy your stay,' the woman said, in a distinct New York accent. 'We're just leaving and can't wait to return.'

'I've only been here a short while and I've fallen in love with the place already,' Kathleen admitted. 'Safe journey.'

Being alone in the walled garden was oddly comforting. Kathleen drank her tea, then wandered about inspecting the plants. Someone with a true passion for gardening was clearly in charge. Each section was divided into colours. One corner boasted predominantly pink shades, which moved towards burnt orange then yellow.

'Sorry to barge in with my wheelbarrow,' said a voice behind her. Spinning around, Kathleen was met with an older yet just as friendly version of Clara. 'I'm Jenny, allegedly the lady of the manor, but I'm a lot happier in my old gardening trousers with my trusty barrow and trowel.'

'I'm Kathleen. I've come to visit with a very old friend who happens to live near here now.'

'Who's your friend?'

'Betty Clarke was her maiden name, but I've just realised I don't know her married name. She's originally from Caracove Bay.' Kathleen looked doubtful.

'Ah that's Betty White. Indeed I do know her. She's a great woman for sharing gardening clippings. She often comes here for tea with her grandchildren.'

Kathleen explained why she'd ended up in Connemara.

'That's just fantastic,' Jenny said. 'Well, I can vouch for Betty. She's a fantastic character. You'll have a great evening with her, I can assure you.'

'I'm so excited about seeing her again. I met with her son, Ben, and he advised me to come here,' she said.

'Glad he's doing my marketing!' She chuckled. 'Did Ben tell you that George, his partner, is my son?'

'I had no idea,' Kathleen said, laughing. 'It's lucky I didn't say anything bad about him. I really need to remember to watch my Ps and Qs around here.'

'Ireland is still a very small island. Everyone is related to someone. Never say a word unless you're willing to say it at the top of your voice through a megaphone.'

'That's sound advice.'

'I'd better plant my little primulas before they shrivel up and die in the wheelbarrow,' she said.

'I'm going to settle into my room, see you later on,' Kathleen said.

As she went back into the hotel she was smiling. Ever since she'd stepped off the plane from Orlando, she had been meeting warm, friendly and genuine people. Not for the first time, she thanked her lucky stars that Jackson had insisted she come here.

Moments later, Kathleen had an urge to bounce on the bed. The vast four-poster was draped with the thinnest, wispiest layers of lightest pink voile with tiny dark pink embroidered butterflies.

Unzipping her bag, she pulled out her dress for dinner and hung it in the antique walnut wardrobe. The ensuite was beautifully presented with gorgeous lace-trimmed towels. This, Kathleen mused, was the difference between a massive impersonal hotel chain and a country house. All the personal touches delighted her.

Remembering Lexie, Kathleen pulled out her mobile phone and sent a quick text to say she'd arrived. The fan of magazines on the coffee table caught her eye and before she knew it Kathleen had been sitting and flicking for over an hour.

It was nearing dinnertime, so instead of rushing or fussing, Kathleen decided to luxuriate in a deep bubble bath. 'You'd love this place, Jackson,' she said. Her voice echoed in the tiled surface of the steamy bathroom. 'Hold my hand this evening, won't you? This could be a horrific mistake. Betty might be a bore. She might be loud as a drain and full of obnoxious opinions. What will I do if she's cross and cranky?' The lapping of the water and the shifting of the suds in the bath seemed to answer. 'Okay, I'll stop with the negativity, Jackson. I'm sure she's a great old gal. Her son seemed very normal. Plus Jenny's a darling and they're friends, so it'll be fine, right?'

Kathleen wound the chain from the plug around her big toe and pulled it free. Gurgling noises made her grin. It was a long time since she'd heard old pipes groaning in this way. It reminded her of the stand-alone bath that used to wash every one of them at number three Cashel Square once upon a time.

Soon she was slipping into her jersey wrap dress and high heels. 'I might be seventy-five but I can still rock killer heels, eh, Jackson?' she said to her reflection.

As she descended the stairs she heard voices at the reception desk. She broke into a wide smile when she spotted Betty. Although almost seventy years had passed, she still recognised her flame-haired friend. Gone were the flowing unruly curls. Instead this elegant woman had a slicked-back ponytail with the same porcelain skin.

'Kathleen!' Betty said, rushing to the foot of the staircase.

'Betty!' She hurried down the last few stairs. They embraced and stood apart, still holding hands. 'Jeez, Louise, you look *good*, honey!'

'So do you. You have the lovely sun-kissed look that non-Irish citizens enjoy.'

'I've skin like a rhino, you mean?' Kathleen laughed.

'Not quite! I'm actually overwhelmed to see you. You really haven't changed much.'

'Neither have you, Betty. I'd know you anywhere. It's amazing that, no matter what our poor old bodies and skin have been through, the eyes remain the same.'

'Let's go and get a glass of something nice.'

Jenny greeted Kathleen and led the way to the drawing room. 'It's a lot quieter in here than it is in the bar,' Jenny said. 'I reckon a glass of bubbly is in order. What do you think, ladies?'

'That sounds wonderful for me,' Kathleen said. 'Betty?'

'Delicious!'

'So tell me everything,' Kathleen said, as she sank into the chair opposite Betty. 'I know from Ben that you have a son and two daughters and that you look after your grandchildren.'

Kathleen needn't have worried about conversation or a sense of awkwardness with Betty. The night flew. Both women went from belly laughs to dabbing their eyes when Kathleen told her old friend about Jackson.

'Poor you,' Betty said. 'It sounds as if he had a really tough few years.'

'We made the best of it, and we were lucky he had as much time as he did.'

'My husband was a good man,' Betty said, 'but he was very set in his ways and most certainly didn't advocate any kind of alternative living. Ben was never able to tell James he was gay. I was a housewife in the old-fashioned sense of the word. I never worked outside the home.'

'But you were happy?' Kathleen asked hopefully.

'Yes, I was,' Betty said. 'But I'm enjoying this part of my life too. It's different – I'm able to get out and about more. I feel truly blessed.'

'I know Jackson is still with me all the time,' Kathleen said. 'From the second I arrived on Irish soil I've met one angel after another. Lexie and her husband, Sam, who live at number three now, have been so generous and kind. I have to remind myself that I haven't known them for ever.'

'That's lovely,' Betty said. 'I'd say you'll stay in touch now too.'

'I hope so,' Kathleen said. 'I've gained a little granddaughter along the way also,' she said, and explained about Britta and Agata.

It was after eleven by the time Jenny managed to join them. 'It's been one of those non-stop evenings,' she said, dragging a chair to the table. 'Clara is bringing me a gin and tonic. Sometimes that's the poison I require.'

'So,' Betty said, 'we've had the most fantastic catch-up, haven't we?' She looked at Kathleen.

'It's been wonderful. I'll admit I was begging Jackson to hold my hand as I left my room earlier on. It suddenly occurred to me that we mightn't have a single thing in common.'

'I've come to the conclusion that people don't really change that much,' Jenny said. 'Of course we all grow up – life and responsibility teach us a hell of a lot – but at the end of the day, we're still the same people.'

'Even though we were eight years old last time we knew one another, I have to agree with Jenny,' said Betty. 'Apart from the high heels and the sophisticated dress, you're still the girl who marched into the murkiness of your basement ahead of me and stood with her hands on her hips defying the darkness.'

Kathleen laughed. 'Lexie and Sam have done a wonderful job of renovating it. If you feel like having a little trip, the two of you might come visit me?'

'That would be a bit of fun, wouldn't it, Jenny?' Betty said. 'We could travel up on the train. Ben and George are always badgering us to come and we don't do it half enough.'

'All right. It's a promise. We'll have a Golden Girls day out!' Jenny agreed.

'Morris might even drive us if we play our cards right,' Betty said.

'As long as he doesn't expect us to go in the hearse. I'm not going near one of those until I have to.'

'Whoa! Hold up a second,' Kathleen said in amusement. 'Who is Morris and why would he want you to travel in a hearse?'

'He's Betty's fancy man,' Jenny teased. 'His family own the local undertaker's.'

'I'll never forget seeing him pull up outside my house,' Betty said. 'I had to touch up my makeup in the hall mirror before opening the front door. I was actually crying with laughter.'

'Morris isn't blessed with a sense of humour and has reached the ripe old age of seventy-five still living with his mammy,' Jenny added. 'Old Mrs Monahan must be tipping towards a hundred and she's still shuffling around cooking for Morris and ironing his shirts.'

'That's kind of sweet,' Kathleen observed.

'You must be joking,' Betty said, with a grin. 'The woman is like a ninja. Four foot tall with more wrinkles than a raisin and a brain as sharp as a Stanley blade. She'd strangle you with the Hoover flex if you tried to get your claws into her Morris.'

'So what possessed you to date him?' Kathleen wondered.

'He was persistent,' Betty said. 'It was a long time since any man had pursued me, and I decided it wouldn't do any harm to share a meal with him. I'll never forget it. My clothes reeked of incense and lily-of-the-valley afterwards. He sat like a mannequin for the entire evening. As he dropped me home he said it was the best date he'd ever been on.'

'That's because it was the only one!' Jenny giggled.

'But the worst part is that he asked me to promise not to tell his mammy!' Betty said.

The three women laughed until they cried, and Kathleen added, 'He must've thought you were as much fun as dating Joan Rivers. All he had to compare you to was a corpse. I'd say you're on to a winner there.'

'That's what I said,' Jenny agreed, holding her hands up dramatically. 'Mammy can't possibly last much longer and they must be loaded. Funerals cost a fortune, as we all know.'

It was two thirty by the time Kathleen finally crawled into bed. She'd drunk far too much wine and knew she'd pay for it next day. But as she lay down, instead of the usual intense, gripping pain, she felt a tiny kindling of hope in her soul. The two women had demonstrated such warmth and positivity that Kathleen couldn't help being drawn to them. It transpired that both had survived widowhood and seemed to have found a new equilibrium. A part of her wanted never to move away from the love she and Jackson had known. But in her heart of hearts she knew he would hate her to waste the time she had left mourning the past.

Chapter 38

LEXIE WOKE WITH A START. SITTING BOLT UPRIGHT, she stared at the alarm clock and cursed. She'd thought she hit the snooze button but she had unwittingly turned the damn thing off. With Sam gone to London there'd been nobody to give her a nudge. She pulled on her frilly shower cap – she hadn't enough time to wash her hair.

The gallery would probably be busy as it was Saturday and Kate was away at a wedding. Normally Lexie didn't mind covering the weekend shift alone. Sam would help out and most of her customers were patient enough if there was a queue. An art gallery didn't normally attract the sort who expected to be zoomed through at the cash desk.

Today, for the first time ever, she briefly considered not opening at all and berated herself for not accompanying Sam. She thought of Amélie and her heart ached. She knew her niece was fiery, but she'd really hoped they'd be friends again this morning. Poking her head into Amélie's room, she decided to pretend everything was cool and hope she'd go along with that.

'Hi, lovie,' she said. 'Sorry to wake you, but Kate is away and I need you to come and help me today, remember?'

Amélie stirred and groaned. 'Sure thing,' she said. Sitting up, she stared at Lexie with bedhead hair. 'Auntie Lex?'

'Yes?'

'I'm so sorry,' she said. She staggered out of bed and wrapped her arms around Lexie. 'I'm a cow and I hope you can forgive me. You always back me up and I should've done the same for you. I know you and Sam are having a shit time at the moment.'

'Oh,' Lexie said, in shock. 'I didn't think you'd noticed.'

'I'm not three,' Amélie said drily. 'Anyhow, hopefully you guys will sort it and I'm going to get myself together too. I want to be a business person like you so I need to knuckle down.'

'Are you kidding me?' Lexie said delightedly. 'You've no idea how happy that makes me. I'm so proud of you, darling. But I really need you today, so let's go and rock this gallery, right?'

'You got it!' Amélie said.

A short while later, as they went out of the front door, they bumped into Agata and Britta. 'Good morning, you two,' Lexie said.

'Hello,' Agata said. 'Did Kathleen mention we were coming?' she asked, blushing.

'Yes.' Lexie thumped her forehead with the heel of her hand. 'She did, of course. And she asked me to give you keys. I'm such a featherhead. I'm running a bit late so I'm hassled. Don't mind me,' she apologised.

'No problem!' Agata said, looking relieved. 'We weren't meant to be here until tomorrow, but I have a few things to do.'

'As a matter of fact, I was going to ask you and Britta to join me for dinner one evening. How about tonight?'

'That would be lovely, Lexie.'

'It's just us. Sam is away so we can suit ourselves pretty much. If the sun keeps shining we could eat in the garden. That way you can put Britta to bed if you need to and we can still hear her through the back door. It'll be a girls' night,' she said, putting her arm around Amélie.

'I'm going to a party, actually. Hope that's cool?'

'Of course,' Lexie said. 'So it's only the three of us. That still okay?'

'Superb!' Agata said. 'I'll really look forward to it.'

'I'll be home by six thirty at the latest. I'll grab something for us to eat on my way home later.'

'I'll do dessert.'

'Let me get the keys to the basement,' Lexie said. She ran back up the steps and grabbed the keys for Agata. Britta waved her chubby hand and grinned.

''Bye, Britta,' she said, feeling ridiculously emotional that the baby had engaged with her.

As they walked swiftly to the gallery, Lexie tried to imagine what it would be like if Britta were hers. When Amélie was that age, Lexie wasn't even in the zone of thinking about being a parent so it had all gone over her head. She had vague recollections of baby Amélie being wheeled around restaurants and bobbed on knees during Christmas dinners, but none of it had seemed like a big deal. Now that she was considering bringing a baby into her life, it all seemed vitally important.

The day flew at the gallery. Lexie was so impressed with Amélie that she gave her a large tip.

'This is so much money!' Amélie exclaimed.

'You deserve it,' Lexie said. 'When you work hard you get paid. Simple!'

They walked home and Lexie began to cook the meat she'd bought that afternoon.

'See you!' Amélie said, as she wafted by leaving a trail of cologne in her wake.

''Bye, sugar plum,' Lexie called. She peeped out and saw Amélie bouncing down the road wearing a gorgeous little mini dress. She looked like a fashion model.

Agata and Britta waved from outside and Lexie rushed to open the door. 'Hi, ladies,' she said, kissing Agata, then Britta. The baby waddled around babbling as Lexie placed a gorgeous feta cheese and watermelon salad on the table.

'Make yourself useful and open the bottle of wine in the fridge,' she said. 'That cake looks divine. It's lovely outside – are you happy to eat out?'

'Um, totally,' Agata said, popping a piece of watermelon into her mouth.

The meat and salad complemented each other beautifully. After a large glass of wine, Lexie finally began to relax. It was a relief not to have to talk about anything too taxing. Agata was such easy company and the baby was a constant source of entertainment.

By the time the sun went down and the evening became chilly, Agata said she'd hit her bed. 'I can't believe this little one has stayed awake for so long.'

'She's a little gem,' Lexie said.

When Agata and Britta had gone, Lexie brought all the dishes into the kitchen and stacked them in the dishwasher. She switched off the lights and remembered not to bolt the front door so Amélie could get in later. She'd leave her bedroom door ajar so she'd hear her come in. She never slept properly until she knew Amélie was home safely. The landline rang. Lexie groaned and considered letting it go to the answer machine, then picked it up.

'Is that Lexie?' a young girl's voice said frantically.

'Yes? Who is this, please?'

'I'm Yvonne. I'm a friend of Amélie's. We're at a party. She was talking to this guy. He was really pushy and we didn't like the look of him. The guy who owns the flat told him to go but we reckon he spiked Amélie's drink.'

'Where is she now?' Lexie asked, as fear shivered through her. 'How do you know he spiked her drink? What's she doing?'

'She started going all floppy and her eyes were rolling. She slumped off the chair and we couldn't wake her—'

'Oh, Jesus. Did you call an ambulance?'

'Yeah, she's gone off in it. She told me she was staying with you so I got your number from her phone. She hadn't any credit so I'm using the phone at Jake's flat.'

'Thank you, Yvonne. I'll follow her to the hospital right now.'

'She's gone to St Mary's.'

Lexie put the phone down and panicked. She couldn't drive after the wine, so she rang a taxi and pulled some clothes on. She was in the car by the time she managed to get hold of Dee and Billy.

'Which hospital is she in?' Billy asked.

'St Mary's.'

'Oh, shit – that place is meant to be like something from *M*A*S*H*.'

Lexie hung up and begged the driver to hurry.

When Lexie ran into Accident and Emergency, the usual weekend carnage was beginning. Drunk and bewildered people staggered around, and a man with what looked like a stab wound groaned from a trolley.

Lexie forced herself not to collapse in panic. If anything happened to Amélie she didn't know what she'd do.

Minutes later Billy and Dee appeared.

'Any news?' Billy asked.

'Nothing yet,' Lexie said. 'I've notified the receptionist that I'm here. She said a doctor will speak to us when they know more.'

A minute later a doctor appeared, looking grave. 'Are you Amélie's family?'

'We're her parents and this is her aunt,' Billy said.

'We've performed a gastric lavage, or stomach pump,' he said. 'She'd ingested a small amount of beer and what we reckon were several Rohypnol tablets.'

'Oh, God, that's the date-rape drug, right?' Lexie said.

The doctor nodded. They'd administered an antidote. 'She's a lucky girl. Her friends reacted quickly and thankfully she hadn't drunk much alcohol.'

'When can we see her?' Dee asked, shaking.

'We need to make sure she's stable and get some fluids into her.'

They thanked the doctor and huddled in a corner of the waiting area.

By the time they were allowed in, Amélie was propped up against pillows with drips in either arm. In a hospital gown, she looked like a tiny child. Her pallor and large, frightened eyes broke Lexie's heart. She hung back and allowed Dee and Billy to hug her first.

Amélie peeped past her parents. 'I'm so sorry,' she managed. 'I wanted to make you all proud. I didn't want to cause more trouble.'

'You didn't know,' Dee said. 'We're just relieved you're all right.'

Lexie left Dee and Billy with their daughter and made her way home. She called Sam's mobile and wasn't surprised when it went directly to his voicemail. She left a brief message telling him what had happened and said she'd call again when she had further news.

Lexie thought morning would never come. Very early, she heard Britta's voice from the garden, so she went down and knocked on the door.

'You're up very early,' Agata said, with a smile. Her face clouded as soon as she saw Lexie's. 'What's happened?' Lexie told Agata about the eventful night and how scary it had all been.

'I'm so shocked. That poor girl has been through so much lately, hasn't she?'

'She's certainly had a lot of growing up to do, that's for sure. But I think she's going to be fine. She's a good girl and she'll come out the other side.'

The two women drank coffee and watched Britta waddle about. Moving out to the early-morning sunshine, they sat on the comfy chairs.

'She's so chilled out,' Lexie said in admiration. 'You're amazing with her.'

'Well, she's my little treasure, aren't you?' Agata kissed her nose. 'She's no trouble. I'd be lost without her.'

Britta was happily munching a mini rice cake while picking individual blades of grass and examining them intently.

'Kathleen is so kind,' said Agata. 'She left a note to say she's been shopping and to help myself to the cupboards.'

'You couldn't meet a nicer person,' Lexie agreed. 'From the first second I met her I knew I was going to get on with her. I admire her hugely too. It takes a lot of courage to jet halfway across the world by yourself.'

'Totally,' Agata agreed. 'I really hope to stay in touch with her after the summer.'

'Me too,' said Lexie.

As the heat from the sun warmed the air, Lexie shrugged off her cardigan. Britta watched and did the same thing. Both women giggled.

'She's so cute!'

'Thanks. I think so too.' Agata laughed.

'Aren't you going to ask me why I don't have children?'

'No,' Agata said immediately. 'But if you want to tell me, feel free.'

Lexie laughed. 'I always thought I was a straight shooter, but you'd give me a run for my money. Sam and I had it all worked out. We never wanted children. We agreed on it. And it wasn't an issue for us until recently.'

'What's changed?'

'Well, it's sort of complicated ...' Lexie told Agata about her mother and the misunderstanding, and how the entire world, Sam included, seemed to think her approaching birthday should signal baby season.

'I can see both sides of the argument,' Agata said. 'Your mother wants you to be certain you won't regret it if your fertility goes. That's hardly unusual coming from a mother, if you think about it. What you really need to discover is whether you're deciding *not* to have a baby just to oppose your mother because she clearly irritates you.'

Lexie rubbed her temples. 'I fully admit I can be as stubborn as a mule. But the fact of the matter is that Sam and I had it all sorted in our heads.'

'Then forget it. Don't give it another thought,' Agata said matter-of-factly. 'If you don't engage in constant conversations about the subject, your family and friends will have to stop too.'

'I'm doubting myself now. Sam and I aren't in a great place at the moment either. We never used to argue and lately I'm as wound up as a spring. I'm afraid we're not on the same page just now.'

'That's hardly surprising,' Agata said. 'All the drama with Amélie can't have helped. And she's not even Sam's family. He's very patient but I can imagine he's getting pretty tired of the hassle.'

'I'd say he's really at a point where he thinks my entire family should be shipped off to a remote island for ever.'

'Maybe you should let him know you get that. Give him a life raft.'

'All the colours of the trees and the sea are so much brighter now,' Lexie mused. 'It's as if I'm seeing the world afresh. I don't know what I would've done if Amélie had died.'

'It doesn't bear thinking about,' Agata agreed.

'As I said, I have a feeling in my waters that she'll be okay now.'

'You always go by your gut,' Agata said. 'You did with me. You did with Kathleen. You've a strong sense of what's right, Lexie.'

Lexie had always known her own mind. It was only lately that she'd started questioning herself. She needed to get back to being the person she'd always been.

She decided to leave the gallery shut that Sunday. She hadn't the heart to go in and pretend she was fine. She phoned Billy and discovered Amélie was being discharged from hospital the following day: they wanted to keep her for another twenty-four hours for observation.

'Fingers crossed she'll be released tomorrow evening,' she said.

'Yeah, but she wants to go to your place. Is that cool?'

'Of course. Whatever helps,' Lexie said.

'The thing is, Dee and I need to talk to her. Would you mind if we collect her and we'll all pop over?'

'Sure. I'll be here.'

As soon as she'd hung up, her phone rang again. 'Hello?'

'Hey.'

'Sam!'

'I've just got your message. How's poor Amélie?'

'She's going to be fine, but she gave us a serious shock.'

'I'll say.'

'Listen, Sam, I was thinking of calling my mother to say that I'll go ahead with the party idea. We all need a positive focus at the moment. Something frivolous to take the heat off Amélie and stop my parents looking at me as if I've murdered the next generation before it's even born.'

'Good plan,' he said, then paused. 'Lex … I wish I was with you. I need to hold you. I miss you.'

'I miss you too,' she said sadly. As they were about to hang up,

Lexie said something that surprised her as much as Sam. 'I think I want to have your baby.'

There was another pause. A brief one, but a pause all the same.

'Did you have to tell me this when I'm hundreds of miles away from you?' he said quietly.

'Sorry,' she said.

'Don't be. Listen, we need to talk some more and know that we're doing this for all the right reasons. I love you, Lexie, and I know we'll make the right decision for us. I'll be back tomorrow evening. Let's talk then.'

Chapter 39

KATHLEEN ENJOYED EVERY LAST MOMENT OF HER time in Connemara. She visited the quaint fishing village of Roundstone where all that separated her from the sea was a higgledy-piggledy stone wall. The twinkling of the sunlight on the calm waters helped distinguish them from the flawless blanket of azure sky.

She happened upon a café immaculately painted in shades of sea blue and cream. The wooden chairs and round tables spilled from inside onto the pavement. A young waitress took her order and confirmed that they sold stamps, so Kathleen turned the metal carousel bursting with postcards and scanned the different designs.

Being left behind was never easy. She knew Jackson would approve of her writing to Rodger. All the same, it felt a little odd as she began to write to another man …

> Dear Rodger
> Hope you like the pictures of the wild west. I think you'd enjoy it here. From one dinosaur to another, I trust you will appreciate this card! I know it's not the same coming from me, but it's better than none at all. Hope to see you soon, all the best,
> Kathleen

She paid for the card and a stamp, then posted it in a nearby box. She sincerely hoped the arrival of the card wouldn't upset Rodger. She understood he longed to receive a card, but she was afraid it might bring a bitter-sweet sadness as it wasn't from Claudia.

All too soon it was time for Kathleen to return to Caracove Bay. Betty and Jenny had agreed to visit her in two weeks' time.

She didn't feel ready to tell the ladies, but that weekend would be Jackson's birthday too. Kathleen knew she'd be on tenterhooks waiting to see if her rainbow materialised.

The train journey was oddly quick and she wondered why going home always seemed quicker than leaving. Just as she was about to wallow in the fact that she now lived alone, she remembered Agata and Britta were waiting for her. Sighing happily, she found a cab outside the train station.

Kathleen knocked on her own front door, and Agata opened it with Britta in her arms.

'Hello, girls!' Kathleen said.

'Hi!' Britta shouted, as she jigged in her mother's arms. 'Hi! Hi!'

'She's talking!' Kathleen exclaimed, dropping her bag and putting her arms out to the baby.

'She's suddenly become really chatty.' Agata giggled. 'She mostly babbles in an incomprehensible way, but every now and then she says something I can understand.'

'And she has such a gravelly little voice. It's just the sweetest thing.'

Britta went to Kathleen and smiled broadly. 'Ooh, look at your beautiful pearly whites!' Kathleen said approvingly. 'So, tell me about your weekend so far,' she said.

'It's been unusual,' said Agata.

'Oh?'

'There was a terrible shock concerning poor Amélie,' she said, and filled Kathleen in on what had happened.

'Oh, dear Lord, how dreadful,' she said. 'Thank goodness she's okay now.'

'I think she's still in shock, poor thing.'

'How have you and Britta been?'

'All good. Now, tell me. How was your friend Betty? Did you two get along okay? I've made us some Swedish meatballs and *Jansson's frestelse*. It's a delicious potato gratin dish and I've a bottle of white wine chilling.'

'You're such a thoughtful girl to do that for me. I'm a little overcome.'

'I didn't mean to upset you,' Agata said, looking guilty.

'Don't mind me!' Kathleen said, flapping a hand in front of her face. 'I'm being a silly old fool. I guess I've become accustomed to being alone. So having you gals to come back to and a home-cooked meal on top … well, it's just divine. Thank you, dear.'

They sat and enjoyed their meal as Britta busied herself with a little stacking game on the floor. Chirping and babbling, it was clear she was just as happy as the two women.

By the time the baby was rubbing her eyes and looking for her bottle, Kathleen was ready for bed too. 'I think I'll hit the sack,' she said. 'By the way, my friends Betty and Jenny are coming in two weeks' time. They'll stay with their sons but I'd like to have them here for dinner.'

'They sound lovely,' said Agata, yawning.

'They are. Maybe you'll come and meet them.'

'Let's see how you go,' Agata said. 'You don't want to be bombarded with people.'

'I told them all about you and Britta,' Kathleen said proudly. 'It's lovely to have my own little person to introduce into conversations.'

'We're lucky to have met one another,' Agata confirmed.

Chapter 40

NEXT MORNING, AS LEXIE WAS GETTING SORTED IN the gallery, Kathleen arrived pushing Britta's buggy. 'Greetings, ladies!' she said cheerfully.

'Hi! Hi! Hi!' Britta shrilled, to everyone's delight.

'Hello!' they answered in unison. Kate rushed to coo over Britta and Lexie hugged Kathleen.

'How was your trip to the west?'

'Wonderful,' Kathleen said. 'Betty and her friend Jenny, who owns the country-house hotel, were such fabulous company. I thoroughly enjoyed myself. You'll get to meet them – they're coming up in two weeks.'

'That sounds like a resounding success,' Lexie said. 'I'm delighted for you.'

'Agata told me about Amélie,' Kathleen said quietly. 'I'm so sorry. Have you heard anything this morning?'

'Yeah,' Lexie said, sighing. 'I could've lived my whole life without experiencing that. It was terrifying. She's coming out of the hospital this evening.'

'Will she go back home?' Kathleen asked.

'Not yet,' Lexie said, biting her lip. 'She wants to come to Cashel Square for a couple more days.'

'But you can't really care for her at the moment. Surely she needs round-the-clock attention for a while.'

'I was going to take a few days off,' Lexie said. 'I considered asking Agata to stand in here at the gallery. That's where you come in. Would you be able to mind little Britta in the afternoons? I know Kate can definitely do the mornings. Amélie and I will be around too, so maybe the four of us could hang out.'

'That sounds superb,' Kathleen said. 'I'm sure Agata would jump at the chance to have a bit of time in the gallery, and I'd love nothing more than being a proper grandma for a week.'

'Thanks, Kathleen. I knew I could count on you,' Lexie said.

Lexie made all her calls to activate the plan. Then she texted Sam and asked if he minded Amélie staying for a bit longer.

That's fine but we need some alone time too. Our situation needs your attention also ...

Lexie texted back that she totally understood and thanked Sam for being so great.

When she looked up, Kathleen and Britta were on the point of leaving. 'I'm going into Dublin on the DART,' Kathleen said. 'I'm going to show Britta Trinity College so that she knows there are wonderful places she can aspire to attend in later years.'

'No harm in raising her expectations at a young age, I suppose. Even if she can't talk much yet.' Lexie grinned.

'I'm trying to fit in as much grandparenting as I can in a short space of time.'

'Enjoy it, and I'll see you later on.'

Lexie explained the plans for the rest of the week to Kate, who was incredibly supportive. 'I'm happy to do as much time as you need. I have so many travelling things to buy that any extra hours you can throw my way are much appreciated. If Agata needs me to hang on for a bit when we're busy, that's no problem.'

'Thanks, Kate. You're a star,' Lexie said. Her phone rang again. Lexie groaned. She wasn't going to get a minute to do any work today.

'Hello, Lexie,' Penelope said. 'I've just spoken to poor Dee. She's putting a brave face on it, but are you sure you should be whisking Amélie off to your house? She's not your daughter, after all. In fact, you've made it crystal clear you don't like children yet you're taking over Dee and Billy's.'

'Mum,' Lexie said, trying with all her might to remain calm, 'I'm not doing anything I haven't been asked to do. Billy gave me his blessing to fulfil Amélie's wishes. *She* asked *me*. Not the other way around. I honestly don't want a row but I need to draw a line in the sand right here and right now.'

'Go on,' Penelope said.

'What I decide with regard to having a baby is none of your business. You are banned from bringing it up. I do not want it mentioned again. Is that clear?'

'Well, I was only trying—'

'I know what you were trying to do and I'm sick to death of it. Give it up, Mum. Second, I may not have ten children but that doesn't mean I don't love Amélie. I am well aware she is not my daughter. She is at breaking point. This is a crisis situation. We all need to pull together and do what's best for her. This is not about you or me or any kind of ego trip. This is about doing anything in our power to help Amélie.'

'I want to help her just as much as you do. I'm her grandmother, don't forget.'

'Mum,' Lexie said, sounding utterly beaten, 'grow up, please.' She hung up and didn't give a damn whether or not her mother liked it. She'd finished taking crap from her. The phone rang again immediately.

'Hi, Dad.'

'Don't hang up, love,' he said. 'I heard your conversation with your mother and I'm on your side. We won't interfere any more. Your mother agrees she's overstepped the mark and right now I'm with you. We need to get Amélie better.'

'Thank you,' Lexie said. 'Praise be to God, someone is finally listening to me.' She filled him in on the plans for the rest of the week and said she needed to go. 'Can you put Mum back on for a second?' she asked.

'Hello,' came a meek and distant-sounding voice.

'Mum,' Lexie said, ignoring the dying-swan act, 'is the offer of the party still open? I'd love to go ahead if it is. Sam and I can pay for it but I'd really appreciate your help with the organisation.'

'Oh,' Penelope said. 'I wasn't expecting that. Well, of course Dad and I would love to help you. As I said before, we could organise it in a heartbeat.' Lexie closed her eyes and smiled as her mother took off and began to recite all the things she could do. 'Leave it to me. All I need is your and Sam's list and I'll even have the invites organised. I had some in mind and I've spoken to lovely Mr Vard, at Dad's remaining printing shop. He has the most gorgeous designs there.'

'That sounds super, Mum,' Lexie said. 'There's another thing I'd love to do. Could we have it in August? I know that's before my actual birthday but I couldn't imagine having a party without Kathleen.'

'That's a wonderful plan,' Penelope said. 'I'm so delighted you've come around to the idea, I quite frankly wouldn't mind when you want to host it. I'll get on to the club and make sure they have a free date in late August and we'll be in business!'

By the time she put the phone down, she was actually laughing into her sleeve. Her mother had clearly organised the party to the last detail and had pretty much set it all up before she'd said no. No wonder she'd been so put out when Lexie objected.

Lexie was ready to do some work at last. Then, her phone buzzed and bleated, letting her know there was a text.

Can you email your guest list by this evening? Just confirmed the yacht club for August and I need final numbers. Love Mum.

Lexie had to smile. It was either that or she'd go utterly insane and blow a gasket. She'd sit with Amélie and Sam later on at home and draw up a list of friends to invite. It would be something fun for them all to do.

She didn't get far with her work before the landline rang.

'Caracove Bay Gallery,' she said cheerfully.

'Hey, it's Amélie. You sound cheerful. I was hoping you weren't going to be furious with me for dumping you in it and asking if I could stay at Cashel Square.'

'Don't you worry about a thing,' Lexie said. 'It's all sorted with your folks. You're all coming over this evening for pizza and then you'll stay but, meanwhile, I need your help.'

'With what?' Amélie asked.

'I'm having a fortieth birthday party and I need to send a list to Grandma.'

'Is she organising it?' Amélie asked. 'Be careful. It'll be all string quartets on lawns with immaculate waiters serving perfect sandwiches and stuck-up fogeys raising their pinkies.'

'Well, that's where you come in. You should have a table of rowdy teenagers to liven us all up.'

'Okay,' Amélie said, 'I'll get a list sorted over the next few days. I'm not really in the mood for a party at the minute.'

'I can imagine. Just mull it over in your head, yeah?'

'Sure. Thanks, Lexie.'

'Meanwhile I'm calling out my list. We can finish it later, but seeing as I'm on a roll, here goes …'

Lexie read out a whole host of people and Amélie said nothing until she came to one couple. 'No!' she said. 'They're far too boring. And they'd bring you a crap present, like a creepy ornament.'

'Ooh, no nasty ornaments for me. I'm forty, not four hundred, right?'

'I think you should do a gift list,' Amélie said.

'I was going to say your presence is the only present I require.'

'What?' Amélie said incredulously. 'But that's the whole reason you have a party, so you can get tonnes of cool stuff. If you don't want the presents I'll have them.'

Lexie laughed. 'You're a scream, but I think I'll do the no-gifts thing all the same.'

'Your loss,' Amélie said. 'Jeez, forty really is old, isn't it? You're getting so bloody sensible.'

'I am, I suppose. See you later. I've done absolutely no work so far today.'

By closing time Lexie decided to write the day off and called the pizza delivery company. She'd only just let herself into her home when Billy's car pulled up. 'Let's go into the living room and get comfortable,' Lexie said brightly. She told them that the pizza was on the way and offered them all a drink.

'Listen,' Billy began. 'We need to clear the air. I can't even sit down until things are sorted.' He looked at Amélie.

'The day you were born was the best day of my life,' Dee said.

'Amélie.' Billy took her hand and crouched at the side of the sofa. 'You are the best thing that's ever happened to us. We wouldn't know what to do without you. We couldn't cope.'

'We certainly wish we were in a better financial situation, that's for certain. I've been made redundant,' Dee said. 'And your father has suffered three wage cuts over the last eighteen months. Our biggest dread was having to take you out of your school. For a while we thought we were goosed and couldn't pay your fees.'

'But Grandma and Granddad have said they'll pay for next year,' Billy said.

'And the reason Dad and I have been so unbelievably stressed,' Dee looked at Billy, who took her hand, 'is because I'm pregnant.'

There was silence in the room as Amélie stared open-mouthed at her parents, then at Lexie. 'Did you know about this?'

'It's all news to me,' she said, as a smile spread across her face. 'Wowzers! Congratulations, folks,' she said, standing to hug Dee and then Billy. 'When did you find out?'

'Only a few weeks ago,' Billy said.

'I thought I was going through menopause,' Dee explained. 'But it turns out I'm having a baby. I'm— Please don't be angry, Amélie, but I'm six months pregnant already.'

'Seriously?' Amélie said. 'But I thought – I thought you two hated one another. I thought you were only together because you were forced.'

'Oh, no, pet,' Dee said. 'We were ushered down the aisle with no hesitation, that's for certain, but Dad and I are still very much in love.'

'You are?' Amélie looked unsure.

'We've only been at each other's throats lately because of me being made redundant along with the money issue and then discovering about the baby. It was a bit of a shock, to be honest. But since you ran away,' Billy looked like he was going to cry, 'we've realised that none of the money stuff matters. We've no mortgage left on the house, your fees will be paid next year and Mum can stay home with the baby.'

'I'm going to be a big sister,' Amélie said, in astonishment, as the news began to sink in.

'What are you thinking?' Lexie asked bravely.

'I – I'm blown away,' Amélie said.

'In a good or bad way?' Dee asked.

'Good. I'd never have guessed this one in a million years,' she said. 'I was so certain I was the bane of your lives and that you were cursed to have a child. I kept looking at Lexie and Sam and all the fun they have.' She turned to Lexie. 'You guys are the perfect couple in my eyes. I know you're having some stupid row right now but when I look at your house, your cool gallery, your car … And you're such a sophisticated and gorgeous person. I honestly figured it was all because you don't have kids.'

Lexie looked stricken.

'Mum and Dad,' Amélie continued, 'I thought I was the root of all your unhappiness.'

'I'm so sorry you thought that.' Dee began to cry. 'If we'd lost you, darling, even this baby wouldn't have made me feel better. Nothing could ever replace you in our lives. Clearly we've failed you if you feel so unloved.'

'Mum, I'm sorry,' Amélie said, hugging her. 'Wow,' she said, jerking backwards. 'Your tummy! It's so hard! Can I touch it?'

'Sure,' Dee said, looking at Billy. 'The doctor actually commented on how neat I am. I was the same when I was expecting you, I guess the fact I'm not exactly a skinny Minnie hides a multitude too!' Billy put his arm around her as Amélie reached over and placed her hand on her mum's belly.

'It's a miracle,' she breathed. She looked up at her parents. 'Kind of gross in a way because it's proof you've been having sex,' she said.

'Amélie!' Billy said.

'I hate to tell you,' Dee said, 'but you weren't an immaculate conception either.'

They all laughed, happy to have some light relief.

The pizza arrived so Lexie left them alone together. In the silence of the kitchen, she pondered on the news. She was delighted that her brother and wife were on the right track. She'd have hated to see them split after all these years.

But another baby? Like Amélie, she hadn't seen this one coming at all.

She knew it would be tough for Billy and Dee financially, but she was delighted for them. A thought struck her. Amélie had known something was up and she'd been right.

A while later, as she made her way back into the living room to call them for food, Lexie took comfort from the scene that met her. Dee and Amélie were chatting animatedly as Billy watched with a grin.

They followed Lexie to the kitchen where they all relaxed and enjoyed the food. An hour later Dee yawned. 'Sorry, folks. I'm bushed. I can barely stay awake past eight o'clock now. I'm relieved that's down to my pregnancy rather than simply being old.'

'I was beginning to think she'd been lying about her age all these years,' Billy said, 'that she was in fact in her seventies, but looked remarkably well.'

Dee and Billy made their way to the hall.

'Are you sure it's cool with you two that Amélie stays here for another few days?' Lexie whispered, as her niece ran to the bathroom.

'Let's just take this in baby steps,' Billy said. 'We want Amélie to come home of her own accord, not because she's being bamboozled by us laying on guilt.'

'Fair enough. But, equally, I don't want you to think I'm butting in.'

'Sis, you're being a total superstar,' Billy said. 'For someone who doesn't have kids, you've got it all sussed – you're streets ahead of us anyway.' He smiled wryly.

Their daughter reappeared to say goodnight and they hugged.

Then Lexie let them out. Glancing at Amélie, she felt a wave of affection. She loved the very bones of her. She'd curl up and die if anything happened to her. Instead of feeling as if she'd been saddled with a problem, she felt privileged that her niece wanted to be with her.

A ripple of nerves shot through her as she glanced at her watch. Sam should be here any minute. Lexie knew it was ludicrous to be nervous of her own husband, but things were on a knife edge.

Dear Diary

I can barely get my head around all that's happened in the past forty-eight hours. I honestly didn't think I'd be writing here again. I was going to burn this book. It contains too many inner thoughts and far too many reasons to want to crawl into a ball and expire.

But I always feel better when I write stuff down. Why? I've no idea. It's not as if writing solves anything, is it? Maybe once it's on paper it's out of my head in some way.

I'm stunned by Mum and Dad's news. I'm going to have a brother or sister. Wow. Now that I see it written down it seems real.

Do you know what? I'm really glad. First, I know I wasn't imagining all the weirdness at home. Second, it takes the focus off me for a change. This little person is going to be a whole new chapter for us all. Actually, I feel a little sorry for it already. The poor mite will arrive with so many pairs of hopeful eyes staring at it, willing it to make us all feel better.

I'm going to protect him or her. I know how it feels to be watched so intently. I'll do things that will detract from the glare, if necessary. One thing I know for certain – I'm good at causing scenes.

I know Mum and Dad were watching me with such trepidation when they made the announcement. I guess they expected me to explode and say I hated the baby before it's even born. But I can't wait to see him or her.

I'm going to use the next three months to get my head together. I want to be the best big sister possible. I'm not actually sure how I'll manage it, but I'm going to ensure that baby has a smiling and über-cool big sis to look up to.

Amélie

Chapter 41

IT WAS AFTER ELEVEN THAT NIGHT BEFORE SAM eventually arrived home. Lexie was in the living room and Amélie had gone to bed, wiped out. Heart pounding, she walked out to greet him.

'Hi,' he said tenderly. 'Sorry I'm so late. The flight was delayed. I didn't bother calling because I figured you'd all be here chatting and having a few drinks.'

'Dee and Billy left early. Dee is wrecked on account of her pregnancy.'

'Her what?' Sam was flabbergasted.

'Yup.' Lexie smiled nervously. 'She's having another baby. Not only that but she's already six months gone.'

Sam took her hand and they went into the living room. Lexie could feel her shoulders relaxing as his touch reassured her he wasn't going to be hostile.

'How are they doing?'

'They're a bit shell-shocked but I think they're relieved we all know now. Amélie took it really well. In fact, she's delighted.'

They chatted for a while and Lexie poured Sam a glass of wine. Then silence prevailed but, unlike recent times, it was comfortable.

'So, have you thought about what I said?' she asked.

'Yeah.' He raked his fingers through his hair. 'I've been trying to concentrate on work but it's been zooming around my brain non-stop. What about you? Have you any further thoughts?'

'I've been eyeballing Britta and now that I'm surrounded by pregnant women it's sort of difficult to avoid the issue.'

Sam gazed into her eyes and took her hand. 'Contrary to what your mother believes,' he said, 'we don't need to rush this. Let's just take stock and try to get ourselves back on track for the moment, yeah? Baby or no baby, nothing is going to work if you and I aren't strong.'

'I know.' She sighed. 'It's been horrible lately. It's not like us to be so ratty with one another. I hate it.'

'Me too, so let's just enjoy being us again and see where we are in a while.'

'Deal.'

That night they slept spooned together, just like old times.

The following morning Amélie was bright and breezy, adding to the jovial atmosphere at breakfast.

'Hey, junkie,' Sam said, kissing her cheek. 'I believe you frightened the bejesus out of everyone while I was gone.'

'I did my best,' Amélie said, with a wink.

'I'm glad you're okay, kiddo,' he said, pulling out a chair for her. 'Come and sit and have some toast. I'll even make you a cup of coffee.'

'Woo, you're in a good mood,' she said, glancing at Lexie.

'Yeah, we've been a bit stressed lately but things are getting back on track now. Hey, I believe you're about to become big sister *extraordinaire*!'

'Yeah! Isn't it mint?'

As they chatted over breakfast Lexie could see that Amélie was in good form and knew there was no reason why she shouldn't go to work. In fact, Amélie wanted to go too, so Lexie went down to the basement to tell Agata that she wouldn't need her after all.

'That's no problem,' Agata said. 'I can do some painting at home. If you need help again, just ask.'

Lexie heard the disappointment in her voice. 'Listen, I'm going to need someone while Kate is travelling. I was going to advertise the position but obviously I'd much rather have someone I know. All the better if that someone is an artist.'

'Really?' Agata brightened.

'I'm not sure how the commute would work for you, though,' Lexie mused.

'Well, I'm going home soon so maybe you could rent the flat to Agata?' Kathleen suggested. 'Sorry! I'll butt out.'

'No, butt in,' Lexie said. 'I think that's a great idea. Would you think about it or are you blissfully happy in Glendalough?'

'I love it there, and if I was alone I'd stay until I was old and haggard. But being here and seeing Britta with Kathleen and you has shown me that it's not really fair to stay in such a secluded albeit beautiful setting.'

'So you'd consider the "Lexie package"?' She grinned.

'I really would.'

'Let's mull it over and chat again in a few days, okay?'

With that, Lexie shot off to the gallery with Amélie.

Kathleen couldn't believe how quickly the time was passing. Now that she'd said it out loud her return date seemed to loom even faster.

'I'm going to miss you terribly when you go back to America,' Agata said. 'I've never had anyone so unconditionally supportive in my life.'

'I'm not going anywhere for quite a while, honey,' Kathleen assured her. 'At least, that's what I'm trying to convince myself. I can't imagine how bitter-sweet it's gonna be when I have to board that flight to America, but for now I'm not shifting. Although I am venturing to the zoo with Rodger tomorrow,' she said. 'I could take Britta with me, if you like.'

'That would be too much for you and Rodger. She'd love to do a smaller trip another day, though, if that suited,' said Agata. 'I'm going back to Glendalough today to have a chat with my landlord. I was hinting that I would sign the lease for another six months, but now that Lexie has offered me this golden opportunity I should take stock.'

'That's fine, dear,' Kathleen said. 'I'm excited for you and Britta. I think it could be a whole new adventure.'

Alone in the house now that Lexie and Amélie had left for the gallery, Sam pressed the button on the Nespresso machine and leaned against the counter to wait for his coffee. He'd been bricking it about coming home. Lexie saying she wanted to have a baby had taken the wind out of his sails.

All the animosity between them of late had become exhausting. He'd actually begun to doubt his feelings for her. In the seventeen years they'd been together he'd thought they were rock solid. But over recent weeks she'd turned into a person he didn't recognise. If he was totally honest, she was becoming a woman he didn't particularly like.

Last night they'd shared a bottle of wine, made love and actually laughed as he'd told her about an incident at the airport.

He knew that life was all about ups and downs. He didn't expect Lexie to be Mrs Fun and Games all day every day. But he couldn't carry on with the relentless doom and gloom either.

Being away had shown Sam that he was still crazy about Lexie, their home and the wonderful life they'd built. As he'd pulled up at number three Cashel Square last night, he'd smiled. He couldn't imagine not living there with Lexie. There were so many plans he wanted to implement at the house. Lots of bits and bobs that needed finishing and fixing up. For the first few years after moving in, they'd poured everything into the house until they'd run out of steam and funds. But Sam felt it was about time he kick-started some more refurbishments.

His mother had always said, 'It takes two to tango,' and Sam was aware that he, too, had a role to play in making their marriage strong again. He'd been irritable and impatient lately. He'd cut himself off from Lexie and he desperately wanted to rekindle their closeness. Now he had an idea and he hoped it would do the trick.

Tuesday came around swiftly and Kathleen got up early to ensure she had everything she needed for the picnic at the zoo. She'd arranged to meet Rodger in Dublin city centre where they'd take a shuttle bus out to the Phoenix Park where the zoo was housed.

'I haven't been to Dublin Zoo since I was five years old,' Kathleen said, when Rodger suggested it. 'It's wonderful that you're accompanying me as it's one of my tasks for Jackson too.'

'I hope you don't think it odd that I'm going with you, seeing as it's partially at Jackson's suggestion.'

'No, it feels right. I'm happy you're coming. Besides, you wanted to go too. So it's a shared suggestion,' she said.

'Well, I was there last year with my grandchildren,' Rodger said, 'but my hip was so bad I could hardly walk. I missed out on so much of it. At least I won't be in such awful pain this time. I could be a bit slow all the same. I was thinking I could always hire a wheelchair if the walking gets too much for me. I don't want to hold you up.'

'We won't be in a hurry. If you're uncomfortable or tired we'll get you a supersonic wheelchair. Either way we'll take it at our own pace.'

As the DART pulled into the station in Dublin, Kathleen spotted Rodger instantly as he waved from the platform. He looked very smart in his chinos and sports jacket.

'I feel a little underdressed,' she joked, as they hugged. 'A cravat?'

'The monkeys insist on it. Didn't you know?'

'Of course. Silly me, I forgot.' She was pulling her bag behind her.

'What on earth have you got there? Are we spending a week in the elephant enclosure?'

'It's my new suitcase. It came to Connemara with me. I was thinking of asking Lexie for the loan of a picnic basket when it occurred to me that we'd have to lug it around for the day. So I have everything we could possibly require in here, and neither of us has to dislocate a shoulder carrying it.'

Rodger laughed, and the bottles clinked in his wine bag.

'Let me take the wine too, no point in you struggling with that.'

They zipped Kathleen's case open and added it.

'How are you at walking now?' she asked.

'Much better,' said Rodger. 'As you can see, I've no crutches. I brought a fold-up walking stick just in case but I'm better than I've been for years.'

'That's fantastic,' Kathleen said. 'I could always pop you into my suitcase if you're sore.' He laughed out loud as they fell into step with one another.

'Yes it's all good. My daughter Bee has stopped being quite so cross with me too, which is a relief.'

'How is she?' Kathleen asked, out of politeness. She found Bee obnoxious.

'She's doing well. It's not easy for her with Amy and Justin being so full-on. She misses Claudia dreadfully. My wife used to take care of the children a lot.'

'Don't they come to you still?' Kathleen asked.

'Not really. Bee reckons they're too much for me. Says I wouldn't be able to chase after them if they decided to dash off across a road or, God forbid, if there was an accident.' Rodger looked sad.

'Why don't you tell her that you're steadier on your feet now? Unless you agree with her.'

'Of course I don't,' Rodger said emphatically. 'But she's a strong-willed woman.'

'It's a pity we didn't think of bringing them today,' Kathleen mused.

'Ah, no, I wouldn't inflict that on you.' He chuckled.

'Another day let's do something with them. I'd love to meet them and help out. I don't get to play Grandma that often.'

'All right, then.' Rodger smiled.

They boarded a bus and chatted happily as they crossed the city, then went through the grand gates into the Phoenix Park.

'I can see why the president likes to live here,' Kathleen said. 'I would too, if I had the choice. It's like a little slice of Heaven in the heart of the bustling city.' Curious deer trotted into the undergrowth as they made their way through the massive park.

The driver brought them right up to the entrance, remarking

that they were lucky to get there before the crowds. The sun was playing hide and seek with the woolly clouds. 'At least it's not raining,' Rodger said cheerfully, as they walked through the turnstiles. He accepted a map from a staff member just inside the gate. 'Why don't you take the map and be the navigator and I'll pull the bag?' he asked.

'You're not getting your paws on my bag.' She giggled. 'You're a dear to offer, but I'm more than happy dragging it. Besides, I'm terrible at reading maps. We'll only end up in the wrong place. You lead the way.'

Kathleen couldn't believe how amazing the zoo was. Her childhood memories involved a rather sparse and mildly depressing concrete environment with grey skies and dejected animals. Now it was beautifully landscaped, with trees and shrubs, and each species had an imaginatively designed habitat.

'Wow! Look at the tiger mama!' Kathleen exclaimed. 'Rodger, she's got a cub. Isn't that the most divine fuzzball you ever saw?'

'That divine fuzzball would take your arm off with one swipe of his paw if the mood took him.'

'You'd never think it when you see them lolling in the long grass like that. You know my Jackson was the vet at Disney's Animal Kingdom? He used to take some amazing photos of the tigers. He'd have loved to see these,' she said wistfully.

'I reckon he can see,' Rodger assured her, patting her hand.

They moved towards the African plains to visit the giraffes, zebra and elephants. 'Let's go around on the little train,' Kathleen suggested.

'Won't we look like two old fools mixed in with the toddlers?'

'Do you care?' Kathleen asked.

'No, now you mention it.'

'That's without doubt my favourite thing about getting older,' Kathleen said, as they climbed aboard. 'I care less and less what others think and, as a result, I'm enjoying things more and more.'

As they bumbled around the vast expanse of the park, weaving through trees past a host of animals, the ones that Kathleen wanted to return to were the flamingos and the red pandas.

'The flamingos were over in that direction,' Rodger said, pointing. 'I spied a picnic area too. How would you feel about dining soon, m' lady?'

'Sounds great. I'm starving,' she said.

They ambled past an island riddled with monkeys and found the flamingo pool.

'Aren't they just fabulous?' Kathleen clasped her hands under her chin. 'They're the most amazing colour. They look as if they were dipped in liquid bubble gum!'

'Speaking of which, let's go and eat,' Rodger said.

Kathleen smiled to herself. Jackson would've been so different if he were here today. He'd have enjoyed the animals for sure, but he'd have made veterinary-style comments and would have been itching to examine them.

The picnic area was bathed in sunshine, making the wooden benches wonderfully warm and comfortable to sit on.

'I even have a tablecloth,' Kathleen said. She propped the case on the seat part of the bench and began to unload their lunch.

'This looks amazing,' Rodger said, as he opened a bottle of wine.

Kathleen produced proper glasses, which she'd wrapped in two tea towels for safety. 'I reckon we could charge to allow folk to sit here,' she whispered.

'Too right,' said Rodger. 'If we had our wits about us, we could load up several cases each day, take over this area and make a small fortune.'

'The people who run the restaurant might be unhappy if we did.' Kathleen giggled. She produced a delicious-looking quiche and several square plastic boxes.

'What have you got in there?' Rodger asked.

'Salads and dips,' Kathleen said proudly. 'Will you open these tortillas and pour them into the wooden bowl for me?'

'We should do these days out more often,' Rodger quipped. Kathleen cut into the quiche and happily served them both.

'This quiche is delicious,' Rodger said. He placed his knife and fork on the table and dabbed at his eyes with a paper napkin. 'Ugh, look at me getting teary, silly old fool that I am … I haven't tasted homemade quiche like this since my Claudia died.'

'That's tough,' Kathleen sympathised. 'The same thing happens to me all the time. I'm doing really well, enjoying my day, and I see, smell or taste something that reminds me of Jackson and I feel like lying on the floor and sobbing.'

'It's hard learning to live without them, isn't it?'

'It is. All we can do is take each day as it comes. I'm hoping that time will heal my pain. Everyone insists it will and they can't all be wrong.'

They took their time over lunch and finished the bottle of wine before clearing everything away into the case again.

'I have to hand it to you,' Rodger said. 'That's a fantastic bag. Everything fits into it and there's no chance you'll lose it.'

Kathleen insisted on going to the red pandas next. They were her all-time favourite, furry and cuddly, like a cross between the giant black-and-white panda and a marmalade cat.

'Oh, my God, look at the babies! That has to be one of the sweetest little things I've ever laid eyes on,' she exclaimed. 'I'd happily steal one and take it home to hand-rear.'

'It'd fit in your magic bag. Will I keep sketch while you climb over the fence and coax that tiny one over with a bit of quiche?'

'Keep sketch!' Kathleen laughed. 'Now there's a phrase I haven't heard in a lifetime.'

Rodger smiled. 'Should I say I'll keep an eye then?'

'No! I love hearing these things again, but I think I'll pass on stealing a baby panda!'

Eventually Kathleen sensed Rodger's boredom, so they moved on to the reptiles. 'I could stay in here all day,' Rodger said, pinning his face to the window. 'Look at the chameleon. Isn't it astonishing?'

'I'd go for the red panda any day,' Kathleen said. 'But he's certainly amazing-looking, with his leathery skin and beady eyes. His claws and tail make him look like something from *Jurassic Park*.'

Rodger laughed, and stayed with the creatures for some time. Kathleen excused herself and waited outside where she could hear a group of people huddled around the parrot cage. The children were giggling as the bird repeated everything they said.

This place was a far cry from Animal Kingdom at Disney and she missed Jackson. It seemed slightly surreal that she was there with another man. 'You don't mind, do you, Jackson?' she whispered. As the group moved from the parrot she stood in front of it and stared at it.

'Everything okay?' Rodger asked, as he joined her.

'You don't mind, do you, Jackson?' the parrot squawked.

Her cheeks burned as she turned to Rodger. 'How embarrassing. I was just whispering to Jackson — I talk to him regularly. I'm sure you'll find me silly. But it helps me get through. That way I can fool my mind into thinking he's still with me in some shape or form.'

'You don't have to explain,' he said. 'I talk to Claudia morning, noon and night. So if you're crazy I am too.'

'Claudia, if you're crazy I am too,' added the parrot. They burst out laughing.

'Maybe that's what we both need to help fill the silence at home in the evenings,' Kathleen said.

'I'd probably welcome a little beggar like that at first but I reckon if he actually lived in my kitchen I'd soon be pretty fed up with him. Is it illegal to serve parrot pie?'

'I've no idea,' she said. She smiled at Rodger — she was glad she had a friend with her while she'd ticked off another task on her 'to do' list. It felt good.

Chapter 42

LEXIE WAS PLEASANTLY SURPRISED WHEN MAIA arrived in the gallery. 'What brings you here on a weekday? Why aren't you chained to your office, like a good little slavey?'

'I had an appointment with the gearbox doctor,' Maia said, snooping around.

'Charming! How's everything?'

'Fine, as far as I know,' Maia said, dropping her gaze.

'Aren't you going ahead with the amniocentesis test then?'

Maia sauntered over to the desk where Lexie was sitting and perched on the end. 'I was all set to go. I had the appointment and everything. But I backed out.'

'Why?' Lexie asked. 'Isn't it better to know what you're headed for?'

'Josh and I thought so too ... for a while. But we've come to the conclusion that we don't need to do all the poking and prodding. The test carries risks and we want this baby no matter what.'

'But what on earth will you do if the child has Down's like Calvin?' Lexie wondered. 'I can ask you that but millions wouldn't. I'm only trying to get you to face the worst-case scenario.'

'Josh and I agree on this one. Whatever happens we'll take what we're given. Besides Calvin has Trisomy 21, which isn't genetic. We managed last time and we'd no warning ...' Maia stared into the middle distance. 'Do you remember how winded we all were just after the birth? The first couple of weeks of Calvin's life were Hell on Earth.'

'I'll never forget it,' Lexie said, becoming quite emotional. 'He was such a sweet little mite but it was all so shrouded in shock, wasn't it?'

'It was horrendous. The pits. But we got through and we're flying now. I can't say it's easy because it's not,' Maia said. 'In fact, our choice to skip the extra testing brought it all back,' she admitted.

'How so?'

'Josh and I never really talked about that time. I still feel strangled by guilt when I think of the days following Calvin's birth,' she said. 'I prayed with all my heart that he would die. I'm so ashamed to say it out loud, but I have to tell someone. I can't even say that to Josh. I hoped and prayed that Calvin would stop breathing. That way I'd be let out of the Hell I'd been trapped in.'

Lexie swallowed hard. She'd had no idea poor Maia had felt that way.

'When he was still alive the following morning, I wanted to bribe a nurse. The midwife who'd stayed with me during the birth was a darling. I was this close,' Maia pinched her thumb and forefinger together, 'to asking her to swap my baby with another woman's "normal" child.'

'Oh, Maia,' Lexie said. 'I'm so sorry you had such an awful time. I knew you were shocked and shaken and bitterly disappointed but I had no notion of how totally devastating it was for you. I was such a crap friend. I should've known how bad it was.'

'How could you? I'd no idea of the wrecking ball that was about to hit me. I'd gone into labour full of fear at the pain I'd go through. I was terrified of giving birth.'

'Well, I knew that,' Lexie said. 'And I was shag-all help there. I'd say I made you worse by looking like a startled chicken any time you brought it up. I remember you showing me one of those books you had with photos of births. I couldn't even look at them.'

'Yeah,' Maia recalled. 'You were kind of averse to the whole shebang.'

'Sorry,' Lexie said.

'Don't apologise. You were fabulous. Both you and Sam were. You were with us all the time. You kept telling me how cute Calvin was,' she said, rocking back and forth.

'He was a darling,' Lexie said.

'All I saw were the tell-tale signs that my boy wasn't perfect.'

'And now? You wouldn't change him for all the tea in China, right?'

Maia sat up straight. 'You know what? If someone told me they could get rid of Calvin's Down's syndrome tomorrow morning, I'd do it. I'd love nothing more than to know that he could fend for himself in later life. But it's not going to happen. Hand on heart, I adore him. I love him more than anyone else in the entire universe. But it's not easy.' Maia gazed sadly at Lexie. 'I know I'm meant to say I wouldn't change him, but I would. I actually would. Every now and again I still wish he didn't have Down's. I wish he wasn't going to struggle more than the average kid. But he will.'

Lexie listened, barely able to breathe. She and Maia told one another everything. They were as close as sisters, but she'd never heard her friend speak so candidly about Calvin.

'I'm adamant he won't ever have a bowl haircut or wear ugly shoes and nasty clothes. He'll always have amazing birthday parties and fabulous toys. He has Down's but he'll never be a poor little thing. Not on my watch,' she said, as some of her usual fight resurfaced.

'I know,' Lexie said sadly. 'And if he even attempts to do the lame-duck act, you'll kick his butt,' she finished.

'I'll kick his butt,' Maia repeated. Tears trickled, then flowed.

Lexie put her arms around Maia. 'It'll all work out, you'll see. This little baby will be the best brother or sister Calvin could hope for.'

'It won't hate me for bringing it into a family with a special-needs sibling, will it?' Maia asked.

'Do any of us hate Calvin?' Lexie shot back.

'*Touché*,' Maia said, nodding.

'Look, Maia, I'm the worst person to discuss any of this with,' Lexie said, 'but I'm honest if nothing else. I don't have a massive amount of patience with small children. I can't do the gooey lovey-dovey chit-chat about how sweet that baby is. I'm not a gushy person. But your son rocks. He's quirky and funny and knows what he wants when he wants it. If you ask me, he's more together than a lot of adults we know.'

Maia laughed. 'You're just the right person for me to discuss this with,' she said. 'You say all the right things and you don't talk crap. If one more person tells me Calvin is a gift from God I swear I'll punch them.'

'Ah, they mean well. They're only trying to say he's a great kid.'

'I know, but it galls me. I can't scowl and say, "Why don't you see how it feels to accept your son's destiny has been altered at birth?"'

'Yeah, I'd hold off on doing that,' Lexie said. 'You might end up having nobody to talk to after a while.'

'I'm actually being acutely honest all the time at the moment,' she admitted. 'I'm fairly direct at the best of times, but even I'm a bit stunned by what's coming out of my mouth lately. I'm blaming the hormones.'

'That's okay,' Lexie said. 'Friends will forgive you and folk who were teetering on the brink with you will be gone by the time the next child comes along.' She smirked.

'I love Calvin so much – you know that, right? Just because I've released all the evil and dark thoughts that have haunted my mind for the past four years, it doesn't mean I don't adore him.'

'I know, doll.'

'I've been even more protective of him lately. We were at the park last night and a little boy tried to yank his Transformer out of his hand. I had to stop myself dive-bombing him and whacking him with it. I had this dreadful slow-motion image of myself, freeze-frame by freeze-frame, biffing a six-year-old with that robot. That's pure evil, right? But I can't bear the thought of anyone messing with my child.'

'That's your job, one hundred per cent. Well, it's your job to stick up for him without resorting to mindless violence, of course. And that's not because he has Down's, that's simply because he's your son. For the record, that little toad at the park is damn lucky I wasn't there. I don't have your motherly instinct, but I'd have decked him.'

'Thanks, Lexie,' Maia said.

'For what?'

'Letting me say the hateful and insufferable things I just said.'

'You're allowed to feel emotions, Maia. They may not be ones you're proud of, but they happened. You had plenty of reason to feel the way you did. The important thing is that Calvin will never know you felt that way and, more than that, you never act in any way negatively with him. So rest easy. You're an amazing mum. I salute you. I couldn't do what you do.'

The gallery phone rang and Lexie ended up chatting to a customer for a few minutes as she tried to sort out the shipment of a painting. She watched Maia as she walked around examining the various pieces. Her bump was only small but it was visible. She admired Josh and Maia. They were fabulous parents, and even though they had struggled for the first few days after Calvin had come along, they'd pulled together ever since.

Lexie thought about the shambles that had been her and Sam's marriage over the last while. When she'd finished her call she walked over to Maia. 'I know you don't go in for airy-fairy stuff and you hate the whole "It's God's will" rant, but you and Josh are brilliant. You've coped with Calvin's diagnosis and you've moved on together, as a family. Look at you having another baby now!' Lexie took her hands. 'Ever heard the theory that we're never dealt a blow in life that we can't cope with? Well, I reckon you guys have Calvin because he chose you.'

'Oh, Lex. Not this notion that babies choose their parents again ...'

'Yes!' she said. 'But hear me out. Calvin chose you and Josh because he knew you'd give him a deadly name, turn your lives around to fit in with him and, most of all, that you'd love him to bits.' Maia looked stumped. 'You've said yourself that he's doing really well with his milestones. That he's coming on in leaps and bounds. That's down to you guys. So don't let me hear any more of the woe-is-us crap. You guys have it sorted and this new baby is going to add to your family in a positive way. Just imagine if it's a girl. You can organise a whole nest of fairies to come and sprinkle glitter from a jet plane all over the housing estate at her birthday parties. Lauren won't know what hit her!'

'Do you think it's a girl?' Maia asked, turning to the side and flattening her hands over her clothes to reveal her tummy better.

'Do I look like an ultrasound machine?' Lexie asked.

'Well, you're into that loopy idea that our babies choose us, so why not take it a step further and become *au fait* with how they lie in the womb so that you can determine the sex?'

'Nah, too crazy, even for me.'

'Would you paint me with my bump?' Maia suddenly asked.

'Huh?' Lexie was stunned.

'I have the portrait you did of Josh and me for our wedding gift. I'd love a similar one of me with a bump. Odds are this'll be my last pregnancy. The world won't survive my hormone surges another time. Would you do it?'

'You know I can't paint any more,' Lexie said, looking at Maia as if she'd lost her marbles. 'Why would you ask me to do something you know I can't?'

'Because I think you gave up too soon.'

'Maia, I tried,' Lexie said. Tears were threatening. How could Maia be so insensitive? If she could paint or draw, she'd be doing it morning, noon and night.

'Why don't you try a different technique or style?'

'That's impossible,' she said grumpily.

'So it's okay for me to have a meltdown and say I'm struggling with my special-needs child and my pregnancy, but I'm expected to get on with it, yet you can sit for the rest of your life licking your wounds? Piss off, Lexie.'

Lexie stared at her. 'You *are* fiery right now, aren't you?' The tension dissolved as they burst out laughing. 'Cripes, I feel so sorry for Josh and Calvin. Do they know you're an emotional landmine right now?'

Maia wrinkled her nose. 'That's why I'm here on my own. We were meant to go to the park for the afternoon, but I bit Josh's head off and stomped away.'

'I see,' Lexie said. 'Why don't you pop into Ramona next door and get a couple of doorsteps of her carrot cake and two cappuccinos and we'll call a truce in the advice-and-badgering session?'

Maia grinned sheepishly, but Lexie noted she hadn't apologised for suggesting she should try painting again.

As Maia walked past the window to Ramona's, Lexie flexed her fingers on her left hand. She was able to do most things now, but on days when they had a lot of lifting to do or it was extremely cold, her joints ached.

She thought of her brushes, paints and easels at home, stuffed into boxes gathering dust. They'd been abandoned for such a long time now. The gallery and the house had kept her busy and, if she was honest, Lexie hadn't allowed her mind to wander to thoughts of her own art. She'd become so accustomed to pouring her heart into other people's work that she'd almost forgotten her own talent.

Amélie had gone to lunch with her friend Yvonne. She arrived back in time to see Maia.

'How's it going?' Maia asked. 'I heard you met some mad dealer person who tried to have his wicked way with you. Horrible bastard,' she said.

'It was pretty awful,' Amélie said. 'I don't know how people take drugs for fun.'

'Maia is having a let's-be-frank phase. It happens in conjunction with pregnancy hormones,' Lexie said, in case Amélie got upset.

'Good on you,' Amélie said, picking a tiny piece off Lexie's cake. 'I *do* straight talking. There's nothing worse than people tiptoeing around whispering. I should know. My folks have been acting all cloak-and-dagger for ages and it turns out Mum's pregnant.'

'Feck off!' Maia shouted, nearly choking on her cake.

'Yeah,' Lexie said, sipping her coffee. 'I totally forgot to tell you. Dee and Billy are expecting.'

'In three months,' Amélie finished. 'Gross – it's proof they're at it like rabbits still, but once I block that image from my mind I kind of like the idea of a baby around the place.'

Maia hugged Amélie. 'I hope I have a girl and she turns out like you. You're a rock star.'

'Thanks, Maia,' Amélie said, beaming.

Lexie listened as Maia gave Amélie the details of her pregnancy, complete with a quick flash of her belly and stretch marks.

'Ugh, I'm never having a baby,' Amélie said.

'Yeah, stick with me, girls. I'm the best advertisement for contraception ever invented. If you'd like, I can go into episiotomy details next.'

'No, thank you,' Lexie and Amélie said in unison.

By the time Maia left, Lexie was emotionally exhausted. But a seed had been planted in her head. Should she try to use her hand again after all this time? Maia had a point. Lexie had encouraged her to get on with the challenges that had been handed to her but she wasn't so great at taking her own advice. For the first time in ten years she had an urge to paint again.

Chapter 43

TWO WEEKS HAD PASSED SINCE KATHLEEN HAD visited Connemara. She couldn't quite believe it was time to see Betty and Jenny again.

'We'll be with you by midday,' Betty promised. 'We'll drop our things and walk around to your flat. I'm so looking forward to seeing it. It's been a lifetime.'

Kathleen hadn't wanted to promise anything, but she'd had a word with Lexie and Sam and they'd agreed to let the ladies see the rest of the house.

'Of course,' Lexie said. 'It would be lovely for Betty to see it all these years later.'

Kathleen had made another quiche for lunch. Rodger had complimented the one they'd had on the zoo trip so she figured it must have been good. There was green salad, tomato and basil salad and wild mushrooms with lemon juice. For dessert she'd made a chocolate biscuit cake to go with coffee.

Just as she'd put the finishing touches to the table there was a rap on the door. 'Hello!' Betty and Jenny carolled.

They stepped inside, full of oohs and aahs.

'This is just perfect, isn't it?' Betty said. 'I can't believe how different it is from when we were kids.'

'If you'd only seen it, Jenny,' Kathleen said. 'It was dark and scary. Nothing like this gorgeous bright place.'

'It was like a spider hotel,' Betty agreed.

'Lexie gave me a key for upstairs too, so let's go up before we have lunch.'

'We have a tiny gift for you,' Betty said, handing Kathleen a small box. 'We wanted to get you something Irish and it had to be small enough that you can take it back to Orlando when you go.'

'Oh, you shouldn't have done that,' Kathleen said. Excitedly, she untied the ribbon and opened the box. Inside, nestled in soft tissue paper, was a stunning heart-shaped crystal on a chain.

'You can hang it in the window or wherever you wish. It's genuine Waterford crystal,' Jenny said.

'I love it. Thank you, both. That's so generous and thoughtful,' Kathleen said, perching it on the window sill. 'Now let's go and have a quick look-see upstairs and then I reckon it'll be time for a little glass of wine.'

They gazed in awe at each room in the main house.

'They've done such an amazing job on the place, haven't they?' Jenny said. 'I love their taste. It's so fresh yet in keeping with the age of the building.'

'Is this them?' Betty asked, as she squinted at a wedding photo on a side table.

'Yes,' said Kathleen. 'Aren't they a darling couple?'

'They look very happy,' Jenny agreed.

Kathleen said they'd just have a quick glance at the bedrooms. 'I don't want them to feel we were snooping through all their stuff,' she said, as they ventured upstairs.

'Oh, gosh, no,' said Betty.

'Ah, they've a daughter,' said Jenny.

'No, their niece is staying with them.'

'Don't Lexie and Sam have any children of their own?' Betty asked.

'Not at the moment,' Kathleen said. 'As you can see, some of the rooms are still waiting for furniture and decoration. But a big building like this would absorb money like a sponge.'

They made their way back downstairs and out of the front door. 'You can see the garden from my back door,' Kathleen explained. 'But now I think it's wine o'clock!'

'Wine o'clock it is!' Jenny agreed.

The three went into the basement kitchen as Kathleen served lunch and took a bottle of white wine out of the fridge. Just as she was going to pour, she stopped in her tracks and stared at the back wall. 'Look,' she breathed.

It was covered with a vibrant display of rainbows.

'They're coming from the crystal on the windowsill,' Jenny said.

'But the sun seems to have moved over the roof towards the back,' Betty said. 'Odd. I don't see the shaft of sunlight making the pattern.'

'It's Jackson,' Kathleen said, her voice cracking. Although she was smiling broadly, tears were streaming down her cheeks. 'It's Jackson's birthday today. He promised me a rainbow to let me know he's with me.'

'That's amazing,' said Jenny.

'A sceptic would say that your crystal created them and I'm just being a silly old fool,' said Kathleen, 'but I'm choosing to believe that Jackson is here with me and letting me know.'

Gradually the rainbows faded.

'I'm not really a believer in the supernatural,' Jenny said. 'I'm afraid I don't have a strong faith. But every now and again, just like now, I get a strong sense that there's something else out there.'

'I firmly believe in life after death,' Betty said. 'I believe in spirits too. At first after James died I could feel him in the room. Now that that time has passed and I'm less frantic about losing him, he's here less and less.'

'Do you ever turn around suddenly and feel he's there?' Kathleen asked.

'Oh, yes,' Betty said. 'I've become more accustomed to it now, but it used to freak me out no end.'

'Well, if my fella is ever standing there when I turn around he'd want to run pretty fast,' Jenny said. 'Because he deserves a good hiding for walking out and leaving me high and dry.'

They all laughed and Kathleen waited until the other two were eating and chatting amicably before she excused herself and went to the bathroom. She locked the door and leaned against the wall.

'Thank you, Jackson. I got my rainbow. You remembered. It was lovely to be able to share it with the ladies too. I wish you were here with me. I can't help feeling that. Do you think I'll ever make it through a day without longing for you?' She was beginning to feel tearful. She didn't want to appear from the bathroom red-eyed, so she washed her hands and concentrated on feeling upbeat.

'All okay?' Betty said, as she rejoined them.

'Yes, thanks,' said Kathleen. 'I'd like to propose a toast.' She raised her glass. 'To friendship and companionship.'

'To friendship and companionship,' the others repeated.

'And happy birthday, Jackson,' Betty added.

Kathleen winked and they sipped their wine.

'So have you had any more attention from Mr Grim Reaper?' Kathleen asked Betty, in an attempt to lighten the mood.

'Ah, no. I don't think Morris and I are exactly a match made in Heaven,' she said.

'I went to the zoo last week with my friend Rodger,' Kathleen said. 'We had a lovely day out. I hadn't been to Dublin Zoo for over sixty years.' Despite her attempts to remain upbeat, come what may, Kathleen heard her voice wobble. 'It was strange spending the day with another man,' she confessed. 'It's totally platonic and poor Rodger feels a little odd too – he lost his wife, Claudia, not so long ago so we were well suited. But it was what I would call bitter-sweet,' she said. She reminded the ladies of her three tasks.

'You told us about them,' Betty said. 'How lovely that you had company.'

'I really need to get out more,' Jenny said. 'All I do is work at the hotel and do the odd errand. Even this trip here today is totally out of character for me. George is always rattling on about my insular ways.'

'Maybe he has a point,' Betty said. 'Clara and Mark are wonderful at the hotel. You really ought to allow yourself more treats.'

'True,' she agreed. 'But what would I do? Where would I go? There's no point in deciding to take time off and end up wandering like a lonely nomad, is there?'

'Why don't you come visit me in Orlando?' Kathleen said. 'I'll be longing for company. Both of you should come.'

'I doubt I'd be able to leave Ruth with the children,' Betty said.

'Why not?' Jenny asked. 'You give up so much time to them, and you're entitled to a holiday. If you gave Ruth enough notice I'm sure she'd be able to take the time off work or find someone to fill in for you.'

Betty's eyes lit up. 'Do you know what? You're both right. I'm not getting any younger, but we're all able-bodied and in good health so what's stopping us?'

'Attagirl!' Kathleen said, delighted. 'It would be so fantastic to see you gals.'

'What about spending Thanksgiving in Orlando?' Betty said. 'We could get some Christmas shopping done and lap up a bit of last-minute sun before the winter really sets in over here.'

'That sounds gorgeous,' Jenny agreed. 'I can't really go AWOL once Christmas kicks in, so it would suit me. What do you think, Kathleen?'

Her face, followed by the pop of another cork, answered the question.

The sun was shining so they ventured out into the little garden.

'Can we have a snoop around the upper part?' Betty asked.

'Of course. There are comfy chairs up there so let's take our wine up,' Kathleen suggested.

It was so warm they had to borrow hats and sun cream from Kathleen. By late afternoon, they were almost comatose.

'I think all my bones have fallen out,' Jenny muttered.

'Uh-huh,' Kathleen agreed. 'I'm transforming into a slug.'

Betty giggled and sat up, suddenly finding energy from somewhere. 'Let's go to the beach and paddle,' she said.

'*Whaaat?*' Jenny drawled. 'I'd drown! If I was any more relaxed here I'd be dead.'

'Precisely,' said Betty. 'Let's go for a revitalising stroll on the beach.'

When they thought about it, it was a good idea, so they went back into the basement and out of the front door. Kathleen brought a towel, with the sun cream and her swimming costume. Then she stuffed a bottle of Prosecco and some paper cups into her bag – it might come in handy.

The walk involved quite a bit of zigzagging and bashing shoulders off walls. All three were giggling involuntarily at nothing.

'We're a disgrace,' Kathleen said. 'We're meant to have more sense at our age.'

'Ah, bugger sense,' said Jenny. 'I for one have spent more than my fair share of days being the sensible and reliable one. So what if we decide to break the mould every once in a while?'

'I'm going to have my swim,' Kathleen announced. 'Then I'm going to eat chips!'

'Your last task!' Betty said.

'We won't let you go alone. Let's duck into your old house, Betty, and grab our swimming things,' Jenny said. 'We have all sorts of things stashed in the spare room,' she explained to Kathleen.

Ben was there and tried to talk them out of it. 'You're all half cut. You can't go swimming unless you want to be rescued and rushed to A&E.'

'Don't be such a bore, Ben,' Betty said, kissing him. 'We'll call you when we finish so you know we're not dead.' All three dissolved into giggles and refused to allow him to accompany them.

'I'd feel much happier if I was there,' he argued.

'We'll be embarrassed enough getting our bodies out in public without you staring at us,' Betty said.

They arrived at the beach and found a lovely spot not too far from the promenade where they changed into their swimming things.

'If one of us is drunkenly drowning, someone will see us and throw us a life belt,' Betty said.

'Let's dump our stuff here. I'll put the towel over it,' Kathleen said.

They giggled as they picked their way barefoot across the stones and shells to the water's edge. Kathleen walked right in without hesitation. 'Oh, dear sweet Jesus!' she shouted, retreating at speed. 'That is unmercifully cold! Why on earth would an ocean want to be that freezing?'

'That's the Irish Sea for you,' Betty said.

'Oh, girls, you are just gonna love the Atlantic Ocean at Daytona Beach when you come visit. We'll go there and pitch up for the day and you will adore it,' Kathleen promised.

'That sounds fabulous,' Jenny said, 'but you're not getting away that easily now. We're here so we're going in.'

'Even if we end up losing a couple of toes from hypothermia?' Kathleen joked.

They walked in and out of the water, and Kathleen wasn't sure if her feet had turned numb or if she'd become accustomed to the cold, but they stayed for quite a time, paddling and chatting then finally submerging.

The feeling of exhilaration afterwards was incredible. Kathleen's skin tingled all over and she felt like an eight-year-old girl once more. 'I'm starving again,' she announced.

'So am I, now that you mention it,' Betty agreed.

'I'll go and get us some chips from the van parked over there. You girls stay with the stuff and I'll be back in a jiffy.'

A little later they were perched happily in a row munching chips and swigging from the Prosecco bottle.

'I actually have paper cups,' Kathleen pointed out.

'It's more fun drinking from the bottle,' Jenny said.

'We could actually get arrested for doing this,' Betty said. 'Isn't it an offence to drink in a public area like this?'

They burst out laughing and polished off the bottle.

'I haven't behaved like this since I was a teenager,' Jenny said, as they linked arms and walked towards Ben and George's house.

'I don't think I've *ever* behaved like this,' Betty admitted.

'I did when I was a lot younger, but I'd thought my days of hanging out and drinking on beaches were well over.'

Betty rang the doorbell and they got a fit of the giggles when Ben opened it.

They filled him in on their adventure.

'There's nothing quite like chipper chips doused in salt and vinegar straight from the paper on the beach, is there?' Jenny mused.

'Nope,' Kathleen agreed. 'The sea-salty fingers add to the whole experience.'

'Not to mention the odd sandy crunch,' said Betty.

By the time George came in, the three women were in full flow, reminiscing about old times.

'Save me,' Ben said dramatically, clinging to George. 'They're on a trip down Memory Lane. I feel like I'm that cartoon man Mr Benn and I've stepped back to the nineteen-fifties.'

By early evening Kathleen knew she needed to get home. Ben offered to run her back.

'It's only around the corner, but you're in danger of falling down a drain the state you're in,' he said. The other two cackled as Kathleen blew kisses and waved.

Lexie must have spotted her from the kitchen window as she was walking towards the steps to the apartment because now she skipped down to her. 'How's it going? Did you have a nice day with your friends?'

Kathleen hiccupped, swaying slightly.

'Oh, it's like that, is it?' Lexie said, grinning.

'Come down for a few minutes, will you, dear?' Kathleen begged. 'I need to tell you about my rainbow.'

'I forgot! It's today, isn't it?' Lexie said. 'I'm so sorry, Kathleen.'

'Don't be silly! You can't be expected to remember all my ludicrous notions.'

As they closed the door, Kathleen waddled over to the couch and plonked down heavily. 'Oh dear, I'm not very good at all-day drinking. I used to be *faaaaa*bulous at it,' she said, batting her hand and sounding much more American than usual. 'But I guess age makes everything less efficient. My poor liver is probably turning to marble as I speak.'

'Let's hope not.' Lexie smiled. 'So tell me about the rainbow.'

'Ah, it was just exquisite, Lexie ...'

Lexie perched on the arm of the sofa and listened as Kathleen regaled her with the tale. 'The entire back wall was covered. It was spectacular. Jackson, honey, you outdid yourself. Mwah!' she said, blowing a kiss skywards.

'I think you should get to bed shortly or else you're going to wake up feeling stiff and cold at four in the morning, wondering how on earth you got here,' Lexie suggested.

'You're probably right,' she said, hauling herself up. 'Goodnight, then, dear.'

Lexie said she'd let herself out, so Kathleen shuffled into the bathroom. Deciding against a full facial cleanse, she pulled out a wipe, did half a job on her face and teeth, then fell into bed. She kicked off her shoes and curled up, momentarily wondering if she ought to undress.

The last thing that went through her mind as she drifted off was an image of Jackson's smiling face as he bent to kiss her cheek.

Chapter 44

KATHLEEN DIDN'T VENTURE OUT OF THE BASEMENT all the next day. She tried to get out of bed twice, but each time she felt nauseous and her head was spinning.

'Jackson, what's going on, honey? I think I've pickled my innards.' Knowing she should eat, she tried some dry toast but even the smell made her retch. She took a cup of weak tea back to bed and propped herself against the pillows. Swallowing two Tylenol, she prayed the pain would subside.

She could hear toing and froing from above and longed to be able to emerge and make conversation. Her legs were heavy and she racked her brains to recall an accident.

'Was I hit by a truck last night, Jackson?' she asked the ceiling.

When she woke next it was three thirty in the afternoon. Her belly ached and she knew that, no matter what, she had to make herself eat.

She shuffled into the kitchen and found yoghurt in the fridge. Leaning against the counter, she peeled the foil lid back and spooned the creamy pink contents into her mouth with a quivering hand until the pot was empty.

A banana followed a slice of dry bread. Then she forced down a pint of tap water. Knowing it might take her stomach a while to settle, she ventured out of the back door and dragged a chair to the sunny section of the patio.

As she sat down the strangest feeling came over her. She could see everything with renewed vigour. The leaves on the trees and the petals of the flowers were astonishingly crisp. The colours were vivid and enticing. The sound of birdsong was distorted, though, and her head ached. Not in a normal way. It felt as if a tiny man had crawled into her ear and was busily hammering a thick blunt nail through her skull.

The food churned inside her, creating a bloated knot in her stomach. She clamped a hand over her mouth and tried to stand up, terrified that she was going to vomit there and then on Lexie's lovely patio. She took a deep breath. Her stomach settled. Her head continued to throb.

As soon as the ground slowed down and the trees stopped spinning, she moved back into the apartment and towards the bathroom. Leaning against the door, she waited for the nausea to return. Sweat poured down her spine. Perhaps a shower would refresh her. Kathleen staggered to the bedroom to fetch sweat pants and a clean T-shirt.

Confusion overwhelmed her. She had no idea where she was or what she was doing there. The fear was paralysing as her eyes darted around the room. She tried desperately to control her breathing. Her shoes lay upturned near the bed. She knew they were hers. Jackson had bought them at the mall last year. She'd teased him and said he was losing his marbles. 'They cost the same as a month's pay when you started out,' she said.

'That was then, this is now. Besides, you're worth it.'

The jewellery on the dressing table was hers too. She'd found that powder-blue cameo years ago and still loved it. The books beside the bed, one of which had a marker in it, seemed vaguely familiar. But the rest of the stuff ... none of it was from their home.

'Jackson?' she called tentatively. 'Honey?'

The silence haunted her. She needed to find Jackson but her head was pounding and those pillows looked so inviting. Lurching forward, she fumbled with the covers. She managed to pull the corner of the duvet down and climb in. The pillow felt so comforting and soothing against her throbbing head. She felt like Goldilocks commandeering a strange bed. But she hadn't the energy to wonder whom she might be offending or why she'd ended up there.

Closing her eyes helped tremendously. The daylight glared and hurt them.

'Stay here with me, darling Jackson,' she said, as she tried to sleep.

Chapter 45

LEXIE SHOWERED AND TOOK EXTRA CARE APPLYING her body lotion. She'd worn the same Jo Malone scent since they'd met. He'd surprised her with a beautifully wrapped box of perfume, shower gel and body lotion a couple of months ago. 'Sam! This must've cost you a fortune.'

'It did, but I'll get the benefit. You'll feel all wonderful and I'll be on the receiving end of Happy Lexie afterwards.'

'Cheeky!'

She smiled as she covered her arms and chest with the luxurious cream, then switched on her hairdryer and wafted it over her skin, encouraging it to dry. Padding into the dressing room, she pulled a brush through her hair as she flicked through a rail of clothes.

She glanced out of the window to check that it was still sunny and warm. She wanted to look her best. Sam had invited her for dinner. 'An official date,' he'd said, with a smile.

The idea had made Lexie want to cry. She was so relieved he was making an effort. 'Oh, wow,' she said. 'What a lovely idea.'

'And, to add to the fun, I'm going home,' Amélie said, appearing with her bag.

'You don't have to leave, honey,' Lexie said.

'I know, but I need to get settled back at home. I feel bad for Mum and Dad too. They don't deserve the added stress.'

'If that's what you want,' Lexie said.

'It is. Besides, you two lovebirds are a bit nauseating. I'm happier living with people who are less saccharine,' she said, raising her eyes to Heaven.

'I'll drop Amélie home – I've to do a few bits in the office,' Sam said.

'But it's Sunday,' Lexie said.

'I need to sort a couple of things and I'll meet you at the fish restaurant on the promenade at six.'

Wanting to feel comfortable and able to eat her dinner without holding her tummy in, Lexie selected a pair of light drawstring linen trousers and a pastel-coloured, kaftan-style top. The neckline and cuffs had gorgeous twinkling jewels, which meant she didn't need to go rummaging for a necklace and bracelet.

Her skin had enough of a glow to allow her to use a tinted moisturiser rather than foundation. A quick flick of mascara and some lip balm completed her summery look.

Not wanting to take the car, she opted for a pair of ornate Swarovski-crystal-encrusted sandals so she could walk easily.

Tiddles appeared and rubbed against her legs, miaowing up at her. 'Yes, Tiddles, I'll feed you before I go, don't worry.' She scooped him up and buried her nose in his soft fur. He stayed in her arms, purring, as they ventured downstairs where she opened a pouch of food and squeezed it into his dish. 'God bless us and save us, Tiddles, that smells vile,' she said, grimacing. The cat shot over to the dish and began to eat hungrily. 'There's the difference between you and me, Tiddles. My kitchen Hell is your Heaven.'

She'd pottered into the garden when it occurred to her that there was no sign of Kathleen. From the silence and lack of movement, Lexie assumed she was out with Betty and Jenny before they went back to Connemara.

Wanting to make the most of the lovely evening, she set off for the restaurant. There were plenty of people, young and old, rambling around, enjoying the balmy evening. As she arrived she glanced at her watch. She was fifteen minutes early so she ordered a glass of Prosecco. The waiter was chatty and friendly, telling her the place had been hopping all day.

She sipped and closed her eyes momentarily. 'Delicious.' The menu offered the usual starters, then a fantastic array of fresh fish. She and Sam usually shared a mixed platter of antipasti.

By the time she was halfway through her glass of bubbly Lexie could feel her shoulders relaxing. She sat back into her chair and looked around at the other diners.

Sam appeared and bent to kiss her, with a cheeky look on his face.

'What have you been up to?' she asked suspiciously.

'You know me too well.' He grinned. The waiter greeted him and offered him a glass of bubbly.

'Yes, please, and another for my wife, the alcoholic,' he joked.

Moments later, as they toasted one another, Sam produced a small red box.

'What's this?' Lexie asked, in complete shock.

'Open it.'

Lexie gasped as she stared at the pretty diamond cluster ring. 'Sam!'

'It's for your birthday,' he said. 'But I thought you needed it now.'

'I didn't expect anything like this,' she said.

'You deserve it. I love you so much, Lexie. Things have been awful lately but I know we'll work it out. I wanted to make sure you realise how much I want us to be together. What better way to say it than with diamonds?'

'I'm hearing you loud and clear,' she said, as she stood up to hug him. 'I love it. And I love you.'

'Let's just have a main course and go home,' Sam said, arching an eyebrow suggestively.

'Good idea.' She giggled.

The waiter looked slightly confused as they gobbled their food, paid and ran out of the place just over half an hour later. 'No drink on the house?' he asked. 'Beautiful evening, you no want stay longer?'

'We have more important things to do,' Sam said, banging him on the back.

They left hand in hand to walk home. As they came around the corner at Cashel Square Lexie was surprised to see there were still no lights on in the basement. They were just about to go up the steps when they heard a faint voice calling from just inside the basement door.

'Kathleen?' Lexie shouted. The muffled answer alarmed her. 'Are you okay? It's Lexie.'

'Help.'

'I'm coming in,' Lexie said, fumbling with her keys. Mercifully she found the right one and opened the door. 'Kathleen?' she called again.

'Help me.'

Her voice sounded really odd. Lexie and Sam found her slumped against the wall just inside the door.

'Kathleen! Oh, my God, are you okay?'

The older woman shook her head and began to cry. 'I don't know what's happened to me. I have a dreadful pain in my head and I can't figure out what I'm doing here. I've been calling out to Jackson for the longest time and he hasn't come. Can you help me?'

Lexie rushed to her side while Sam called the emergency services. 'It's okay, Kathleen. Help is on the way,' she promised.

Sam had ordered a taxi too, and said he'd meet them at the hospital as the ambulance workers would only allow one person to accompany Kathleen. Lexie had never been in an ambulance before, but she'd had a strange notion that it would be serene and calm. Instead it was like travelling in an out-of-control tin can: everything rattled and clattered while walkie-talkies crackled and beeped non-stop.

Kathleen was wheeled away by a waiting medical team as soon as they arrived. Lexie climbed out of the ambulance and made her way to Accident and Emergency. Not sure what to do, she went to the reception desk and gave her details, explaining she was with Kathleen.

'Thanks for letting us know,' the woman said. 'Take a seat and we'll inform you of any news as we have it.'

Perching on the edge of the yellow plastic chair, Lexie glanced around at the other anxious people sitting there. She'd never been to Accident and Emergency until Amélie was brought in and here she was again. She shuddered, and wondered how on earth the doctors and nurses managed to work there. She'd be terrified. Sam appeared and she ran to him.

'Any news?'

'Not yet,' she said, as they found seats together.

What seemed like a lifetime later, a doctor appeared. 'Are you the lady who brought Kathleen Williams in?'

'Yes,' she said. 'I'm Lexie Collins and this is my husband, Sam.'

'It seems Mrs Williams has suffered a mild stroke.'

'Oh, no! Poor Kathleen,' Lexie cried.

'She's slowly beginning to remember things. It appears she's had an ischaemic stroke, which is caused by a blood clot. That's the most common type and can be treated successfully if we get to it in time.'

'And have you?' Lexie asked.

'It appears so,' the doctor said. 'We've given Mrs Williams an intravenous injection of a blood-thinning drug that should dissolve the clot. We'll need to run some more tests and keep a very close eye on her over the next few days. She's been asking for her husband, Jackson. Is he contactable?'

'No,' Sam said. 'He passed away a couple of months ago.'

'Ah, I see,' said the doctor.

'Do you think the stroke was caused by stress? She was so close to him and she seemed to be doing very well, but maybe when she was alone she was in a terrible state.'

'There are many reasons why people have strokes,' he said. 'The important thing is that Mrs Williams is in the best place now. We'll look after her.'

'Can we see her?' Lexie asked.

'Give us another while to ensure the drug is doing what we want it to and then I'll let you go in to her.'

'Thank you,' Sam said, shaking the doctor's hand.

They went back to the plastic chairs and sat down.

'Poor Kathleen. She must've been so scared earlier,' Lexie said.

'Thank God we found her when we did,' Sam said. Lexie nodded and laid her head on his chest.

Knowing they'd want to be informed, Lexie phoned her parents and Agata.

'Oh how awful,' Agata said. 'Please let me know if there's anything

I can do. Tell her Britta and I send our love. We'll come and visit as soon as the doctors allow it.'

'I'll keep you in the loop,' Lexie promised.

Her parents were equally shocked. 'The poor woman. She's been through a terrible lot lately, hasn't she?' Penelope sympathised. 'Still, good for you for acting so swiftly, dear.'

'I'm just glad we found her when we did,' Lexie said.

It was after midnight before the hospital staff would allow Lexie and Sam to see Kathleen. Not sure if the older woman would recognise them, they tiptoed into the room, hoping they wouldn't cause further confusion.

'Hello, Lexie darling,' Kathleen murmured. 'And Sam. You're my knights in shining armour.' Her lips were chapped and dry and she seemed to have aged.

'You remember us.' Lexie breathed a sigh of relief. 'You gave us a bit of a shock earlier on. How are you feeling?'

'Pretty rough,' Kathleen said. 'Seems you found me just in time. Thank you, my darling friends. You really have been sent to me by an angel. Where would I be without you both?' Tears slipped down her wan cheeks as she closed her eyes. 'This isn't really how I envisaged my life.'

'I know,' Lexie said. 'But, fingers crossed, you're over the worst of it now.'

'I'll be fine,' Kathleen sobbed. 'I'm just feeling super-emotional.'

'Of course you are,' Lexie soothed. 'I called Agata and my parents. They all send their love and Mum and Dad are praying for you.'

'That's so kind.'

'Is there anyone else you'd like me to call? Maybe Rodger or Betty?'

'Oh, thank you, dear, but I think I'll leave it until tomorrow. It's too late. We don't want them thinking there's something wrong.'

In spite of the awful situation, Lexie and Sam burst out laughing.

'Eh, maybe something isn't quite right, Kathleen. Correct me if I'm wrong, but you just made a pretty good attempt at wiping yourself out,' Sam said.

'I did, didn't I? I'm a tough old bird, though. I'll hang in there.'

'You'd better,' Lexie said, as Sam nodded. 'Now we're going to let you sleep – you look exhausted.' Lexie took her hand gently. 'I'll bring you some essentials in the morning. Is there anything special you'd like from the flat?'

'Just some nightdresses and my washbag, if you don't mind,' Kathleen said. 'Call me narrow-minded, but I'm not crazy about these hospital gowns.'

'They're not the most attractive.' Lexie smiled. 'The nurses have our details, but if you need us during the night, please call, okay?'

'Thank you, sweet girl. Thank you, Sam.'

They kissed her and left the hospital.

As they lay entwined in bed a while later, Lexie and Sam had never felt more grateful to have one another.

Chapter 46

KATHLEEN SPENT THE NIGHT CAUGHT BETWEEN drugged slumber and semi-consciousness, a horrible sensation, but the nurses were kind. She was beyond relieved when the morning rounds began and her breakfast arrived on a tray.

She hadn't realised she had her cell phone with her until it rang. Cautiously she reached out and caught hold of the cardigan she'd been wearing on admission and took it out of the pocket. 'Hello?'

'Kathleen, it's Agata.'

'Hello, dear,' she said.

'Lexie called to tell me about your stroke. You poor love. How are you feeling today?'

'I've been better, and I was lucky Lexie and Sam found me when they did.'

'None of it sounds at all lucky if you ask me,' Agata said. 'In fact it sounds horrendous.'

'Ah, you know how it is. We need to look on the bright side, eh?'

'There is no bright side with a stroke. Enough of that. When can I come and visit? Britta has only just found a grandma so you're not allowed to die yet.'

Kathleen laughed. 'Nobody else could put it quite like that.'

'I mean it! If you die I'll be furious with you,' Agata said.

'I'll do my best not to,' Kathleen answered, as a nurse popped her head around the door. 'Just a second, Agata. Nurse, am I allowed to have a visit from my granddaughter?'

'I don't see why not, just so long as it's a short one,' the nurse replied.

'I heard that,' Agata said. 'We'll be there this afternoon, okay?'

'Lovely.'

The nurse checked her vital signs and said they'd be running several tests throughout the day.

Then Kathleen decided to call Rodger.

'Ah, hello, my friend,' he answered cheerfully. 'You're up early today. Isn't it great to see the sun shining again?'

'Well, it's not a whole lot of use to me at the moment,' Kathleen said. She told Rodger all she could remember. He was understandably shocked and said how sorry he was.

'One good turn deserves another. Would you like a visitor?'

'Indeed I would!'

Rodger had nothing planned so he said he'd finish his breakfast and head straight over.

Betty and Jenny would be hurt if she didn't let them know what had happened so next she dialled Betty's number.

'Hi, Kathleen!' Betty answered. 'I'm just about to leave the house to go to Ruth's and mind the children. How are things?'

Kathleen filled her in. 'A lot of it is very fuzzy. Apparently I came to the hospital by ambulance and I don't remember a single bit of that.'

'Do you think all the wine we drank contributed to the whole thing?'

'No, dear. I'd say that's a total coincidence,' Kathleen reassured her.

'What can I do for you?' Betty asked. 'Will I come back up to Caracove? I could stay with you in the flat until you feel stronger.'

'You are a darling,' Kathleen said. 'I wouldn't hear of it. Besides, your grandchildren need you there. I'll be here for another few days minimum and I'll have Lexie and Sam upstairs.'

Kathleen was suddenly exhausted so they hung up. It would take her a while to regain her strength but she was grateful for all the support she had.

She felt as if she'd only just closed her eyes when there was a knock at the door. 'Hello,' she said, trying not to sound groggy.

'It's Rodger. Is it okay if I come in?' said a voice from outside the half-open door.

'Please do.' She made certain that her hospital gown wasn't gaping anywhere.

'Hi,' he said, smiling. 'Fancy meeting you here!'

'The tables have turned,' she answered. 'Musical hospital beds!'

'It comes with the territory when you reach our age,' Rodger said, rolling his eyes. 'Some of the old parts don't work as well as they once did.'

'That's a fact,' Kathleen said. 'It's a funny thing, this getting older business, isn't it?'

'I still feel forty in my head. It's only when I see myself in the mirror or a bit of me breaks that I discover I'm not as young as I feel.' He grinned.

'I know what you mean. You'd think with all the technology someone might've come up with a way of staying young for ever, wouldn't you?'

'Would you honestly take it if they did?' Rodger asked, with his head to the side.

'No,' she said. 'I reckon when my time comes I'll be done, in every sense of the word.'

'I agree,' he said. 'God, we're morbid!'

'Just aware,' Kathleen said. 'I think it's because my Jackson and your Claudia are gone – we don't have the insatiable hunger to live for ever any more.'

'You said it, girl. I'm enjoying my days. I'm happier than I thought I would be … When Claudia died I assumed I'd never belly-laugh again. I thought my world would a horrible shade of grey and eventually stop turning. But life goes on. It may not be the same, but it still happens.'

Kathleen lay back against the pillows.

'The fear that used to grip me before Jackson died was awful,' she admitted. 'I used to wake in the small hours of the morning and stare at him in the darkness. I'd torture myself with the notion that he was slipping away from me. Slowly ebbing towards a place I'd never find.'

'Do you think they can see and hear us?' Rodger asked.

'I know they can,' Kathleen answered.

For a while they sat in companionable silence.

'Until yesterday I thought I secretly wanted to die too,' Kathleen said.

'But now?'

'I've surprised myself,' she mused. 'I knew something bad was happening to me. The pain in my head was appalling and I wanted it to stop, but this instinct kicked in. I wanted to survive, Rodger. I didn't feel ready to go just yet.'

'Then your time hasn't come,' he stated.

'I've been doing well, even if I say so myself,' she said. 'But it's been a constant struggle.'

'Jackson has only been gone a matter of weeks.'

'I know. But the way I've come to see it is this. If I don't alter my mind-set I'll spend the rest of my time on this planet making do. Merely existing. It's never going to be the same but that's okay. I see that now. I'm going to embrace each new day and try to find the best things on offer in this world.'

'Good for you.'

Rodger stayed for a while longer. They talked about the past, the present and, most importantly, the future. They agreed that life had to be appreciated.

Kathleen dozed off again and woke as Lexie stepped into the room laden with bags, flowers and fresh fruit.

'Hello there,' Kathleen said, stretching. 'Aren't I the popular one today?'

'You look a thousand times better than you did last night,' Lexie said. 'Which wouldn't be hard.'

'I'm sorry for scaring you, honey.'

'Don't worry about it,' she said. 'Now, I need you to do something for me. This party my mother's organising ...'

'Oh, yes.'

'You're to have your own table and invite your friends.'

'That's out of the question, Lexie. This is for you and your family.'

'I decided in the ambulance last night that if you survived you were hosting a table. Here you are, so the decision has been made.'

Lexie sat on the chair beside the bed and dropped the bags on to the floor. 'Flowers,' she said, shoving the bunch into an empty vase on the bedside locker. 'Fruit.' She put grapes and apples into the bowl. 'They think of everything in here, don't they?' she commented.

'I guess all folk bring the same stuff.'

Finding a pen and notepad, she leafed through the pages. 'Who do you want to invite?'

'Really?' Kathleen raised an eyebrow.

'Yes, shoot!'

'Britta and Agata, Betty and Jenny, Ben and George, Rodger and Tiddles.'

Lexie giggled. 'Tiddles is inviting his own friends, including the budgie from number six that he's been salivating over for the past eight months. It sits in a cage in full view of all the neighbourhood cats and teases them.'

'Like Tweetie Pie from the old cartoon.'

'That's exactly what he is,' Lexie said.

'So I won't ask Tiddles.'

'No, he's sorted. Besides, you have a perfect table of eight. My mother will approve. She likes things to be just so.'

'Isn't the party in September?' Kathleen asked.

'It was going to be, but we've changed it to August so you can come.'

Kathleen had to bite back tears. 'That's just precious of you, Lexie.'

'I couldn't have my party without you there and, correct me if I'm wrong, but your wedding anniversary is in August, isn't it?'

'Certainly is,' she said wistfully.

'So maybe we'll have a rainbow to add to the occasion.'

'Maybe we will,' Kathleen said, smiling.

'You should get some sleep,' Lexie said a few minutes later.

'I need a nap all right,' she agreed. 'I know you've only just arrived, but strokes are kind of exhausting.'

Chapter 47

KATHLEEN HAD GONE FROM BEING AS WEAK AS A kitten to feeling better than she had in years. Ben and George had been amazing. 'Knock, knock,' they called, at the door to the flat. 'We have supper!'

'You're my two guardian angels, did you know that?'

'You've only told us about a thousand times,' George quipped.

'I don't know how I would've managed without you, boys, over the last couple weeks,' she said.

'We know, we know,' Ben said. 'As we said before, it's totally our pleasure.'

It was the day before Lexie's party and the two men had brought a Thai green curry to share. 'Mum can't bear anything with spices so we never make it for her,' Ben said.

'What time are the girls arriving?' Kathleen asked, as she tossed the salad.

'Their train gets in just after nine. I'll fly to the station and collect them,' George said. 'They don't want to wear you out so they said they'll see you tomorrow.'

'I'm looking forward to it already,' Kathleen said excitedly. 'It's going to be a superb weekend.'

'It certainly will,' Ben agreed. 'We need to make the most of it, seeing as you're leaving us next week.'

'I have to go home some time,' Kathleen said. 'Much as I'd love to stay here longer, I need to face our house and all of Jackson's things.'

'We understand,' George said, 'but we'll all miss you.'

'Who knows? Maybe you'll come over with your mothers for a visit,' she said hopefully.

'We'd be there in a heartbeat, Kathleen, you know we would. It's just a matter of money. If I get the job I attended the interview for,' Ben said, 'we'll try to sort something.'

By the time they'd had supper George had to leave for the station.

'I'll wander back to the house and make sure it's shipshape for the beady eyes of our mothers,' Ben said, with a wink.

Kathleen cleared the plates and pottered about before going to bed to read. She was truly excited about the party the following night. Penelope had dropped in several times to let her in on the plans. Kathleen could understand why she and Lexie didn't see eye to eye at times, but she couldn't fault her. During the last few weeks as she was convalescing, Penelope had been unbelievably kind and thoughtful.

As she climbed into bed Kathleen knew she was going to miss Cashel Square and Caracove Bay dreadfully. Ireland had become a new and different life for her. Jackson had never been to Caracove so it was easier to bear the separation there. This bed, this bathroom, the sofa and kitchen table had never hosted her darling husband, so his absence didn't seem quite as cruel. But the ghost of him would echo through every corridor of their home in Orlando. She longed to touch his clothes, see all their framed photos and immerse herself in the life they'd once had. But she wasn't sure she would stay there. She didn't know if she'd be able to live out the rest of her days in a place where Jackson had been king. Her king.

Lexie finished putting on a layer of fake tan. The pretty coral chiffon dress she'd chosen for the party would look so much better if she had an extra glow.

'You smell,' Sam said, wrinkling his nose, as she padded into the dressing room wearing nothing but slippers.

'Thanks.' She grinned, and he attempted to pull her into his arms. 'Naughty,' she said, slapping his hand away. 'You can't touch me until I'm dry.'

'Yet another reason why most men despise fake tan,' Sam mused. 'It stinks and there's no hanky-panky while it dries.'

'You'll appreciate it when I look sun-kissed at the party.'

'Do I really have to wear that silk shirt you bought me?' he asked, like a grumpy teenager.

'You can wear whatever you like tomorrow night. But you might end up having to stay here on your own.'

'How's Penelope holding up?' Sam asked.

'Fine.' Lexie rolled her eyes. 'You'd swear she was organising the return of the Messiah the way she's carrying on. She must have four clipboards stuffed with bits of paper.'

'She loves it all,' Sam said. 'It'll give poor Dee a break too. I'd say Penelope has a stop-watch counting backwards till her due date.'

'Talk about a doting grandmother, I think she's more excited than Dee, Billy and Amélie put together.'

'It's nice to see. And better than her showing no interest, I guess.'

'True,' Lexie agreed.

In spite of the fake tan, he wrapped his arms around her and spooned close to her in bed.

Chapter 48

THE DAY OF THE PARTY WAS LIKE ARMAGEDDON.

'Oh, Sam, it's vile out there,' Lexie said, pulling back the curtains and looking at the squally rain. 'Mum will do her nut. She'd been hoping to serve drinks on the veranda so people could have a lovely view of the boats.'

'Well, she'll have to settle for drinks inside, won't she?' Sam said matter-of-factly. 'Your mother can organise a lot of things but the weather is beyond even Penelope's control.'

The phone rang and Lexie dashed to grab it. 'Hi, Mum! Yes, I know … I know … Yes, of course … No, don't worry … Yes, of course people realise this is Ireland. As you say yourself, one can't depend on the weather around here … Okay … Yes, I'll see you then. If you need me to do any last-minute jobs you know where I am … Okay … Okay, Mum.' Lexie was looking cross. 'I'm not being snippy. I was just trying to help.'

By the time she hung up Lexie was agitated. 'How does Mum always manage to turn everything into a row?'

'She's highly strung, you're highly strung. You're probably too alike,' Sam observed.

'I am *not* like her,' Lexie fumed.

Sam raised his eyebrows. '"Mirror, mirror, on the wall, I am my mother after all."'

'Run like the wind, Sam, before I do damage to you.' Lexie laughed as he shot off down the stairs.

'Coffee is ready and the toast is on,' he shouted, a few minutes later.

She padded downstairs in her dressing gown. In the kitchen, he nudged her. 'So you're nearly forty!'

'You're already forty.' She elbowed him back.

'Yup, but I don't give a toss what age I am. Ladies seem to have more of a problem with all this.'

'I actually don't mind turning forty,' Lexie said. 'In fact, I think there's a certain advantage to it.'

'How?'

'Well, a person in their forties is probably taken a little more seriously than a person in their twenties or thirties. It's sort of accepted that you've grown into yourself, that you're *au fait* with your life and all it entails.'

'That's very profound of you.' He grinned.

'Um, that's because I'm going into my forties,' she said, raising her pinkie to drink her coffee. 'I'm going to get my hair done with Kathleen in a while. What are your plans?'

'Well, I'll do my own hair,' he said, shaking his head like a sheepdog. 'I'm meeting your father at the yacht club to do a few chores.'

'Oh? Like what?'

'All will be revealed!' Sam said, tapping the side of his nose and winking.

'God, I *hate* secrets.' Lexie scowled.

'You don't hate surprises, though, and that's what these are, little surprises. There's a difference.'

'I suppose,' she agreed reluctantly.

They finished breakfast in companionable silence, both lost in their own thoughts.

A knock at the front door made Lexie jump. Glancing at her watch, she cursed under her breath as she opened it. 'Kathleen! Hello, love, come on in. I'll be with you in two seconds. I was in a world of my own there. Sam will make you a cuppa while I throw some clothes on.'

'Take your time, Lexie. I'm probably a bit early. I'm so excited, you wouldn't believe it.'

'Ha! You are sweet,' Lexie said, hugging her. 'How are you feeling today?'

'On top of the world, my dear,' she said cheerfully. 'I'm better with each passing day. I'll be back to my old self in no time.'

'Good for you!'

As Lexie ran up the stairs she said a silent prayer of thanks that Kathleen was doing so well.

Fifteen minutes later they pitched up at the Caracove Bay hair salon.

'Hello, Lexie!'

'Hi, Shelly,' Lexie answered. 'Are you ready to make Kathleen and me look like movie stars?'

'I certainly am,' she said. 'As it's a special occasion I'm putting you both into the private room upstairs.'

'Really?'

'Follow me,' Shelly instructed. 'This is where we do all the graduation girls, brides and hen nights. It's a self-contained salon where you can have a little glass of bubbly and chat without anybody interfering. I'll be looking after you, with Kaylee, so it'll be fun.'

'Super! Is it feasible for us to take the room when there's only Kathleen and me?' Lexie asked.

'Sure it'll be fine,' Shelly said.

'After you,' Kathleen said, as they reached the bottom of the stairs.

Lexie ran up and opened the door at the top.

'Surprise!'

'Oh, my God! I wasn't expecting this,' Lexie said, nearly falling backwards. There, looking thrilled with themselves, were her mother, Maia, Dee, Amélie, Agata and little Britta.

'Did you know about this?' Lexie asked Kathleen.

'I arranged it.'

'Thank you!'

'I didn't know what to give you as a present so I thought I'd do something you'd remember.'

'You're so kind,' Lexie said, glassy-eyed.

'Not only are we having our hair done, but I've booked a makeup lady too,' Kathleen said proudly. 'She does lots of TV makeup and she sounded lovely over the phone.'

'Brilliant!' Lexie rushed to kiss everyone.

'I'm having GHD curls and I'm going to ask the makeup lady to put on these.' Amélie held out the craziest pair of false eyelashes Lexie had ever seen.

'Amélie! How are you going to see through those electric-blue feathers?' Lexie laughed.

'Aren't they mint-bomb?'

'I love them,' Kathleen said. 'If I was fifty years younger I'd wear them too.'

'Why don't you get some extra-long luscious lashes?' Amélie asked, with one eyebrow raised.

'I might just do that.' Kathleen giggled.

Maia handed Lexie a lurid pink bathrobe and feather boa.

'It's my birthday, not my hen night,' Lexie remonstrated.

'Stop nit-picking,' Maia said. 'You wouldn't allow me do any of this when you got married so I'm doing it now. I'm feeling quite calm at the moment but I could turn on you at any second, so don't annoy me.'

'Okay, crazy lady, I'll wear it all.'

'And you have to let me take photos of you and put them on Facebook,' she continued.

'What?' Lexie looked stricken. 'But I thought you hated Facebook!'

'I've become obsessed with it lately. It's like a drug. Seeing as I can't drink wine in the evenings I've started messing around on my computer. I was buying loads of baby things on-line, but figured Josh and I would be broke by the time I give birth, so I've substituted Facebook.' She sighed.

'That's healthy.' Lexie rolled her eyes.

'It's shameful but I can't help it. I'm not downloading the app on my phone or I won't do any work. I've become so nosy. I think of people from way back when and start trying to find them. I've got over three hundred friends already.'

Lexie laughed. 'I never go near it, but maybe I'm missing out.'

'Oh, you are! Please join and then at least I can converse with you. If I'm sharing too much information you can call me and tell me to stop. I don't trust myself any longer.'

Penelope and Agata went first as there were only two basins in the room. The others sat on the shocking pink sofas and admired the pony-print laminated table.

'This place is sick!' Amélie said, as she bounced baby Britta on her lap.

'Doncha just love it?' Shelly asked. 'I would actually live here if my husband didn't object. I put in all the décor I'm not allowed have at home.'

'When I get my own place it's *soooo* going to be like this,' Amélie vowed.

Agata decided to have her hair straightened and Penelope opted for an up-style. A tray of drinks arrived, with a three-tiered stand of divine cupcakes. Decorated in pastel colours, they looked almost too good to eat. 'They come with love and compliments of Ramona from the café,' Shelly said.

A little envelope was tucked into the cakes. 'Aw,' said Lexie. 'She's written, "Happy birthday to one of my best and favourite customers. See you this evening, love Ramona."'

'How lovely,' Penelope exclaimed.

'She's a doll,' said Kathleen. 'I asked her to do them for me and she insisted on giving them as her pressie.'

By the time they'd all had their hair done, the makeup lady arrived.

'Hi, all, I'm Cat and I'm here to make you even more beautiful.'

'As long as she doesn't make us look like she does, I'll be happy,' Penelope hissed to Lexie.

'Shush, Mum! She'll hear you.'

Cat had bright violet bobbed hair and looked as if baby Britta had got at her with a packet of face paints. Her eyelids were coloured with stripes of fluorescent pink and black, her skin was Sudocrem pale and, the *pièce de résistance*, her lips were blue.

'So, who's first, then?' she asked, popping some bubble gum into her mouth.

'Me!' Amélie jumped up and went to sit at a mirrored dressing table.

'At least she's enthusiastic,' Dee whispered to Lexie.

'I couldn't agree more,' Lexie said. 'Although I'd prefer her not to look like a drag queen when Cat's finished with her.'

'I'm loving your eye shadow,' Maia said. 'Can you do mine like yours?' Lexie had to stifle her giggles as her friend started rooting through Cat's selection.

'Maia,' Lexie whispered, 'I don't think those are your colours.'

'Exactly.' Maia winked. 'I'm milking this pregnancy thing. I'll have a few more months of madness while I can.'

They were all pleasantly surprised by the wonderful job Cat did.

'We look like models,' Kathleen said. 'Would you mind taking a group photo?' Cat agreed readily.

As they all left, Penelope reminded them of the party's arrival time. 'So we'll see you there at seven thirty,' she said. 'On the dot, please.'

Lexie grinned. Her mother was never going to change. She'd always be a fusspot but, for some reason, Lexie didn't find that as annoying as she used to.

Maybe on hitting forty she was learning some tolerance ...

Chapter 49

AS KATHLEEN, BRITTA, AGATA, LEXIE AND MAIA walked back towards Cashel Square, they chatted amicably.

'That was such fun, Kathleen. Thank you so much,' Lexie said.

'You're welcome. I enjoyed it too. Nothing like a bit of girly time to lift the spirits.'

'I'm delighted to have a day without the boys,' Maia agreed. 'I love them dearly but there's only so much I can take of car noises and digging in the sand pit.'

Lexie put her arm through Maia's. 'I'm glad you're honest about motherhood,' she said. 'You don't act like a Mary Poppins style Mum when I know you're not.'

'Josh and I are a perfect match,' she said. 'He has the patience of a saint and loves nothing more than wiling away the hours at Calvin's pace. He's doing potty training with him at the moment and I can't get over how encouraging he is.'

'Calvin's doing so well,' Lexie said. 'But I'm guessing it would be great to have him out of nappies when the baby comes.'

'The carer at the centre we take Calvin to from time to time was really impressed. She said it obviously varies but that he's pretty young to be almost trained, considering he has DS.'

'All children differ, of course,' Agata said, 'but you and Josh are a great team. Calvin is lucky to have you as parents.'

'Thanks, Agata,' Maia said, as her eyes filled with tears. 'Every now and again it's lovely to hear I'm doing something right.'

Lexie laughed.

'What's so funny?' Maia shot back.

'You! Sorry, honey, I shouldn't laugh but you really are a looney! One minute you're like a Rottweiler, the next you're Mrs Sincere and then you're blubbing.'

'Yeah.' She sighed. 'Being pregnant is a crazy bat-shit thing, my friend.'

'Will we have a snack and some tea?' Lexie suggested, as they arrived at the house.

'Sounds lovely, but we don't want to impose,' Agata said.

'You're not at all.'

Britta had fallen asleep in her buggy, so Lexie wheeled her into the sitting room. The inky sky rumbled menacingly as they sat down.

'What an awful day,' Lexie said, her hands on her hips. 'Hey!' She jumped as Sam appeared behind her. 'Are you creeping up on us?'

'No, I live here.'

'What are you up to? You look guilty,' Lexie said.

'You do, actually,' Maia agreed.

'None of your business, either of you,' he said, tapping the side of his nose with his finger.

They finished their snack and Maia went home to change and pick up Josh. Downstairs there was great excitement as Kathleen and Agata dressed Britta.

'Oh, she looks just darling,' Kathleen exclaimed.

'Well, that isn't surprising, seeing as she's wearing head-to-toe designer clothing,' Agata said, with mild disapproval. 'I still cannot believe you bought her Prada. She's a baby!'

'She's my granddaughter so I'll spoil her if I like – isn't that right, Britta?' Kathleen cooed.

Britta looked edible in a sugar pink and white gingham dress with a soft tulle underskirt, pale pink ballerina tights and the most stunning shoes Kathleen had ever laid eyes on. They were Mary-Janes with a diamanté bow at the front in shiny supple patent leather.

'Look!' Britta shouted, and pointed at her shoes.

'New shoes for Britta,' Kathleen said, encouraging her to talk.

'Sooz,' Britta repeated, and clapped.

'I've died and gone to Heaven,' Kathleen exclaimed. 'She's just precious. That was worth every cent.'

'You're a sucker,' Agata said drily.

The tiny bolero cardigan with diamanté clasp made Agata giggle.

'That is just the limit! It's so tiny! How on earth do they make these things so small?'

'Isn't it heavenly?' Kathleen agreed. 'That's what set me off on the whole shopping spree. I was in the store looking for a little gift for Britta and I spotted it on a shelf. Well, I was a goner. When I realised there was an entire outfit to match, I just *had* to have it.'

'Did you say thank you to Grandma Kathleen?' Agata asked.

'Tata!' Britta said, puckering her lips. Kathleen leaned in and they did a sucker-fish style kiss.

'You're welcome, baby girl.' Kathleen laughed. 'Oh you do bring such joy to my heart,' she said. 'It's wonderful to have you both here!'

Agata hugged her. 'I'm going to miss you when you go,' she said.

'And I'm going to miss you two more than you'll ever know,' Kathleen said. 'Maybe you'll come visit.'

'I'd love that, you know I would,' Agata said. 'Let's see how my finances work out.'

Amélie was having a rare moment of compatibility with Dee. 'Mum, you look really great in that.'

'Do I?' Dee looked doubtful. 'I've tried on everything I own and it all makes me look like a beached whale.'

'That dress is gorgeous. Pale lilac is so this year,' Amélie said. 'It would be a trillion times better if you put a fun necklace and earrings with it. I have just the thing, if you want to try?'

'Eh … I'm not sure your stuff would work on me, love. I wasn't even sure about the colour of this dress, but the girl in the maternity shop insisted I buy it. I might be a bit long in the tooth …'

'Mum, if you're young enough to have a baby, you can certainly rock it in some bling.'

Amélie ran to her room and came back with a diamanté choker and matching earrings. She fastened the choker around her mother's throat and handed her the earrings to put on. 'I reckon this would be mega too,' she said, producing a cream goose-down bolero.

'I'd never fit into that,' Dee said. 'And it's a step too far for me.'

Amélie was having none of it and insisted her mother at least try it on. 'See? It fits! You look wowzers, Mum!'

'I do?'

'Of course.' Amélie seemed a little puzzled. 'You're very pretty, Mum, but you stick to rather stuffy clothes so you rarely stand out. You should put yourself out there a little more.'

'Thank you,' Dee said. 'Now let's see you in your finery. Grandma will be very proud of us both, which is good, seeing as she kindly bought all the new stuff.'

'I'm sorry things are so hard financially for you and Dad at the moment,' Amélie said. 'I've realised since I've worked in the gallery how hard it is to make money. I always assumed Auntie Lexie was loaded and didn't do much work. But she's there all the time and never stops. Just because she charges three hundred for a painting, it doesn't mean she has three hundred to go and spend on makeup. There are rents and rates and wages and all that to be paid first.'

Dee smiled. 'I'm glad you've learned so much.' She stroked her daughter's hair tenderly. 'It's good that you understand the value of things a little better. I wish Dad and I could give you more things, but it's not going to be that easy once this little baby's arrived.'

'I know,' Amélie said. 'I was thinking maybe I could get a summer job that pays proper money next year. You've been more than generous with pay, but I want to plan my strategy and try to make money for all of next summer.'

'That's a good idea,' she said, smiling. 'For now, though, you need to knuckle down and do your best at school.'

'I will.'

The front door opening let them know Billy was home. Amélie ran to her room to get dressed.

Penelope and Reggie were getting into their taxi as the rain persisted.

'This is ghastly,' Penelope complained. 'I stupidly assumed we'd have a gorgeous sunny evening.'

'It'll be splendid either way, love. Don't get yourself in a tizzy.

There's no point. As long as people show up and enjoy themselves, your job has been well done.'

'That's true.' Penelope sighed. 'You know, it was strange at the salon today. I haven't seen Lexie so relaxed or cheerful for a long time.'

'That's great.' Reggie nodded.

'Dee is blooming, and she and Amélie seem to have called a truce on their constant snapping.'

'That's a relief. Poor Dee doesn't need any added stress right now. Please God Amélie is back on track now too.'

'Agata – the artist – was there with her baby,' Penelope said. 'She's a dotey little thing, I must say. Typically Scandinavian, with white-blonde hair, big blue eyes and divine sallow skin.'

'She sounds very sweet,' Reggie said, patting his wife's hand.

'You met her at the gallery one night, Reggie,' she snapped.

'Did I? If you say so, dear.'

Penelope clicked her tongue off the roof of her mouth. 'Anyway, Lexie was terribly good with the little cherub. Very natural with her … I've no idea why she won't have a baby, Reggie. What's the big deal? Most people do it!'

'Most people,' Reggie repeated. 'But that doesn't mean Lexie and Sam ought to. You said yourself, dear, she was happy today. It's her birthday party tonight. Don't bring up Babygate. Let it slide and maybe it's time we accepted her decision. All I ever wanted was for our children to be happy. We can still be there if they need us but, equally, we ought to keep quiet when they don't. They're all adults now, Penelope.'

'But mothers know best, Reggie. What if she's making a mistake she comes to regret?'

'Then that's her lookout,' Reggie said. 'One woman's happiness can be another woman's nightmare. Don't you see? We can't tell Lexie how to be happy. She needed to find her own version of happiness and I think she has.'

Penelope sat in silence for the rest of the journey. What Reggie had said made perfect sense. She just wasn't sure she liked it.

Chapter 50

LEXIE, SAM, KATHLEEN, AGATA AND BRITTA ARRIVED
just after Penelope and Reggie.

'Hello!' Reggie said, kissing each of them in turn. 'Isn't it just
dreadful out there?'

'Hi, Daddy,' Lexie said. 'It's like winter. The wind is unbelievable.'

'All the more reason to have a nice drink,' Sam said, shaking hands
with Reggie.

'My thoughts exactly! Let's get to the bar.'

The women chatted to Penelope in the reception area just inside
the main entrance.

'As Lexie knows, I had intended hosting the drinks reception out
on the veranda but unless we all want to be blown to Wales that's not
an option,' Penelope said.

'It's lovely in here,' Agata said. 'I love the old-world style of the
place. The heavy gold and burgundy tones suit the Georgian building
so well.'

'Reggie and I have socialised here for years. It's lovely to have as
a facility,' Penelope agreed. 'Kathleen, how are you feeling now? I
hope the day hasn't been too much for you, with the salon earlier
on.'

'Oh, no, I'm feeling great, thank you, Penelope. I can really
notice the difference in my stamina. Even this time last week when
you called to me in the evening I was quite tired.'

'I remember,' Penelope said, looking concerned.

'But now I'm so much better. I've actually been given clearance to
fly home, which is rather handy. I didn't fancy the swim.'

'No.' Penelope laughed.

'I'm so excited about tonight. I can't tell you how pleased I am to be in a position to invite my friends too. That was such a wonderfully kind idea.'

'We're delighted to do it,' Penelope said. 'Lexie is so fond of you. She's enjoyed your company this summer no end. We all have.'

Just then the other guests started to arrive.

Maia looked stunning in a rather daring backless black dress. 'Rocking the sexy pregnant style,' Lexie said, whistling.

'I love it from the back, but then I turn around and I'm like the girl who ate all the pies,' she said.

'I reckon that bright eye shadow you insisted Cat put on is distracting from your bump big-time,' Lexie said.

'Calvin adored it. He kept hugging and kissing me.' She giggled.

The inclement weather drove the guests inside rapidly so within forty minutes everyone was there, drink in hand. The meal was delicious, with either tian of crab or chicken satay to start, followed by watercress soup, then *boeuf en croûte* or sea bass. When dessert was nowhere to be seen, Lexie feared the worst. The entire room erupted into an alcohol-fuelled version of 'Happy Birthday' and she knew she was scuppered.

'Speech!' Sam shouted. The momentum built so Lexie knew she'd no choice but to say a few words.

'I'll attempt to murder Sam later for making me stand up here,' she said, and went on to thank her family and friends, then sat again as quickly as possible.

'Before we all start dancing the night away,' Sam said, 'I'd like you to join us on the balcony. The rain has mercifully stopped and we have a little surprise for you all.'

All the guests milled towards the back doors and outside into the evening air. Waiters with trays of champagne offered a glass to each guest. Before anyone could question why they were standing there, a magnificent fireworks display was sending popping colours into the sky.

Kathleen and Rodger joined Lexie and Sam, Maia and Josh, Penelope and Reggie to gaze at them, entranced. As they came to a crescendo there were gasps from everyone as Lexie's name was written in golden sparkles across the sky. The very final display was a sparkling rainbow, which lit the entire bay.

Lexie turned to Kathleen and held her hand out. As they gazed into the night sky, the older woman's smile couldn't have been wider.

'Happy anniversary,' Lexie whispered.

'Thank you, dear.' Kathleen smiled. 'I honestly didn't expect to see a rainbow today. Sam is a sweetheart to do that for me.'

'Do what?' Sam asked.

'The rainbow!' she said.

'Oh, right.' He looked confused.

'You did tell him?' Kathleen asked Lexie. 'He does know, I presume?'

'Know what? Are you drunk, Kathleen?' Sam laughed. 'What on earth are you talking about, woman?'

'You mean you didn't tell the fireworks people to do the rainbow for me?'

'Eh … Should I lie and pretend I did?' he asked.

'No!' Lexie said. 'Definitely not, but just answer me this. Did you know about Jackson's promise?'

'No.' Sam looked more confused still.

'Well, I'll be damned,' Kathleen said, and tears coursed down her cheeks.

'What did I do? Kathleen, don't cry,' Sam said, in panic. 'All I asked the fireworks crew to do was spell out Lexie!'

'That's perfect, thank you,' Lexie said, kissing him. 'I'll explain in a minute, but suffice it to say you've just made Kathleen very happy.'

'Why is she sobbing, then?' he asked. Once Lexie had explained Jackson's message, Sam looked even more concerned.

'Jeez, Kathleen,' he said. 'I'm a little creeped out if I'm totally honest.'

Kathleen burst out laughing. 'You look it! Well done. Jackson! Honey, look what you've done!'

'Cheers, Jackson,' Sam said, raising his glass to the sky. 'You freaked me out no end. I'll have to drink myself into a coma now or I'll be awake all night thinking about the afterlife and other things that scare the living daylights out of me.'

Once the music started, the crowd poured back inside to dance. Lexie spotted Amélie sitting alone. 'Hey,' she said. 'Aren't you having fun?'

'Yeah,' Amélie said. 'It's such a mint party. I'm just taking a moment to chill. I can't help thinking how different things could've been if you hadn't come to France with Dad. Or if those drugs had left me in a stupor and that weird guy had done Lord only knows what.'

'It's scary,' Lexie agreed. 'But you've got to move past it all and grab life by the coat-tails now.'

'I will,' Amélie promised. 'My friends are having a blast. Thanks for letting me host a table.' Her pals were singing like chipmunks and falling around laughing. 'Even if they are inhaling all the helium balloons Grandma put up!'

Amélie's gaze fixed on a group of Lexie's friends. 'What are they doing to themselves?' she asked, aghast.

'I think it's called being middle-aged and pissed,' Lexie said, giggling.

'Did people dance like that in discos and nightclubs years ago?' Amélie asked, as her father waved, red-faced and sweaty, while doing a hitch-hiker-style movement. 'He's *sooo* embarrassing. He should have his arms and legs tied together so he can't move. That's off the Richter scale in mortification. I hope nobody films him on a phone. That's grounds for suicide if he ever sees it,' Amélie said, with a watery grin.

'I'm glad your dad's letting his hair down,' Lexie said, tucking her hair behind her ear. 'I hope things get better for you all soon. I love you. You know that, don't you?'

'Yeah.' She grinned. 'You're slurring wildly. I'm holding my drink better than you.'

'You're not meant to be drinking. You're under age.'

'Oops! I'm off to show these old farts how to move on the dance floor,' she said, dashing to grab her friend Yvonne.

Lexie burst out laughing.

'What's so funny?' Sam asked, as he hugged her from behind.

'Amélie,' she managed. 'She can't cope with middle-aged drunken dancing. I think she's gone to wash her eyeballs with acid!'

Sam looked over at the carnage on the dance floor and cracked up too. 'It's pretty hideous, isn't it?'

'Ah, they're having a ball. So what if they look like they've been let out of the lunatic asylum for the night?'

Once some of the eighties classics came on, Lexie and Sam took to the floor, where they stayed for the rest of the night. Penelope and Reggie left as soon as they could. Agata kept telling Lexie how guilty she felt, leaving Britta asleep in her pram.

'She's in the private lounge with one of the waitresses keeping an eye on her. She's perfect!' Lexie said, flapping her hand. 'Don't you worry. Dance the night away!'

The music stopped at two but the drinking continued until three, by which time Lexie felt as if her head was separating. 'I have to go to bed, Sam,' she whimpered. 'I'm broken.'

They swayed up the road together.

'Where did Kathleen and Agata go?' she asked suddenly.

'They left a while ago. It was only the hard core crew left!'

'I'm very hard core, me,' Lexie said, hiccupping.

'You're about as hard as a marshmallow,' Sam said, kissing the top of her head.

Lexie's bed had never felt so wonderful as she fell into it.

Chapter 51

THE FOLLOWING WEEK, KATHLEEN WANTED TO DO something nostalgic with her last day in Ireland. She'd asked Lexie to join her on an early-morning walk. 'I've invited Betty, Jenny, Agata, Britta and Rodger to afternoon tea. Rodger can't make it but said he'd come by later in the evening.'

'The two ladies are so kind to come and visit you again,' Lexie said. 'You're going to leave a rather large hole in many lives.'

'I'm going to miss you all desperately,' Kathleen said. 'I'm actually quite nervous about returning to Orlando. I don't know how I'll cope.'

'I'm sure you have heaps of friends who are longing to see you and welcome you back.'

'Oh, I do,' she said. 'That's not my worry. It's the familiarity that should include Jackson I'm fretting about.'

They sped off towards Cloon woods at the foot of the Wicklow Mountains. As the little Fiat 500 climbed the hill to the pretty woodland walk they were lost in their own worlds.

'This is just amazing,' Lexie exclaimed eventually. 'I'm ashamed to say I've never been here before.'

'You work too hard, young lady,' Kathleen said, wagging a finger.

Lexie laughed.

'So the plan today,' Kathleen said, as they got out of the car, 'is to collect as many blackberries as we can.'

'Is that why you brought me up here at the crack of dawn?' Lexie yawned.

'If there's rain and the fruit is left on the bushes for too long, it'll be full of creepy-crawlies.'

'Not so nice.'

'Certainly not. Jam made with wild fruit equals delicious. Jam with added maggots equals ick.'

The picking was decidedly therapeutic, the serene surroundings lulling them as they inhaled the clear, pure air and allowed the early-morning sunshine to warm their skin.

'This is sort of addictive, isn't it?' Lexie asked, as her fingers turned a delicious shade of mulberry from the oozing juice.

'I used to spend hour upon hour doing this as a child,' Kathleen said. 'Then Mum and I would throw the berries into her huge preserving pan and I'd be allowed to stand on a chair and watch it bubble. I used to pretend I was a wicked witch bubbling up my cauldron.'

'Is this why you asked me to keep all my empty jars for the last while?' she asked, suddenly understanding.

'Sure is! I even went to the trouble of sourcing a large saucepan from Ben and George's house to make our jam.'

By mid-morning they had two sizeable bags of fruit and decided to go home.

'I'd love to have the jam ready for when the guests arrive. I baked fruit scones last night and have clotted cream in the fridge.'

'My mouth's watering already,' Lexie said. 'I'll be the one with my face pressed up against your window drooling when we get home!'

'You won't need to do that. I was hoping you'd come in with me and help me make the jam.'

'I'd love to.'

Lexie was feeling decidedly sad as they pulled up at Cashel Square. 'Sam's car is here,' she said. 'I'll just run in and let him know I'm downstairs.'

'No!' Kathleen said. 'Eh … don't do that. We have very little time to get things done. He'll guess where you are when he sees your car. Let's just get going, if you don't mind, dear.'

Lexie thought Kathleen was behaving slightly oddly, but she made no comment as she followed her into the flat.

Kathleen showed her how to measure the fruit and sugar quantities and explained how to test the juice after it had all been boiling for a while. 'I'll put a saucer in the fridge and once I think the juice is thickening I'll spoon some onto the chilled saucer. If I push it with my finger ever so gently, it should have formed a skin on top, which will wrinkle.'

'How do you know these things?' Lexie marvelled.

'My mother passed them down to me and I'm so thrilled to be in a position to share them with you now.'

'I'll pass them on to Amélie. Although she'd probably spit like a cat if I even suggest an early-morning excursion to the hills, but I'm going to insist. I'll bribe her with money, if need be. I want her to experience this. I know she'll thank me afterwards.'

'Do let me know how you get on,' Kathleen said, with a twinkle in her eye. 'Email me photos too.'

'I will,' Lexie promised.

By early afternoon the jam had been ladled into sterilised jars with wax lids placed on top before their screw tops.

'Why did you put those on?' Lexie asked.

'Because the wax melts with the heat of the jam, then cools and seals it so it doesn't go mouldy.'

'Well, you learn something new every day. How come shop-bought stuff doesn't have that?'

'Because it's full of preservatives. This stuff is all natural.'

The other guests arrived and admired the pretty table Kathleen and Lexie had set in the garden. The sun was still shining and the scene was idyllic.

'Oh, this brings me back to when we were children,' Betty exclaimed. 'Kathleen's mother was a great woman for jam-making. Do you remember the delicious Victoria sponge she used to bake? It melted in the mouth and tasted so buttery.'

Kathleen raised a finger and dashed inside.

'One like this?' she asked proudly, when she returned with an identical cake that had a thick coating of icing sugar on top.

Betty clapped in delight as Agata and Britta arrived.

'Hello, all!' Agata said, looking mildly hassled.

'Hello there,' Kathleen said. 'You're just in time. We're about to cut some cake and have scones.'

'Hiya!' Britta shouted, waving vigorously at everyone.

'Ooh, she is just the cutest thing I've ever seen,' Kathleen exclaimed. 'I want to eat her.'

'I felt like eating her last night too, but not in a nice way,' Agata said, sighing. 'She was so cranky.'

'Her cheeks are red,' Kathleen said, putting her arms out to her. 'Poor little darling.' She kissed her.

'She's probably teething terribly but sometimes I get to a point where I need some distraction. Still,' she said brightly, 'it'll be a different story when I begin work at the gallery.'

'When are you starting?' Betty asked.

'As soon as I can organise a minder,' Agata said. 'There are a few agencies in the area, so I won't have a problem finding someone, I hope.'

Kathleen stood back and watched as her guests chatted and laughed. She would struggle to keep her composure when she boarded the plane the following day.

'Gaga,' Britta said, and pointed at her.

'Oh, dear Lord,' Kathleen said. 'She tried to say "Grandma".'

'She certainly did,' Lexie agreed.

'You've made my day, sweet baby girl,' she crooned. 'I never thought I'd hear anyone call me that.' Tears slipped down her cheeks.

'Don't cry, Kathleen,' Betty said. 'You'll be back soon and we're going to try and make it to Orlando.'

'If Agata and Britta are living here, you can have our spare room,' Lexie said firmly, 'so don't ever feel you've no place to stay.'

'And there'll always be a room for you in Connemara,' Betty said.

'Thank you,' Kathleen said, wiping her eyes. 'I know I'll be back.'

'Don't let it take so long this time,' Betty warned.

'I don't think I'll be around in another sixty-odd years, Betty.'

It was six o'clock by the time Betty and Jenny decided to leave.

'We could stay all night, but you've to get up really early in the morning for your flight,' Jenny said. 'Oh, give me a hug.'

Kathleen embraced her and thanked her for making the summer so wonderful.

Betty hugged her too. 'I'm already looking forward to our visit in November.'

'I am too,' Kathleen said, holding her hands.

Agata and Britta waited for an hour or so before attempting to say goodbye.

'Oh dear, this isn't easy,' Kathleen said. 'Thank you for sharing the joy of your precious little girl with me,' she said to Agata.

'Thank you for being her grandma,' Agata said, her voice wobbly. 'Say bye-bye to Grandma,' she instructed, as the little girl went into Kathleen's arms.

'Bye-bye, Gaga,' she said, grinning and showing her little pearly teeth.

Kathleen buried her face in the baby's curls and closed her eyes for a moment. 'I'll definitely be back here soon. I can't bear the thought of being without this little one.'

'Good,' Agata said, as she hugged Kathleen and took Britta from her arms.

'I'll see you tomorrow afternoon,' Agata said to Lexie.

'See you then,' Lexie said, waving sadly.

Once they were alone, Lexie and Kathleen sat on the garden chairs and opened a bottle of wine.

'Seems I came out here at just the right time,' Sam said, joining them in the garden.

'Sam!' Lexie said, standing to kiss him. 'How was your day? Sorry I didn't pop in to see you. We got caught up making jam, then people arrived.'

'So I guessed,' he said easily. 'Not to worry, I've been busy too,' he said. 'How was your farewell tea party?'

'Lovely,' Kathleen said. 'But also quite sad. I really will miss this place and the friends I've made.'

'You'll probably be happy to get back to some decent weather all the same,' Sam said, accepting a glass of wine from Lexie. 'I bought some lobster from our old pal Larry.'

'How divine! We'll have a feast,' Kathleen said.

'Is Rodger coming for dinner?' Lexie asked casually.

'I didn't think that far ahead,' Kathleen said, looking worried.

'There's plenty to eat,' Sam said. 'You know Larry – he gave me enough for six people, let alone three.'

'Why don't you text him and let him know?' Lexie said.

'And if he has any sense he'll be here,' Sam joked. 'I wouldn't turn down a lobster dinner with two beautiful ladies if I were him.'

Kathleen did as Sam suggested and was delighted to get an immediate response. She giggled. 'He says he was going to come over at about eight thirty but he's getting into his car this second. He's driving again and is delighted.'

'Super,' Sam said.

The front door opened and Amélie walked in. 'Hi, Lex, hi, Sam, hi, Kathleen,' she said, out of breath. 'I can't do the goodbye thing. I wasn't going to come over but I couldn't not say farewell,' she said, as tears rolled down her cheeks. Here,' she said, thrusting a letter into Kathleen's hand. 'Safe journey.' She flapped her hands in front of her eyes. 'Ugly crying on the way. Mind yourself, Kathleen. You rock.'

Kathleen pulled her into her arms and whispered in her ear, 'Don't ever lose sight of what an awesome person you are. Be the best big sis you can be.'

'I will,' Amélie said, and rushed out of the door.

'I hate goodbyes too,' Kathleen said, with a shrug.

Kathleen opened the letter. 'It's handwritten on gorgeous butterfly paper. I'll read it out.'

Dear Kathleen

It was so great to get to know you this summer. Thanks for the chats and totally awesome stories about Disney and Jackson. I hope your heart doesn't hurt too much when you go home. I'll mail you and please try to stay in touch.

I'd love it if you'd come back some time. You could see my new brother or sister.

You rock. I hope I end up being like you some day.

Thanks for 'getting' me and being my friend and never looking at me as if I'm crazy.

Respect, kudos and I hope you know you are totally mint-bomb.

Your biggest fan

Amélie ❤

'That is one of the sweetest letters I've ever received,' Kathleen said. 'She's a good girl.'

'Before Rodger arrives and we sit down to a delicious dinner I need you to follow me,' Sam announced.

'What's all this about?' Lexie asked. Kathleen grinned. 'Are you two in cahoots here or what?' Sam nodded.

They filed up the stairs towards the messy back bedroom. 'Close your eyes,' Sam instructed. Lexie did as she was told and shuffled forward as Kathleen guided her shoulders.

'Open your eyes,' Sam said.

Lexie peered nervously into the room and a little yelp escaped her lips. 'Oh, Sam,' she breathed. 'What have you done?'

'It was Maia's idea and Kathleen backed it up. So if you want to blame anyone you'll have to line us all up.'

'I'm stunned,' she said, as she gazed around. All the junk was gone and Sam had installed a massive drawing-table in the room with two easels. Her paints, brushes and charcoals were neatly stored where she could access them easily.

'It's wonderful,' she breathed.

'Maia has been ranting and raving saying she wants you to start painting again,' Sam said. 'I thought you might be able to do some sort of sketching at least ...'

Lexie hugged him and Kathleen. Then she rang Maia and blubbed down the phone at her.

'Now there are no excuses. I want my portrait.'

'I hear you,' Lexie said.

'I'll be over one evening this week so we can start.'

'Jeez, you're scary bossy today. By the time that child is born you'll be like a sergeant major.'

They made their way downstairs where Lexie began to prepare the dinner. She was so excited at the thought of doing some art again. Maia was right: it didn't have to be the same as before. Perhaps she'd be able to work in a new style.

Shortly afterwards Rodger pulled up outside.

'Holy cow!' said Sam. 'That's a serious machine he's driving there.'

Lexie and Kathleen were momentarily silenced as they took in the top-of-the-range Porsche.

'He didn't buy that on the wage he earned being a tour guide,' Lexie said drily.

'Certainly not.' Kathleen laughed.

They all went to welcome him.

'Nice wheels,' Sam said. 'We're all wildly impressed here.'

'She's a beauty, isn't she?' Rodger said. 'I was gutted that I couldn't drive her for a while. My hip was giving me such gyp I couldn't manage the gears. But now that I'm recovering I'm zooming about again.'

'It's stunning,' Lexie said.

'I bought her just after Claudia died. My daughter was furious with me and said I was behaving like a drug-crazed teenager tearing around the countryside in a younger man's machine.'

'Don't mind her,' Kathleen said. 'She's just jealous.'

'I've started to realise that no matter what I do, that girl won't be happy,' Rodger said, shaking his head regretfully. 'I had a similar car before which I used at weekends. Claudia was afraid to sit into it. So I know she wouldn't mind me having it now she's gone.'

'Indeed she wouldn't,' Kathleen assured him.

They enjoyed their dinner and the conversation flowed. By eleven o'clock Kathleen was yawning. 'Gosh, I'm sorry, here we are at the last supper and I'm falling asleep into my dessert.'

'You need to take things easy,' Lexie said. 'We were trawling the hedgerows at the crack of dawn this morning,' she explained to Rodger. 'Little did I know she and Sam had planned to remove me from the house so he could transform our spare room into a studio.'

'What a lovely surprise,' Rodger said. 'I should get going anyway. I've a long drive back to Howth.'

'Lovely to see you, Rodger,' Lexie said. 'If you're ever out for a spin, call in, won't you?'

'Thank you,' he said, then kissed her cheek and shook Sam's hand.

Kathleen and Rodger made their way to the front door.

'Rodger, I've got to thank you for being so kind to me,' Kathleen said.

'You took the words right out of my mouth,' he said sincerely. 'It's been a long time since I've enjoyed female company. You've made my summer so special.'

'I'll miss you,' she stated simply.

'And I you. But we'll stay in touch, won't we?'

'You bet. We might be many miles apart but we're still at the end of a telephone or Skype.'

They hugged for the longest time and then Rodger strode out to his car. Feeling a little like a lost teenager, Kathleen stood inside the front door and waved until he was out of sight.

'Thank you for sending him to me, Jackson,' she whispered. 'In another space, and at another time, he could have been more than a friend. But right now my heart still thinks it belongs to you.'

Lexie and Sam were chatting about holiday plans when she rejoined them in the kitchen.

'Okay?' Lexie asked.

'Just about,' Kathleen said honestly. 'He's a darling man.'

'Seems he has a few notes in the bank too,' Sam joked, elbowing her gently.

'Stop it, Sam, you cheeky article,' Lexie said.

Kathleen threw her head back and laughed. 'You're dead right, Sam. He's what my mother might have deemed a good catch.'

'Did you snog him?' Sam wondered.

'No!' Kathleen said, in mock astonishment. 'I'm a lady, I'll have you know.'

'Pity.' He sighed. 'If you don't want him can I have a shot with him then?'

They all chuckled and Sam ducked as Lexie swiped at him.

'Lex and I were just saying, if you don't make it back here soon, we could come and visit.'

'Oh, I'd love that,' she said. 'I'm dreading going. If I knew I'd see you two again soon it would soften the blow slightly.'

'Well, let's make a pact that we'll meet up with one another in the near future. Your place or mine, only time will tell,' Lexie said.

They walked Kathleen to her door.

'I wish you'd let me take you to the airport,' Lexie said.

'I've told you, sweet girl, I'm not dragging either of you out there at four in the morning. I'd never get over the guilt. Besides, I'd only dissolve at the departure gate. I'm happier doing it this way. Honestly.'

'Okay,' Sam interjected. 'I'm going to give you a bear hug and leave you gals to your goodbyes.' He scooped her up and swung her around. 'Safe journey until we meet again.'

'Thank you for everything, Sam,' she said.

'It was our pleasure,' he said.

'Look after this gorgeous girl, won't you? Look after you two as well,' she said. 'Don't lose sight of what you have. Some people spend their whole lives searching for the magic you've found. Don't waste it. A day will come when one of you has to depart. Live for the moment and relish the time you have together.'

'We will,' Sam said gruffly. 'Now you're making me all emotional,' he croaked. 'I'm out of here. This is not my forte!'

Kathleen waved as he took the steps two at a time. She held her arms open to Lexie. 'What can I say?' They held each other tightly. 'The angels sent me to you. You've been a wonderful friend when I needed it most. I will never forget you for this. Thank you for opening your home and your heart to me, dear Lexie.'

'Oh, Kathleen, I promised myself I wasn't going to cry,' she sobbed.

'I'll miss you so much. We will *definitely* see each other soon. Come Hell or high water we will.'

'I know we will. I'll make it happen,' Kathleen said.

Eventually Lexie reluctantly dragged herself back up the steps to the main house and then to her bedroom.

'All okay?' Sam asked, as she joined him in bed.

'Yeah,' she said, sighing heavily. 'She's a gem, isn't she?'

'Certainly is,' Sam mused. 'She's right about one thing, Lex,' he said, pulling her into his arms. 'We need to make sure we look after *us*.'

'If I've learned nothing else over the last while, I can assure you I know that. Are you happy that it's just you and me?' she asked, gazing into his eyes.

'I've never been more certain that I am,' he responded. 'I thought you'd understand that when I turned the spare room into an art studio.'

'Thank you so much. I'm flabbergasted. I can't wait to start doing some art again.'

'Are we happy as a family of two, then?' Sam raised an eyebrow.

Lexie nodded, feeling as if a massive weight had been lifted from her shoulders. 'Are *you* happy with that?' she asked tentatively.

'Lex, the fear in your eyes is heartbreaking,' he said. 'I got so caught up in the baby-boom thing ... Everywhere I turned there were pregnant people. I think I had a total panic and felt we needed to conform.'

'And now?'

'I realised I was losing you. That was never the plan, Lexie. We're a great team. I'm sorry I lost sight of us.'

'I'm sorry for being so difficult,' she said. 'But I had to be true to myself. You've no idea how happy I am that I'm not going to lose you, Sam. I would've had a baby to keep you. If push had come to shove, I would've done it.'

'That was actually what turned me. No matter what happens going forward, as long as you and I are together we'll be okay.'

It was just after seven o'clock the next morning when Kathleen stared out of the airport window. She wanted to take one last look at the green grass of Ireland before she boarded the plane.

'I'm looking forward to getting away from all this rain,' she overheard a fellow passenger say, as their flight was called.

'I've loved every second of my time here,' Kathleen said.

The other woman stopped in her tracks. 'It's a beautiful country but I'm craving the sunshine of Florida, I've never been so cold,' she quipped.

'I've realised that warmth comes from within,' Kathleen stated. 'I was expecting Siberian conditions and I can honestly tell you I found it positively tropical here.'

Epilogue

LEXIE WOKE WITH A START. SITTING UP, SHE LOOKED around the room and reached over for Sam, but he was gone. It was a bright, crisp December morning and, although the heating had come on, the cold was seeping through the bay window of her bedroom.

'Sam?'

She remembered he had a meeting and needed to be in work early. A smile spread across her face as she thought of the excitement and the flurry of phone calls the evening before.

'I'm a big sister,' Amélie shouted, as soon as Lexie answered her mobile.

'What flavour is the baby?' Lexie asked.

'It's a girl! Mum and Dad have said I can choose her name,' she said, choking with emotion. 'She's so tiny and so perfect, Auntie Lex.'

'I can't wait to see her.'

'I could be a total nightmare and insist they call her something like Madonna,' Amélie said.

'You wouldn't!'

'No, course not. She's so pure and unscathed by life, Lex. I'm going to do everything I can to be a good mentor to her. I want her to grow up and become this rock-solid, confident yet sensitive woman.'

'I'm sure she will,' she said. 'How's your mum after her Caesarean section?'

'She looks a bit stoned.' Amélie giggled. 'But she's thrilled. Dad is strutting about with his chest out like the king of the peacocks.'

'Good for Billy,' Lexie said. 'I can't wait to see you all. I'll be in tomorrow morning.'

'Cool. Here's Dad.' She passed the phone to Billy.

He and Lexie chatted for a few moments as she congratulated him.

'It was so different from Amélie's birth,' he said. 'I was just telling her how sorry I am that we allowed our parents to dictate to us back then. We were young and scared and didn't have the guts to stand up and tell them all to back off.'

'Well, it's great that all three of you can celebrate with this little girl.'

'I agree,' Billy said. 'No more secrets and, as Amélie is saying here, this baby is going to know it all!'

Lexie texted Agata and told her the great news, then asked if she was okay to open the gallery. A local woman was minding Britta and so far it was going swimmingly. Lexie wanted to pop into Caracove Bay shopping centre and buy clothes for the baby. She couldn't wait to browse through all the tiny things. Sam had warned her not to go too crazy. 'She'll grow at a rate of knots, so don't buy shedloads or she won't be able to wear them all.'

'Leave me alone,' she had said, pouting good-naturedly. 'It's not every day I become an auntie. Besides, we agreed I'm allowed to spoil Amélie and this baby as much as I like. They're our family.'

'Too true,' he agreed.

'Maia will give us another opportunity to go crazy in the next few months. It's lucky we're sticking to our original plan of not having kids or we'd have no money to clothe all these babies.'

Rodger was about to get into his car and go for a drive when the most extraordinary sight almost knocked him off his feet.

It was see-your-breath cold yet two beautiful butterflies flapped past him. They circled and fluttered, then disappeared around the side of the house. He turned his face to the sky and waved, then sat in a stunned silence in his car.

Lexie was just pulling on her warm winter coat when the landline rang. She was so eager to get to the hospital she was going to leave it and hope the person might call her mobile, but something stopped her. Rushing to the kitchen, she managed to grab the call before it went to the answer machine. 'Hello,' she said cheerfully.

'Am I speaking with Lexie Collins?' said a male American voice.

'Yes, this is Lexie.'

'My name is Dr Jim Kenny. I'm calling from Orlando General Hospital.'

'Kathleen!' Lexie said instantly. 'Is Kathleen okay?'

'I'm so sorry to be the bearer of sad tidings,' he said, 'but your friend Kathleen passed away last night.'

'No,' Lexie sobbed. 'How?'

'She suffered a massive stroke. We did all we could but by the time she was brought here by the emergency services it was too late. I'm so sorry.'

Lexie leaned against the wall and cried silently.

'Ma'am?'

'Yes?' Lexie managed.

'A member of the ambulance crew handed me a note, which they found in her jacket pocket. She had written several things addressed to a few people. One had your name and number with a short entry. May I read it to you?'

'Okay,' Lexie sobbed.

'The message reads, "I promised you I would see you soon. Now I can see you any time I like. When you're lonely look to the sky and know I'm near by. Thank you for being a friend when I needed it most. Jackson says hello."'

'Thank you,' Lexie managed, and hung up. Numbed by sadness, she pulled out a kitchen chair and sat down heavily. How dreadfully ironic that Billy and Dee's baby girl had arrived to such joy and fanfare as her dear friend Kathleen departed.

Lexie knew Kathleen would approve of that. She was a great

believer in things happening for a reason. That did nothing to ease the pain that was gripping her heart, though.

'Sleep well, darling friend,' she said out loud. 'I hope you and Jackson are delighted to be reunited. Thank you for blessing us with your friendship. I'm so glad you got to spend your last summer at Caracove Bay.'

Once she'd called Sam, Agata, Betty and her parents, Lexie washed her face and willed herself to carry on with her plan to see the new baby, knowing Kathleen would want that.

Rodger sprang to mind. She didn't have his mobile number so she couldn't call him.

The scene that met her at the hospital a short while later was quite simply beautiful. The smiling faces of Dee, Billy and Amélie were heart-warming.

'Say hello to your auntie Lexie,' Amélie said, holding the baby up. 'She's really cool and buys the best pressies. You're gonna love her.'

'She's a little cherub,' Lexie said.

'Meet Katie,' Dee said. 'We all love the name but she'll be Kathleen on her birth cert.'

'Did Mum tell you the news?' Lexie asked, trying not to cry again.

'What news?' Amélie asked, as Lexie took the baby in her arms.

'Kathleen passed away last night,' Lexie said, and the tears raced down her cheeks.

'We had no idea,' Amélie said, as she began to sob. 'We wanted little Katie to have a strong and inspirational namesake.'

'Now we know we've definitely made the right choice,' Dee said, wiping her eyes.

Lexie brought baby Katie to the window. She had no idea why she felt a sudden urge to look upwards, but the answer was clear as she drank in the spectacle above: a perfect arc of colours adorned the sky.

Acknowledgements

ALL AUTHORS KNOW THAT BOOKS APPEAR ON shelves after a plethora of work. The shiny new novel doesn't descend from the sky by magic. No, it's the fruit of many months of labour by a team of hard working people. I cannot thank Ciara Doorley enough for her wise and gentle guidance. She's a wonderful editor whose encouragement and championing of me knows no bounds. Thanks also to the rest of the team at Hachette Books Ireland, Breda Purdue, Jim Binchy, Joanna Smyth, Bernard Hoban, Siobhan Tierney and Ruth Shern. My job never feels like a chore, you all make it seem easy.

Thanks to my new team at Headline UK. You've all been so welcoming, friendly and enthusiastic from the moment I stepped into your huge swanky London office. I'm excited and nervous in equal measure about unleashing my work upon new audiences! Special thanks to Sherise Hobbs, it's an honour and a pleasure to have a second editor working on my books. Huge hugs to Emily Furniss, Jo Liddiard, Christina Demosthenous and Helena Towers.

Thank you Hazel Orme for doing the copyedit and giving this story its final polish and allowing it to shine!

My agent Sheila Crowley of Curtis Brown UK, known from this moment forth as Special Agent Sheila, is always by my side and on my side. I am privileged to have your support, thank you, thank you, thank you.

If you've read any of my previous books you'll know I've battled cancer a number of times. I wouldn't be able to continue the fight if it weren't for the unbending support of my husband Cian and our children Sacha and Kim. I have reached a point where I embarrass

Sacha and Kim constantly. I'm quite proud of that. I'd like to thank them for allowing me to exist and I promise to try and do it in a less mortifying manner going forward. Cian, you're my rock. I couldn't do any of this without you. I'm glad we have each other, it's especially nice to have someone who is still talking to me when teenage hormones are raging.

Mum and Dad are still there to mind and protect me even though I'm over forty. Thank you both for everything you do. All the good parts of me are from both of you. The bad parts I made up on my own.

Thanks to my brother Tim his partner Hilary, Steffy, Stan and Camille, Robyn and Jo for being the best family I could wish for. Thanks to the Mc Graths, Synnotts and O'Brics for flying the in-law flags! Thanks Michelle for the relaxing reflexology that keeps me sane.

My uncle Neil lost his battle with cancer recently. He was brave, stoic and valiant to the end. This book is dedicated to his memory and for his wife Jackie and my amazing cousins Kate, Juliette and Rebecca. I know Neil is looking down on all of you, bursting with pride.

There are many angels walking among us and they work at Blackrock Clinic and St Vincent's private hospital in Dublin. The care, expertise and treatments these amazing people have given me have kept me alive. No words can thank you all for what you've done and continue to do for me. Three cheers for the radiation therapists at St Vincent's Private, together with Professor John Armstrong and Dr Sharif. Dr David Fennelly's halo is still shining brightly along with the nurses and staff of Blackrock Clinic oncology day unit. Thank you seems feeble and inadequate. Suffice to say if I knew the winning lotto numbers I'd tell you all first.

Big hugs and bundles of kisses to my many friends who are always there to help with school runs (especially Trish Mc Govern) to chat, drink coffee and support me. I never take any of you for granted and know how lucky I am to have each and every one of you in my life.

To all my author friends Cathy Kelly, Patricia Scanlan, Caroline Grace-Cassidy, Sinead Moriarty, Sarah Webb, Maria Duffy, Sheila O'Flanagan, Zoe Miller, Claire Allan and many more who are constant cheerleaders and supporters of my work, you are a special and lovely group of people. I am so proud to be part of the talent pool that constantly produces incredible stories. When I read your books it fires me up and makes me want to keep going. Thank you all.

Special thanks to Elaine Crowley, Paul Blake, Jenn Mc Guirk, Nicola Dooley, Lorianne King and all the team at Midday for the endless hours of fun and frolics you add to my days. Big hugs to my fellow lady panellists who make me laugh out loud on a regular basis.

I have recently become an ambassador for Breast Cancer Ireland. They do incredible work for cancer research. They are aiming to change cancer from a life threatening disease to a chronic illness. I am privileged to be associated with such an awesome organisation. I look forward to lots of fun fundraising ideas! Special thanks to Triona Mc Carthy who introduced me to Aisling Hurley, Proff Arnie Hill and Samantha Mc Gregor at Breast Cancer Ireland.

Thanks to Norah Casey, an inspiring and irrepressible force of nature who has given me incredible support and recognition.

Lastly but by no means least-ly (I know that's not a word but I like the sound of it) – I would like to thank my marvellous and fabulous readers. You cheer me up constantly via Twitter (@MsEmmaHannigan), Facebook (Author Emma Hannigan) and my website (emmahannigan.com). I have a dreadful habit of forgetting that people actually read my stories. When I write I get so caught up in the characters and the world they inhabit that it often slips my mind that other people end up dipping into that universe too. So thank you for buying and reading my books and going to the trouble of sending me gorgeous messages to let me know you've enjoyed them.

I feel so privileged to be an author. It's my dream job and I cannot thank you all enough for supporting my work. I send you all a bear hug and I hope that *The Summer Guest* pleases you.

Love and light,
Emma

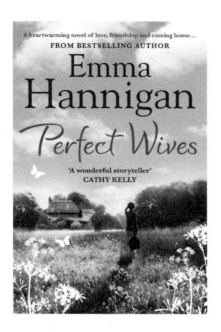

A heartwarming novel of love, friendship and coming home from this bestselling author ...

When actress Jodi Ludlum returns to the Dublin village of Bakers Valley to raise her young son, she's determined to shield him from the media glare that follows her in LA. But coming home means leaving her husband behind – and waking old ghosts.

Francine Hennessy was born and raised in Bakers Valley. To all appearances, she is the model wife, mother, home-maker and career woman. But, behind closed doors, Francine's life is crumbling around her.

As Jodi struggles to conceal her secrets and Francine faces some shocking news, the two become unlikely confidants. Suddenly having the perfect life seems less important than finding friendship, and the perfect place to belong ...

Reading is so much more than the act of moving from page to page. It's the exploration of new worlds; the pursuit of adventure; the forging of friendships; the breaking of hearts; and the chance to begin to live through a new story each time the first sentence is devoured.

We at Hachette Ireland are very passionate about what we read, and what we publish. And we'd love to hear what you think about our books.

If you'd like to let us know, or to find out more about us and our titles, please visit www.hachette.ie or our Facebook page www.facebook.com/hachetteireland, or follow us on Twitter @HachetteIre